KU-664-730

Blood Meridian

CORMAC MCCARTHY is the author of eleven
acclaimed novels. Among his honours are the National
Book Award, the National Book Critics Circle
Award and the Pulitzer Prize for Fiction.

ALSO BY CORMAC MCCARTHY

The Road

The Sunset Limited

No Country for Old Men

Cities of the Plain

The Crossing

All the Pretty Horses

The Stonemason
(a play)

The Gardener's Son
(a screenplay)

Suttree

Child of God

Outer Dark

The Orchard Keeper

The Counselor
(a screenplay)

CORMAC McCARTHY

Blood Meridian

OR

The Evening Redness in the West

<small>WITH AN INTRODUCTION BY PHILIPP MEYER</small>

<small>PICADOR CLASSIC</small>

First published 1985 by Random House, Inc., New York

First published in the UK 1989 by Picador

First published in paperback 1990 by Picador

This Picador Classic edition first published 2015 by Picador
an imprint of Pan Macmillan
20 New Wharf Road, London N1 9RR
Associated companies throughout the world
www.panmacmillan.com

ISBN 978-1-4472-8945-6

Copyright © Cormac McCarthy 1985
Introduction copyright © Philipp Meyer 2015

The right of Cormac McCarthy to be identified as the
author of this work has been asserted by him in accordance
with the Copyright, Designs and Patents Act 1988.

All rights reserved. No part of this publication may be reproduced,
stored in a retrieval system, or transmitted, in any form, or by any means
(electronic, mechanical, photocopying, recording or otherwise)
without the prior written permission of the publisher.

7 9 8 6

A CIP catalogue record for this book is available from the British Library.

Printed and bound by CPI Group (UK) Ltd, Croydon, CR0 4YY

This book is sold subject to the condition that it shall not, by way
of trade or otherwise, be lent, hired out, or otherwise circulated without
the publisher's prior consent in any form of binding or cover other than
that in which it is published and without a similar condition including
this condition being imposed on the subsequent purchaser.

Visit **www.picador.com/classic** to read more about all our books
and to buy them. You will also find features, author interviews and
news of any author events, and you can sign up for e-newsletters
so that you're always first to hear about our new releases.

Introduction

THIRTY YEARS AGO, if you'd asked someone to name the most important writers in America, Cormac McCarthy would not have been one of them. His masterpiece, *Blood Meridian*, had drifted out of print. In fact, all of his books had. McCarthy had lived most of his adult life in near-poverty, shunning publicity, turning down teaching and speaking engagements, and—one suspects—guessing his books would not sell much.

McCarthy was born in 1933 and grew up in Knoxville, Tennessee, the son of a prominent lawyer. His family had servants and lived in a big sprawling house; young Cormac likely did not want for much. But, like Ernest Hemingway, who also grew up in comfortable surroundings, McCarthy has never showed any interest in writing about domestic life.

His early works are all set in Appalachia or Tennessee, but in 1976 he moved to El Paso, Texas, on the U.S./Mexico border.

Blood Meridian was the first product of this move. And this book—his masterpiece—marks both a pinnacle and a turning point in his career. It is the first of his western novels and the last of his darker, meaner books. With one exception, all the books that follow *Blood Meridian* have a softer edge—sympathetic protagonists engaged in sympathetic quests.

Initial reactions were mixed. *The New York Times* gave this novel a lukewarm review, calling aspects of the book "facile," and it sold only a handful of copies. This is not an unusual path for literary masterpieces. F. Scott Fitzgerald was dead by the time *The Great Gatsby* became popular and it was the same with Melville and *Moby Dick*. McCarthy, thankfully, has lived long enough to see his work reach its proper standing.

*

McCarthy is in a bit of a strange box. He is the only living writer with a prose style that stacks up against the great modernists—Faulkner, Joyce, Hemingway, and Virginia Woolf—and yet he is a very different writer from any of them. He has no interest in internality: we rarely get a sense of what his characters are thinking. We are not privy to their internal or emotional lives. McCarthy is working in an older—perhaps the oldest—narrative register.

When you are judging a literary masterpiece, you are judging first the substance and ideas behind the work. Are they true, are they worth saying, does the book articulate them organically (without talking over the characters) and in a way no one has done before? You are judging the artist's ability to capture a world and the people in it and the ability to work in a mode so distinct it can only be hers or his. You would not confuse a Van Gogh with a Rembrandt—in fact you would be able to identify both at a glance. At the highest level, prose should be no different.

*

In the conventional sense, the protagonist of this book is a young man called "The Kid." He is never given a proper name and for most of the book he is more observer than participant. Dozens of pages pass without him saying a word or having a thought.

The early parts of the book see the kid grow up, develop "a taste for mindless violence," and, at fourteen, run away from home. He is shot, stabbed, and beaten, reaches Texas and enlists in a guerilla army which plans (insanely) to invade Mexico. In Mexico, the kid meets up with another guerilla army—a group of men hunting Indians for their scalps. In their company, he rides across most of the American Southwest.

At the time the book takes, 1849–1850, this part of North America was an ungoverned space. The Spanish had been there about three centuries, and, while some Indian tribes had been there several millennia, the two most violent tribes—the Comanche and the Apache—were relative newcomers. The Apache arrived around 1650—well after the Spanish—and the Comanche even later.

It's worth pointing out that the group of people we monolithically refer to as "Native Americans" or "American Indians" were in reality composed of thousands of small nations which had nothing in common except skin color. They spoke hundreds of different languages. Their cultures and societies varied radically: they ranged from pacifistic to extremely violent. Some were farmers, others were engineers, others yet were pure warriors and raiders.

The Comanche and Apache were nomadic warrior tribes. The Comanche in particular treated Mexico the way Europeans treated Africa—as a place to capture slaves and other plunder. They would ride down from the north, wipe out a village, and carry off as many horses and captives as they could. The Apache were not much better.

Into this ungoverned space—fought over by the Mexicans, the Americans, the Apache, the Comanche, and various other Indian tribes—rode the Glanton gang. Both in real life and in this novel, John Glanton was a former Texas Ranger who was paid to hunt Apaches in Northern Mexico. He led only forty men, but they were heavily armed with advanced weapons. (In 1849, repeating firearms were extremely rare—only a few thousand existed on the entire planet—and yet every member of the gang had one.) Glanton's aim was to get rich collecting the bounty on Native American scalps that various Mexican states were offering.

*

The two writers McCarthy is most often compared to are Herman Melville and William Faulkner. But, as is commonly the case when comparing great artists, there are more differences than similarities. Faulkner's works are deeply internal; McCarthy's are almost entirely external. Faulkner is always searching for redemptive qualities—in his Nobel Prize lecture, he talks about how humans will survive anything (even nuclear war)—he was fascinated by the human capacity to overcome and endure. McCarthy holds the opposite view. Both in his novels and in his real life interviews, he is a stern pessimist. He is sure we are all doomed.

In terms of prose style, McCarthy learned and appropriated enormously from Faulkner, though he tends to exceed his mentor in artistic discipline. While on the surface they are working in the same biblical, incantatory register, McCarthy is relentless about keeping the language tight. The sentences might go on for half a page, but every word needs to be there. This is not always the case with Faulkner.

Comparisons to Melville suffer from the same problem—he and McCarthy are not actually that much alike. What they mostly share is a thematic interest in life and death. Both *Moby Dick* and *Blood Meridian* are obsessed with the idea of man's destiny—or, more precisely, with the question of who among us might control his or her fate.

Both are meticulous with the details of their respective worlds. *Moby Dick* is a natural history of whaling and life at sea; *Blood Meridian* is a natural history of the southwest, of horse warfare and combat against the Indians. Every flower is in its proper season, every animal, rock, and tree in its proper place. Even the hallucinations and apparitions are real—the desert in those areas is known for exactly the types of mirages that McCarthy describes.

And yet here the similarities with Melville end. McCarthy wants nothing to do with internality. None of his characters are as developed as Melville's Ishmael—we see them only from the outside.

This is a bold choice, given that the thing the novel does

better than any other art form is innerness. Giving a sense of human consciousness, the workings of a mind. So if McCarthy leaves out so much of what makes the novel so powerful—indeed, if he leaves out most of what makes human life interesting—how can it be that this book is such a masterpiece?

Because he is drawing from older traditions. The Bible. The *Odyssey* and the *Iliad*. Works primarily concerned with man's fate and his place in the universe. Like Aeneas and Odysseus, McCarthy's characters materialize on the page fully formed. They depart fully formed as well: there is no change nor progression in the conventional sense. Details that might humanize them are left out: such as the fact that in real life, John Glanton's young wife was brutally murdered by Apaches, which eventually turned Glanton himself into a brutal killer. But this is not something McCarthy is interested in telling us. His John Glanton is a murderer simply because that is what men do.

This is a book full of sermonizing, lecturing, instruction about the nature of mankind. Novels like this typically fail completely; this one works because every sentence is organic to the situation and characters. We believe the Judge when he discourses on philosophy because we recognize him as a kind of devil or war god—his actions are consonant with his lecturing. His tone is biblical, magisterial, and perfectly fitted to a narrative of flesh and blood and damnation.

*

Most of the book's storyline is taken directly from a memoir by Samuel Chamberlain, a decorated veteran of both the Mexican–American and the American Civil wars. The memoir was discovered in 1941, long after Chamberlain's death—the bulk of it describes Chamberlain's (mostly true) adventures in the Mexican–American war. The final section of the memoir describes Chamberlain's (possibly false) tales of riding with the Glanton gang.

In addition to Glanton, we also have historical documentation on a few of the other characters—Brown, Davey Walker, and Marcus Webster. As best we can guess, Samuel Chamberlain met Brown or Webster in California and wrote his "memoir" based on their accounts.

Judge Holden, the most important character in *Blood Meridian*, was probably an invention of Samuel Chamberlain's. As Chamberlain describes him, the Judge is an enormous hairless giant possessed of inhuman strength and intelligence. He speaks numerous languages and is acquainted with all the great cities of the world. He is an excellent dancer, horseman, tracker, marksman, and musician, he knows "the nature of all the strange plants and their botanical names, [he is] great in Geology and Mineralogy." He is also a rapist and a murderer.

McCarthy takes Holden and ups the ante—he makes the Judge the hero of the book, in the most ancient sense of the word. The ancient hero (think again of Aeneas, Odysseus) is not quite fully divine, but is certainly more than human. Like any other demi-god, he does not develop psychologically over the course of the story—he is fully formed from the first page, and moves through the landscape fighting—and triumphing over—both gods and men. The only creature in American literature anything like the Judge is Melville's whale—Moby Dick himself.

The Judge, of course, can speak. He tells us that war is all that matters. War, as he sees it, is the ultimate expression of free will; the individual asserting himself over society, other men, and even death. So as McCarthy and the Judge see it, this is a story about free will. About creation and authorship: the Judge is constantly recording things in his notebooks, sketches and observations, in attempt to replace or supplant the real item (which he physically destroys when possible). This is not so different from what the artist hopes to do. Few of us know anything about fifteenth-century Danish kings, but most of us know the story of Hamlet. Such as it is with Chamberlain and Cormac McCarthy. Art has eclipsed the Real.

*

And in reality, life in the 1850s Southwest did not bear much resemblance to the world described in *Blood Meridian*. At the same time the book takes place, Thoreau was writing *Walden*, Whitman was writing *Leaves of Grass*, and Melville was writing *Moby Dick*.

Americans were flooding into Texas and New Mexico because life in those places was so good. The 1850s saw the population of Texas triple, while New Mexico's doubled. Meanwhile, reading this book, you get the sense that not a single person was left alive in either place.

This is what Great Art does. It becomes more real than the real, more true than the truth. It is the mechanism by which our mythologies form.

*

For writers a few generations behind McCarthy, he is the presence that looms over all of us. None of us has ever met him, but we all refer to him as Cormac. I have read this book dozens of times; I used to walk around reading *Blood Meridian* to myself out loud. Like Joyce's *Ulysses*, *Blood Meridian* pushes the boundaries of what a book can do.

Cormac's style is infectious. He exerts a kind of gravitational force on the minds of younger writers, both in terms of style and tone. A lot of authors seem to have used him as a handbook and even the more conscientious among us is affected. I once had a very strange dream and at the risk of revealing how insane I really am, I will share it: Along with some friends, I was standing outside the ruins of an old Greek temple. Cormac and his followers were barricaded inside, all armed with automatic weapons. My friends and I were topping off magazines, checking our carbines, preparing our assault. When I woke up I thought it was a pretty great dream, but the truth is I have deleted entire chapters of my own novels because they sounded too much like Cormac. Apparently I cannot not escape his influence, even in my sleep.

As for the real-life Cormac, no other novelist since Ernest

Hemingway has inspired such legions of imitators. McCarthy is—at least in the English language—the biggest stylistic influence of the past fifty years. A friend suggested that for this reason alone, McCarthy should win the Nobel Prize. He is probably right.

*

A lot has been made of this book as a gnostic text—an examination of the idea that some men are closer to God, more touched with a divine fire. Certainly the Judge is, for better or worse. And in the book's epilogue, a man moves about a barren plain "striking fire that God has placed" in the earth. He is digging holes for fenceposts, creating the demarcation between civilization and the wild; or, depending on your point of view, between a new civilization and an old one. Other men follow him blindly. They see only the holes he has dug. They don't see the man. They don't see his fire.

The man leads them alone, and in isolation, calling this divine fire from the raw materials of existence. This of course is what Great Artists do. They follow their inner voice into places others will not understand; they work knowing they will be ignored and misunderstood. The lucky few—like Cormac McCarthy—will live to see their masterpieces recognized.

PHILIPP MEYER

Blood Meridian

OR

The Evening Redness in the West

The author wishes to thank the Lyndhurst Foundation,
the John Simon Guggenheim Memorial Foundation, and the
John D. and Catherine T. MacArthur Foundation.
He also wishes to express his appreciation to
Albert Erskine, his editor of twenty years.

Your ideas are terrifying and your hearts are faint. Your acts of pity and cruelty are absurd, committed with no calm, as if they were irresistible. Finally, you fear blood more and more. Blood and time.

PAUL VALÉRY

It is not to be thought that the life of darkness is sunk in misery and lost as if in sorrowing. There is no sorrowing. For sorrow is a thing that is swallowed up in death, and death and dying are the very life of the darkness.

JACOB BOEHME

Clark, who led last year's expedition to the Afar region of northern Ethiopia, and UC Berkeley colleague Tim D. White, also said that a re-examination of a 300,000-year-old fossil skull found in the same region earlier shows evidence of having been scalped.

The Yuma Daily Sun, June 13, 1982

I

SEE THE CHILD. He is pale and thin, he wears a thin and ragged linen shirt. He stokes the scullery fire. Outside lie dark turned fields with rags of snow and darker woods beyond that harbor yet a few last wolves. His folk are known for hewers of wood and drawers of water but in truth his father has been a schoolmaster. He lies in drink, he quotes from poets whose names are now lost. The boy crouches by the fire and watches him.

Night of your birth. Thirty-three. The Leonids they were called. God how the stars did fall. I looked for blackness, holes in the heavens. The Dipper stove.

The mother dead these fourteen years did incubate in her own bosom the creature who would carry her off. The father never speaks her name, the child does not know it. He has a sister in this world that he will not see again. He watches, pale and unwashed. He can neither read nor write and in him broods already a taste for mindless violence. All history present in that visage, the child the father of the man.

At fourteen he runs away. He will not see again the freezing kitchenhouse in the predawn dark. The firewood, the washpots. He wanders west as far as Memphis, a solitary migrant upon that flat and pastoral landscape. Blacks in the fields, lank and stooped, their fingers spiderlike among the bolls of cotton. A shadowed agony in the garden. Against the sun's declining figures moving in the slower dusk across a paper skyline. A lone dark husbandman pursuing mule and harrow down the rain-blown bottomland toward night.

A year later he is in Saint Louis. He is taken on for New Orleans aboard a flatboat. Forty-two days on the river. At night the steamboats hoot and trudge past through the black waters all alight like cities adrift. They break up the float and sell the lumber and he walks in the streets and hears tongues he has not heard before. He lives in a room above a courtyard behind a tavern and he comes down at night like some fairybook beast to fight with the sailors. He is not big but he has big wrists, big hands. His shoulders are set close. The child's face is curiously untouched behind the scars, the eyes oddly innocent. They fight with fists, with feet, with bottles or knives. All races, all breeds. Men whose speech sounds like the grunting of apes. Men from lands so far and queer that standing over them where they lie bleeding in the mud he feels mankind itself vindicated.

On a certain night a Maltese boatswain shoots him in the back with a small pistol. Swinging to deal with the man he is shot again just below the heart. The man flees and he leans against the bar with the blood running out of his shirt. The others look away. After a while he sits on the floor.

He lies in a cot in the room upstairs for two weeks while the tavernkeeper's wife attends him. She brings his meals, she carries out his slops. A hardlooking woman with a wiry body like a man's. By the time he is mended he has no money to pay her and he leaves in the night and sleeps on the riverbank until he can find a boat that will take him on. The boat is going to Texas.

Only now is the child finally divested of all that he has been. His origins are become remote as is his destiny and not again in all the world's turning will there be terrains so wild and barbarous to try whether the stuff of creation may be shaped to man's will or whether his own heart is not another kind of clay. The passengers are a diffident lot. They cage their eyes and no man asks another what it is that brings him here. He sleeps on the deck, a pilgrim among others. He watches the dim shore rise and fall. Gray seabirds gawking. Flights of pelicans coastwise above the gray swells.

They disembark aboard a lighter, settlers with their chattels, all studying the low coastline, the thin bight of sand and scrub pine swimming in the haze.

He walks through the narrow streets of the port. The air smells of salt and newsawn lumber. At night whores call to him from the dark like souls in want. A week and he is on the move again, a few dollars in his purse that he's earned, walking the sand roads of the southern night alone, his hands balled in the cotton pockets of his cheap coat. Earthen causeways across the marshland. Egrets in their rookeries white as candles among the moss. The wind has a raw edge to it and leaves lope by the roadside and skelter on in the night fields. He moves north through small settlements and farms, working for day wages and found. He sees a parricide hanged in a crossroads hamlet and the man's friends run forward and pull his legs and he hangs dead from his rope while urine darkens his trousers.

He works in a sawmill, he works in a diphtheria pesthouse. He takes as pay from a farmer an aged mule and aback this animal in the spring of the year eighteen and forty-nine he rides up through the latterday republic of Fredonia into the town of Nacogdoches.

THE REVEREND GREEN had been playing to a full house daily as long as the rain had been falling and the rain had been falling for two weeks. When the kid ducked into the ratty canvas tent there was standing room along the walls, a place or two, and such a heady reek of the wet and bathless that they themselves would sally forth into the downpour now and again for fresh air before the rain drove them in again. He stood with others of his kind along the back wall. The only thing that might have distinguished him in that crowd was that he was not armed.

Neighbors, said the reverend, he couldnt stay out of these here hell, hell, hellholes right here in Nacogdoches. I said to him, said: You goin to take the son of God in there with ye? And he said: Oh no. No I aint. And I said: Dont you know that he said I will foller ye always even unto the end of the road?

Well, he said, I aint askin nobody to go nowheres. And I said: Neighbor, you dont need to ask. He's a goin to be there with ye ever step of the way whether ye ask it or ye dont. I said: Neighbor, you caint get shed of him. Now. Are you going to drag him, *him*, into that hellhole yonder?

You ever see such a place for rain?

The kid had been watching the reverend. He turned to the man who spoke. He wore long moustaches after the fashion of teamsters and he wore a widebrim hat with a low round crown. He was slightly walleyed and he was watching the kid earnestly as if he'd know his opinion about the rain.

I just got here, said the kid.

Well it beats all I ever seen.

The kid nodded. An enormous man dressed in an oilcloth slicker had entered the tent and removed his hat. He was bald as a stone and he had no trace of beard and he had no brows to his eyes nor lashes to them. He was close on to seven feet in height and he stood smoking a cigar even in this nomadic house of God and he seemed to have removed his hat only to chase the rain from it for now he put it on again.

The reverend had stopped his sermon altogether. There was no sound in the tent. All watched the man. He adjusted the hat and then pushed his way forward as far as the crateboard pulpit

6

where the reverend stood and there he turned to address the reverend's congregation. His face was serene and strangely childlike. His hands were small. He held them out.

Ladies and gentlemen I feel it my duty to inform you that the man holding this revival is an imposter. He holds no papers of divinity from any institution recognized or improvised. He is altogether devoid of the least qualification to the office he has usurped and has only committed to memory a few passages from the good book for the purpose of lending to his fraudulent sermons some faint flavor of the piety he despises. In truth, the gentleman standing here before you posing as a minister of the Lord is not only totally illiterate but is also wanted by the law in the states of Tennessee, Kentucky, Mississippi, and Arkansas.

Oh God, cried the reverend. Lies, lies! He began reading feverishly from his opened bible.

On a variety of charges the most recent of which involved a girl of eleven years—I said eleven—who had come to him in trust and whom he was surprised in the act of violating while actually clothed in the livery of his God.

A moan swept through the crowd. A lady sank to her knees.

This is him, cried the reverend, sobbing. This is him. The devil. Here he stands.

Let's hang the turd, called an ugly thug from the gallery to the rear.

Not three weeks before this he was run out of Fort Smith Arkansas for having congress with a goat. Yes lady, that is what I said. Goat.

Why damn my eyes if I wont shoot the son of a bitch, said a man rising at the far side of the tent, and drawing a pistol from his boot he leveled it and fired.

The young teamster instantly produced a knife from his clothing and unseamed the tent and stepped outside into the rain. The kid followed. They ducked low and ran across the mud toward the hotel. Already gunfire was general within the tent and a dozen exits had been hacked through the canvas walls and people were pouring out, women screaming, folk stumbling, folk trampled underfoot in the mud. The kid and his friend reached the hotel gallery and wiped the water from their eyes and turned to watch. As they did so the tent began to sway and buckle and like a huge and wounded medusa it slowly settled to the ground trailing tattered canvas walls and ratty guyropes over the ground.

The baldheaded man was already at the bar when they entered. On the polished wood before him were two hats and a double handful of coins. He raised his glass but not to them. They stood up to the bar and ordered whiskeys and the kid laid his money down but the barman pushed it back with his thumb and nodded.

These here is on the judge, he said.

They drank. The teamster set his glass down and looked at the kid or he seemed to, you couldnt be sure of his gaze. The kid looked down the bar to where the judge stood. The bar was that tall not every man could even get his elbows up on it but it came just to the judge's waist and he stood with his hands placed flatwise on the wood, leaning slightly, as if about to give another address. By now men were piling through the doorway, bleeding, covered in mud, cursing. They gathered about the judge. A posse was being drawn to pursue the preacher.

Judge, how did you come to have the goods on that no-account?

Goods? said the judge.

When was you in Fort Smith?

Fort Smith?

Where did you know him to know all that stuff on him?

You mean the Reverend Green?

Yessir. I reckon you was in Fort Smith fore ye come but here.

I was never in Fort Smith in my life. Doubt that he was.

They looked from one to the other.

Well where was it you run up on him?

I never laid eyes on the man before today. Never even heard of him.

He raised his glass and drank.

There was a strange silence in the room. The men looked like mud effigies. Finally someone began to laugh. Then another. Soon they were all laughing together. Someone bought the judge a drink.

IT HAD BEEN raining for sixteen days when he met Toadvine and it was raining yet. He was still standing in the same saloon and he had drunk up all his money save two dollars. The teamster had gone, the room was all but empty. The door stood open and you could see the rain falling in the empty lot behind the hotel. He drained his glass and went out. There were boards laid across the mud and he followed the paling band of doorlight down toward the batboard jakes at the bottom of the lot. Another man was coming up from the jakes and they met halfway on the narrow planks. The man before him swayed slightly. His wet hatbrim fell to his shoulders save in the front where it was pinned back. He held a bottle loosely in one hand. You better get out of my way, he said.

The kid wasnt going to do that and he saw no use in discussing it. He kicked the man in the jaw. The man went down and got up again. He said: I'm goin to kill you.

He swung with the bottle and the kid ducked and he swung again and the kid stepped back. When the kid hit him the man shattered the bottle against the side of his head. He went off the boards into the mud and the man lunged after him with the jagged bottleneck and tried to stick it in his eye. The kid was fending with his hands and they were slick with blood. He kept trying to reach into his boot for his knife.

Kill your ass, the man said. They slogged about in the dark of the lot, coming out of their boots. The kid had his knife now and they circled crabwise and when the man lurched at him he cut the man's shirt open. The man threw down the bottleneck and unsheathed an immense bowieknife from behind his neck. His hat had come off and his black and ropy locks swung about his head and he had codified his threats to the one word kill like a crazed chant.

That'ns cut, said one of several men standing along the walkway watching.

Kill kill slobbered the man wading forward.

But someone else was coming down the lot, great steady sucking sounds like a cow. He was carrying a huge shellalegh. He reached the kid first and when he swung with the club the kid went face down in the mud. He'd have died if someone hadn't turned him over.

When he woke it was daylight and the rain had stopped and he was looking up into the face of a man with long hair who was completely covered in mud. The man was saying something to him.

What? said the kid.

I said are you quits?

Quits?

Quits. Cause if you want some more of me you sure as hell goin to get it.

He looked at the sky. Very high, very small, a buzzard. He looked at the man. Is my neck broke? he said.

The man looked out over the lot and spat and looked at the boy again. Can you not get up?

I dont know. I aint tried.

I never meant to break your neck.

No.

I meant to kill ye.

They aint nobody done it yet. He clawed at the mud and pushed himself up. The man was sitting on the planks with his boots alongside him. They aint nothin wrong with you, he said.

The kid looked about stiffly at the day. Where's my boots? he said.

The man squinted at him. Flakes of dried mud fell from his face.

I'm goin to have to kill some son of a bitch if they got my boots.

Yonder looks like one of em.

The kid labored off through the mud and fetched up one boot. He slogged about in the yard feeling likely lumps of mud.

This your knife? he said.

The man squinted at him. Looks like it, he said.

The kid pitched it to him and he bent and picked it up and wiped the huge blade on his trouserleg. Thought somebody'd done stole you, he told the knife.

The kid found his other boot and came and sat on the boards. His hands were huge with mud and he wiped one of them briefly at his knee and let it fall again.

They sat there side by side looking out across the barren lot. There was a picket fence at the edge of the lot and beyond the fence a boy was drawing water at a well and there were chickens in the yard there. A man came from the dramshop door down the walk toward the outhouse. He stopped where they sat and looked at them and then stepped off into the mud. After a while he came back and stepped off into the mud again and went around and on up the walk.

The kid looked at the man. His head was strangely narrow and his hair was plastered up with mud in a bizarre and primitive coiffure. On his forehead were burned the letters H T and lower and almost between the eyes the letter F and these markings were splayed and garish as if the iron had been left too long. When he turned to look at the kid the kid could see that he had no ears. He stood up and sheathed the knife and started up the walk with the boots in his hand and the kid rose and followed. Halfway to the hotel the man stopped and looked out at the mud and then sat down on the planks and pulled on the boots mud and all. Then he rose and slogged off through the lot to pick something up.

I want you to look here, he said. At my goddamned hat.

You couldnt tell what it was, something dead. He flapped it about and pulled it over his head and went on and the kid followed.

The dramhouse was a long narrow hall wainscotted with varnished boards. There were tables by the wall and spittoons on the floor. There were no patrons. The barman looked up when they entered and a nigger that had been sweeping the floor stood the broom against the wall and went out.

Where's Sidney? said the man in his suit of mud.

In the bed I reckon.

They went on.

Toadvine, called the barman.

The kid looked back.

The barman had come from behind the bar and was looking after them. They crossed from the door through the lobby of the hotel toward the stairs leaving varied forms of mud behind them on the floor. As they started up the stairs the clerk at the desk leaned and called to them.

Toadvine.

He stopped and looked back.

He'll shoot you.

Old Sidney?

Old Sidney.

They went on up the stairs.

At the top of the landing was a long hall with a windowlight at the end. There were varnished doors down the walls set so close they might have been closets. Toadvine went on until he came to the end of the hall. He listened at the last door and he eyed the kid.

You got a match?

The kid searched his pockets and came up with a crushed and stained wooden box.

The man took it from him. Need a little tinder here, he said. He was crumbling the box and stacking the bits against the

12

door. He struck a match and set the pieces alight. He pushed the little pile of burning wood under the door and added more matches.

Is he in there? said the boy.

That's what we're fixin to see.

A dark curl of smoke rose, a blue flame of burning varnish. They squatted in the hallway and watched. Thin flames began to run up over the panels and dart back again. The watchers looked like forms excavated from a bog.

Tap on the door now, said Toadvine.

The kid rose. Toadvine stood up and waited. They could hear the flames crackling inside the room. The kid tapped.

You better tap louder than that. This man drinks some.

He balled his fist and lambasted the door about five times.

Hell fire, said a voice.

Here he comes.

They waited.

You hot son of a bitch, said the voice. Then the knob turned and the door opened.

He stood in his underwear holding in one hand the towel he'd used to turn the doorknob with. When he saw them he turned and started back into the room but Toadvine seized him about the neck and rode him to the floor and held him by the hair and began to pry out an eyeball with his thumb. The man grabbed his wrist and bit it.

Kick his mouth in, called Toadvine. Kick it.

The kid stepped past them into the room and turned and kicked the man in the face. Toadvine held his head back by the hair.

Kick him, he called. Aw, kick him, honey.

He kicked.

Toadvine pulled the bloody head around and looked at it and let it flop to the floor and he rose and kicked the man himself. Two spectators were standing in the hallway. The door was completely afire and part of the wall and ceiling. They went out and down the hall. The clerk was coming up the steps two at a time.

Toadvine you son of a bitch, he said.

Toadvine was four steps above him and when he kicked him he caught him in the throat. The clerk sat down on the stairs. When the kid came past he hit him in the side of the head and the clerk slumped over and began to slide toward the landing. The kid stepped over him and went down to the lobby and crossed to the front door and out.

Toadvine was running down the street, waving his fists above his head crazily and laughing. He looked like a great clay voodoo doll made animate and the kid looked like another. Behind them flames were licking at the top corner of the hotel and clouds of dark smoke rose into the warm Texas morning.

He'd left the mule with a Mexican family that boarded animals at the edge of town and he arrived there wildlooking and out of breath. The woman opened the door and looked at him.

Need to get my mule, he wheezed.

She looked at him some more, then she called toward the back of the house. He walked around. There were horses tethered in the lot and there was a flatbed wagon against the fence with some turkeys sitting on the edge looking out. The old lady had come to the back door. Nito, she called. Venga. Hay un caballero aquí. Venga.

He went down the shed to the tackroom and got his wretched saddle and his blanketroll and brought them back. He found the mule and unstalled it and bridled it with the rawhide hackamore and led it to the fence. He leaned against the animal with his shoulder and got the saddle over it and got it cinched, the mule starting and shying and running its head along the fence. He led it across the lot. The mule kept shaking its head sideways as if it had something in its ear.

He led it out to the road. As he passed the house the woman came padding out after him. When she saw him put his foot in the stirrup she began to run. He swung up into the broken saddle and chucked the mule forward. She stopped at the gate and watched him go. He didnt look back.

When he passed back through the town the hotel was burning and men were standing around watching it, some holding empty buckets. A few men sat horseback watching the flames and one of these was the judge. As the kid rode past the judge turned and watched him. He turned the horse, as if he'd have the animal watch too. When the kid looked back the judge smiled. The kid touched up the mule and they went sucking out past the old stone fort along the road west.

II

NOW COME DAYS OF begging, days of theft. Days of riding where there rode no soul save he. He's left behind the pinewood country and the evening sun declines before him beyond an endless swale and dark falls here like a thunderclap and a cold wind sets the weeds to gnashing. The night sky lies so sprent with stars that there is scarcely space of black at all and they fall all night in bitter arcs and it is so that their numbers are no less.

He keeps from off the king's road for fear of citizenry. The little prairie wolves cry all night and dawn finds him in a grassy draw where he'd gone to hide from the wind. The hobbled mule stands over him and watches the east for light.

The sun that rises is the color of steel. His mounted shadow falls for miles before him. He wears on his head a hat he's made from leaves and they have dried and cracked in the sun and he looks like a raggedyman wandered from some garden where he'd used to frighten birds.

Come evening he tracks a spire of smoke rising oblique from among the low hills and before dark he hails up at the doorway of an old anchorite nested away in the sod like a groundsloth. Solitary, half mad, his eyes redrimmed as if locked in their cages with hot wires. But a ponderable body for that. He watched wordless while the kid eased down stiffly from the mule. A rough wind was blowing and his rags flapped about him.

Seen ye smoke, said the kid. Thought you might spare a man a sup of water.

The old hermit scratched in his filthy hair and looked at the ground. He turned and entered the hut and the kid followed.

Inside darkness and a smell of earth. A small fire burned on the dirt floor and the only furnishings were a pile of hides in one corner. The old man shuffled through the gloom, his head bent to clear the low ceiling of woven limbs and mud. He pointed down to where a bucket stood in the dirt. The kid bent and took up the gourd floating there and dipped and drank. The water was salty, sulphurous. He drank on.

You reckon I could water my old mule out there?

The old man began to beat his palm with one fist and dart his eyes about.

Be proud to fetch in some fresh. Just tell me where it's at.

What ye aim to water him with?

The kid looked at the bucket and he looked around in the dim hut.

I aint drinkin after no mule, said the hermit.

Have you not got no old bucket nor nothin?

No, cried the hermit. No. I aint. He was clapping the heels of his clenched fists together at his chest.

The kid rose and looked toward the door. I'll find somethin, he said. Where's the well at?

Up the hill, foller the path.

It's nigh too dark to see out here.

It's a deep path. Foller ye feet. Foller ye mule. I caint go.

He stepped out into the wind and looked about for the mule

but the mule wasnt there. Far to the south lightning flared soundlessly. He went up the path among the thrashing weeds and found the mule standing at the well.

A hole in the sand with rocks piled about it. A piece of dry hide for a cover and a stone to weight it down. There was a rawhide bucket with a rawhide bail and a rope of greasy leather. The bucket had a rock tied to the bail to help it tip and fill and he lowered it until the rope in his hand went slack while the mule watched over his shoulder.

He drew up three bucketfuls and held them so the mule would not spill them and then he put the cover back over the well and led the mule back down the path to the hut.

I thank ye for the water, he called.

The hermit appeared darkly in the door. Just stay with me, he said.

That's all right.

Best stay. It's fixin to storm.

You reckon?

I reckon and I reckon right.

Well.

Bring ye bed. Bring ye possibles.

He uncinched and threw down the saddle and hobbled the mule foreleg to rear and took his bedroll in. There was no light save the fire and the old man was squatting by it tailorwise.

Anywheres, anywheres, he said. Where's ye saddle at?

The kid gestured with his chin.

Dont leave it out yonder somethinll eat it. This is a hungry country.

He went out and ran into the mule in the dark. It had been standing looking in at the fire.

Get away, fool, he said. He took up the saddle and went back in.

Now pull that door to fore we blow away, said the old man.

The door was a mass of planks on leather hinges. He dragged it across the dirt and fastened it by its leather latch.

I take it ye lost your way, said the hermit.

No, I went right to it.

He waved quickly with his hand, the old man. No, no, he said. I mean ye was lost to of come here. Was they a sandstorm? Did ye drift off the road in the night? Did thieves beset ye?

The kid pondered this. Yes, he said We got off the road someways or another.

Knowed ye did.

How long you been out here?

Out where?

The kid was sitting on his blanketroll across the fire from the old man. Here, he said. In this place.

The old man didnt answer. He turned his head suddenly aside and seized his nose between his thumb and forefinger and blew twin strings of snot onto the floor and wiped his fingers on the seam of his jeans. I come from Mississippi. I was a slaver, dont care to tell it. Made good money. I never did get caught. Just got sick of it. Sick of niggers. Wait till I show ye somethin.

He turned and rummaged among the hides and handed through the flames a small dark thing. The kid turned it in his hand. Some man's heart, dried and blackened. He passed it back and the old man cradled it in his palm as if he'd weigh it.

They is four things that can destroy the earth, he said. Women, whiskey, money, and niggers.

They sat in silence. The wind moaned in the section of stovepipe that was run through the roof above them to quit the place of smoke. After a while the old man put the heart away.

That thing costed me two hundred dollars, he said.

You give two hundred dollars for it?

I did, for that was the price they put on the black son of a bitch it hung inside of.

He stirred about in the corner and came up with an old dark brass kettle, lifted the cover and poked inside with one finger. The remains of one of the lank prairie hares interred in cold grease and furred with a light blue mold. He clamped the lid back on the kettle and set it in the flames. Aint much but we'll go shares, he said.

I thank ye.

Lost ye way in the dark, said the old man. He stirred the fire, standing slender tusks of bone up out of the ashes.

The lad didnt answer.

The old man swung his head back and forth. The way of the transgressor is hard. God made this world, but he didnt make it to suit everbody, did he?

I dont believe he much had me in mind.

Aye, said the old man. But where does a man come by his notions. What world's he seen that he liked better?

I can think of better places and better ways.

Can ye make it be?

No.

No. It's a mystery. A man's at odds to know his mind cause his mind is aught he has to know it with. He can know his heart, but he dont want to. Rightly so. Best not to look in there. It aint the heart of a creature that is bound in the way that God has set for it. You can find meanness in the least of creatures, but when God made man the devil was at his elbow. A creature that can do anything. Make a machine. And a machine to make the machine. And evil that can run itself a thousand years, no need to tend it. You believe that?

I dont know.

Believe that.

When the old man's mess was warmed he doled it out and they ate in silence. Thunder was moving north and before long it was booming overhead and starting bits of rust in a thin trickle down the stovepipe. They hunkered over their plates and wiped the grease up with their fingers and drank from the gourd.

The kid went out and scoured his cup and plate in the sand and came back banging the tins together as if to fend away some drygulch phantom out there in the dark. Distant thunderheads reared quivering against the electric sky and were sucked away in the blackness again. The old man sat with one ear cocked to the howling waste without. The kid shut the door.

Dont have no bacca with ye do ye?

No I aint, said the kid.

Didnt allow ye did.

You reckon it'll rain?

It's got ever opportunity. Likely it wont.

The kid watched the fire. Already he was nodding. Finally he raised up and shook his head. The hermit watched him over the dying flames. Just go on and fix ye bed, he said.

He did. Spreading his blankets on the packed mud and pulling off his stinking boots. The fluepipe moaned and he heard the mule stamp and snuffle outside and in his sleep he struggled and muttered like a dreaming dog.

He woke sometime in the night with the hut in almost total darkness and the hermit bent over him and all but in his bed.

What do you want? he said. But the hermit crawled away and in the morning when he woke the hut was empty and he got his things and left.

All that day he watched to the north a thin line of dust. It seemed not to move at all and it was late evening before he could see that it was headed his way. He passed through a forest of live oak and he watered at a stream and moved on in the dusk and made a fireless camp. Birds woke him where he lay in a dry and dusty wood.

By noon he was on the prairie again and the dust to the north was stretched out along the edge of the earth. By evening the first of a drove of cattle came into view. Rangy vicious beasts with enormous hornspreads. That night he sat in the herders' camp and ate beans and pilotbread and heard of life on the trail.

They were coming down from Abilene, forty days out, headed for the markets in Louisiana. Followed by packs of wolves, coyotes, indians. Cattle groaned about them for miles in the dark.

They asked him no questions, a ragged lot themselves. Crossbreeds some, free niggers, an indian or two.

I had my outfit stole, he said.

They nodded in the firelight.

They got everthing I had. I aint even got a knife.

You might could sign on with us. We lost two men. Turned back to go to Californy.

I'm headed yon way.

I guess you might be goin to Californy ye own self.

I might. I aint decided.

Them boys was with us fell in with a bunch from Arkansas. They was headed down for Bexar. Goin to pull for Mexico and the west.

I'll bet them old boys is in Bexar drinkin they brains out.

I'll bet old Lonnie's done topped ever whore in town.

How far is it to Bexar?

It's about two days.

It's furthern that. More like four I'd say.

How would a man go if he'd a mind to?

You cut straight south you ought to hit the road about half a day.

You going to Bexar?

I might do.

You see old Lonnie down there you tell him get a piece for me. Tell him old Oren. He'll buy ye a drink if he aint blowed all his money in.

In the morning they ate flapjacks with molasses and the herders saddled up and moved on. When he found his mule there was a small fibre bag tied to the animal's rope and inside the bag there was a cupful of dried beans and some peppers and an old greenriver knife with a handle made of string. He saddled up the mule, the mule's back galled and balding, the hooves cracked. The ribs like fishbones. They hobbled on across the endless plain.

He came upon Bexar in the evening of the fourth day and

he sat the tattered mule on a low rise and looked down at the town, the quiet adobe houses, the line of green oaks and cottonwoods that marked the course of the river, the plaza filled with wagons with their osnaburg covers and the whitewashed public buildings and the Moorish churchdome rising from the trees and the garrison and the tall stone powderhouse in the distance. A light breeze stirred the fronds of his hat, his matted greasy hair. His eyes lay dark and tunneled in a caved and haunted face and a foul stench rose from the wells of his boot tops. The sun was just down and to the west lay reefs of bloodred clouds up out of which rose little desert nighthawks like fugitives from some great fire at the earth's end. He spat a dry white spit and clumped the cracked wooden stirrups against the mule's ribs and they staggered into motion again.

He went down a narrow sandy road and as he went he met a deadcart bound out with a load of corpses, a small bell tolling the way and a lantern swinging from the gate. Three men sat on the box not unlike the dead themselves or spirit folk so white they were with lime and nearly phosphorescent in the dusk. A pair of horses drew the cart and they went on up the road in a faint miasma of carbolic and passed from sight. He turned and watched them go. The naked feet of the dead jostled stiffly from side to side.

It was dark when he entered the town, attended by barking dogs, faces parting the curtains in the lamplit windows. The light clatter of the mule's hooves echoing in the little empty streets. The mule sniffed the air and swung down an alleyway into a square where there stood in the starlight a well, a trough, a hitchingrail. The kid eased himself down and took the bucket from the stone coping and lowered it into the well. A light splash echoed. He drew the bucket, water dripping in the dark. He dipped the gourd and drank and the mule nuzzled his elbow. When he'd done he set the bucket in the street and sat on the coping of the well and watched the mule drink from the bucket.

He went on through the town leading the animal. There was

no one about. By and by he entered a plaza and he could hear guitars and a horn. At the far end of the square there were lights from a cafe and laughter and highpitched cries. He led the mule into the square and up the far side past a long portico toward the lights.

There was a team of dancers in the street and they wore gaudy costumes and called out in Spanish. He and the mule stood at the edge of the lights and watched. Old men sat along the tavern wall and children played in the dust. They wore strange costumes all, the men in dark flatcrowned hats, white nightshirts, trousers that buttoned up the outside leg and the girls with garish painted faces and tortoiseshell combs in their blueblack hair. The kid crossed the street with the mule and tied it and entered the cafe. A number of men were standing at the bar and they quit talking when he entered. He crossed the polished clay floor past a sleeping dog that opened one eye and looked at him and he stood at the bar and placed both hands on the tiles. The barman nodded to him. Dígame, he said.

I aint got no money but I need a drink. I'll fetch out the slops or mop the floor or whatever.

The barman looked across the room to where two men were playing dominoes at a table. Abuelito, he said.

The older of the two raised his head.

Qué dice el muchacho.

The old man looked at the kid and turned back to his dominoes.

The barman shrugged his shoulders.

The kid turned to the old man. You speak american? he said.

The old man looked up from his play. He regarded the kid without expression.

Tell him I'll work for a drink. I aint got no money.

The old man thrust his chin and made a clucking noise with his tongue.

The kid looked at the barman.

The old man made a fist with the thumb pointing up and the

24

little finger down and tilted his head back and tipped a phantom drink down his throat. Quiere hecharse una copa, he said. Pero no puede pagar.

The men at the bar watched.

The barman looked at the kid.

Quiere trabajo, said the old man. Quién sabe. He turned back to his pieces and made his play without further consultation.

Quieres trabajar, said one of the men at the bar.

They began to laugh.

What are you laughing at? said the boy.

They stopped. Some looked at him, some pursed their mouths or shrugged. The boy turned to the bartender. You got something I could do for a couple of drinks I know damn good and well.

One of the men at the bar said something in spanish. The boy glared at them. They winked one to the other, they took up their glasses.

He turned to the barman again. His eyes were dark and narrow. Sweep the floor, he said.

The barman blinked.

The kid stepped back and made sweeping motions, a pantomime that bent the drinkers in silent mirth. Sweep, he said, pointing at the floor.

No está sucio, said the barman.

He swept again. Sweep, goddamnit, he said.

The barman shrugged. He went to the end of the bar and got a broom and brought it back. The boy took it and went on to the back of the room.

A great hall of a place. He swept in the corners where potted trees stood silent in the dark. He swept around the spittoons and he swept around the players at the table and he swept around the dog. He swept along the front of the bar and when he reached the place where the drinkers stood he straightened up and leaned on the broom and looked at them. They conferred silently among themselves and at last one took his glass from the bar and stepped away. The others followed. The lad swept past them to the door.

The dancers had gone, the music. Across the street sat a man on a bench dimly lit in the doorlight from the cafe. The mule stood where he'd tied it. He tapped the broom on the steps and came back in and took the broom to the corner where the barman had gotten it. Then he came to the bar and stood.

The barman ignored him.

The kid rapped with his knuckles.

The barman turned and put one hand on his hip and pursed his lips.

How about that drink now, said the lad.

The barman stood.

The kid made the drinking motions that the old man had made and the barman flapped his towel idly at him.

Andale, he said. He made a shooing motion with the back of his hand.

The kid's face clouded. You son of a bitch, he said. He started down the bar. The barman's expression did not change. He brought up from under the bar an oldfashioned military pistol with a flint lock and shoved back the cock with the heel of his hand. A great wooden clicking in the silence. A clicking of glasses all down the bar. Then the scuffling of chairs pushed back by the players at the wall.

The kid froze. Old man, he said.

The old man didnt answer. There was no sound in the cafe. The kid turned to find him with his eyes.

Está borracho, said the old man.

The boy watched the barman's eyes.

The barman waved the pistol toward the door.

The old man spoke to the room in spanish. Then he spoke to the barman. Then he put on his hat and went out.

The barman's face drained. When he came around the end

of the bar he had laid down the pistol and he was carrying a bung-starter in one hand.

The kid backed to the center of the room and the barman labored over the floor toward him like a man on his way to some chore. He swung twice at the kid and the kid stepped twice to the right. Then he stepped backward. The barman froze. The kid boosted himself lightly over the bar and picked up the pistol. No one moved. He raked the frizzen open against the bartop and dumped the priming out and laid the pistol down again. Then he selected a pair of full bottles from the shelves behind him and came around the end of the bar with one in each hand.

The barman stood in the center of the room. He was breathing heavily and he turned, following the kid's movements. When the kid approached him he raised the bungstarter. The kid crouched lightly with the bottles and feinted and then broke the right one over the man's head. Blood and liquor sprayed and the man's knees buckled and his eyes rolled. The kid had already let go the bottleneck and he pitched the second bottle into his right hand in a roadagent's pass before it even reached the floor and he backhanded the second bottle across the barman's skull and crammed the jagged remnant into his eye as he went down.

The kid looked around the room. Some of those men wore pistols in their belts but none moved. The kid vaulted the bar and took another bottle and tucked it under his arm and walked out the door. The dog was gone. The man on the bench was gone too. He untied the mule and led it across the square.

HE WOKE IN the nave of a ruinous church, blinking up at the vaulted ceiling and the tall swagged walls with their faded frescos. The floor of the church was deep in dried guano and the droppings of cattle and sheep. Pigeons flapped through the piers of dusty light and three buzzards hobbled about on the picked bone carcass of some animal dead in the chancel.

His head was in torment and his tongue swollen with thirst. He sat up and looked around him. He'd put the bottle under his saddle and he found it and held it up and shook it and drew the cork and drank. He sat with his eyes closed, the sweat beaded on his forehead. Then he opened his eyes and drank again. The buzzards stepped down one by one and trotted off into the sacristy. After a while he rose and went out to look for the mule.

It was nowhere in sight. The mission occupied eight or ten ares of enclosed land, a barren purlieu that held a few goats and burros. In the mud walls of the enclosure were cribs inhabited by families of squatters and a few cookfires smoked thinly in the sun. He walked around the side of the church and entered the sacristy. Buzzards shuffled off through the chaff and plaster like enormous yardfowl. The domed vaults overhead were clotted with a dark furred mass that shifted and breathed and chittered. In the room was a wooden table with a few clay pots and along the back wall lay the remains of several bodies, one a child. He went on through the sacristy into the church again and got his saddle. He drank the rest of the bottle and he put the saddle on his shoulder and went out.

The facade of the building bore an array of saints in their niches and they had been shot up by American troops trying their rifles, the figures shorn of ears and noses and darkly mottled with leadmarks oxidized upon the stone. The huge carved and paneled doors hung awap on their hinges and a carved stone Virgin held in her arms a headless child. He stood blinking in the noon heat. Then he saw the mule's tracks. They were just the palest disturbance of the dust and they came out of the door of the church and crossed the lot to the gate in the east wall. He hiked the saddle higher onto his shoulder and set out after them.

A dog in the shade of the portal rose and lurched sullenly out into the sun until he had passed and then lurched back. He took the road down the hill toward the river, a ragged figure enough. He entered a deep wood of pecan and oak and the road took a rise and he could see the river below him. Blacks were washing a carriage in the ford and he went down the hill and stood at the edge of the water and after a while he called out to them.

They were sopping water over the black lacquerwork and one of them raised up and turned to look at him. The horses stood to their knees in the current.

What? called the black.

Have you seen a mule.

Mule?

I lost a mule. I think he come this way.

The black wiped his face with the back of his arm. Somethin come down the road about a hour back. I think it went down the river yonder. It might of been a mule. It didnt have no tail nor no hair to speak of but it did have long ears.

The other two blacks grinned. The kid looked off down the river. He spat and set off along the path through the willows and swales of grass.

He found it about a hundred yards downriver. It was wet to its belly and it looked up at him and then lowered its head again into the lush river grass. He threw down the saddle and took up the trailing rope and tied the animal to a limb and kicked it halfheartedly. It shifted slightly to the side and continued to graze. He reached atop his head but he had lost the crazy hat somewhere. He made his way down through the trees and stood looking at the cold swirling waters. Then he waded out into the river like some wholly wretched baptismal candidate.

III

HE WAS LYING NAKED under the trees with his rags spread across the limbs above him when another rider going down the river reined up and stopped.

He turned his head. Through the willows he could see the legs of the horse. He rolled over on his stomach.

The man got down and stood beside the horse.

He reached and got his twinehandled knife.

Howdy there, said the rider.

He didnt answer. He moved to the side to see better through the branches.

Howdy there. Where ye at?

What do you want?

Wanted to talk to ye.

What about?

Hell fire, come on out. I'm white and christian.

The kid was reaching up through the willows trying to get his breeches. The belt was hanging down and he tugged at it but the breeches were hung on a limb.

Goddamn, said the man. You aint up in the tree are ye?

Why dont you go on and leave me the hell alone.

Just wanted to talk to ye. Didnt intend to get ye all riled up.

You done got me riled.

Was you the feller knocked in that Mexer's head yesterday evenin? I aint the law.

Who wants to know?

Captain White. He wants to sign that feller up to join the army.

The army?

Yessir.

What army?

Company under Captain White. We goin to whip up on the Mexicans.

The war's over.

He says it aint over. Where are you at?

He rose and hauled the breeches down from where he'd hung them and pulled them on. He pulled on his boots and put the knife in the right bootleg and came out from the willows pulling on his shirt.

The man was sitting in the grass with his legs crossed. He was dressed in buckskin and he wore a plug hat of dusty black silk and he had a small Mexican cigar in the corner of his teeth. When he saw what clawed its way out through the willows he shook his head.

Kindly fell on hard times aint ye son? he said.

I just aint fell on no good ones.

You ready to go to Mexico?

I aint lost nothin down there.

It's a chance for ye to raise ye self in the world. You best make a move someway or another fore ye go plumb in under.

What do they give ye?

Ever man gets a horse and his ammunition. I reckon we might find some clothes in your case.

I aint got no rifle.

Well find ye one.

What about wages?

Hell fire son, you wont need no wages. You get to keep everthing you can raise. We goin to Mexico. Spoils of war. Aint a man in the company wont come out a big landowner. How much land you own now?

I dont know nothin about soldierin.

The man eyed him. He took the unlit cigar from his teeth and turned his head and spat and put it back again. Where ye from? he said.

Tennessee.

Tennessee. Well I dont misdoubt but what you can shoot a rifle.

The kid squatted in the grass. He looked at the man's horse. The horse was fitted out in tooled leather with worked silver trim. It had a white blaze on its face and four white stockings and it was cropping up great teethfuls of the rich grass. Where you from, said the kid.

I been in Texas since thirty-eight. If I'd not run up on Captain White I dont know where I'd be this day. I was a sorrier sight even than what you are and he come along and raised me up like Lazarus. Set my feet in the path of righteousness. I'd done took to drinkin and whorin till hell wouldnt have me. He seen somethin in me worth savin and I see it in you. What do ye say?

I dont know.

Just come with me and meet the captain.

The boy pulled at the halms of grass. He looked at the horse again. Well, he said. Dont reckon it'd hurt nothin.

They rode through the town with the recruiter splendid on the stockingfooted horse and the kid behind him on the mule like something he'd captured. They rode through narrow lanes where the wattled huts steamed in the heat. Grass and prickly pear grew on the roofs and goats walked about on them and somewhere off in that squalid kingdom of mud the sound of the little deathbells tolled thinly. They turned up Commerce Street through the Main Plaza among rafts of wagons and they crossed another plaza where boys were selling grapes and figs from little trundlecarts. A few bony dogs slank off before them. They rode through the Military Plaza and they passed the little street where the boy and the mule had drunk the night before and there were clusters of women and girls at the well and many shapes of wickercovered clay jars standing about. They passed a little house where women inside were wailing and the little hearsecart stood at the door with the horses patient and motionless in the heat and the flies.

The captain kept quarters in a hotel on a plaza where there were trees and a small green gazebo with benches. An iron gate at the hotel front opened into a passageway with a courtyard at the rear. The walls were whitewashed and set with little ornate colored tiles. The captain's man wore carved boots with tall heels that rang smartly on the tiles and on the stairs ascending from the courtyard to the rooms above. In the courtyard there were green plants growing and they were freshly watered and steaming. The captain's man strode down the long balcony and rapped sharply at the door at the end. A voice said for them to come in.

He sat at a wickerwork desk writing letters, the captain. They stood attending, the captain's man with his black hat in his hands. The captain wrote on nor did he look up. Outside the kid could hear a woman speaking in Spanish. Other than that there was just the scratching of the captain's pen.

When he had done he laid down the pen and looked up. He looked at his man and then he looked at the kid and then he bent his head to read what he'd written. He nodded to himself and dusted the letter with sand from a little onyx box and folded it. Taking a match from a box of them on the desk he lit it and held it to a stick of sealing wax until a small red medallion had pooled onto the paper. He shook out the match, blew briefly at the paper and knuckled the seal with his ring. Then he stood the letter between two books on his desk and leaned back in his chair and looked at the kid again. He nodded gravely. Take seats, he said.

They eased themselves into a kind of settle made from some dark wood. The captain's man had a large revolver at his belt and as he sat he hitched the belt around so that the piece lay cradled between his thighs. He put his hat over it and leaned back. The kid folded his busted boots one behind the other and sat upright.

The captain pushed his chair back and rose and came around to the front of the desk. He stood there for a measured minute and then he hitched himself up on the desk and sat with his boots dangling. He had gray in his hair and in the sweeping moustaches that he wore but he was not old. So you're the man, he said.

What man? said the kid.

What man sir, said the captain's man.

How old are you, son?

Nineteen.

The captain nodded his head. He was looking the kid over. What happened to you?

What?

Say sir, said the recruiter.

Sir?

I said what happened to you.

The kid looked at the man sitting next to him. He looked down at himself and he looked at the captain again. I was fell on by robbers, he said.

Robbers, said the captain.

Took everthing I had. Took my watch and everthing.

Have you got a rifle?

Not no more I aint.

Where was it you were robbed.

I dont know. They wasnt no name to it. It was just a wilderness.

Where were you coming from?

I was comin from Naca, Naca . . .

Nacogdoches?

Yeah.

Yessir.

Yessir.

How many were there?

The kid stared at him.

Robbers. How many robbers.

Seven or eight, I reckon. I got busted in the head with a scantlin.

The captain squinted one eye at him. Were they Mexicans?

Some. Mexicans and niggers. They was a white or two with em. They had a bunch of cattle they'd stole. Only thing they left me with was a old piece of knife I had in my boot.

The captain nodded. He folded his hands between his knees. What do you think of the treaty? he said.

The kid looked at the man on the settle next to him. He had his eyes shut. He looked down at his thumbs. I dont know nothin about it, he said.

I'm afraid that's the case with a lot of Americans, said the captain. Where are you from, son?

Tennessee.

You werent with the Volunteers at Monterrey were you?

No sir.

Bravest bunch of men under fire I believe I ever saw. I suppose more men from Tennessee bled and died on the field in northern Mexico than from any other state. Did you know that?

No sir.

They were sold out. Fought and died down there in that desert and then they were sold out by their own country.

The kid sat silent.

The captain leaned forward. We fought for it. Lost friends and brothers down there. And then by God if we didnt give it back. Back to a bunch of barbarians that even the most biased in their favor will admit have no least notion in God's earth of honor or justice or the meaning of republican government. A people so cowardly they've paid tribute a hundred years to tribes of naked savages. Given up their crops and livestock. Mines shut down. Whole villages abandoned. While a heathen horde rides over the land looting and killing with total impunity. Not a hand raised against them. What kind of people are these? The Apaches wont even shoot them. Did you know that? They kill them with rocks. The captain shook his head. He seemed made sad by what he had to tell.

Did you know that when Colonel Doniphan took Chihuahua City he inflicted over a thousand casualties on the enemy and lost only one man and him all but a suicide? With an army of unpaid irregulars that called him Bill, were half naked, and had walked to the battlefield from Missouri?

No sir.

The captain leaned back and folded his arms. What we are dealing with, he said, is a race of degenerates. A mongrel race, little better than niggers. And maybe no better. There is no government in Mexico. Hell, there's no God in Mexico. Never will be. We are dealing with a people manifestly incapable of governing themselves. And do you know what happens with people who cannot govern themselves? That's right. Others come in to govern for them.

There are already some fourteen thousand French colonists in the state of Sonora. They're being given free land to settle. They're being given tools and livestock. Enlightened Mexicans encourage this. Paredes is already calling for secession from the Mexican government. They'd rather be ruled by toadeaters than thieves and imbeciles. Colonel Carrasco is asking for American intervention. And he's going to get it.

Right now they are forming in Washington a commission to come out here and draw up the boundary lines between our country and Mexico. I dont think there's any question that ultimately Sonora will become a United States territory. Guaymas a U S port. Americans will be able to get to California without having to pass through our benighted sister republic and our citizens will be protected at last from the notorious packs of cutthroats presently infesting the routes which they are obliged to travel.

The captain was watching the kid. The kid looked uneasy. Son, said the captain. We are to be the instruments of liberation in a dark and troubled land. That's right. We are to spearhead the drive. We have the tacit support of Governor Burnett of California.

He leaned forward and placed his hands on his knees. And we will be the ones who will divide the spoils. There will be a section of land for every man in my company. Fine grassland. Some of the finest in the world. A land rich in minerals, in gold and silver I would say beyond the wildest speculation. You're young. But I dont misread you. I'm seldom mistaken in a man. I think you mean to make your mark in this world. Am I wrong?

No sir.

No. And I don't think you're the sort of chap to abandon a land that Americans fought and died for to a foreign power. And mark my word. Unless Americans act, people like you and me who take their country seriously while those mollycoddles in Washington sit on their hindsides, unless we act, Mexico—and I mean the whole of the country—will one day fly a European flag. Monroe Doctrine or no.

The captain's voice had become soft and intense. He tilted his head to one side and regarded the kid with a sort of benevolence. The kid rubbed the palms of his hands on the knees of his filthy jeans. He glanced at the man beside him but he seemed to be asleep.

What about a saddle? he said.

Saddle?

Yessir.

You dont have a saddle?

No sir.

I thought you had a horse.

A mule.

I see.

I got a old hull on the mule but they aint much left of it. Aint a whole lot left of the mule. He said I was to get a horse and a rifle.

Sergeant Trammel did?

I never promised him no saddle, said the sergeant.

We'll get you a saddle.

I did tell him we might find him some clothes, Captain.

Right. We may be irregulars but we dont want to look like bobtails, do we?

No sir.

We aint got no more broke horses neither, said the sergeant.

Well break one.

That old boy that was so good about breakin em is out of commission.

I know that. Get somebody else.

Yessir. Maybe this man can break horses. You ever break horses?

No sir.

Aint no need to sir me.

Yessir.

Sergeant, said the captain, easing himself down from the desk.

Yessir.

Sign this man up.

THE CAMP WAS upriver at the edge of the town. A tent patched up from old wagon canvas, a few wickiups made of brush and beyond them a corral in the form of a figure eight likewise made from brush where a few small painted ponies stood sulking in the sun.

Corporal, called the sergeant.

He aint here.

He dismounted and strode toward the tent and threw back the fly. The kid sat on the mule. Three men were lying in the shade of a tree and they studied him. Howdy, said one.

Howdy.

You a new man?

I reckon.

Captain say when we leavin this pesthole?

He never said.

The sergeant came from the tent. Where's he at? he said.

Gone to town.

Gone to town, said the sergeant. Come here.

The man rose from the ground and ambled over to the tent and stood with his hands resting in the small of his back.

This here man aint got no outfit, said the sergeant.

The man nodded.

The captain give him a shirt and some money to get his boots mended. We need to get him somethin he can ride and we need to get him a saddle.

A saddle.

Ought to be able to sell that mule for enough to get him one of some kind.

The man looked at the mule and turned back and squinted at the sergeant. He leaned and spat. That there mule wont bring ten dollars.

What it brings it brings.

They done killed another beef.

I dont want to hear about it.

I caint do nothin with em.

I aint tellin the captain. He'll roll them eyes around till they come unscrewed and fall out in the ground.

The man spat again. Well, that's the gods truth anyway.

See to this man now. I got to get.

Well.

Aint nobody sick is they?

No.

Thank God for that.

He stood up into the saddle and touched the horse's neck lightly with the reins. He looked back and shook his head.

In the evening the kid and two other recruits went into town. He'd bathed and shaved himself and he wore a pair of blue cord trousers and the cotton shirt the captain had given him and save for the boots he looked a new man altogether. His friends rode small and colorful horses that forty days ago had been wild animals on the plain and they shied and skittered and snapped like turtles.

Wait till you get you one of these, said the second corporal. You aint never had no fun.

These horses is all right, said the other.

There's one or two in there yet that might make ye a horse.

The kid looked down at them from his mule. They rode either side like escorts and the mule trotted with its head up, its eyes shifting nervously. They'll all stick ye head in the ground, said the second corporal.

They rode through a plaza thronged with wagons and stock. With immigrants and Texans and Mexicans and with slaves and Lipan indians and deputations of Karankawas tall and austere, their faces dyed blue and their hands locked about the shafts of their sixfoot spears, all but naked savages who with their painted skins and their whispered taste for human flesh seemed outrageous presences even in that fabled company. The recruits rode with their animals close reined and they turned up past the courthouse and along the high walls of the cárcel with the broken glass imbedded in the topmost course. In the Main Plaza a band had assembled and were at tuning their instruments. The riders turned down Salinas Street past small gaminghouses and coffee-stands and there were in this street a number of Mexican harnessmakers and traders and keepers of gamechickens and cobblers and bootmakers in little stalls or shops of mud. The second corporal was from Texas and spoke a little Spanish and he meant to trade the mule. The other boy was from Missouri. They were in good spirits, scrubbed and combed, clean shirts all. Each foreseeing a night of drink, perhaps of love. How many youths have come home cold and dead from just such nights and just such plans.

They traded the mule accoutred as it was for a Texas stock saddle, bare tree with rawhide cover, not new but sound. For a bridle and bit that was new. For a woven wool blanket from Saltillo that was dusty new or not. And lastly for a two and a half dollar gold piece. The Texan looked at this small coin in the kid's palm and demanded more money but the harnessmaker shook his head and held up his hands in utter finality.

What about my boots? said the kid.

Y sus botas, said the Texan.

Botas?

Sí. He made sewing motions.

The harnessmaker looked down at the boots. He cupped his fingers in a little gesture of impatience and the kid took off the boots and stood barefoot in the dust.

When all was done they stood in the street and looked at one another. The kid had his new tack slung up on his shoulder. The second corporal looked at the boy from Missouri. You got any money, Earl?

Not a copper cent.

Well I aint neither. We might's well get our asses back on out to that hole of misery.

The kid shifted the weight of the gear on his shoulder. We got this quarter eagle to drink up yet, he said.

ALREADY IT IS twilight down in the Laredito. Bats fly forth from their roostings in courthouse and tower and circle the quarter. The air is full of the smell of burning charcoal. Children and dogs squat by the mud stoops and gamecocks flap and settle in the branches of the fruit trees. They go afoot, these comrades, down along a bare adobe wall. Band music carries dimly from the square. They pass a watercart in the street and they pass a hole in the wall where by the light of a small forgefire an old man beats out shapes of metal. They pass in a doorway a young girl whose beauty becomes the flowers about.

They arrive at last before a wooden door. It is hinged into a larger door or gate and all must step over the foot-high sill where a thousand boots have scuffed away the wood, where fools in their hundreds have tripped or fallen or tottered drunkenly into the street. They pass along a ramada in a courtyard by an old grape arbor where small fowl nod in the dusk among the gnarled and barren vines and they enter a cantina where the lamps are lit and they cross stooping under a low beam to a bar and belly up one two three.

There is an old disordered Mennonite in this place and he turns to study them. A thin man in a leather weskit, a black and straightbrim hat set square on his head, a thin rim of whiskers. The recruits order glasses of whiskey and drink them down and order more. There are monte games at tables by the wall and there are whores at another table who look the recruits over. The recruits stand sideways along the bar with their thumbs in their belts and watch the room. They talk among themselves of the expedition in loud voices and the old Mennonite shakes a rueful head and sips his drink and mutters.

They'll stop you at the river, he says.

The second corporal looks past his comrades. Are you talking to me?

At the river. Be told. They'll jail you to a man.

Who will?

The United States Army. General Worth.

The hell they will.

Pray that they will.

He looks at his comrades. He leans toward the Mennonite. What does that mean, old man?

Do ye cross that river with yon filibuster armed ye'll not cross it back.

Dont aim to cross it back. We goin to Sonora.

What's it to you, old man?

The Mennonite watches the enshadowed dark before them as it is reflected to him in the mirror over the bar. He turns to them. His eyes are wet, he speaks slowly. The wrath of God lies sleeping. It was hid a million years before men were and only men have power to wake it. Hell aint half full. Hear me. Ye carry war of a madman's making onto a foreign land. Yell wake more than the dogs.

But they berated the old man and swore at him until he moved off down the bar muttering, and how else could it be?

How these things end. In confusion and curses and blood. They drank on and the wind blew in the streets and the stars that had been overhead lay low in the west and these young men fell afoul of others and words were said that could not be put right again and in the dawn the kid and the second corporal knelt over the boy from Missouri who had been named Earl and they spoke his name but he never spoke back. He lay on his side in the dust of the courtyard. The men were gone, the whores were gone. An old man swept the clay floor within the cantina. The boy lay with his skull broken in a pool of blood, none knew by whom. A third one came to be with them in the courtyard. It was the Mennonite. A warm wind was blowing and the east held a gray light. The fowls roosting among the grapevines had begun to stir and call.

There is no such joy in the tavern as upon the road thereto, said the Mennonite. He had been holding his hat in his hands and now he set it upon his head again and turned and went out the gate.

IV

FIVE DAYS LATER on the dead man's horse he followed the riders and wagons through the plaza and out of the town on the road downcountry. They rode through Castroville where coyotes had dug up the dead and scattered their bones and they crossed the Frio River and they crossed the Nueces and they left the Presidio road and turned north with scouts posted ahead and to the rear. They crossed the del Norte by night and waded up out of the shallow sandy ford into a howling wilderness.

Dawn saw them deployed in a long file over the plain, the dry wood wagons already moaning, horses snuffling. A dull thump of hooves and clank of gear and the constant light chink of harness. Save for scattered clumps of buckbrush and prickly-pear and the little patches of twisted grass the ground was bare and there were low mountains to the south and they were bare too. Westward the horizon lay flat and true as a spirit level.

Those first days they saw no game, no birds save buzzards. They saw in the distance herds of sheep or goats moving along the skyline in scarves of dust and they ate the meat of wild asses shot on the plain. The sergeant carried in his saddle scabbard a heavy Wesson rifle that used a false muzzle and paper patch and fired a coneshaped ball. With it he killed the little wild pigs of the desert and later when they began to see herds of antelope he would halt in the dusk with the sun off the land and screwing a bipod into the threaded boss on the underside of the barrel would kill these animals where they stood grazing at distances of half a mile. The rifle carried a vernier sight on the tang and he would eye the distance and gauge the wind and set the sight like a man using a micrometer. The second corporal would lie at his elbow with a glass and call the shots high or low should he miss and the wagon would wait by, until he had shot a stand of three or four and then rumble off across the cooling land with the skinners jostling and grinning in the bed. The sergeant never put the rifle up but what he wiped and greased the bore.

They rode well armed, each man with a rifle and many with the smallbore fiveshot Colt's revolvers. The captain carried a pair of dragoon pistols in scabbards that mounted across the pommel of the saddle so that they rode at each knee. These guns were United States issue, Colt's patent, and he had bought them from a deserter in a Soledad livery stable and paid eighty dollars in gold for them and the scabbards and the mold and flask they came with.

The rifle the kid carried had been sawed down and rebored till it weighed very light indeed and the mold for it was so small he had to patch the balls with buckskin. He had fired it a few times and it carried much where it chose. It rode before him on the saddlebow, he having no scabbard. It had been carried so before, God's years of it, and the forestock was much worn beneath.

In the early dark the wagon came back with the meet. The skinners had piled the wagonbed with mesquite brush and stumps they'd drug out of the ground with the horses and they unloaded the firewood and commenced cutting up the gutted antelopes in the floor of the wagon with bowieknives and hand-axes, laughing and hacking in a welter of gore, a reeking scene in the light of the handheld lanterns. By full dark the blackened ribracks leaned steaming at the fires and there was a jousting over the coals with shaven sticks whereon were skewered gobs of meat and a clank of canteens and endless raillery. And sleep that night on the cold plains of a foreign land, forty-six men wrapped in their blankets under the selfsame stars, the prairie wolves so like in their yammering, yet all about so changed and strange.

They caught up and set out each day in the dark before the day yet was and they ate cold meat and biscuit and made no fire. The sun rose on a column already ragged these six days out. Among their clothes there was small agreement and among their hats less. The little painted horses stepped shifty and truculent and a vicious snarl of flies fought constantly in the bed of the gamewagon. The dust the party raised was quickly dispersed and lost in the immensity of that landscape and there was no dust other for the pale sutler who pursued them drives unseen and his lean horse and his lean cart leave no track upon such ground or any ground. By a thousand fires in the iron blue dusk he keeps his commissary and he's a wry and grinning tradesman good to follow every campaign or hound men from their holes in just those whited regions where they've gone to hide from God. On this day two men fell sick and one died before dark. In the morning there was another ill to take his place. The two of them were laid among sacks of beans and rice and coffee in the supply-wagon with blankets over them to keep them from the sun and they rode with the slamming and jarring of the wagon half shirring the meat from their bones so that they cried out to be left and then they died. The men turned out in the early morning darkness to dig their graves with the bladebones of antelope and they covered them with stones and rode on again.

They rode on and the sun in the east flushed pale streaks of light and then a deeper run of color like blood seeping up in sudden reaches flaring planewise and where the earth drained up into the sky at the edge of creation the top of the sun rose out of nothing like the head of a great red phallus until it cleared the unseen rim and sat squat and pulsing and malevolent behind them. The shadows of the smallest stones lay like pencil lines across the sand and the shapes of the men and their mounts advanced elongate before them like strands of the night from which they'd ridden, like tentacles to bind them to the darkness yet to come. They rode with their heads down, faceless under their hats, like an army asleep on the march. By midmorning another man had died and they lifted him from the wagon where he'd stained the sacks he'd lain among and buried him also and rode on.

Now wolves had come to follow them, great pale lobos with yellow eyes that trotted neat of foot or squatted in the shimmering heat to watch them where they made their noon halt. Moving on again. Loping, sidling, ambling with their long noses to the ground. In the evening their eyes shifted and winked out there on the edge of the firelight and in the morning when the riders rode out in the cool dark they could hear the snarling and the pop of their mouths behind them as they sacked the camp for meatscraps.

The wagons drew so dry they slouched from side to side like dogs and the sand was grinding them away. The wheels shrank and the spokes reeled in their hubs and clattered like loomshafts and at night they'd drive false spokes into the mortices and tie them down with strips of green hide and they'd drive wedges between the iron of the tires and the suncracked felloes. They wobbled on, the trace of their untrue labors like sidewinder tracks in the sand. The duledge pegs worked loose and dropped behind. Wheels began to break up.

Ten days out with four men dead they started across a plain of pure pumice where there grew no shrub, no weed, far as the eye could see. The captain called a halt and he called up the Mexican who served as guide. They talked and the Mexican gestured and the captain gestured and after a while they moved on again.

This looks like the high road to hell to me, said a man from the ranks.

What does he reckon for the horses to eat?

I believe they're supposed to just grit up on this sand like chickens and be ready for the shelled corn when it does come.

In two days they began to come upon bones and cast-off apparel. They saw halfburied skeletons of mules with the bones so white and polished they seemed incandescent even in that blazing heat and they saw panniers and packsaddles and the bones of men and they saw a mule entire, the dried and blackened carcass hard as iron. They rode on. The white noon saw them through the waste like a ghost army, so pale they were with dust, like shades of figures erased upon a board. The wolves loped paler yet and grouped and skittered and lifted their lean snouts on the air. At night the horses were fed by hand from sacks of meal and watered from buckets. There was no more sickness. The survivors lay quietly in that cratered void and watched the whitehot stars go rifling down the dark. Or slept with their alien hearts beating in the sand like pilgrims exhausted upon the face of the planet Anareta, clutched to a namelessness wheeling in the night. They moved on and the iron of the wagontires grew polished bright as chrome in the pumice. To the south the blue cordilleras stood footed in their paler image on the sand like reflections in a lake and there were no wolves now.

They took to riding by night, silent jornadas save for the trundling of the wagons and the wheeze of the animals. Under the moonlight a strange party of elders with the white dust thick on their moustaches and their eyebrows. They moved on and the stars jostled and arced across the firmament and died beyond the inkblack mountains. They came to know the nightskies well.

Western eyes that read more geometric constructions than those names given by the ancients. Tethered to the polestar they rode the Dipper round while Orion rose in the southwest like a great electric kite. The sand lay blue in the moonlight and the iron tires of the wagons rolled among the shapes of the riders in gleaming hoops that veered and wheeled woundedly and vaguely navigational like slender astrolabes and the polished shoes of the horses kept hasping up like a myriad eyes winking across the desert floor. They watched storms out there so distant they could not be heard, the silent lightning flaring sheetwise and the thin black spine of the mountain chain fluttering and sucked away again in the dark. They saw wild horses racing on the plain, pounding their shadows down the night and leaving in the moonlight a vaporous dust like the palest stain of their passing.

All night the wind blew and the fine dust set their teeth on edge. Sand in everything, grit in all they ate. In the morning a urinecolored sun rose blearily through panes of dust on a dim world and without feature. The animals were failing. They halted and made a dry camp without wood or water and the wretched ponies huddled and whimpered like dogs.

That night they rode through a region electric and wild where strange shapes of soft blue fire ran over the metal of the horses' trappings and the wagonwheels rolled in hoops of fire and little shapes of pale blue light came to perch in the ears of the horses and in the beams of the men. All night sheetlightning quaked sourceless to the west beyond the midnight thunderheads, making a bluish day of the distant desert, the mountains on the sudden skyline stark and black and livid like a land of some other order out there whose true geology was not stone but fear. The thunder moved up from the southwest and lightning lit the desert all about them, blue and barren, great clanging reaches ordered out of the absolute night like some demon kingdom summoned up or changeling land that come the day would leave them neither trace nor smoke nor ruin more than any troubling dream.

They halted in the dark to recruit the animals and some of the men stowed their arms in the wagons for fear of drawing the lightning and a man named Hayward prayed for rain.

He prayed: Almighty God, if it aint too far out of the way of things in your eternal plan do you reckon we could have a little rain down here.

Pray it up, some called, and kneeling he cried out among the thunder and the wind: Lord we are dried to jerky down here. Just a few drops for some old boys out here on the prairie and a long ways from home.

Amen, they said, and catching up their mounts they rode on. Within the hour the wind cooled and drops of rain the size of grapeshot fell upon them out of that wild darkness. They could smell wet stone and the sweet smell of the wet horses and wet leather. They rode on.

They rode through the heat of the day following with the waterkegs empty and the horses perishing and in the evening these elect, shabby and white with dust like a company of armed and mounted millers wandering in dementia, rode up off the desert through a gap in the low stone hills and down upon a solitary jacal, crude hut of mud and wattles and a rudimentary stable and corrals.

Bone palings ruled the small and dusty purlieus here and death seemed the most prevalent feature of the landscape. Strange fences that the sand and wind had scoured and the sun bleached and cracked like old porcelain with dry brown weather cracks and where no life moved. The corrugated forms of the riders passed jingling across the dry bistre land and across the mud facade of the jacal, the horses trembling, smelling water. The captain raised his hand and the sergeant spoke and two men dismounted and advanced upon the hut with rifles. They pushed open a door made of rawhide and entered. In a few minutes they reappeared.

Somebody's here somewheres. They's hot coals.

The captain surveyed the distance with an air of vigilance.

He dismounted with the patience of one used to dealing with incompetence and crossed to the jacal. When he came out he surveyed the terrain again. The horses shifted and clinked and stamped and the men pulled their jaws down and spoke roughly to them.

Sergeant.

Yessir.

These people cant be far. See if you can find them. And see if there's any forage here for the animals.

Forage?

Forage.

The sergeant placed a hand on the cantle and looked about at the place they were in and shook his head and dismounted.

They went through the jacal and into the enclosure behind and out to the stable. There were no animals and nothing but a stall half filled with dry sotols in the way of feed. They walked out the back to a sink among the stones where water stood and a thin stream flowed away over the sand. There were hoofprints about the tank and dry manure and some small birds ran mindlessly along the rim of the little creek.

The sergeant had been squatting on his heels and now he rose and spat. Well, he said. Is there any direction you caint see twenty mile in?

The recruits studied the emptiness about.

I dont believe the folks here is gone that long.

They drank and walked back toward the jacal. Horses were being led along the narrow path.

The captain was standing with his thumbs in his belt.

I caint see where they've got to, said the sergeant.

What's in the shed.

Some old dry fodder.

The captain frowned. They ought to have a goat or a hog. Something. Chickens.

In a few minutes two men came dragging an old man from the stable. He was covered with dust and dry chaff and he held one arm across his eyes. He was dragged moaning to the captain's feet where he lay prostrate in what looked like windings of white cotton. He put his hands over his ears and his elbows before his eyes like one called upon to witness some appalling thing. The captain turned away in disgust. The sergeant toed him with his boot. What's wrong with him? he said.

He's pissing himself, Sergeant. He's pissing himself. The captain gestured at the man with his gloves.

Yessir.

Well get him the hell out of here.

You want Candelario to talk to him?

He's a halfwit. Get him away from me.

They dragged the old man away. He had begun to babble but no one listened and in the morning he was gone.

They bivouacked by the tank and the farrier saw to the mules and ponies that had thrown shoes and they worked on the wagons by firelight far into the night. They set forth in a crimson dawn where sky and earth closed in a razorous plane. Out there dark little archipelagos of cloud and the vast world of sand and scrub shearing upward into the shoreless void where those blue islands trembled and the earth grew uncertain, gravely canted and veering out through tinctures of rose and the dark beyond the dawn to the uttermost rebate of space.

They rode through regions of particolored stone upthrust in ragged kerfs and shelves of traprock reared in faults and anticlines curved back upon themselves and broken off like stumps of great stone treeboles and stones the lightning had clove open, seeps exploding in steam in some old storm. They rode past trapdykes of brown rock running down the narrow chines of the ridges and onto the plain like the ruins of old walls, such auguries everywhere of the hand of man before man was or any living thing.

They passed through a village then and now in ruins and they camped in the walls of a tall mud church and burned the fallen timbers of the roof for their fire while owls cried from the arches in the dark.

The following day on the skyline to the south they saw clouds of dust that lay across the earth for miles. They rode on, watching the dust until it began to near and the captain raised his hand for a halt and took from his saddlebag his old brass cavalry telescope and uncoupled it and swept it slowly over the land. The sergeant sat his horse beside him and after a while the captain handed him the glass.

Hell of a herd of something.

I believe it's horses.

How far off do you make them?

Hard to tell.

Call Candelario up here.

The sergeant turned and motioned for the Mexican. When he rode up he handed him the glass and the Mexican raised it to his eye and squinted. Then he lowered the glass and watched with his naked eyes and then he raised it and looked again. Then he sat his horse with the glass at his chest like a crucifix.

Well? said the captain.

He shook his head.

What the hell does that mean? They're not buffalo are they?

No. I think maybe horses.

Let me have the glass.

The Mexican handed him the telescope and he glassed the horizon again and collapsed the tube shut with the heel of his hand and replaced it in his bag and raised his hand and they went on.

They were cattle, mules, horses. There were several thousand head and they were moving quarterwise toward the company. By late afternoon riders were visible to the bare eye, a handful of ragged indians mending the outer flanks of the herd with their nimble ponies. Others in hats, perhaps Mexicans. The sergeant dropped back to where the captain was riding.

What do you make of that, Captain?

I make it a parcel of heathen stockthieves is what I make it. What do you?

Looks like it to me.

The captain watched through the glass. I suppose they've seen us, he said.

They've seen us.

How many riders do you make it?

A dozen maybe.

The captain tapped the instrument in his gloved hand. They dont seem concerned, do they?

No sir. They dont.

The captain smiled grimly. We may see a little sport here before the day is out.

The first of the herd began to swing past them in a pall of yellow dust, rangy slatribbed cattle with horns that grew agoggle and no two alike and small thin mules coalblack that shouldered one another and reared their malletshaped heads above the backs of the others and then more cattle and finally the first of the herders riding up the outer side and keeping the stock between themselves and the mounted company. Behind them came a herd of several hundred ponies. The sergeant looked for Candelario. He kept backing along the ranks but he could not find him. He nudged his horse through the column and moved up the far side. The lattermost of the drovers were now coming through the dust and the captain was gesturing and shouting. The ponies had begun to veer off from the herd and the drovers were beating their way toward this armed company met with on the plain. Already you could see through the dust on the ponies' hides the painted chevrons and the hands and rising suns and birds and fish of every device like the shade of old work through sizing on a canvas and now too you could hear above the pounding of the unshod hooves the piping of the quena, flutes made from human bones, and some among the company had begun to saw back on their mounts and some to mill in confusion when up from the offside of those ponies there rose a fabled horde of mounted lancers and archers bearing shields bedight with bits of broken mirrorglass that cast a thousand unpieced suns against the eyes of their enemies. A legion of horribles, hundreds in number, half naked or clad in costumes attic or biblical or wardrobed out of a fevered dream with the skins of animals and silk finery and pieces of uniform still tracked with the blood of prior owners, coats of slain dragoons, frogged and braided cavalry jackets, one in a stovepipe hat and one with an umbrella and one in white stockings and a bloodstained weddingveil and some in headgear of cranefeathers or rawhide helmets that bore the horns of bull or buffalo and one in a pigeontailed coat worn backwards and otherwise naked and one in the armor of a Spanish conquistador, the breastplate and pauldrons deeply dented with old blows of mace or sabre done in another country by men whose very bones were dust and many with their braids spliced up with the hair of other beasts until they trailed upon the ground and their horse's ears and tails worked with bits of brightly colored cloth and one whose horse's whole head was painted crimson red and all the horsemen's faces gaudy and grotesque with daubings like a company of mounted clowns, death hilarious, all howling in a barbarous tongue and riding down upon them like a horde from a hell more horrible yet than the brimstone land of christian reckoning, screeching and yammering and clothed in smoke like those vaporous beings in regions beyond right knowing where the eye wanders and the lip jerks and drools.

Oh my god, said the sergeant.

A rattling drove of arrows passed through the company and men tottered and dropped from their mounts. Horses were rearing and plunging and the mongol hordes swung up along their flanks and turned and rode full upon them with lances.

The company was now come to a halt and the first shots were fired and the gray riflesmoke rolled through the dust as the lancers breached their ranks. The kid's horse sank beneath

55

him with a long pneumatic sigh. He had already fired his rifle and now he sat on the ground and fumbled with his shotpouch. A man near him sat with an arrow hanging out of his neck. He was bent slightly as if in prayer. The kid would have reached for the bloody hoop-iron point but then he saw that the man wore another arrow in his breast to the fletching and he was dead. Everywhere there were horses down and men scrambling and he saw a man who sat charging his rifle while blood ran from his ears and he saw men with their revolvers disassembled trying to fit the spare loaded cylinders they carried and he saw men kneeling who tilted and clasped their shadows on the ground and he saw men lanced and caught up by the hair and scalped standing and he saw the horses of war trample down the fallen and a little whitefaced pony with one clouded eye leaned out of the murk and snapped at him like a dog and was gone. Among the wounded some seemed dumb and without understanding and some were pale through the masks of dust and some had fouled themselves or tottered brokenly onto the spears of the savages. Now driving in a wild frieze of headlong horses with eyes walled and teeth cropped and naked riders with clusters of arrows clenched in their jaws and their shields winking in the dust and up the far side of the ruined ranks in a piping of bone flutes and dropping down off the sides of their mounts with one heel hung in the withers strap and their short bows flexing beneath the outstretched necks of the ponies until they had circled the company and cut their ranks in two and then rising up again like funhouse figures, some with nightmare faces painted on their breasts, riding down the unhorsed Saxons and spearing and clubbing them and leaping from their mounts with knives and running about on the ground with a peculiar bandy-legged trot like creatures driven to alien forms of locomotion and stripping the clothes from the dead and seizing them up by the hair and passing their blades about the skulls of the living and the dead alike and snatching aloft the bloody wigs and hacking and chopping at the naked bodies, ripping off limbs, heads, gutting the strange white torsos and holding up great handfuls of viscera, genitals, some of the savages so slathered up with gore they might have rolled in it like dogs and some who fell upon the dying and sodomized them with loud cries to their fellows. And now the horses of the dead came pounding out of the smoke and dust and circled with flapping leather and wild manes and eyes whited with fear like the eyes of the blind and some were feathered with arrows and some lanced through and stumbling and vomiting blood as they wheeled across the killing ground and clattered from sight again. Dust stanched the wet and naked heads of the scalped who with the fringe of hair below their wounds and tonsured to the bone now lay like maimed and naked monks in the bloodslaked dust and everywhere the dying groaned and gibbered and horses lay screaming.

V

WITH DARKNESS one soul rose wondrously from among the
new slain dead and stole away in the moonlight. The ground
where he'd lain was soaked with blood and with urine from the
voided bladders of the animals and he went forth stained and
stinking like some reeking issue of the incarnate dam of war
herself. The savages had moved to higher ground and he could
see the light from their fires and hear them singing, a strange
and plaintive chanting up there where they'd gone to roast
mules. He made his way among the pale and dismembered,
among the sprawled and legflung horses, and he took a reckoning by the stars and set off south afoot. The night wore a
thousand shapes out there in the brush and he kept his eyes
to the ground ahead. Starlight and waning moon made a faint

shadow of his wanderings on the dark of the desert and all along the ridges the wolves were howling and moving north toward the slaughter. He walked all night and still he could see the fires behind him.

With daylight he made his way toward some outcroppings of rock a mile across the valley floor. He was climbing among the strewn and tumbled boulders when he heard a voice calling somewhere in that vastness. He looked out over the plain but he could see no one. When the voice called again he turned and sat to rest and soon he saw something moving along the slope, a rag of a man clambering toward him over the talus slides. Picking his way with care, looking behind him. The kid could see that nothing followed.

He wore a blanket over his shoulders and his shirtsleeve was ripped and dark with blood and he carried that arm against him with his other hand. His name was Sproule.

Eight of them had escaped. His horse had carried off several arrows and it caved under him in the night and the others had gone on, the captain among them.

They sat side by side among the rocks and watched the day lengthen on the plain below.

Did you not save any of your possibles? Sproule said.

The kid spat and shook his head. He looked at Sproule.

How bad is your arm?

He pulled it to him. I've seen worse, he said.

They sat looking out over those reaches of sand and rock and wind.

What kind of indians was them?

I dont know.

Sproule coughed deeply into his fist. He pulled his bloody arm against him. Damn if they aint about a caution to the christians, he said.

They laid up in the shade of a rock shelf until past noon, scratching out a place in the gray lava dust to sleep, and they set forth in the afternoon down the valley following the war trail and they were very small and they moved very slowly in the immensity of that landscape.

Come evening they hove toward the rimrock again and Sproule pointed out a dark stain on the face of the barren cliff. It looked like the black from old fires. The kid shielded his eyes. The scalloped canyon walls rippled in the heat like drapery folds.

It might could be a seep, said Sproule.

It's a long ways up there.

Well if you see any water closer let's make for that.

The kid looked at him and they set off.

The site lay up a draw and their way was a jumble of fallen rock and scoria and deadlylooking bayonet plants. Small black and olivecolored shrubs blasted under the sun. They stumbled up the cracked clay floor of a dry watercourse. They rested and moved on.

The seep lay high up among the ledges, vadose water dripping down the slick black rock and monkeyflower and deathcamas hanging in a small and perilous garden. The water that reached the canyon floor was no more than a trickle and they leaned by turns with pursed lips to the stone like devouts at a shrine.

They passed the night in a shallow cave above this spot, an old reliquary of flintknappings and ratchel scattered about on the stone floor with beads of shell and polished bone and the charcoal of ancient fires. They shared the blanket in the cold and Sproule coughed quietly in the dark and they rose from time to time to descend and drink at the stone. They were gone before sunrise and the dawn found them on the plain again.

They followed the trampled ground left by the warparty and in the afternoon they came upon a mule that had failed and been lanced and left dead and then they came upon another. The way narrowed through rocks and by and by they came to a bush that was hung with dead babies.

They stopped side by side, reeling in the heat. These small victims, seven, eight of them, had holes punched in their underjaws and were hung so by their throats from the broken stobs of a mesquite to stare eyeless at the naked sky. Bald and pale and bloated, larval to some unreckonable being. The castaways hobbled past, they looked back. Nothing moved. In the afternoon they came upon a village on the plain where smoke still rose from the ruins and all were gone to death. From a distance it looked like a decaying brick kiln. They stood without the walls a long time listening to the silence before they entered.

They went slowly through the little mud streets. There were goats and sheep slain in their pens and pigs dead in the mud. They passed mud hovels where people lay murdered in all attitudes of death in the doorways and the floors, naked and swollen and strange. They found plates of food half eaten and a cat came out and sat in the sun and watched them without interest and flies snarled everywhere in the still hot air.

At the end of the street they came to a plaza with benches and trees where vultures huddled in foul black rookeries. A dead horse lay in the square and some chickens were pecking in a patch of spilled meal in a doorway. Charred poles lay smoldering where the roofs had fallen through and a burro was standing in the open door of the church.

They sat on a bench and Sproule held his wounded arm to his chest and rocked back and forth and blinked in the sun.

What do you want to do? said the kid.

Get a drink of water.

Other than that.

I dont know.

You want to try and head back?

To Texas?

I dont know where else.

We'd never make it.

Well you say.

I aint got no say.

He was coughing again. He held his chest with his good hand and sat as if he'd get his breath.

What have you got, a cold?

I got consumption.

Consumption?

He nodded. I come out here for my health.

The kid looked at him. He shook his head and rose and walked off across the plaza toward the church. There were buzzards squatting among the old carved wooden corbels and he picked up a stone and squailed it at them but they never moved.

The shadows had grown long in the plaza and little coils of dust were moving in the parched clay streets. The carrion birds sat about the topmost corners of the houses with their wings outstretched in attitudes of exhortation like dark little bishops. The kid returned to the bench and propped up one foot and leaned on his knee. Sproule sat as before, still holding his arm.

Son of a bitch is dealin me misery, he said.

The kid spat and looked off down the street. We better just hold up here for tonight.

You reckon it would be all right?

Who with?

What if them indians was to come back?

What would they come back for?

Well what if they was to?

They wont come back.

He held his arm.

I wish you had a knife on you, the kid said.

I wish you did.

There's meat here if a man had a knife.

I aint hungry.

I think we ought to scout these houses and see what all's here.

You go on.

We need to find us a place to sleep.

Sproule looked at him. I dont need to go nowheres, he said.

Well. You suit yourself.

Sproule coughed and spat. I aim to, he said.

The kid turned and went on down the street.

The doorways were low and he had to stoop to clear the lintel beams, stepping down into the cool and earthy rooms. There was no furniture save pallets for sleeping, perhaps a wooden mealbin. He went from house to house. In one room the bones of a small loom black and smoldering. In another a man, the charred flesh drawn taut, the eyes cooked in their sockets. There was a niche in the mud wall with figures of saints dressed in doll's clothes, the rude wooden faces brightly painted. Illustrations cut from an old journal and pasted to the wall, a small picture of a queen, a gypsy card that was the four of cups. There were strings of dried peppers and a few gourds. A glass bottle that held weeds. Outside a bare dirt yard fenced with ocotillo and a round clay oven caved through where black curd trembled in the light within.

He found a clay jar of beans and some dry tortillas and he took them to a house at the end of the street where the embers of the roof were still smoldering and he warmed the food in the ashes and ate, squatting there like some deserter scavenging the ruins of a city he'd fled.

When he returned to the square Sproule was gone. All about lay in shadow. He crossed the square and mounted the stone steps to the door of the church and entered. Sproule was standing in the vestibule. Long buttresses of light fell from the high windows in the western wall. There were no pews in the church and the stone floor was heaped with the scalped and naked and partly eaten bodies of some forty souls who'd barricaded themselves in this house of God against the heathen. The savages had hacked holes in the roof and shot them down from above and the floor was littered with arrowshafts where they'd snapped them off to get the clothes from the bodies. The altars had been hauled down and the tabernacle looted and the great sleeping God of the Mexicans routed from his golden cup. The primitive painted saints in their frames hung cocked on the walls as if an earthquake had visited and a dead Christ in a glass bier lay broken in the chancel floor.

The murdered lay in a great pool of their communal blood. It had set up into a sort of pudding crossed everywhere with the tracks of wolves or dogs and along the edges it had dried and cracked into a burgundy ceramic. Blood lay in dark tongues on the floor and blood grouted the flagstones and ran in the vestibule where the stones were cupped from the feet of the faithful and their fathers before them and it had threaded its way down the steps and dripped from the stones among the dark red tracks of the scavengers.

Sproule turned and looked at the kid as if he'd know his thoughts but the kid just shook his head. Flies clambered over the peeled and wigless skulls of the dead and flies walked on their shrunken eyeballs.

Come on, said the kid.

They crossed the square in the last of the light and went down the narrow street. In the doorway there lay a dead child with two buzzards sitting on it. Sproule shooed his good hand at the buzzards and they bated and hissed and flapped clumsily but they did not fly.

They set forth in the morning with first light while wolves slank from the doorways and dissolved in the fog of the streets. They went by the southwest road the way the savages had come. A little sandy stream, cottonwoods, three white goats. They waded a ford where women lay dead at their wash.

They struggled all day across a terra damnata of smoking slag, passing from time to time the bloated shapes of dead mules or horses. By evening they had drunk all the water they carried. They slept in the sand and woke in the cool early morning dark and went on and they walked the cinderland till they were near to fainting. In the afternoon they came upon a carreta in the trace, tilted on its tongue, the great wheels cut from rounds of a cottonwood trunk and pinned to the axletrees with tenons. They crawled under it for shade and slept until dark and went on.

The rind of a moon that had been in the sky all day was gone and they followed the trail through the desert by starlight, the Pleiades straight overhead and very small and the Great Bear walking the mountains to the north.

My arm stinks, said Sproule.

What?

I said my arm stinks.

You want me to look at it?

What for? You caint do nothin for it.

Well. You suit yourself.

I aim to, said Sproule.

They went on. Twice in the night they heard the little prairie vipers rattle among the scrub and they were afraid. With the dawn they were climbing among shale and whinstone under the wall of a dark monocline where turrets stood like basalt prophets and they passed by the side of the road little wooden crosses propped in cairns of stone where travelers had met with death. The road winding up among the hills and the castaways laboring upon the switchbacks, blackening under the sun, their eyeballs inflamed and the painted spectra racing out at the corners. Climbing up through ocotillo and pricklypear where the rocks trembled and sleared in the sun, rock and no water and the sandy trace and they kept watch for any green thing that might tell of water but there was no water. The ate pinole from a bag with their fingers and went on. Through the noon heat and into the dusk where lizards lay with their leather chins flat to the cooling rocks and fended off the world with thin smiles and eyes like cracked stone plates.

They crested the mountain at sunset and they could see for miles. An immense lake lay below them with the distant blue mountains standing in the windless span of water and the shape of a soaring hawk and trees that shimmered in the heat and a distant city very white against the blue and shaded hills. They sat and watched. They saw the sun drop under the jagged rim of the earth to the west and they saw it flare behind the mountains and they saw the face of the lake darken and the shape of the city dissolve upon it. They slept among the rocks face up like dead men and in the morning when they rose there was no city and no trees and no lake only a barren dusty plain.

Sproule groaned and collapsed back among the rocks. The kid looked at him. There were blisters along his lower lip and his arm through the ripped shirt was swollen and something foul had seeped through among the darker bloodstains. He turned back and looked out over the valley.

Yonder comes somebody, he said.

Sproule didnt answer. The kid looked at him. I aint lyin, he said.

Indians, said Sproule. Aint it?

I dont know. Too far to tell.

What do you aim to do?

I dont know.

What happened to the lake?

I couldnt tell ye.

We both saw it.

People see what they want to see.

Then how come I aint seein it now? I sure as hell want to.

The kid looked out over the plain below.

What if it's indians? said Sproule.

Likely it will be.

Where can we hide at?

The kid spat dryly and wiped his mouth with the back of his hand. A lizard came out from under a rock and crouched on its small cocked elbows over that piece of froth and drank it dry and returned to the rock again leaving only a faint spot in the sand which vanished almost instantly.

They waited all day. The kid made sorties down into the canyons in search of water but he found none. Nothing moved

in that purgatorial waste save carnivorous birds. By early afternoon they could see the horsemen on the switchbacks coming
up the face of the mountain below them. They were Mexicans.

Sproule was sitting with his legs outstretched before him. I
was worried about my old boots lastin me, he said. He looked
up. Go on, he said. Save yourself. He waved his hand.

They were laid up under a ledge of rock in a narrow shade.
The kid didnt answer. Within the hour they could hear the dry
scrabble of hooves among the rocks and the clank of gear. The
first horse to round the point of rock and pass through the gap
in the mountain was the captain's big bay and he carried the
captain's saddle but he did not carry the captain. The refugees
stood by the side of the road. The riders looked burnt and
haggard coming up out of the sun and they sat their horses as
if they had no weight at all. There were seven of them, eight of
them. They wore broadbrimmed hats and leather vests and they
carried escopetas across the pommels of their saddles and as
they rode past the leader nodded gravely to them from the
captain's horse and touched his hatbrim and they rode on.

Sproule and the kid looked after them. The kid called out
and Sproule had started to trot clumsily along behind the horses.

The riders began to slump and reel like drunks. Their heads
lolled. Their guffaws echoed among the rocks and they turned
their mounts and sat them and regarded the wanderers with
huge grins.

Qué quiere? cried the leader.

The riders cackled and slapped at one another. They had
nudged their horses forward and they began to ride them about
without aim. The leader turned to the two afoot.

Buscan a los indios?

With this some of the men dismounted and fell to hugging one another and weeping shamelessly. The leader looked
at them and grinned, his teeth white and massive, made for
foraging.

Loonies, said Sproule. They're loonies.

The kid looked up at the leader. How about a drink of water? he said.

The leader sobered, he pulled a long face. Water? he said.

We aint got no water, said Sproule.

But my friend, how no? Is very dry here.

He reached behind him without turning and a leather canteen was passed across the riders to his hand. He shook it and offered it down. The kid pulled the stopper and drank and stood panting and drank again. The leader reached down and tapped the canteen. Basta, he said.

He hung on gulping. He could not see the horseman's face darken. The man shucked one boot backward out of the stirrup and kicked the canteen cleanly from between the kid's hands leaving him there for a moment in a frozen gesture of calling with the canteen rising and turning in the air and the lobes of water gleaming about it in the sun before it clattered to the rocks. Sproule scrambled after it and snatched it up where it lay draining and began to drink, watching over the rim. The horseman and the lad watched each other. Sproule sat back gasping and coughing.

The kid stepped across the rocks and took the canteen from him. The leader kneed his horse forward and drew a sword from its place beneath his leg and leaning forward ran the blade under the strap and raised it up. The point of the blade was about three inches from the kid's face and the canteen strap was draped across the flat of it. The kid had stopped and the rider raised the canteen gently from his hands and let it slide down the blade and come to rest at his side. He turned to the men and smiled and they once again began to hoot and to pummel one another like apes.

He swung the stopper up from where it hung by a thong and drove it home with the heel of his hand. He pitched the canteen to the man behind him and looked down at the travelers. Why you no hide? he said.

From you?

From I.

We were thirsty.

Very thirsty. Eh?

They didnt answer. He was tapping the flat of the sword lightly against the horn of his saddle and he seemed to be forming words in his mind. He leaned slightly to them. When the lambs is lost in the mountain, he said. They is cry. Sometime come the mother. Sometime the wolf. He smiled at them and raised the sword and ran it back where it had come from and turned the horse smartly and trotted it through the horses behind him and the men mounted up and followed and soon all were gone.

Sproule sat without moving. The kid looked at him but he would look away. He was wounded in an enemy country far from home and although his eyes took in the alien stones about yet the greater void beyond seemed to swallow up his soul.

They descended the mountain, going down over the rocks with their hands outheld before them and their shadows contorted on the broken terrain like creatures seeking their own forms. They reached the valley floor at dusk and set off across the blue and cooling land, the mountains to the west a line of jagged slate set endwise in the earth and the dry weeds heeling and twisting in a wind sprung from nowhere.

They walked on into the dark and they slept like dogs in the sand and had been sleeping so when something black flapped up out of the night ground and perched on Sproule's chest. Fine fingerbones stayed the leather wings with which it steadied as it walked upon him. A wrinkled pug face, small and vicious, bare lips crimped in a horrible smile and teeth pale blue in the starlight. It leaned to him. It crafted in his neck two narrow grooves and folding its wings over him it began to drink his blood.

Not soft enough. He woke, put up a hand. He shrieked and the bloodbat flailed and sat back upon his chest and righted itself again and hissed and clicked its teeth.

The lad was up and had seized a rock but the bat sprang away and vanished in the dark. Sproule was clawing at his neck and he was gibbering hysterically and when he saw the kid standing there looking down at him he held out to him his bloodied hands as if in accusation and then clapped them to his ears and cried out what it seemed he himself would not hear, a howl of such outrage as to stitch a caesura in the pulsebeat of the world. But the kid only spat into the darkness of the space between them. I know your kind, he said. What's wrong with you is wrong all the way through you.

IN THE MORNING they crossed a dry wash and the kid hiked up it looking for a tank or a hole but there was none. He picked out a sink in the wash and fell to digging with a bone and after he had dug some two feet into the sand the sand turned damp and then a little more and a slow seep of water began to fill into the furrows he dredged with his fingers. He took off his shirt and pushed it down into the sand and watched it darken and he watched the water rise slowly among the folds of cloth until there was perhaps a cupful and then he lowered his head into the excavation and drank. Then he sat and watched it fill again. He did this for over an hour. Then he put on the shirt and went back down the wash.

Sproule didnt want to take off his shirt. He tried sucking up the water and he got a mouthful of sand.

Why dont you let me use your shirt, he said.

The kid was squatting in the dry gravel of the wash. Suck on ye own shirt, he said.

He took off the shirt. It stuck to the skin and a yellow pus ran. His arm was swollen to the size of his thigh and it was garishly discolored and small worms worked in the open wound. He pushed the shirt down into the hole and leaned and drank.

In the afternoon they came to a crossroads, what else to call it. A faint wagon trace that came from the north and crossed their path and went on to the south. They stood scanning the landscape for some guidance in that emptiness. Sproule sat where the tracks crossed and looked out from the great caves in his skull where his eyes lay. He said that he would not rise.

Yonder's a lake, said the kid.

He would not look.

It lay shimmering in the distance. Its edges rimed with salt. The kid studied it and studied the roads. After a while he nodded toward the south. I believe this here is the most traveled.

It's all right, said Sproule. You go on.

You suit yourself.

Sproule watched him set off. After a while he rose and followed.

They had gone perhaps two miles when they stopped to rest, Sproule sitting with his legs out and his hands in his lap and the lad squatting a little ways from him. Blinking and bearded and filthy in their rags.

Does that sound like thunder to you? said Sproule.

The kid raised his head.

Listen.

The kid looked at the sky, pale blue, unmarked save where the sun burned like a white hole.

I can feel it in the ground, said Sproule.

It aint nothin.

Listen.

The kid rose and looked about. To the north a small movement of dust. He watched it. It did not rise nor did it blow away.

It was a carreta, lumbering clumsily over the plain, a small mule to draw it. The driver may have been asleep. When he saw the fugitives in the trace before him he halted the mule and began to saw it around to go back and he did get it turned but by then the kid had seized the raw leather headstall and hauled

71

the animal to a standstill. Sproule came hobbling up. From the rear of the wagon two children peered out. They were so pale with dust, their hair so white and faces pinched, they looked like little gnomes crouched there. At the sight of the kid before him the driver shrank back and the woman next to him set up a high shrill chittering and began to point from one horizon to the other but he pulled himself up into the bed of the cart and Sproule came dragging after and they lay staring up at the hot canvas tarp while the two waifs drew back into the corner and watched blackeyed as woodmice and the cart turned south again and set off with a rising rumble and clatter.

There was a clay jar of water hung by a thong from the bowstay and the kid took it down and drank from it and gave it to Sproule. Then he took it back and drank the rest. They lay in the floor of the cart among old hides and spills of salt and after a while they slept.

It was dark when they entered the town. The jostle of the cart ceasing was what woke them. The kid raised himself up and looked out. Starlight in a mud street. The wagon empty. The mule wheezed and stamped in the traces. After a while the man came from the shadows and led them along a lane into a yard and he backed the mule until the cart was alongside a wall and then he unhitched the mule and led it away.

He lay back in the tilted cartbed. It was cold in the night and he lay with his knees drawn up under a piece of hide that smelled of mold and urine and he slept and woke all night and all night dogs barked and in the dawn cocks called and he heard horses on the road.

In the first gray light flies began to land on him. They touched his face and woke him and he brushed them away. After a while he sat up.

They were in a barren mudwalled courtyard and there was a house made of reeds and clay. Chickens stepped about and clucked and scratched. A small boy came from the house and pulled down his pants and shat in the yard and rose and went in again. The kid looked at Sproule. He was lying with his face to the wagonboards. He was partly covered with his blanket and flies were crawling on him. The kid reached to shake him. He was cold and wooden. The flies rose, then they settled back.

The kid was standing by the cart pissing when the soldiers rode into the yard. They seized him and tied his hands behind him and they looked in the cart and talked among themselves and then they led him out into the street.

He was taken to an adobe building and put in an empty room. He sat in the floor while a wild-eyed boy with an old musket watched him. After a while they came and took him out again.

They led him through the narrow mud streets and he could hear music like a fanfare growing the louder, First children walked with him and then old folk and finally a throng of brown-skinned villagers all dressed in white cotton like attendants in an institution, the women in dark rebozos, some with their breasts exposed, their faces stained red with almagre, smoking small cigars. Their numbers swelled and the guards with their shoul-dered fusils frowned and shouted at the jostlers and they went on along the tall adobe wall of a church and into the plaza.

There was a bazaar in progress. A traveling medicine show, a primitive circus. They passed stout willow cages clogged with vipers, with great limegreen serpents from some more southerly latitude or beaded lizards with their black mouths wet with venom. A reedy old leper held up handfuls of tapeworms from a jar for all to see and cried out his medicines against them and they were pressed about by other rude apothecaries and by vendors and mendicants until all came at last before a trestle whereon stood a glass carboy of clear mescal. In this container with hair afloat and eyes turned upward in a pale face sat a human head.

They dragged him forward with shouts and gestures. Mire, mire, they cried. He stood before the jar and they urged his consideration of it and they tilted it around so that the head should face him. It was Captain White. Lately at war among the heathen. The kid looked into the drowned and sightless eyes of his old commander. He looked about at the villagers and at the soldiers, their eyes all upon him, and he spat and wiped his mouth. He aint no kin to me, he said.

THEY PUT HIM in an old stone corral with three other ragged refugees from the expedition. They sat stunned and blinking against the wall or roved the perimeter around in the dry tracks of mules and horses and retched and shat while small boys hooted from the parapet.

He fell in with a thin boy from Georgia. I was sickern a dog, the boy said. I was afraid I was goin to die and then I was afraid I wasnt.

I seen a rider on the captain's horse up in the country from here, the kid told him.

Aye, said the Georgian. They killed him and Clark and another boy I never did know his name. We come on into town and the very next day they had us in the calabozo and this selfsame son of a bitch is down there with the guards laughin and drinkin and playin cards, him and the jefe, to see who gets the captain's horse and who gets his pistols. I guess you seen the captain's head.

I seen it.

That's the worst thing I ever seen in my life.

Somebody ought to of pickled it a long time ago. By rights they ought to pickle mine. For ever takin up with such a fool.

They drifted as the day advanced from wall to wall to keep out of the sun. The boy from Georgia told him of his comrades displayed on slabs cold and dead in the market. The captain headless in a wallow half eaten by hogs. He ran his heel out in the dust and gouged a little place for it to rest. They fixin to send us to Chihuahua City, he said.

How do you know?

That's what they say. I dont know.

That's what who says?

Shipman yonder. He speaks the lingo some.

The kid regarded the man spoken of. He shook his head and spat dryly.

All day small boys perched on the walls and watched them by shifts and pointed and jabbered. They'd walk around the parapet and try to piss down on sleepers in the shade but the prisoners kept alert. Some at first threw stones but the kid picked one from the dust the size of an egg and with it dropped a small child cleanly from the wall with no sound other than the muted thud of its landing on the far side.

Now you gone and done it, said the Georgian.

The kid looked at him.

They'll be in here with whips and I dont know what all.

The kid spat. They aint about to come in here and eat no whips.

Nor did they. A woman brought them bowls of beans and charred tortillas on a plate of unfired clay. She looked harried and she smiled at them and she had smuggled them sweets under her shawl and there were pieces of meat in the bottom of the bowls that had come from her own table.

Three days later mounted on little malandered mules they set out for the capital as foretold.

THEY RODE five days through desert and mountain and through dusty pueblos where the populace turned out to see them. Their escorts in varied suits of timeworn finery, the prisoners in rags. They'd been given blankets and squatting by the desert fires at night sunblackened and bony and wrapped in these serapes they looked like God's profoundest peons. The soldiers none spoke english and they directed their charges with grunts or gestures. They were indifferently armed and they were much afraid of the indians. They rolled their tobacco in cornhusks and they sat by the fire in silence and listened to the night. Their talk when they talked was of witches or worse and always they sought to parcel from the darkness some voice or cry from among the cries that was no right beast. La gente dice que el coyote es un brujo. Muchas veces el brujo es un coyote.

Y los indios también. Muchas veces llaman como los coyotes.

Y qué es eso?

Nada.

Un tecolote. Nada mas.

Quizás.

When they rode through the gap in the mountains and looked down on the city the sergeant of the expedition halted the horses and spoke to the man behind him and he in turn dismounted and took rawhide thongs from his saddlebag and approached the prisoners and gestured for them to cross their wrists and hold them out, showing how with his own hands. He tied them each in this manner and then they rode on.

They entered the city in a gantlet of flung offal, driven like cattle through the cobbled streets with shouts going up behind for the soldiery who smiled as became them and nodded among the flowers and proffered cups, herding the tattered fortune-seekers through the plaza where water splashed in a fountain and idlers reclined on carven seats of white porphyry and past the governor's palace and past the cathedral where vultures squatted along the dusty entablatures and among the niches in the carved facade hard by the figures of Christ and the apostles, the birds holding out their own dark vestments in postures of strange benevolence while about them flapped on the wind the dried scalps of slaughtered indians strung on cords, the long dull hair swinging like the filaments of certain seaforms and the dry hides clapping against the stones.

They passed old alms-seekers by the church door with their seamy palms outheld and maimed beggars sad-eyed in rags and children asleep in the shadows with flies walking their dreamless faces. Dark coppers in a clackdish, the shriveled eyes of the blind. Scribes crouched by the steps with their quills and inkpots and bowls of sand and lepers moaning through the streets and naked dogs that seemed composed of bone entirely and vendors of tamales and old women with faces dark and harrowed as the land squatting in the gutters over charcoal fires where blackened strips of anonymous meat sizzled and spat. Small orphans were abroad like irate dwarfs and fools and sots drooling and flailing about in the small markets of the metropolis and the prisoners rode past the carnage in the meatstalls and the waxy smell where racks of guts hung black with flies and flayings of meat in great red sheets now darkened with the advancing day and the flensed and naked skulls of cows and sheep with their dull blue eyes glaring wildly and the stiff bodies of deer and javelina and ducks and quail and parrots, all wild things from the country round hanging head downward from hooks.

They were made to dismount and were driven afoot through the crowds and down old stone steps and over a doorsill worn like soap and through an iron sallygate into a cool stone cellar long a prison to take their place among the ghosts of old martyrs and patriots while the gate clanked shut behind them.

When their eyes lost their blindness they could make out figures crouched along the wall. Stirrings in beds of hay like nesting mice disturbed. A light snoring. Outside the rattle of a cart and the dull clop of hooves in the street and through the stones a dim clank of hammers from a smith's shop in another part of the dungeon. The kid looked about. Blackened bits of candlewick lay here and there in pools of dirty grease on the stone floor and strings of dried spittle hung from the walls. A few names scratched where the light could find them out. He squatted and rubbed his eyes. Someone in underwear crossed before him to a pail in the center of the room and stood and pissed. This man then turned and came his way. He was tall and wore his hair to his shoulders. He shuffled through the straw and stood looking down at him. You dont know me, do ye? he said.

The kid spat and squinted up at him. I know ye, he said, I'd know your hide in a tanyard.

VI

WITH DAYLIGHT men rose from the hay and crouched on their haunches and regarded the new arrivals without curiosity. They were half naked and they sucked their teeth and snuffled and stirred and picked at themselves like apes. A chary light had washed a high small window from the dark and an early street-vendor'd begun to cry his wares.

Their morning feed was bowls of cold piñole and they were fitted with chains and routed out into the streets clanking and stinking. Overseen all day by a goldtoothed pervert who carried a plaited rawhide quirt and harried them down the gutters on their knees gathering up the filth. Under the wheels of vending-carts, the legs of beggars, dragging behind them their sacks of refuse. In the afternoon they sat in the shade of a wall and ate their dinner and watched two dogs hung together in the street sidle and step.

How do you like city life? said Toadvine.

I dont like it worth a damn so far.

I keep waitin for it to take with me but it aint done it.

They watched the overseer covertly as he passed, his hands clasped behind his back, his cap cocked over one eye. The kid spat.

I seen him first, said Toadvine.

Seen who first.

You know who. Old Brassteeth yonder.

The kid looked after the sauntering figure.

My biggest worry is that somethin will happen to him. I pray daily for the Lord to watch over him.

How you think you goin to get out of this jackpot that you're in?

We'll get out. It aint like the cárcel.

What's the cárcel?

State penitentiary. There's old pilgrims in there come down the trail back in the twenties.

The kid watched the dogs.

After a while the guard came back along the wall kicking the feet of any who were sleeping. The younger guard carried his escopeta at the ready as if there might be some fabled uprising among these chained and tattered felons. Vamonos, vamonos, he called. The prisoners rose and shuffled out into the sun. A small bell was ringing and a coach was coming up the street. They stood along the curb and took off their hats. The guidon passed ringing the bell and then the coach. It had an eye painted on the side and four mules to draw it, taking the host to some soul. A fat priest tottered after carrying an image. The guards were going among the prisoners snatching the hats from the heads of the newcomers and pressing them into their infidel hands.

When the coach had passed they donned their hats again and moved on. The dogs stood tail to tail. Two other dogs sat a little apart, squatting loosely in their skins, just frames of dogs in napless hides watching the coupled dogs and then watching the prisoners clanking away up the street. All lightly shimmering in the heat, these lifeforms, like wonders much reduced. Rough likenesses thrown up at hearsay after the things themselves had faded in men's minds.

HE'D TAKEN UP a pallet between Toadvine and another Kentuckian, a veteran of the war. This man had returned to claim some darkeyed love he'd left behind two years before when Doniphan's command pulled east for Saltillo and the officers had had to drive back hundreds of young girls dressed as boys that took the road behind the army. Now he would stand in the street solitary in his chains and strangely unassuming, gazing out across the tops of the heads of the townspeople, and at night he'd tell them of his years in the west, an amiable warrior, a reticent man. He'd been at Mier where they fought until the draintiles and the gutters and the spouts from the azoteas ran with blood by the gallon and he told them how the brittle old Spanish bells would explode when hit and how he sat against a wall with his shattered leg stretched out on the cobbles before him listening to a lull in the firing that grew into a strange silence and in this silence there grew a low rumbling that he took for thunder until a cannonball came around the corner trundling over the stones like a wayward bowl and went past and down the street and disappeared from sight. He told how they'd taken the city of Chihuahua, an army of irregulars that fought in rags and underwear and how the cannonballs were solid copper and came loping through the grass like runaway suns and even the horses learned to sidestep or straddle them and how the dames of the city rode up into the hills in buggies and picnicked and watched the battle and how at night as they sat by the fires they could hear the moans of the dying out on the plain and see by its lantern the deadcart moving among them like a hearse from limbo.

They had gravel enough, said the veteran, but they didnt know how to fight. They'd stick. You heard stories about how they found em chained to the trailspades of their pieces, limber-teams and all, but if they was I never seen it. We picked powder in the locks yonder. Blowed them gates open. People in here looked like skinned rats. Whitest Mexicans you'll ever see. Thowed theirselves down and commenced kissin our feet and such. Old Bill, he just turned em all loose. Hell, he didnt know what they'd done. Just told em not to steal nothin. Of course they stole everthing they could get their hands on. Whipped two of em and they both died of it and the very next day another bunch run off with some mules and Bill just flat out hung them fools. Which they did likewise perish of. But I never reckoned I'd be in here my own self.

They were squatting crosslegged by candlelight eating from clay bowls with their fingers. The kid looked up. He poked at the bowl.

What is this? he said.

That's prime bullmeat, son. From the corrida. You'll get it of a Sunday night.

You best keep chewin. Dont let it feel ye to weaken.

He chewed. He chewed and he told them of the encounter with the Comanche and they chewed and listened and nodded.

I'm proud I missed that dance, said the veteran. Them is some cruel sons of bitches. I know of one old boy up on the Llano near the dutch settlements, they caught him, took his horse and all. Left him to walk it. He come crawlin into Fredericksburg on his hands and knees buck naked about six days later and you know what they'd done? Cut the bottoms of his feet off.

Toadvine shook his head. He gestured toward the veteran. Grannyrat here knows em, he told the kid. Fought em. Aint ye, Granny?

The veteran waved his hand. Shot some stealin horses is all. Down towards Saltillo. Wasnt nothin to it. There was a cave down there had been a Lipan burial. Must of been a thousand indians in there all settin around. Had on their best robes and blankets and all. Had their bows and their knives, whatever. Beads. The Mexicans carried everthing off. Stripped em naked. Took it all. They carried off whole indians to their homes and set em in the corner all dressed up but they begun to come apart when they got out of that cave air and they had to be thowed out. Towards the last of it they was some Americans went in there and scalped what was left of em and tried to sell the scalps in Durango. I dont know if they had any luck about it or not. I expect some of them injins had been dead a hundred year.

Toadvine was toweling up grease from his bowl with a folded tortilla. He squinted at the kid in the candlelight. What do you reckon we could get for old Brassteeth's teeth? he said.

THEY SAW patched argonauts from the states driving mules through the streets on their way south through the mountains to the coast. Goldseekers. Itinerant degenerates bleeding westward like some heliotropic plague. They nodded or spoke to the prisoners and dropped tobacco and coins in the street beside them.

They saw blackeyed young girls with painted faces smoking little cigars, going arm in arm and eyeing them brazenly. They saw the governor himself erect and formal within his silkmullioned sulky clatter forth from the double doors of the palace courtyard and they saw one day a pack of viciouslooking humans mounted on unshod indian ponies riding half drunk through the streets, bearded, barbarous, clad in the skins of animals stitched up with thews and armed with weapons of every description, revolvers of enormous weight and bowieknives the size of claymores and short twobarreled rifles with bores you could stick your thumbs in and the trappings of their horses fashioned out of human skin and their bridles woven up from human hair and decorated with human teeth and the riders wearing scapulars or necklaces of dried and blackened human ears and the horses rawlooking and wild in the eye and their teeth bared like feral dogs and riding also in the company a number of half-naked savages reeling in the saddle, dangerous, filthy, brutal, the whole like a visitation from some heathen land where they and others like them fed on human flesh.

Foremost among them, outsized and childlike with his naked face, rode the judge. His cheeks were ruddy and he was smiling and bowing to the ladies and doffing his filthy hat. The enormous dome of his head when he bared it was blinding white and perfectly circumscribed about so that it looked to have been painted. He and the reeking horde of rabble with him passed on through the stunned streets and hove up before the governor's palace where their leader, a small blackhaired man, clapped for entrance by kicking at the oaken doors with his boot. The doors were opened forthwith and they rode in, rode in all, and the doors were closed again.

Gentlemens, said Toadvine, I'll guarangoddamntee ye I know what that there is about.

The following day the judge in the company of others stood in the street smoking a cigar and rocking back on his heels. He wore a pair of good kidskin boots and he was studying the prisoners where they knelt in the gutter clutching up the filth with their bare hands. The kid was watching the judge. When the judge's eyes fell upon him he took the cigar from between his teeth and smiled. Or he seemed to smile. Then he put the cigar between his teeth again.

That night Toadvine called them together and they crouched by the wall and spoke in whispers.

His name is Glanton, said Toadvine. He's got a contract with Trias. They're to pay him a hundred dollars a head for scalps and a thousand for Gómez's head. I told him there was three of us. Gentlemens, we're gettin out of this shithole.

We aint got no outfits.

He knows that. He said he'd find anybody that was a guaranteed hand and take it out of their shares. So dont let on like you aint no seasoned indiankiller cause I claimed we was three of the best.

Three days later they rode out singlefile through the streets with the governor and his party, the governor on a pale gray stallion and the killers on their small warponies, smiling and bowing and the lovely darkskinned girls throwing flowers from the windows and some blowing kisses and small boys running alongside and old men waving their hats and crying out huzzahs and Toadvine and the kid and the veteran bringing up the rear, the veteran's feet tucked into tapaderos slung nearly to the ground, so long were his legs, so short the horse's. Out to the edge of the city by the old stone aqueduct where the governor gave them his blessing and drank their health and their fortune in a simple ceremonial and they took the road upcountry.

VII

IN THIS COMPANY there rode two men named Jackson, one black, one white, both forenamed John. Bad blood lay between them and as they rode up under the barren mountains the white man would fall back alongside the other and take his shadow for the shade that was in it and whisper to him. The black would check or start his horse to shake him off. As if the white man were in violation of his person, had stumbled onto some ritual dormant in his dark blood or his dark soul whereby the shape he stood the sun from on that rocky ground bore something of the man himself and in so doing lay imperiled. The white man laughed and crooned things to him that sounded like the words of love. All watched to see how this would go with them but none would caution either back from his course and when Glanton looked to the rear along the column from time to time he seemed to simply reckon them among his number and ride on.

Earlier that morning the company had met in a courtyard behind a house on the outskirts of the city. Two men carried from a wagon a stenciled ordnance box from the Baton Rouge arsenal and a Prussian jew named Speyer pried open the box with a pritchel and a shoeing hammer and handed up a flat package in brown butcherpaper translucent with grease like a paper of bakery goods. Glanton opened the package and let the paper fall to the dirt. In his hand he held a longbarreled sixshot Colt's patent revolver. It was a huge sidearm meant for dragoons and it carried in its long cylinders a rifle's charge and weighed close to five pounds loaded. These pistols would drive the half-ounce conical ball through six inches of hardwood and there were four dozen of them in the case. Speyer was breaking out the gang-molds and flasks and tools and Judge Holden was unwrapping another of the pistols. The men pressed about. Glanton wiped the bore and chambers of the piece and took the flask from Speyer.

She's a stout looker, said one.

He charged the bores and seated a bullet and drove it home with the hinged lever pinned to the underside of the barrel. When all the chambers were loaded he capped them and looked about. In that courtyard other than merchants and buyers were a number of living things. The first that Glanton drew sight upon was a cat that at that precise moment appeared upon the high wall from the other side as silently as a bird alighting. It turned to pick its way among the cusps of broken glass set upright in the mud masonry. Glanton leveled the huge pistol in one hand and thumbed back the hammer. The explosion in that dead silence was enormous. The cat simply disappeared. There was no blood or cry, it just vanished. Speyer glanced uneasily at the Mexicans. They were watching Glanton. Glanton thumbed back the hammer again and swung the pistol. A group of fowl in the corner of the courtyard that had been pecking in the dry dust stood nervously, their heads at varied angles. The pistol roared and one of the birds exploded in a cloud of feathers. The others began to trot mutely, their long necks craned. He fired again. A second bird spun and lay kicking. The others flared, piping thinly, and Glanton turned with the pistol and shot a small goat that was standing with its throat pressed to the wall in terror and it fell stone dead in the dust and he fired upon a clay garraffa that burst in a shower of potsherds and water and he raised the pistol and swung toward the house and rang the bell in its mud tower above the roof, a solemn tolling that hung on in the emptiness after the echoes of the gunfire had died away.

A haze of gray gunsmoke lay over the courtyard. Glanton set the hammer at halfcock and spun the cylinder and lowered the hammer again. A woman appeared in the doorway of the house and one of the Mexicans spoke to her and she went in again.

Glanton looked at Holden and then he looked at Speyer. The jew smiled nervously.

They aint worth no fifty dollars.

Speyer looked grave. What is your life worth? he said.

In Texas five hundred but you'd have to discount the note with your ass.

Mr Riddle thinks that it's a fair price.

Mr Riddle aint payin it.

He's putting up the money.

Glanton turned the pistol in his hand and examined it.

I thought it was agreed, said Speyer.

Aint nothin agreed.

They were contracted for the war. You'll not see their like again.

Not till some money changes hands it aint agreed.

A detachment of soldiers, ten or a dozen of them, entered from the street with their arms at the ready.

Qué pasa aquí?

Glanton looked at the soldiers without interest.

Nada, said Speyer. Todo va bien.

Bien? The sergeant was looking at the dead birds, the goat.

The woman appeared at the door again.

Está bien, said Holden. Negocios del Gobernador.

The sergeant looked at them and he looked at the woman in the door.

Somos amigos del Señor Riddle, said Speyer.

Andale, said Glanton. You and your halfassedlookin niggers.

The sergeant stepped forward and assumed a posture of authority. Glanton spat. The judge had already crossed the space between them and now he took the sergeant aside and fell to conversing with him. The sergeant came to his armpit and the judge spoke warmly and gestured with a great expansiveness of spirit. The soldiers squatted in the dust with their muskets and regarded the judge without expression.

Dont you give that son of a bitch no money, said Glanton.

But the judge was already bringing the man forward for a formal presentation.

Le presento al sargento Aguilar, he called, hugging the ragged militant to him. The sergeant held out his hand quite gravely. It occupied that space and the attention of all who stood there like something presented for validation and then Speyer stepped forward and took it.

Mucho gusto.

Igualmente, said the sergeant.

The judge escorted him from one to the next of the company, the sergeant formal and the Americans muttering obscenities or shaking their heads silently. The soldiers squatted on their heels and watched each movement in this charade with the same dull interest and at length the judge hove up before the black.

That dark vexed face. He studied it and he drew the sergeant forward the better for him to observe and then he began a laborious introduction in Spanish. He sketched for the sergeant a problematic career of the man before them, his hands drafting with a marvelous dexterity the shapes of what varied paths conspired here in the ultimate authority of the extant—as he told them—like strings drawn together through the eye of a ring. He adduced for their consideration references to the children of Ham, the lost tribes of Israelites, certain passages from the Greek poets, anthropological speculations as to the propagation of the races in their dispersion and isolation through the agency of geological cataclysm and an assessment of racial traits with respect to climatic and geographical influences. The sergeant listened to this and more with great attention and when the judge was done he stepped forward and held out his hand.

Jackson ignored him. He looked at the judge.

What did you tell him, Holden?

Dont insult him, man.

What did you tell him?

The sergeant's face had clouded. The judge took him about the shoulders and leaned and spoke into his ear and the sergeant nodded and stepped back and saluted the black.

What did you tell him, Holden?

That shaking hands was not the custom in your land.

Before that. What did you say to him before that.

The judge smiled. It is not necessary, he said, that the principals here be in possession of the facts concerning their case, for their acts will ultimately accommodate history with or without their understanding. But it is consistent with notions of right principle that these facts—to the extent that they can be readily made to do so—should find a repository in the witness of some third party. Sergeant Aguilar is just such a party and any slight to his office is but a secondary consideration when compared to divergences in that larger protocol exacted by the formal agenda of an absolute destiny. Words are things. The words he is in possession of he cannot be deprived of. Their authority transcends his ignorance of their meaning.

The black was sweating. A dark vein in his temple pulsed like a fuse. The company had listened to the judge in silence. A few smiled. A halfwitted killer from Missouri guffawed softly like an asthmatic. The judge turned again to the sergeant and they spoke together and the judge and he crossed to where the crate stood in the courtyard and the judge showed him one of the pistols and explained its workings with great patience. The sergeant's men had risen and stood waiting. At the gate the judge doled coins into Aguilar's palm and he shook hands formally with each ragged charge and complimented them upon their military bearing and they exited into the street.

At noon that day the partisans rode out each man armed with a pair of the pistols and took the road upcountry as told.

THE OUTRIDERS returned in the evening and the men dismounted for the first time that day and recruited their horses in the sparse swale while Glanton conferred with the scouts. Then they rode on until dark and made camp. Toadvine and the veteran and the kid squatted at a small remove from the fires. They did not know that they were set forth in that company in the place of three men slain in the desert. They watched the Delawares, of whom there were a number in the party, and they too sat somewhat apart, crouched on their heels, one pounding coffeebeans in a buckskin with a rock while the others stared into the fire with eyes as black as gunbores. That night the kid would see one of them sort with his hand among the absolute embers for a right coal with which to light his pipe.

They were about in the morning before daybreak and they caught up and saddled their mounts as soon as it was light enough to see. The jagged mountains were pure blue in the dawn and everywhere birds twittered and the sun when it rose caught the moon in the west so that they lay opposed to each other across the earth, the sun whitehot and the moon a pale replica, as if they were the ends of a common bore beyond whose terminals burned worlds past all reckoning. As the riders came up through the mesquite and pyracantha singlefile in a light clank of arms and chink of bitrings the sun climbed and the moon set and the horses and the dewsoaked mules commenced to steam in flesh and in shadow.

Toadvine had fallen in with a fugitive from Vandiemen's Land named Bathcat who had come west on legbail. He was from Wales by birth and he had but three fingers to his right hand and few teeth. Perhaps he saw in Toadvine a fellow fugitive—an earless and branded felon who had chosen in life much as had he—and he offered to wager as to which Jackson would kill which.

I dont know them boys, said Toadvine.

How do ye think then?

Toadvine spat quietly to one side and looked at the man. I wouldnt want to bet, he said.

Not a gaming man?

Depends on the game.

The blackie will do for him. Take your odds.

Toadvine looked at him. The necklace of human ears he wore looked like a string of dried black figs. He was big and raw-looking and one eyelid sagged where a knife had severed the small muscles there and he was furnished with gear of every class, the fine with the shoddy. He wore good boots and he carried a handsome rifle bound with german silver but the rifle was slung in a cutoff bootleg and his shirt was in tatters and his hat rancid.

Ye've not hunted the aborigines afore, said Bathcat.

Who says it?

I know it.

Toadvine didnt answer.

You'll find em right lively.

So I hear.

The Vandiemenlander smiled. Much is changed, he said. When I first come into this country there was savages up on the San Saba had hardly seen white men. They come into our camp and we shared our mess with em and they couldnt keep their eyes off our knives. Next day they brought whole strings of horses into camp to trade. We didnt know what they wanted. They had knives of their own, such as they was. But what it was, you see, was they'd never seen sawed bones in a stew before.

Toadvine glanced at the man's forehead but the man's hat was pushed down almost to his eyes. The man smiled and forked the hat back slightly with his thumb. The print of the hatband lay on his forehead like a scar but there was no mark other. Only on the inside of his lower arm was there tattooed a number which Toadvine would see in a Chihuahua bathhouse and again when he would cut down the man's torso where it hung skewered by its heels from a treelimb in the wastes of Pimeria Alta in the fall of that year.

They rode up through cholla and nopal, a dwarf forest of spined things, through a stone gap in the mountains and down among blooming artemisia and aloe. They crossed a broad plain of desert grass dotted with palmilla. On the slopes were gray stone walls that followed the ridgelines down to where they lay broached and tumbled upon the plain. They did not noon nor did they siesta and the cotton eye of the moon squatted at broad day in the throat of the mountains to the east and they were still riding when it overtook them at its midnight meridian, sketching on the plain below a blue cameo of such dread pilgrims clanking north.

They spent the night in the corral of a hacienda where all night men kept watchfires burning on the azoteas or roofs. Two weeks before this a party of campesinos had been hacked to death with their own hoes and partly eaten by hogs while the Apaches rounded up what stock would drive and disappeared into the hills. Glanton ordered a goat killed and this was done in the corral while the horses shied and trembled and in the flaring light of the fires the men squatted and roasted the meat and ate it with knives and wiped their fingers in their hair and turned in to sleep upon the beaten clay.

At dusk of the third day they rode into the town of Corralitos, the horses shuffling through the caked ash and the sun glaring redly through the smoke. The smelter chimneys were ranged against an ashen sky and the globy lights of the furnaces glowered under the dark of the hills. It had rained in the day and the windowlights of the low mud houses were reflected in pools along the flooded road out of which great dripping swine rose moaning before the advancing horses like oafish demons routed from a fen. The houses were loopholed and parapeted and the air was filled with the fumes of arsenic. The people had turned out to see the Texans, they called them, standing solemnly along the way and noting the least of their gestures with looks of awe, looks of wonder.

They camped in the plaza, blackening the cottonwoods with their fires and driving forth the sleeping birds, the flames lighting up the wretched town to its darkest pens and bringing forth even the blind tottering with their hands outstretched toward that conjectural day. Glanton and the judge with the Brown brothers rode out to the hacienda of General Zuloaga where they were received and given their dinner and the night passed without incident.

In the morning when they had saddled their mounts and were assembled in the square to ride out they were approached by a family of itinerant magicians seeking safe passage upcountry as far as Janos. Glanton looked down at them from his place at the head of the column. Their goods were piled up in tattered panniers lashed to the backs of three burros and they were a man and his wife and a grown boy and a girl. They were dressed in fools costumes with stars and halfmoons embroidered on and the once gaudy colors were faded and pale from the dust of the road and they looked a set of right wanderfolk cast on this evil terrain. The old man came forward and took the bridle of Glanton's horse.

Get your hands off the horse, said Glanton.

He spoke no english but he did as he was told. He commenced to put forth his case. He gestured, he pointed back toward the others. Glanton watched him, who knows if he heard at all. He turned and looked at the boy and at the two women and he looked down at the man again.

What are you? he said.

The man held his ear toward Glanton and looked up with mouth agape.

I said what are you? Are you a show?

He looked back toward the others.

A show, said Glanton. Bufones.

The man's face brightened. Sí, he said. Sí, bufones. Todo. He turned to the boy. Casimero! Los perros!

The boy ran to one of the burros and began to tug among the packings. He came up with a pair of bald and bat-eared animals slightly larger than rats and pale brown in color and he pitched them into the air and caught them on the palms of his hands where they began to pirouette mindlessly.

Mire, mire! called the man. He was fishing about in his pockets and soon he was juggling four small wooden balls in front of Glanton's horse. The horse snorted and lifted its head and Glanton leaned over the saddle and spat and wiped his mouth with the back of his hand.

Aint that the drizzlin shits, he said.

The man was juggling and calling back over his shoulder to the women and the dogs were dancing and the women were turning to in preparation of something when Glanton spoke to the man.

Dont start no more of that crazy shit. You want to ride with us you fall in in the back. I promise you nothin. Vamonos.

He rode on. The company clanked into motion and the juggler ran shooing the women toward the burros and the boy stood wide-eyed with the dogs under his arm until the man spoke to him. They rode out through the rabble past great cones of slag and tailings. The people watched them go. Some of the men stood hand in hand like lovers and a small child led forth a blind man on a string to a place of vantage.

AT NOON they crossed the stony bottom of the Casas Grandes River and they rode along a benchland above the gaunt rill of water past a place of bones where Mexican soldiers had slaughtered an encampment of Apaches some years gone, women and children, the bones and skulls scattered along the bench for half a mile and the tiny limbs and toothless paper skulls of infants like the ossature of small apes at their place of murder and old remnants of weathered basketry and broken pots among the gravel. They rode on. The river led a limegreen corridor of trees down out of the barren mountains. To the west lay the ragged Carcaj and to the north the Animas peaks dim and blue.

They made camp that night on a windy plateau among piñon and juniper and the fires leaned downwind in the darkness and hot chains of sparks raced among the scrub. The jugglers unloaded the burros and began to set up a large gray tent. The canvas was scrawled with arcana and it flapped and lurched, stood towering, luffed and wrapped them about. The girl lay on the ground holding to one corner. She began to drag through the sand. The juggler took small steps. The woman's eyes were rigid in the light. As the company watched the four of them all clutched to the snapping cloth were towed mutely from sight beyond the reach of the firelight and into the howling desert like supplicants at the skirts of some wild and irate goddess.

The pickets saw the tent lumber horribly away into the night. When the family of jugglers returned they were arguing among themselves and the man went again to the edge of the firelight and peered out upon the wrathful blackness and spoke to it and gestured with his fist nor would he return until the woman sent the boy to fetch him. Now he sat staring at the flames while the family unpacked. They watched him uneasily. Glanton watched him also.

Showman, he said.

The juggler looked up. He put one finger to his chest.

You, said Glanton.

He rose and shuffled forward. Glanton was smoking a slender black cigar. He looked up at the juggler.

You tell fortunes?

The juggler's eyes skittered. Cómo? he said.

Glanton put the cigar in his mouth and mimed a deal of cards with his hands. La baraja, he said. Para adivinar la suerte.

The juggler tossed one hand aloft. Sí, sí, he said, shaking his head with vigor. Todo, todo. He held up one finger and then turned and made his way to the trove of shoddy partly offloaded from the burros. When he returned he was smiling affably and manipulating the cards very nimbly.

Venga, he called. Venga.

The woman followed him. The juggler squatted before Glanton and spoke to him in a low voice. He turned and looked at the woman and he riffled the cards and rose and took her by the hand and led her over the ground away from the fire and seated her facing out into the night. She swept up her skirt and composed herself and he took from his shirt a kerchief and with it bound her eyes.

Bueno, he called, Puedes ver?

No.

Nada?

Nada, said the woman.

Bueno, said the juggler.

He turned with the deck of cards and advanced toward Glanton. The woman sat like a stone. Glanton waved him away.

Los caballeros, he said.

The juggler turned. The black was squatting by the fire watching and when the juggler fanned the cards he rose and came forward.

The juggler looked up at him. He folded the cards and fanned them again and he made a pass over them with his left

97

hand and held them forth and Jackson took a card and looked at it.

Bueno, said the juggler. Bueno. He admonished caution with a forefinger to his thin lips and took the card and held it aloft and turned with it. The card popped once sharply. He looked at the company seated about the fire. They were smoking, they were watching. He made a slow sweep before him with the card outheld. It bore the picture of a fool in harlequin and a cat. El tonto, he called.

El tonto, said the woman. She raised her chin slightly and she began a singsong chant. The dark querent stood solemnly, like a man arraigned. His eyes shifted over the company. The judge sat upwind from the fire naked to the waist, himself like some great pale deity, and when the black's eyes reached his he smiled. The woman ceased. The fire fled down the wind.

Quién, quién, cried the juggler.

She paused. El negro, she said.

El negro, cried the juggler, turning with the card. His clothes snapped in the wind. The woman raised her voice and spoke again and the black turned to his mates.

What does she say?

The juggler had turned and was making small bows to the company.

What does she say? Tobin?

The expriest shook his head. Idolatry, Blackie, idolatry. Do not mind her.

What does she say Judge?

The judge smiled. With his thumb he had been routing small life from the folds of his hairless skin and now he held up one hand with the thumb and forefinger pressed together in a gesture that appeared to be a benediction until he flung something unseen into the fire before him. What does she say?

What does she say.

I think she means to say that in your fortune lie our fortunes all.

And what is that fortune?

The judge smiled blandly, his pleated brow not unlike a dolphin's. Are you a drinking man, Jackie?

No more than some.

I think she'd have you beware the demon rum. Prudent counsel enough, what do you think?

That aint no fortune.

Exactly so. The priest is right.

The black frowned at the judge but the judge leaned forward to regard him. Wrinkle not thy sable brow at me, my friend. All will be known to you at last. To you as to every man.

Now a number of the company seated there seemed to weigh the judge's words and some turned to look at the black. He stood an uneasy honoree and at length he stepped back from the firelight and the juggler rose and made a motion with the cards, sweeping them in a fan before him and then proceeding along the perimeter past the boots of the men with the cards outheld as if they would find their own subject.

Quién, quién, he whispered among them.

They were right loath all. When he came before the judge the judge, who sat with one hand splayed across the broad expanse of his stomach, raised a finger and pointed.

Young Blasarius yonder, he said.

Cómo?

El joven.

El joven, whispered the juggler. He looked about him slowly with an air of mystery until he found with his eyes the one so spoken. He moved past the adventurers quickening his step. He stood before the kid, he squatted with the cards and fanned them with a slow rhythmic motion akin to the movements of certain birds at court.

Una carta, una carta, he wheezed.

The kid looked at the man and he looked at the company about.

Sí, sí, said the juggler, offering the cards.

He took one. He'd not seen such cards before, yet the one he held seemed familiar to him. He turned it upside down and regarded it and he turned it back.

The juggler took the boy's hand in his own and turned the card so he could see. Then he took the card and held it up.

Cuatro de copas, he called out.

The woman raised her head. She looked like a blindfold mannequin raised awake by a string.

Cuatro de copas, she said. She moved her shoulders. The wind went among her garments and her hair.

Quién, called the juggler.

El hombre . . . she said. El hombre más joven. El muchacho.

El muchacho, called the juggler. He turned the card for all to see. The woman sat like that blind interlocutrix between Boaz and Jachin inscribed upon the one card in the juggler's deck that they would not see come to light, true pillars and true card, false prophetess for all. She began to chant.

The judge was laughing silently. He bent slightly the better to see the kid. The kid looked at Tobin and at David Brown and he looked at Glanton himself but they were none laughing. The juggler kneeling before him watched him with a strange intensity. He followed the kid's gaze to the judge and back. When the kid looked down at him he smiled a crooked smile.

Get the hell away from me, said the kid.

The juggler leaned his ear forward. A common gesture and one that served for any tongue. The ear was dark and misshapen, as if in being put forth in this fashion it had suffered no few clouts, or perhaps the very news men had for him had blighted it. The kid spoke to him again but a man named Tate from Kentucky who had fought with McCulloch's Rangers as had Tobin and others among them leaned and whispered to the ragged soothsayer and he rose and made a slight bow and moved away. The woman had ceased her chanting. The juggler stood flapping in the wind and the fire lashed a long hot tail over the ground. Quién, quién, he called.

El jefe, said the judge.

The juggler's eyes sought out Glanton. He sat unmoved. The juggler looked at the old woman where she sat apart, facing the dark, lightly tottering, racing the night in her rags. He raised his finger to his lips and he spread his arms in a gesture of uncertainty.

El jefe, hissed the judge.

The man turned and went along the group at the fire and brought himself before Glanton and crouched and offered up the cards, spreading them in both hands. If he spoke his words were snatched away unheard. Glanton smiled, his eyes were small against the stinging grit. He put one hand forth and paused, he looked at the juggler. Then he took a card.

The juggler folded shut the deck and tucked it among his clothes. He reached for the card in Glanton's hand. Perhaps he touched it, perhaps not. The card vanished. It was in Glanton's hand and then it was not. The juggler's eyes snapped after it where it had gone down the dark. Perhaps Glanton had seen the card's face. What could it have meant to him? The juggler reached out to that naked bedlam beyond the fire's light but in the doing he overbalanced and fell forward against Glanton and created a moment of strange liaison with his old man's arms about the leader as if he would console him at his scrawny bosom.

Glanton swore and flung him away and at that moment the old woman began to chant.

Glanton rose.

She raised her jaw, gibbering at the night.

Shut her up, said Glanton.

La carroza, la carroza, cried the beldam. Invertido. Carta de guerra, de venganza. La ví sin ruedas sobre un rio obscuro . . .

Glanton called to her and she paused as if she'd heard him but it was not so. She seemed to catch some new drift in her divinings.

Perdida, perdida. La carta está perdida en la noche.

The girl standing this while at the edge of the howling darkness crossed herself silently. The old malabarista was on his knees where he'd been flung. Perdida, perdida, he whispered.

Un maleficio, cried the old woman. Qué viento tan maleante . . .

By god you will shut up, said Glanton, drawing his revolver.

Carroza de muertos, llena de huesos. El joven qué . . .

The judge like a great ponderous djinn stepped through the fire and the flames delivered him up as if he were in some way native to their element. He put his arms around Glanton. Someone snatched the old woman's blindfold from her and she and the juggler were clouted away and when the company turned in to sleep and the low fire was roaring in the blast like a thing alive these four yet crouched at the edge of the firelight among their strange chattels and watched how the ragged flames fled down the wind as if sucked by some maelstrom out there in the void, some vortex in that waste apposite to which man's transit and his reckonings alike lay abrogate. As if beyond will or fate he and his beasts and his trappings moved both in card and in substance under consignment to some third and other destiny.

In the morning when they rode out it was that pale day with the sun not risen and the wind had abated in the night and the things of the night were gone. The juggler on his burro trotted out to the head of the column and fell in with Glanton and they rode on together and they were so riding in the afternoon when the company entered the town of Janos.

AN ANCIENT walled presidio composed wholly of mud, a tall mud church and mud watchtowers and all of it rainwashed and lumpy and sloughing into a soft decay. The advent of the riders bruited by scurvid curs that howled woundedly and slank among the crumbling walls.

They rode past the church where old Spanish bells seagreen

with age hung from a pole between low mud dolmens. Darkeyed children watched from the hovels. The air was heavy with the smoke from charcoal fires and a few old pelados sat mute in the doorways and many of the houses were caved and ruinous and stood for pens. An old man with soapy eyes lurched out at them and held forth his hand. Una corta caridad, he croaked to the passing horses. Por Dios.

In the square two of the Delawares and the outrider Webster were squatting in the dust with a weathered old woman the color of pipeclay. Dry old crone, half naked, her paps like wrinkled aubergines hanging from under the shawl she wore. She stared at the ground nor did she look up even when the horses stood all about her.

Glanton looked down the square. The town appeared empty. There was a small company of soldiers garrisoned here but they did not turn out. Dust was blowing through the streets. His horse leaned and sniffed at the old woman and jerked its head and trembled and Glanton patted the animal's neck and dismounted.

She was in a meatcamp about eight mile up the river, said Webster. She caint walk.

How many were there?

We reckoned maybe fifteen or twenty. They didnt have no stock to amount to anything. I dont know what she was doin there.

Glanton crossed in front of his horse, passing the reins behind his back.

Watch her, Cap. She bites.

She had raised her eyes to the level of his knees. Glanton pushed the horse back and took one of the heavy saddle pistols from its scabbard and cocked it.

Watch yourself there.

Several of the men stepped back.

The woman looked up. Neither courage nor heartsink in

those old eyes. He pointed with his left hand and she turned to follow his hand with her gaze and he put the pistol to her head and fired.

The explosion filled all that sad little park. Some of the horses shied and stepped. A fistsized hole erupted out of the far side of the woman's head in a great vomit of gore and she pitched over and lay slain in her blood without remedy. Glanton had already put the pistol at halfcock and he flicked away the spent primer with his thumb and was preparing to recharge the cylinder. McGill, he said.

A Mexican, solitary of his race in that company, came forward.

Get that receipt for us.

He took a skinning knife from his belt and stepped to where the old woman lay and took up her hair and twisted it about his wrist and passed the blade of the knife about her skull and ripped away the scalp.

Glanton looked at the men. They were stood some looking down at the old woman, some already seeing to their mounts or their equipage. Only the recruits were watching Glanton. He seated a pistolball in the mouth of the chamber and then he raised his eyes and looked across the square. The juggler and his family stood aligned like witnesses and beyond them in the long mud facade faces that had been watching from the doors and the naked windows dropped away like puppets in a gallery before the slow sweep of his eyes. He levered the ball home and capped the piece and spun the heavy pistol in his hand and returned it to the scabbard at the horse's shoulder and took the dripping trophy from McGill and turned it in the sun the way a man might qualify the pelt of an animal and then handed it back and took up the trailing reins and led his horse out through the square toward the water at the ford.

They made camp in a grove of cottonwoods across the creek just beyond the walls of the town and with dark they drifted in small groups through the smoky streets. The circus folk had set up a little pitchtent in the dusty plaza and had stood a few poles about mounted with cressets of burning oil. The juggler was beating a sort of snaredrum made of tin and rawhide and calling out in a high nasal voice his bill of entertainments while the woman shrieked Pase pase pase, sweeping her arms about her in a gesture of the greatest spectacle. Toadvine and the kid watched among the milling citizenry. Bathcat leaned and spoke to them.

Look yonder, chappies.

They turned to look where he pointed. The black stood stripped to the waist behind the tent and as the juggler turned with a sweep of his arm the girl gave him a shove and he leaped from the tent and strode about with strange posturings under the lapsing flare of the torches.

VIII

Another cantina, another advisor – Monte – A knifing –
The darkest corner of the tavern the most conspicuous –
The sereño – Riding north – The meatcamp – Grannyrat –
Under the Animas peaks – A confrontation and a killing –
Another anchorite, another dawn.

THEY PAUSED without the cantina and pooled their coins and Toadvine pushed aside the dried cowhide that hung for a door and they entered a place where all was darkness and without definition. A lone lamp hung from a crosstree in the ceiling and in the shadows dark figures sat smoking. They made their way across the room to a claytiled bar. The place reeked of woodsmoke and sweat. A thin little man appeared before them and placed his hands ceremonially upon the tiles.

Dígame, he said.

Toadvine took off his hat and put it on the bar and swept a clawed hand through his hair.

What have you got that a man could drink with just a minimum risk of blindness and death.

Cómo?

He cocked his thumb at his throat. What have you got to drink, he said.

The barman turned and looked behind him at his wares. He seemed uncertain whether anything there would answer their requirements.

Mescal?

Suit everbody?

Trot it out, said Bathcat.

The barman poured the measures from a clay jar into three dented tin cups and pushed them forward with care like counters on a board.

Cuánto, said Toadvine.

The barman looked fearful. Seis? he said.

Seis what?

The man held up six fingers.

Centavos, said Bathcat.

Toadvine doled the coppers onto the bar and drained his cup and paid again. He gestured at the cups all three with a wag of his finger. The kid took up his cup and drained it and set it down again. The liquor was rank, sour, tasted faintly of creosote. He was standing like the others with his back to the bar and he looked over the room. At a table in the far corner men were playing cards by the light of a single tallow candle. Along the wall opposite crouched figures seeming alien to the light who watched the Americans with no expression at all.

There's a game for ye, said Toadvine. Play monte in the dark with a pack of niggers. He raised the cup and drained it and set it on the bar and counted the remaining coins. A man was shuffling toward them out of the gloom. He had a bottle under his arm and he set it on the tiles with care together with his cup and spoke to the barman and the barman brought him a clay pitcher of water. He turned the pitcher so that the handle of it stood to his right and he looked at the kid. He was old and he wore a flatcrowned hat of a type no longer much seen in that country and he was dressed in dirty white cotton drawers and shirt. The huaraches he wore looked like dried and blackened fish lashed to the floors of his feet.

You are Texas? he said.

The kid looked at Toadvine.

You are Texas, the old man said. I was Texas three year. He held up his hand. The forefinger was gone at the first joint and perhaps he was showing them what happened in Texas or perhaps he merely meant to count the years. He lowered the hand and turned to the bar and poured wine into the cup and took up the jar of water and poured it sparingly after. He drank and set the cup down and turned to Toadvine. He wore thin white whiskers at the point of his chin and he wiped them with the back of his hand before looking up again.

You are socieded de guerra. Contra los barbaros.

Toadvine didnt know. He looked like some loutish knight beriddled by a troll.

The old man put a phantom rifle to his shoulder and made a noise with his mouth. He looked at the Americans. You kill the Apache, no?

Toadvine looked at Bathcat. What does he want? he said.

The Vandiemenlander passed his own threefingered hand across his mouth but he allowed no affinity. The old man's full he said. Or mad.

Toadvine propped his elbows on the tiles behind him. He looked at the old man and he spat on the floor. Craziern a runaway nigger, aint ye? he said.

There was a groan from the far side of the room. A man rose and went along the wall and bent to speak with others. The groans came again and the old man passed his hand before his face twice and kissed the ends of his fingers and looked up.

How much monies they pay you? he said.

No one spoke.

You kill Gómez they pay you much monies.

The man in the dark of the far wall moaned again. Madre de Dios, he called.

Gómez, Gómez, said the old man. Even Gómez. Who can

ride against the Tejanos? They are soldiers. Que soldados tan valientes. La sangre de Gómez, sangre de la gente . . .

He looked up. Blood, he said. This country is give much blood. This Mexico. This is a thirsty country. The blood of a thousand Christs. Nothing.

He made a gesture toward the world beyond where all the land lay under darkness and all a great stained altarstone. He turned and poured his wine and poured again from the waterjar, temperate old man, and drank.

The kid watched him. He watched him drink and he watched him wipe his mouth. When he turned he spoke neither to the kid nor Toadvine but seemed to address the room.

I pray to God for this country. I say that to you. I pray. I dont go in the church. What I need to talk to them dolls there? I talk here.

He pointed to his chest. When he turned to the Americans his voice softened again. You are fine caballeros, he said. You kill the barbaros. They cannot hide from you. But there is another caballero and I think that no man hides, from him. I was a soldier. It is like a dream. When even the bones is gone in the desert the dreams is talk to you, you dont wake up forever.

He drained his cup and took up his bottle and went softly away on his sandals into the farther dim of the cantina. The man at the wall moaned again and called upon his god. The Vandiemenlander and the barman spoke together and the barman gestured at the dark in the corner and shook his head and the Americans chambered down their last cups and Toadvine pushed the few tlacos toward the barman and they went out.

That was his son, said Bathcat.

Who was?

The lad in the corner cut with a knife.

He was cut?

One of the chaps at the table cut him. They were playin cards and one of them cut him.

Why dont he leave.

I asked him the same myself.

What did he say?

He had a question for me. Said where would he go to?

They made their way through the narrow walled streets toward the gate and the fires of the camp beyond. A voice was calling. It called: Las diez y media, tiempo sereno. It was the watchman at his rounds and he passed them with his lantern calling softly the hour.

IN THE PREDAWN dark the sounds about describe the scene to come. The first cries of birds in the trees along the river and the clink of harness and the snuffle of horses and the gentle sound of their cropping. In the darkened village roosters have begun. The air smells of horses and charcoal. The camp has begun to stir. Sitting all about in the accruing light are the children from the town. None of the men rising know how long they have been there in darkness and silence.

When they rode through the square the dead squaw was gone and the dust was newly raked. The juggler's lamps were stark and black atop their poles and the fire was cold before the pitchtent. An old woman who had been chopping wood raised up and stood with the axe in both hands as they passed.

They rode through the sacked indian camp at midmorning, the blackened sheets of meat draped across the bushes or hung from poles like strange dark laundry. Deerhides were pegged out on the ground and white or ruddled bones lay strewn over the rocks in a primitive shambles. The horses cocked their ears and stepped quickly. They rode on. In the afternoon black Jackson caught them up, his mount surbated and all but blown. Glanton turned in the saddle and measured him with his eye. Then he nudged his horse forward and the black fell in with his pale wayfellows and all rode on as before.

They did not miss the veteran until that evening. The judge

made his way down through the smoke of the cookfires and squatted before Toadvine and the kid.

What's become of Chambers, he said.

I believe he's quit.

Quit.

I believe he has.

Did he ride out this morning?

Not with us he never.

It was my understanding that you spoke for your group.

Toadvine spat. He appears to of spoke for hisself.

When did you last see him.

Seen him yesterday evenin.

But not this morning.

Not this mornin.

The judge regarded him.

Hell, said Toadvine. I allowed you knowed he was gone. It aint like he was so small you never would miss him.

The judge looked at the kid. He looked at Toadvine again. Then he rose and went back.

In the morning two of the Delawares were gone. They rode on. By noon they had begun to climb toward the gap in the mountains. Riding up through wild lavender or soapweed, under the Animas peaks. The shadow of an eagle that had set forth from those high and craggy fastnesses crossed the line of riders below and they looked up to mark it where it rode in that brittle blue and faultless void. They came up through piñon and scruboak and they crossed the gap through a high pine forest and rode on through the mountains.

In the evening they came out upon a mesa that overlooked all the country to the north. The sun to the west lay in a holocaust where there rose a steady column of small desert bats and to the north along the trembling perimeter of the world dust was blowing down the void like the smoke of distant armies. The crumpled butcherpaper mountains lay in sharp shadowfold under the long blue dusk and in the middle distance the glazed bed of a dry lake lay shimmering like the mare imbrium and herds of deer were moving north in the last of the twilight, harried over the plain by wolves who were themselves the color of the desert floor.

Glanton sat his horse and looked long out upon this scene. Sparse on the mesa the dry weeds lashed in the wind like the earth's long echo of lance and spear in old encounters forever unrecorded. All the sky seemed troubled and night came quickly over the evening land and small gray birds flew crying softly after the fled sun. He chucked up the horse. He passed and so passed all into the problematical destruction of darkness.

They camped that night on the foreplain at the foot of a talus slope and the murder that had been reckoned upon took place. The white man Jackson had been drunk in Janos and he had ridden red-eyed and sullen for two days through the mountains. He now sat disheveled by the fire with his boots off drinking aguardiente from a flask, circumscribed about by his companions and by the cries of wolves and providence of night. He was sitting so when the black approached the fire and threw down his apishamore and sat upon it and fell to stoking his pipe.

There were two fires in this camp and no rules real or tacit as to who should use them. But when the white man looked to the other fire he saw that the Delawares and John McGill and the new men in the company had taken their supper there and with a gesture and a slurred oath he warned the black away.

Here beyond men's judgements all covenants were brittle. The black looked up from his pipebowl. About that fire were men whose eyes gave back the light like coals socketed hot in their skulls and men whose eyes did not, but the black man's eyes stood as corridors for the ferrying through of naked and unrectified night from what of it lay behind to what was yet to come. Any man in this company can sit where it suits him, he said.

The white man swung his head, one eye half closed, his lip loose. His gunbelt lay coiled on the ground. He reached and drew the revolver and cocked it. Four men rose and moved away.

You aim to shoot me? said the black.

You dont get your black ass away from this fire I'll kill you graveyard dead.

He looked to where Glanton sat. Glanton watched him. He put the pipe in his mouth and rose and took up the apishamore and folded it over his arm.

Is that your final say?

Final as the judgement of God.

The black looked once more across the flames at Glanton and then he moved away in the dark. The white man uncocked the revolver and placed it on the ground before him. Two of the others came back to the fire and stood uneasily. Jackson sat with his legs crossed. One hand lay in his lap and the other was outstretched on his knee holding a slender black cigarillo. The nearest man to him was Tobin and when the black stepped out of the darkness bearing the bowieknife in both hands like some instrument of ceremony Tobin started to rise. The white man looked up drunkenly and the black stepped forward and with a single stroke swapt off his head.

Two thick ropes of dark blood and two slender rose like snakes from the stump of his neck and arched hissing into the fire. The head rolled to the left and came to rest at the expriest's feet where it lay with eyes aghast. Tobin jerked his foot away and rose and stepped back. The fire steamed and blackened and a gray cloud of smoke rose and the columnar arches of blood slowly subsided until just the neck bubbled gently like a stew and then that too was stilled. He was sat as before save headless, drenched in blood, the cigarillo still between his fingers, leaning toward the dark and smoking grotto in the flames where his life had gone.

Glanton rose. The men moved away. No one spoke. When they set out in the dawn the headless man was sitting like a murdered anchorite discalced in ashes and sark. Someone had taken his gun but the boots stood where he'd put them. The company rode on. They had not gone forth one hour upon that plain before they were ridden upon by the Apaches.

IX

An ambuscado – The dead Apache – Hollow ground –
A gypsum lake – Trebillones – Snowblind horses –
The Delawares return – A probate – The ghost coach –
The copper mines – Squatters – A snakebit horse –
The judge on geological evidence – The dead boy –
On parallax and false guidance in things past – The ciboleros.

THEY WERE CROSSING the western edge of the playa when Glanton halted. He turned and placed one hand on the wooden cantle and looked toward the sun where it sat new risen above the bald and flyspecked mountains to the east. The floor of the playa lay smooth and unbroken by any track and the mountains in their blue islands stood footless in the void like floating temples.

Toadvine and the kid sat their horses and gazed upon that desolation with the others. Out on the playa a cold sea broke and water gone these thousand years lay riffled silver in the morning wind.

Sounds like a pack of hounds, said Toadvine.

It sounds like geese to me.

Suddenly Bathcat and one of the Delawares turned their horses and quirted them and called out and the company turned and milled and began to line out down the lake bed toward the thin line of scrub that marked the shore. Men were leaping from their horses and hobbling them instantly with loops of rope ready made. By the time the animals were secured and they had thrown themselves on the ground under the creosote bushes with their weapons readied the riders were beginning to appear far out on the lake bed, a thin frieze of mounted archers that trembled and veered in the rising heat. They crossed before the sun and vanished one by one and reappeared again and they were black in the sun and they rode out of that vanished sea like burnt phantoms with the legs of the animals kicking up the spume that was not real and they were lost in the sun and lost in the lake and they shimmered and slurred together and separated again and they augmented by planes in lurid avatars and began to coalesce and there began to appear above them in the dawn-broached sky a hellish likeness of their ranks riding huge and inverted and the horses' legs incredibly elongate trampling down the high thin cirrus and the howling antiwarriors pendant from their mounts immense and chimeric and the high wild cries carrying that flat and barren pan like the cries of souls broke through some misweave in the weft of things into the world below.

They'll swing to their right, called Glanton, and as he spoke they did so, favoring their bow arms. The arrows came lofting up in the blue with the sun on their fletchings and then suddenly gaining speed and passing with a waney whistle like the flight of wild ducks. The first rifle cracked.

The kid was lying on his belly holding the big Walker revolver in both hands and letting off the shots slowly and with care as if he'd done it all before in a dream. The warriors passed within a hundred feet, forty, fifty of them, and went on up the edge of the lake and began to crumble in the serried planes of heat and to break up silently and to vanish.

The company lay under the creosote recharging their pieces. One of the ponies was lying in the sand breathing steadily and others stood that bore arrows with a curious patience. Tate and Doc Irving pulled back to see about them. The others lay watching the playa.

They walked out, Toadvine and Glanton and the judge. They picked up a short rifled musket bound in rawhide and studded about the stock with brassheaded tacks in varied designs. The judge looked north along the pale shore of the dry lake where the heathen had fled. He handed the rifle to Toadvine and they went on.

The dead man lay in a sandy wash. He was naked save for skin boots and a pair of wide Mexican drawers. The boots had pointed toes like buskins and they had parfleche soles and high tops that were rolled down about the knees and tied. The sand in the wash was dark with blood. They stood there in the windless heat at the edge of the dry lake and Glanton pushed him over with his boot. The painted face came up, sand stuck to the eyeball, sand stuck to the rancid grease with which he'd smeared his torso. You could see the hole where the ball from Toadvine's rifle had gone in above the lower rib. The man's hair was long and black and dull with dust and a few lice scuttled. There were slashes of white paint on the cheeks and there were chevrons of paint above the nose and figures in dark red paint under the eyes and on the chin. He was old and he bore a healed lance wound just above the hipbone and an old sabre wound across the left cheek that ran to the corner of his eye. These wounds were decorated their length with tattooed images, perhaps obscure with age, but without referents in the known desert about.

The judge knelt with his knife and cut the strap of the tigreskin warbag the man carried and emptied it in the sand. It held an eyeshield made from a raven's wing, a rosary of fruitseeds, a few gunflints, a handful of lead balls. It held also a calculus or madstone from the inward parts of some beast and this the judge examined and pocketed. The other effects he spread with the palm of his hand as if there were something to be read there. Then he ripped open the man's drawers with his knife. Tied alongside the dark genitals was a small skin bag and this the judge cut away and also secured in the pocket of his vest. Lastly he seized the dark locks and swept them up from the sand and cut away the scalp. Then they rose and returned, leaving him to scrutinize with his drying eyes the calamitous advance of the sun.

They rode all day upon a pale gastine sparsely grown with saltbush and panicgrass. In the evening they entrained upon a hollow ground that rang so roundly under the horses' hooves that they stepped and sidled and rolled their eyes like circus animals and that night as they lay in that ground each heard, all heard, the dull boom of rock falling somewhere far below them in the awful darkness inside the world.

On the day that followed they crossed a lake of gypsum so fine the ponies left no track upon it. The riders wore masks of bone-black smeared about their eyes and some had blacked the eyes of their horses. The sun reflected off the pan burned the undersides of their faces and shadow of horse and rider alike were painted upon the fine white powder in purest indigo. Far out on the desert to the north dustspouts rose wobbling and augered the earth and some said they'd heard of pilgrims borne aloft like dervishes in those mindless coils to be dropped broken and bleeding upon the desert again and there perhaps to watch the thing that had destroyed them lurch onward like some drunken djinn and resolve itself once more into the elements from which it sprang. Out of that whirlwind no voice spoke and the pilgrim lying in his broken bones may cry out and in his anguish he may rage, but rage at what? And if the dried and blackened shell of him is found among the sands by travelers to come yet who can discover the engine of his ruin?

That night they sat at the fire like ghosts in their dusty beards and clothing, rapt, pyrolatrous. The fires died and small coals scampered down the plain and sand crept past in the dark all night like armies of lice on the move. In the night some of the horses began to scream and daybreak found several so crazed with snowblindness they required to be shot. When they rode out the Mexican they called McGill was on his third horse in as many days. He could not have blacked the eyes of the pony he'd ridden coming up from the dry lake short of muzzling it like a dog and the horse he now rode was wilder yet and there were only three animals left in the caballado.

That afternoon the two Delawares that had left them a day out of Janos caught them up where they nooned at a mineral well. They had with them the veteran's horse, still saddled. Glanton walked out to where the animal stood and took up the trailing reins and led it to the fire where he removed the rifle from the scabbard and handed it to David Brown and then began to go through the wallet strapped to the cantle and to pitch the veteran's meagre effects into the fire. He undid the girthstraps and loosed the other accoutrements and piled them onto the flames, blankets, saddle, all, the greasy wool and leather sending up a foul gray smoke.

Then they rode on. They were moving north and for two days the Delawares read the smokes on the distant peaks and then the smokes stopped and there were no more. As they entered the foothills they came upon a dusty old diligence with six horses in the traces grazing the dry grass in a fold among the barren scrag.

A deputation cut for the carriage and the horses jerked their heads and shied and went trotting. The riders harried them about the basin until they were circling like paper horses in a windtrap and the diligence rattling after with one broken wheel. The black walked out waving his hat and called them off and he approached the yoked horses with the hat outheld and talked to them where they stood trembling until he could reach the trailing straps.

Glanton walked past him and opened the carriage door. The inside of the coach was splintered up with new wood and a dead man slumped out and hung head down. There was another man inside and a young boy and they lay enhearsed with their weapons in a stink to drive a buzzard off a gutcart. Glanton took the guns and ammunition and handed them out. Two men climbed to the freightdeck and cut away the ropes and the tattered tarp and they kicked down a steamer trunk and an old rawhide dispatch box and broke them open. Glanton cut the straps on the dispatch box with his knife and tipped the box out in the sand. Letters penned for any destination save here began to skitter and drift away down the canyon. There were a few tagged bags of ore samples in the box and he emptied them on the ground and kicked at the lumps of ore and looked about. He looked inside the coach again and then he spat and turned and looked the horses over. They were big American horses but badly used up. He directed two of them cut out of the traces and then he waved the black away from the lead horse and wafted his hat at the animals. They set off down the floor of the canyon, mismatched and sawing in the harness, the diligence swaying on its leather springs and the dead man dangling out of the clapping door. They diminished upon the plain to the west first the sound and then the shape of them dissolving in the heat rising off the sand until they were no more than a mote struggling in that hallucinatory void and then nothing at all. The riders rode on.

All afternoon they rode singlefile up through the mountains. A small gray lanneret flew about them as if seeking their banner and then it shied away over the plain below on its slender falcon wings. They rode on through sandstone cities in the dusk of that day, past castle and keep and windfashioned watchtower and stone granaries in sun and in shadow. They rode through marl and terracotta and rifts of copper shale and they rode through a wooded swag and out upon a promontory overlooking a bleak and barren caldera where lay the abandoned ruins of Santa Rita del Cobre.

Here they made a dry and fireless camp. They sent down scouts and Glanton walked out on the bluff and sat in the dusk watching the darkness deepen in the gulf below to see if any light should show itself down there. The scouting party returned in the dark and it was still dark in the morning when the company mounted and rode out.

They entered the caldera in a condition of half gray dawn, riding singlefile through the shaley streets between rows of old adobes abandoned these dozen years past when the Apaches cut off the wagontrains from Chihuahua and laid the works under siege. The starving Mexicans had set out afoot on the long journey south but none ever arrived. The Americans rode past the slag and rubble and the dark shapes of shaft mouths and they rode past the smeltinghouse where piles of ore stood about and weathered wagons and orecarts bonewhite in the dawn and the dark iron shapes of abandoned machinery. They crossed a stony arroyo and rode on through that gutted terrain to a slight rise where sat the old presidio, a large triangular building of adobe with round towers at the corners. There was a single door in the east wall and as they approached they could see rising the smoke that they had smelled on the morning air.

Glanton pounded on the door with his rawhidecovered club like a traveler at an inn. A bluish light suffused the hills about and the tallest peaks to the north stood in the only sun while all the caldera lay in darkness yet. The echo of his knocking clapped about the stark and riven walls of rock and returned. The men sat their horses. Glanton gave the door a kick.

Come out if you're white, he called.

Who's there? called a voice.

Glanton spat.

Who is it? they called.

Open it, said Glanton.

They waited. Chains were drawn rattling across the wood. The tall door creaked inward and a man stood before them at the ready with a rifle. Glanton touched his horse with his knee and it raised its head along the door and forced it open and they rode through.

In the gray murk within the compound they dismounted and tied. A few old freightwagons stood about, some looted of their wheels by travelers. There was a lamp burning in one of the offices and several men stood in the door. Glanton crossed the triangle. The men stepped aside. We thought you was injins they said.

They were four left out of a party of seven that had set out for the mountains to prospect for precious metals. They had been barricaded in the old presidio for three days, fled here from the desert to the south pursued by the savages. One of the men was shot through the lower chest and he lay propped against the wall in the office. Irving came in and looked at him.

What have you done for him? he said.

Aint done nothin.

What do you want me to do for him?

Aint asked you to do nothin.

That's good, said Irving. Because there aint nothing to be done.

He looked at them. They were foul and ragged and half crazed. They'd been making forays at night up the arroyo for wood and water and they had been feeding off a dead mule that lay gutted and stinking in the far corner of the yard. The first thing they asked for was whiskey and the next was tobacco. They had but two animals and one of these had been snakebit in the desert and this thing now stood in the compound with its head enormously swollen and grotesque like some fabled equine ideation out of an Attic tragedy. It had been bitten on the nose and its eyes bulged out of the shapeless head in a horror of agony and it tottered moaning toward the clustered horses of the company with its long misshapen muzzle swinging and drooling and its breath wheezing in the throttled pipes of its throat. The skin had split open along the bridge of its nose and the bone shone through pinkish white and its small ears looked like paper spills twisted into either side of a hairy loaf of dough. The American horses began to mill and separate along the wall at its approach and it swung after them blindly. There was a flurry of thumps and kicks and the horses began to circle the compound. A small mottled stallion belonging to one of the Delawares came out of the remuda and struck at the thing twice and then turned and buried its teeth in its neck. Out of the mad horse's throat came a sound that brought the men to the door.

Why dont you shoot that thing? said Irving.

Sooner it dies the sooner it'll rot, they said.

Irving spat. You aim to eat it and it snakebit?

They looked at one another. They didnt know.

Irving shook his head and went out. Glanton and the judge looked at the squatters and the squatters looked at the floor. Some of the roofbeams were half down into the room and the floor was filled with mud and rubble. Into these ruinous works the morning sun now slanted and Glanton could see crouched in a corner a Mexican or halfbreed boy maybe twelve years old. He was naked save for a pair of old calzones and makeshift sandals of uncured hide. He glared back at Glanton with a sort of terrified insolence.

Who's this child? said the judge.

They shrugged, they looked away.

Glanton spat and shook his head.

They posted guards atop the azotea and unsaddled the horses and drove them out to graze and the judge took one of the packanimals and emptied out the panniers and went off to explore the works. In the afternoon he sat in the compound breaking ore samples with a hammer, the feldspar rich in red oxide of copper and native nuggets in whose organic lobations he purported to read news of the earth's origins, holding an extemporary lecture in geology to a small gathering who nodded and spat. A few would quote him scripture to confound his ordering up of eons out of the ancient chaos and other apostate supposings. The judge smiled.

Books lie, he said.

God dont lie.

No, said the judge. He does not. And these are his words.

He held up a chunk of rock.

He speaks in stones and trees, the bones of things.

The squatters in their rags nodded among themselves and were soon reckoning him correct, this man of learning, in all his speculations, and this the judge encouraged until they were right proselytes of the new order whereupon he laughed at them for fools.

That evening the main part of the company quartered themselves on the dry clay of the compound under the stars. Before morning rain would drive them in, huddled in the dark mud cubicles along the south wall. In the office of the presidio they'd built a fire in the floor and the smoke rose through the ruined roof and Glanton and the judge and their lieutenants sat about the blaze and smoked their pipes while the squatters stood off to one side chewing the tobacco they'd been given and spitting at the wall. The halfbreed boy watched them with his dark eyes. To the west among the low dark hills they could hear the howling of a wolf that the squatters did mistrust and the hunters smiled among themselves. In a night so beclamored with the jackal-yapping of coyotes and the cries of owls the howl of that old dog wolf was the one sound they knew to issue from its right form, a solitary lobo, perhaps gray at the muzzle, hung like a marionette from the moon with his long mouth gibbering.

It grew cold in the night and it blew stormy with wind and rain and soon all the wild menagerie of that country grew mute. A horse put its long wet face in at the door and Glanton looked up and spoke to it and it lifted its head and curled its lip and withdrew into the rain and the night.

The squatters observed this as they observed everything with their shifting eyes and one of them allowed that he would never make a pet of a horse. Glanton spat at the fire and looked at the man where he sat horseless in his rags and he shook his head at the wonderful invention of folly in its guises and forms. The rain had slacked and in the stillness a long crack of thunder rolled overhead and clanged among the rocks and then the rain came harder until it was pouring through the blackened opening in the roof and steaming and hissing in the fire. One of the men rose and dragged up the rotted ends of some old beams and piled them onto the flames. The smoke spread along the sagging vigas above them and little streams of liquid clay started down from the sod roof. Outside the compound lay under sheets of water that slashed about in the gusts and the light of the fire falling from the door laid a pale band upon that shallow sea along which the horses stood like roadside spectators waiting an event. From time to time one of the men would rise and go out and his shadow would fall among the animals and they would raise and lower their dripping heads and dap their hooves and then wait in the rain again.

The men who had been on watch entered the room and stood steaming before the fire. The black stood at the door neither in nor out. Someone had reported the judge naked atop the walls, immense and pale in the revelations of lightning, striding the perimeter up there and declaiming in the old epic mode. Glanton watched the fire silently and the men composed themselves in their blankets in the drier places about the floor and soon they were asleep.

In the morning the rain had ceased. The water stood in pools in the courtyard and the snakebit horse lay dead with its shapeless head stretched in the mud and the other animals had gathered in the northeast corner under the tower and stood facing the wall. The peaks to the north were white with snow in the new risen sun and when Toadvine stepped out into the day the sun was just touching the upper walls of the compound and the judge was standing in the gently steaming quiet picking his teeth with a thorn as if he had just eaten.

Morning, said the judge.

Morning, said Toadvine.

Looks fair to clear.

It done has cleared, said Toadvine.

The judge turned his head and looked toward the pristine cobalt keep of the visible day. An eagle was crossing the gorge with the sun very white on its head and tailfeathers.

So it has, said the judge. So it has.

The squatters emerged and stood about the cantonment blinking like birds. They had elected among themselves to join the company and when Glanton came across the yard leading his horse the spokesman for their group stepped forward to inform him of their decision. Glanton didnt even look at him. He entered the cuartel and got his saddle and gear. In the meantime someone had found the boy.

He was lying face down naked in one of the cubicles. Scattered about on the clay were great numbers of old bones. As if he like others before him had stumbled upon a place where something inimical lived. The squatters crowded in and stood about the corpse in silence. Soon they were conversing senselessly about the merits and virtues of the dead boy.

In the compound the scalphunters mounted up and turned their horses toward the gates that now stood open to the east to welcome in the light and to invite their journey. As they rode out the doomed men hosteled in that place came dragging the boy out and laid him in the mud. His neck had been broken and his head hung straight down and it flopped over strangely when they let him onto the ground. The hills beyond the minepit were reflected grayly in the pools of rainwater in the courtyard and the partly eaten mule lay in the mud with its hindquarters missing like something from a chromo of terrific war. Within the doorless cuartel the man who'd been shot sang church hymns and cursed God alternately. The squatters stood about the dead boy with their wretched firearms at rest like some tatterdemalion guard of honor. Glanton had given them a half pound of rifle-powder and some primers and a small pig of lead and as the company rode out some looked back at them, three men standing there without expression. No one raised a hand in farewell. The dying man by the ashes of the fire was singing and as they rode out they could hear the hymns of their childhood and they could hear them as they ascended the arroyo and rode up through the low junipers still wet from the rain. The dying man sang with great clarity and intention and the riders setting forth upcountry may have ridden more slowly the longer to hear him for they were of just these qualities themselves.

THEY RODE that day through low hills barren save for the scrub evergreens. Everywhere in this high parkland deer leapt and scattered and the hunters shot several from their saddles and gutted and packed them and by evening they had acquired a retinue of half a dozen wolves of varying size and color that trotted behind them singlefile and watched over their own shoulders to see that each should follow in his place. At dusk they halted and built a fire and roasted the deer. The night was much enclosed about them and there were no stars. To the north they could see other fires that burned red and sullen along the invisible ridges. They ate and moved on, leaving the fire on the ground behind them, and as they rode up into the mountains this fire seemed to become altered of its location, now here, now there, drawing away, or shifting unaccountably along the flank of their movement. Like some ignis fatuus belated upon the road behind them which all could see and of which none spoke. For this will to deceive that is in things luminous may manifest itself likewise in retrospect and so by sleight of some fixed part of a journey already accomplished may also post men to fraudulent destinies.

As they rode that night upon the mesa they saw come toward them much like their own image a party of riders pieced out of the darkness by the intermittent flare of the dry lightning to the north. Glanton halted and sat his horse and the company halted behind him. The silent riders hove on. When they were a hundred yards out they too halted and all sat in silent speculation at this encounter.

Who are you? called Glanton.

Amigos, somos amigos.

They were counting each the other's number.

De dónde viene? called the strangers.

A dónde va? called the judge.

They were ciboleros down from the north, their packhorses laden with dried meat. They were dressed in skins sewn with the ligaments of beasts and they sat their animals in the way of men seldom off them. They carried lances with which they hunted the wild buffalo on the plains and these weapons were dressed with tassels of feathers and colored cloth and some carried bows and some carried old fusils with tasseled stoppers in their bores. The dried meat was packed in hides and other than the few arms among them they were innocent of civilized device as the rawest savage of that land.

They parleyed without dismounting and the ciboleros lighted their small cigarillos and told that they were bound for the markets at Mesilla. The Americans might have traded for some of the meat but they carried no tantamount goods and the disposition to exchange was foreign to them. And so these parties divided upon that midnight plain, each passing back the way the other had come, pursuing as all travelers must inversions without end upon other men's journeys.

X

Tobin – The skirmish on the Little Colorado – The Katabasis –
How came the learned man – Glanton and the judge –
A new course – The judge and the bats – Guano – The deserters –
Saltpeter and charcoal – The malpais – Hoofprints – The volcano –
Brimstone – The matrix – The slaughter of the aborigines.

IN THE DAYS to follow all trace of the Gileños faded and
they pushed deeper into the mountains. By fires of highland
driftwood pale as bone they crouched in silence while the
flames yawed in the nightwinds ascending those stony draws.
The kid sat with his legs crossed mending a strap with an awl
he'd borrowed from the expriest Tobin and the frockless one
looked on as he worked.

You've done this afore, said Tobin.

The kid wiped his nose with a swipe of his greasy sleeve and
turned the piece in his lap. Not me, he said.

Well you've the knack. More so than me. There's little equity
in the Lord's gifts.

The kid looked up at him and then bent to his work again.

That's so, said the expriest. Look around you. Study the
judge.

I done studied him.

Mayhaps he aint to your liking, fair enough. But the man's a hand at anything. I've never seen him turn to a task but what he didnt prove clever at it.

The kid drove the greased thread through the leather and hauled it taut.

He speaks dutch, said the expriest.

Dutch?

Aye.

The kid looked at the expriest, he bent to his mending.

He does for I heard him do it. We cut a parcel of crazy pilgrims down off the Llano and the old man in the lead of them he spoke right up in dutch like we were all of us in dutchland and the judge give him right back. Glanton come near fallin off his horse. We none of us knew him to speak it. Asked where he'd learned it you know what he said?

What did he say.

Said off a dutchman.

The expriest spat. I couldnt of learned it off ten dutchmen. What about you?

The kid shook his head.

No, said Tobin. The gifts of the Almighty are weighed and parceled out in a scale peculiar to himself. It's no fair accountin and I dont doubt but what he'd be the first to admit it and you put the query to him boldface.

Who?

The Almighty, the Almighty. The expriest shook his head. He glanced across the fire toward the judge. That great hairless thing. You wouldnt think to look at him that he could out-dance the devil himself now would ye? God the man is a dancer, you'll not take that away from him. And fiddle. He's the greatest fiddler I ever heard and that's an end on it. The greatest. He can cut a trail, shoot a rifle, ride a horse, track a deer. He's been all over the world. Him and the governor they sat up till breakfast and it was Paris this and London that in five languages, you'd have give something to of heard them. The governor's a learned man himself he is, but the judge . . .

The expriest shook his head. Oh it may be the Lord's way of showin how little store he sets by the learned. Whatever could it mean to one who knows all? He's an uncommon love for the common man and godly wisdom resides in the least of things so that it may well be that the voice of the Almighty speaks most profoundly in such beings as lives in silence themselves.

He watched the kid.

For let it go how it will, he said, God speaks in the least of creatures.

The kid thought him to mean birds or things that crawl but the expriest, watching, his head slightly cocked, said: No man is give leave of that voice.

The kid spat into the fire and bent to his work.

I aint heard no voice, he said.

When it stops, said Tobin, you'll know you've heard it all your life.

Is that right?

Aye.

The kid turned the leather in his lap. The expriest watched him.

At night, said Tobin, when the horses are grazing and the company is asleep, who hears them grazing?

Dont nobody hear them if they're asleep.

Aye. And if they cease their grazing who is it that wakes?

Every man.

Aye, said the expriest. Every man.

The kid looked up. And the judge? Does the voice speak to him?

The judge, said Tobin. He didn't answer.

I seen him before, said the kid. In Nacogdoches.

Tobin smiled. Every man in the company claims to have encountered that sootysouled rascal in some other place.

Tobin rubbed his beard on the back of his hand. He saved us all, I have to give him that. We come down off the Little Colorado we didnt have a pound of powder in the company. Pound. We'd not a dram hardly. There he set on a rock in the middle of the greatest desert you'd ever want to see. Just perched on this rock like a man waitin for a coach. Brown thought him a mirage. Might have shot him for one if he'd had aught to shoot him with.

How come you to have no powder?

Shot it up all at the savages. Holed up nine days in a cave, lost most of the horses. We were thirty-eight men when we left Chihuahua City and we were fourteen when the judge found us. Mortally whipped, on the run. Every man jack of us knew that in that godforsook land somewhere was a draw or a cul-de-sac or perhaps just a pile of rocks and there we'd be driven to a stand with those empty guns. The judge. Give the devil his due.

The kid held the tack in one hand, the awl in the other. He watched the expriest.

We'd been on the plain all night and well up into the next day. The Delawares kept callin halts and droppin to the ground to give a listen. There was no place to run and no place to hide. I dont know what they wanted to hear. We knew the bloody niggers was out there and speakin for myself that was already an abundance of information, I didnt need more. That sunrise we'd looked to be our last. We were all watchin the backtrack, I dont know how far you could see. Fifteen, twenty miles.

Then about the meridian of that day we come upon the judge on his rock there in that wilderness by his single self. Aye and there was no rock, just the one. Irving said he'd brung it with him. I said that it was a merestone for to mark him out of nothing at all. He had with him that selfsame rifle you see with him now, all mounted in german silver and the name that he'd give it set with silver wire under the checkpiece in latin: *Et In Arcadia Ego*. A reference to the lethal in it. Common enough

for a man to name his gun. I've heard Sweetlips and Hark From
The Tombs and every sort of lady's name. His is the first and
only ever I seen with an inscription from the classics.

And there he set. No horse. Just him and his legs crossed,
smilin as we rode up. Like he'd been expectin us. He'd an old
canvas kitbag and an old woolen benjamin over the one
shoulder. In the bag was a brace of pistols and a good assortment
of specie, gold and silver. He didnt even have a canteen. It was
like . . . You couldnt tell where he'd come from. Said he'd been
with a wagon company and fell out to go it alone.

Davy wanted to leave him there. Didnt set well with his
honor and it dont to this day. Glanton just studied him. It was a
day's work to even guess what he made of that figure on that
ground. I dont know to this day. They've a secret commerce.
Some terrible covenant. You mind. You'll see I'm right. He
called for the last of two packanimals we had and he cut the
straps and left the wallets to lay where they fell and the judge
mounted up and he and Glanton rode side by side and soon
they was conversin like brothers. The judge sat that animal
bareback like an indian and rode with his grip and his rifle
perched on the withers and he looked about him with the
greatest satisfaction in the world, as if everything had turned out
just as he planned and the day could not have been finer.

We'd not rode far before he struck us a new course about
nine points to the east. He pointed out a range of mountains
maybe thirty mile distant and we pulled for those mountains and
none of us asked what for. By then Glanton had give him the
particulars of the situation in which he'd installed himself but if
bein naked of arms in that wilderness and half of all Apacheria
in pursuit worried him at all he kept it to himself entire.

The expriest had paused to rekindle his pipe, reaching into
the raw fire for a coal as did the red scouts and then setting it
back among the flames as if it had a proper place there.

Now what do you reckon it was in them mountains that we

set out for? And how did he come to know of it? How to find it? How to put it to use?

Tobin seemed to frame these questions to himself. He was regarding the fire and pulling on his pipe. How indeed, he said. We reached the foothills in the early evenin and rode up a dry arroyo and pushed on I guess till midnight and made camp with neither wood nor water. Come mornin we could see them on the plain to the north maybe ten mile out. They were ridin four and six abreast and there was no short supply of them and they were in no hurry.

The judge had been up all the night by what the videttes said. Watchin the bats. He would go up the side of the mountain and make notes in a little book and then he would come back down. Could not have been more cheerful. Two men had deserted in the night and that made us down to twelve and the judge thirteen. I gave him my best study, the judge. Then and now. He appeared to be a lunatic and then not. Glanton I always knew was mad.

We left out with the first light up a little wooded draw. We were on the north slope and there was willow and alder and cherry growin out of the rock, just little trees. The judge would stop to botanize and then ride to catch up. My hand to God. Pressing leaves into his book. Sure I never saw the equal to it and all the time the savages in plain view below us. Ridin on that pan. God I'd put a crick in my neck I couldnt keep my eyes off of them and they were a hundred souls if they were one.

We come out on some flinty ground where it was all juniper and we just went on. No attempt to put their trackers at fault. We rode all that day. We saw no more of the savages for they were come under the lee of the mountain and were somewhere on the slopes below us. As soon as it was dusk and the bats was about the judge he altered our course again, ridin along holdin onto his hat, lookin up at the little animals. We got broke up and scattered all in the junipers and we halted to regroup and to recruit the horses. We sat around in the dark, no one spoke a word. When the judge got back he and Glanton whispered among themselves and then we moved on.

We led the horses in the dark. There was no trail, just steep scrabbly rock. When we reached the cave some of the men thought that he meant for us to hide there and that he was for a fact daft altogether. But it was the nitre. The nitre, you see. We left all that we owned at the mouth of that cave and we filled our wallets and panniers and our mochilas with the cave dirt and we left out at daybreak. When we topped the rise above that place and looked back there was a great spout of bats being sucked down into the cave, thousands of the creatures, and they continued so for an hour or more and even then it was just that we could no longer see them.

The judge. We left him at a high pass, a little clearwater creek. Him and one of the Delawares. He told us to circle the mountain and to return to that place in forty-eight hours. We unloaded all the containers onto the ground and took the two horses with us and him and the Delaware commenced luggin the panniers and the wallets up that little creek. I watched him go and I said that I would never set eyes on that man again.

Tobin looked at the kid. Never in this world. I thought Glanton would leave him. We went on. The next day on the far side of the mountain we encountered the two lads that had deserted us. Hangin upside down in a tree. They'd been skinned and I can tell ye it does very little for a man's appearance. But if the savages had not guessed it already now they knew for sure. That we'd none of us any powder.

We would not ride the animals. Just lead them, keep them off the rocks, hold their noses if they snuffled. But in those two days the judge leached out the guano with creekwater and woodash and precipitated it out and he built a clay kiln and burned charcoal in it, doused the fire by day and fired it again come dark. When we found him him and the Delaware was settin in the creek stark naked and they appeared at first to be

drunk but on what none could surmise. The entire top of that
mountain was covered with Apache indians and there set he.
He got up when he seen us and went to the willows and come
back with a pair of wallets and in one was about eight pounds
of pure crystal saltpetre and in the other about three pounds of
fine alder charcoal. He'd ground the charcoal to a powder in the
hollow of a rock, you could have made ink of it. He lashed
the bags shut and put them across the pommel of Glanton's
saddle and him and the indian got their clothes and I was glad
of it for I never seen a grown man with not a hair to his body
and him weighin twenty-four stone which he did then and does
now. And by my own warrant, for I added up the counters on
the bar with my own and sober eyes at a stockscale in Chihuahua
City in that same month and year.

We went down the mountain with no scouts, nothin. Just
straight out. We were dead for sleep. It was dark when we
reached the plain and we grouped and took a headcount and
then we rode out. The moon was about three quarters full and
waxing and we were like circus riders, not a sound, the horses
on eggshells. We'd no way of knowin where the savages was.
The last clue we'd had of their vicinity was the poor buggers
flayed in the tree. We set out dead west across the desert. Doc
Irving was before me and it was that bright I could count the
hairs on his head.

We rode all night and toward the morning just as the moon
was down we come upon a band of wolves. They scattered and
come back, not a sound out of them no more than smoke.
They'd drift off and quarter around and circle the horses. Bold
as brass. We cut at them with our hobbles and they would slip
past, you couldnt hear them on the hardpan just their breath or
they would mutter and grouse or pop their teeth. Glanton halted
and the things swirled around and slank off and come back. Two
of the Delawares backtracked off to the left a bit—braver souls
than me—and sure they found the kill. Twas a young buck
antelope new killed the evenin before. It was about half con-

sumed and we set upon it with our knives and took the rest of the meat with us and we ate it raw in the saddle and it was the first meat we'd seen in six days. Froze for it we were. Foragin on the mountain for piñon nuts like bears and glad to get them. We left little more than bones for the lobos, but I would never shoot a wolf and I know other men of the same sentiments.

In all this time the judge had spoke hardly a word. So at dawn we were on the edge of a vast malpais and his honor takes up a position on some lava rocks there and he commences to give us a address. It was like a sermon but it was no such sermon as any man of us had ever heard before. Beyond the malpais was a volcanic peak and in the sunrise it was many colors and there was dark little birds crossin down the wind and the wind was flappin the judge's old benjamin about him and he pointed to that stark and solitary mountain and delivered himself of an oration to what end I know not, then or now, and he concluded with the tellin us that our mother the earth as he said was round like an egg and contained all good things within her. Then he turned and led the horse he had been ridin across that terrain of black and glassy slag, treacherous to man and beast alike, and us behind him like the disciples of a new faith.

The expriest broke off and tapped the dead pipe against the heel of his boot. He looked at the judge over the way where he sat with his torso bared to the flames as was his practice. He turned and regarded the kid.

The malpais. It was a maze. Ye'd run out upon a little promontory and ye'd be balked about by the steep crevasses, you wouldnt dare to jump them. Sharp black glass the edges and sharp the flinty rocks below. We led the horses with every care and still they were bleedin about their hooves. Our boots was cut to pieces. Clamberin over those old caved and rimpled plates you could see well enough how things had gone in that place, rocks melted and set up all wrinkled like a pudding, the earth stove through to the molten core of her. Where for aught any man knows lies the locality of hell. For the earth is a globe in the void and truth there's no up nor down to it and there's men in this company besides myself seen little cloven hoofprints in the stone clever as a little doe in her going but what little doe ever trod melted rock? I'd not go behind scripture but it may be that there has been sinners so notorious evil that the fires coughed em up again and I could well see in the long ago how it was little devils with their pitchforks had traversed that fiery vomit for to salvage back those souls that had by misadventure been spewed up from their damnation onto the outer shelves of the world. Aye. It's a notion, no more. But someplace in the scheme of things this world must touch the other. And somethin put them little hooflet markings in the lava flow for I seen them there myself.

The judge, he seemed not to take his eyes from that dead cone where it rose off the desert like a great chancre. We followed solemn as owls so that he turned to look back and he did laugh when he seen our faces. At the foot of the mountain we drew lots and we sent two men to go on with the horses. I watched them go. One of them is at this fire tonight and I saw him lead them horses away over the slaglands like a doomed man.

And we were not doomed ourselves I dont reckon. When I looked up he was already upon the slope hand and foot, the judge was, his bag over his shoulder and his rifle for alpenstock. And so did we all go. Not halfway up we could already see the savages out on the plain. We climbed on. I thought at worst we'd throw ourselves into the caldron rather than be taken by those fiends. We climbed up and I reckon it was midday when we reached the top. We were done in. The savages not ten miles out. I looked at the men about me and sure they didnt look much. The dignity was gone out of them. They were good hearts all, then and now, and I did not like to see them so and I thought the judge had been sent among us for a curse. And yet he proved me wrong. At the time he did. I'm of two minds again now.

He was the first to the rim of the cone for all the size of him and he stood gazin about like he'd come for the view. Then he set down and he begun to scale at the rock with his knife. One by one we straggled up and he set with his back to that gapin hole and he was chippin away and he called upon us to do the same. It was brimstone. A weal of brimstone all about the rim of the caldron, bright yellow and shining here and there with the little flakes of silica but most pure flowers of sulphur. We chipped it loose and chopped it fine with our knives till we had about two pounds of it and then the judge took the wallets and went to a cupped place in the rock and dumped out the charcoal and the nitre and stirred them about with his hand and poured the sulphur in.

I didnt know but what we'd be required to bleed into it like freemasons but it was not so. He worked it up dry with his hands and all the while the savages down there on the plain drawin nigh to us and when I turned back the judge was standin, the great hairless oaf, and he'd took out his pizzle and he was pissin into the mixture, pissin with a great vengeance and one hand aloft and he cried out for us to do likewise.

We were half mad anyways. All lined up. Delawares and all. Every man save Glanton and he was a study. We hauled forth our members and at it we went and the judge on his knees kneadin the mass with his naked arms and the piss was splashin about and he was cryin out to us to piss, man, piss for your very souls for cant you see the redskins yonder, and laughin the while and workin up this great mass in a foul black dough, a devil's batter by the stink of it and him not a bloody dark pastryman himself I dont suppose and he pulls out his knife and he commences to trowel it across the southfacin rocks, spreadin it out thin with the knifeblade and watchin the sun with one eye and him smeared with blacking and reekin of piss and sulphur and grinnin and wieldin the knife with a dexterity that was wondrous like he did it every day of his life. And when he was done he set back and wiped his hands on his chest and then he watched the savages and so did we all.

They were on the malpais by then and they had a tracker who followed us every step on that naked rock, fallin back at each blind head and callin out to the others. I dont know what he followed. Scent perhaps. We could soon hear them talkin down there. Then they seen us.

Well, God in his glory knows what they thought. They were scattered out across the lava and one of them pointed and they all looked up. Thunderstruck no doubt. To see eleven men perched on the topmost rim of that scalded atoll like misflown birds. They parleyed and we watched to see would they dispatch any of their number after the horses but they did not. Their greed overcame all else and they started for the base of the cone, scramblin over the lava for to see who would be first.

We had I would suppose an hour. We watched the savages and we watched the judge's foul matrix dryin on the rocks and we watched a cloud that was making for the sun. One by one we give up watchin the rocks or the savages either one, for the cloud did look to be dead set for the sun and it would have took the better part of an hour to have crossed it and that was the last hour we had. Well, the judge was sittin making entries in his little book and he saw the cloud same as every other man and he put down the book and watched it and we did all. No one spoke. There was none to curse and none to pray, we just watched. And that cloud just cut the corner from the sun and passed on and there was no shadow fell upon us and the judge took up his ledger and went on with his entries as before. I watched him. Then I clambered down and tested a patch of the stuff with my hand. There was heat comin off of it. I walked along the rim and the savages was ascendin by every quarter for there was no route to favor on that bald and gravel slope. I looked for rocks of any size to send down but there was none there larger than your fist, just fine gravel and plates of scrag. I looked at Glanton and he was watchin the judge and he seemed to have had his wits stole.

Well the judge closed up his little book and took his leather shirt and spread it out in the little cupped place and called for us to bring the stuff to him. Every knife was out and we went to scrapin it up and him cautionin us not to strike fire on them flints. And we heaped it up in the shirt and he commenced to chop and grind it with his knife. And Captain Glanton, he calls out.

Captain Glanton. Would ye believe it? Captain Glanton, he says. Come charge that swivelbore of yours and let's see what manner of thing we have here.

Glanton come up with his rifle and he scooped his charger full and he charged both barrels and patched two balls and drove them home and capped the piece and made to step to the rim. But that was never the judge's way.

Down the maw of that thing, he says, and Glanton never questioned it. He went down the pitch of the inner rim to where lay the terminus of that terrible flue and he held his piece out over it and pointed it straight down and cocked the hammer and fired.

You wouldnt hear a sound like it in a long day's ride. It give me the fidgets. He fired both barrels and he looked at us and he looked at the judge. The judge just waved and went on with his grindin and then he called us all about to fill our horns and flasks and we did, one by one, circlin past him like communicants. And when all had shared he filled his own flask and he got out his pistols and saw to the priming. The foremost of the savages was not more than a furlong on the slope. We were ready to lay into them but again the judge would not have it. He fired off his pistols down into the caldron, spacin out the shots, and he fired all ten chambers and cautioned us back from sight while he reloaded the pieces. All this gunfire had give the savages some pause no doubt for they very likely reckoned us to be without powder altogether. And then the judge, he steps up to the rim and he had with him a good white linen shirt from out of his bag and he waved it to the redskins and he called down to them in spanish.

Well it would have brought tears to your eyes. All dead save me, he called. Have mercy on me. Todos muertos. Todos. Wavin the shirt. God it set them yappin on the slope like dogs and he turns to us, the judge, with that smile of his, and he says: Gentlemen. That was all he said. He had the pistols stuck in his belt at the back and he drew them one in each hand and he is as eitherhanded as a spider, he can write with both hands at a time and I've seen him to do it, and he commenced to kill indians. We needed no second invitation. God it was a butchery. At the first fire we killed a round dozen and we did not let up. Before the last poor nigger reached the bottom of the slope there was fifty-eight of them lay slaughtered among the gravels. They just slid down the slope like chaff down a hopper, some turned this way, some that, and they made a chain about the base of the mountain. We rested our rifle barrels on the brimstone and we shot nine more on the lava where they ran. It was a stand, what it was. Wagers was laid. The last of them shot was a reckonable part of a mile from the muzzles of the guns and that on a dead run. It was sharp shootin all around and not a misfire in the batch with that queer powder.

The expriest turned and looked at the kid. And that was the judge the first ever I saw him. Aye. He's a thing to study.

The lad looked at Tobin. What's he a judge of? he said.

What's he a judge of?

What's he a judge of.

Tobin glanced off across the fire. Ah lad, he said. Hush now. The man will hear ye. He's ears like a fox.

XI

Into the mountains – Old Ephraim – A Delaware carried off –
The search – Another probate – In the gorge – The ruins –
Keet seel – The solerette – Representations and things –
The judge tells a story – A mule lost – Mescal pits –
Night scene with moon, blossoms, judge – The village –
Glanton on the management of animals – The trail out.

THEY RODE ON into the mountains and their way took them through high pine forests, wind in the trees, lonely birdcalls. The shoeless mules slaloming through the dry grass and pine needles. In the blue coulees on the north slopes narrow tailings of old snow. They rode up switchbacks through a lonely aspen wood where the fallen leaves lay like golden disclets in the damp black trail. The leaves shifted in a million spangles down the pale corridors and Glanton took one and turned it like a tiny fan by its stem and held it and let it fall and its perfection was not lost on him. They rode through a narrow draw where the leaves were shingled up in ice and they crossed a high saddle at sunset where wild doves were rocketing down the wind and passing through the gap a few feet off the ground, veering wildly among the ponies and dropping off down into the blue gulf below. They rode on into a dark fir forest, the little Spanish ponies sucking at the thin air, and just at dusk as Glanton's horse was clambering over a fallen log a lean blond bear rose up out of the swale on the far side where it had been feeding and looked down at them with dim pig's eyes.

Glanton's horse reared and Glanton flattened himself along the horse's shoulder and drew his pistol. One of the Delawares was next behind him and the horse he rode was falling backward and he was trying to turn it, beating it about the head with his balled fist, and the bear's long muzzle swung toward them in a stunned articulation, amazed beyond reckoning, some foul gobbet dangling from its jaws and its chops dyed red with blood. Glanton fired. The ball struck the bear in the chest and the bear leaned with a strange moan and seized the Delaware and lifted him from the horse. Glanton fired again into the thick ruff of fur forward of the bear's shoulder as it turned and the man dangling from the bear's jaws looked down at them cheek and jowl with the brute and one arm about its neck like some crazed defector in a gesture of defiant camaraderie. All through the woods a bedlam of shouts and the whack of men beating the screaming horses into submission. Glanton cocked the pistol a third time as the bear swung with the indian dangling from its mouth like a doll and passed over him in a sea of honey-colored hair smeared with blood and a reek of carrion and the rooty smell of the creature itself. The shot rose and rose, a small core of metal scurrying toward the distant beltways of matter grinding mutely to the west above them all. Several rifleshots rang out and the beast loped horribly into the forest with his hostage and was lost among the darkening trees.

The Delawares trailed the animal three days while the party moved on. The first day they followed blood and they saw where the thing had rested and where the wounds had stanched and the next day they followed the dragmarks through the duff of a high forest floor and the day after they followed only the faintest trace across a high stone mesa and then nothing. They cut for sign until dark and they slept on the naked flints and the next day they rose and looked out on all that wild and stony country to the north. The bear had carried off their kinsman like some fabled storybook beast and the land had swallowed them up beyond all ransom or reprieve. They caught up their horses and turned back. Nothing moved in that high wilderness save the wind. They did not speak. They were men of another time for all that they bore christian names and they had lived all their lives in a wilderness as had their fathers before them. They'd learnt war by warring, the generations driven from the eastern shore across a continent, from the ashes at Gnadenhutten onto the prairies and across the outlet to the Woodlands of the west. If much in the world were mystery the limits of that world were not, for it was without measure or bound and there were contained within it creatures more horrible yet and men of other colors and beings which no man has looked upon and yet not alien none of it more than were their own hearts alien in them, whatever wilderness contained there and whatever beasts.

They cut the trail of the party early the next day and by nightfall of the day following they had overtaken them. The lost warrior's horse stood saddled in the caballado as they had left it and they took down the bags and divided his estate among them and that man's name was never said again. In the evening the judge came to the fire and sat with them and questioned them and made a map upon the ground and scrutinized it. Then he rose and trod it out with his boots and in the morning all rode on as before.

Their way led now through dwarf oak and ilex and over a stony ground where black trees stood footed in the seams on the slopes. They rode through sunlight and high grass and in the late afternoon they came out upon an escarpment that seemed to rim the known world. Below them in the paling light smoldered the plains of San Agustin stretching away to the northeast, the earth floating off in a long curve silent under looms of smoke from the underground coal deposits burning there a thousand years. The horses picked their way along the rim with care and the riders cast varied glances out upon that ancient and naked land.

In the days to come they would ride up through a country where the rocks would cook the flesh from your hand and where other than rock nothing was. They rode in a narrow enfilade along a trail strewn with the dry round turds of goats and they rode with their faces averted from the rock wall and the bake-oven air which it rebated, the slant black shapes of the mounted men stenciled across the stone with a definition austere and implacable like shapes capable of violating their covenant with the flesh that authored them and continuing autonomous across the naked rock without reference to sun or man or god.

They rode down from this country through a deep gorge, clattering over the stones, rifts of cool blue shade. In the dry sand of the arroyo floor old bones and broken shapes of painted pottery and graven on the rocks above them pictographs of horse and cougar and turtle and the mounted Spaniards helmeted and bucklered and contemptuous of stone and silence and time itself. Lodged in faults and crevices a hundred feet above them were nests of straw and jetsam from old high waters and the riders could hear the mutter of thunder in some nameless distance and they kept watch on the narrow shape of sky overhead for any darkness of impending rain, threading the canyon's close pressed flanks, the dry white rocks of the dead river floor round and smooth as arcane eggs.

That night they camped in the ruins of an older culture deep in the stone mountains, a small valley with a clear run of water and good grass. Dwellings of mud and stone were walled up beneath an overhanging cliff and the valley was traced with the work of old acequias. The loose sand in the valley floor was strewn everywhere with pieces of pottery and blackened bits of wood and it was crossed and recrossed with the tracks of deer and other animals.

The judge walked the ruins at dusk, the old rooms still black with woodsmoke, old flints and broken pottery among the ashes and small dry corncobs. A few rotting wooden ladders yet leaned against the dwelling walls. He roamed through the ruinous kivas picking up small artifacts and he sat upon a high wall and sketched in his book until the light failed.

The moon rose full over the canyon and there was stark silence in the little valley. It may be it was their own shadows kept the coyotes from abroad for there was no sound of them or wind or bird in that place but only the light rill of water running over the sand in the dark below their fires.

The judge all day had made small forays among the rocks of the gorge through which they'd passed and now at the fire he spread part of a wagonsheet on the ground and was sorting out his finds and arranging them before him. In his lap he held the leather ledgerbook and he took up each piece, flint or potsherd or tool of bone, and deftly sketched it into the book. He sketched with a practiced ease and there was no wrinkling of that bald brow or pursing of those oddly childish lips. His fingers traced the impression of old willow wicker on a piece of pottery clay and he put this into his book with nice shadings, an economy of pencil strokes. He is a draftsman as he is other things, well sufficient to the task. He looks up from time to time at the fire or at his companions in arms or at the night beyond. Lastly he set before him the footpiece from a suit of armor hammered out in a shop in Toledo three centuries before, a small steel tapadero frail and shelled with rot. This the judge sketched in profile and in perspective, citing the dimensions in his neat script, making marginal notes.

Glanton watched him. When he had done he took up the little footguard and turned it in his hand and studied it again and then he crushed it into a ball of foil and pitched it into the fire. He gathered up the other artifacts and cast them also into the fire and he shook out the wagonsheet and folded it away among his possibles together with the notebook. Then he sat with his hands cupped in his lap and he seemed much satisfied with the world, as if his counsel had been sought at its creation.

A Tennessean named Webster had been watching him and he asked the judge what he aimed to do with those notes and sketches and the judge smiled and said that it was his intention to expunge them from the memory of man. Webster smiled and the judge laughed. Webster regarded him with one eye asquint and he said: Well you've been a draftsman somewheres and them pictures is like enough the things themselves. But no man can put all the world in a book. No more than everthing drawed in a book is so.

Well said, Marcus, spoke the judge.

But dont draw me, said Webster. For I dont want in your book.

My book or some other book said the judge. What is to be deviates no jot from the book wherein it's writ. How could it? It would be a false book and a false book is no book at all.

You're a formidable riddler and I'll not match words with ye. Only save my crusted mug from out your ledger there for I'd not have it shown about perhaps to strangers.

The judge smiled. Whether in my book or not, every man is tabernacled in every other and he in exchange and so on in an endless complexity of being and witness to the uttermost edge of the world.

I'll stand for my own witness, said Webster, but by now the others had begun to call to him his conceit, and who would want to see his bloody portrait anyway and would there be fights break out in the great crowds awaiting its unveiling and perhaps they could tar and feather the picture, lacking the article itself. Until the judge raised his hand and called for amnesty and told them that Webster's feelings were of a different kind and not motivated by vanity at all and that he'd once drawn an old Hueco's portrait and unwittingly chained the man to his own likeness. For he could not sleep for fear an enemy might take it and deface it and so like was the portrait that he would not suffer it creased nor anything to touch it and he made a journey across the desert with it to where he'd heard the judge was to be found and he begged his counsel as to how he might preserve the thing and the judge took him deep into the mountains and they buried the portrait in the floor of a cave where it lies yet for aught the judge knew.

When he was done telling this Webster spat and wiped his mouth and eyed the judge again. That man, he said, was no more than a ignorant heathen savage.

That's so, said the judge.

It aint like that with me.

Excellent, said the judge, reaching for his portmanteau. You've no objection to a sketch then?

I'll sit for no portrait, said Webster. But it aint like you said.

The company fell silent. Someone rose to stoke the fire and the moon ascended and grew small over the ruined dwellings and the little stream braided over the sands in the valley floor shone like woven metal and save for the sound it made there was no sound other.

What kind of indians has these here been, Judge?

The judge looked up.

Dead ones I'd say, what about you, Judge?

Not so dead, said the judge.

They was passable masons, I'd say that. These niggers here-abouts now aint no kind.

Not so dead, said the judge. Then he told them another story and it was this story.

In the western country of the Alleghenies some years ago when it was yet a wilderness there was a man who kept a harness shop by the side of the Federal road. He did so because it was his trade and yet he did little of it for there were few travelers in that place. So that he fell into the habit before long of dressing himself as an indian and taking up station a few miles above his shop and waiting there by the roadside to ask whoever should come that way if they would give him money. At this time he had done no person any injury.

One day a certain man came by and the harnessmaker in his beads and feathers stepped from behind his tree and asked this certain man for some coins. He was a young man and he refused and having recognized the harnessmaker for a white man spoke to him in a way that made the harnessmaker ashamed so that he invited the young man to come to his dwelling a few miles distant on the road.

This harnessmaker lived in a bark house he had built and he kept a wife and two children all of whom reckoned the old man mad and were only waiting some chance to escape him and the wild place he'd brought them to. They therefore welcomed the guest and the woman gave him his supper. But while he ate the old man again began to try to wheedle money from him and he said that they were poor as indeed they were and the traveler listened to him and then he took out two coins which like the old man had never seen and the old man took the coins and studied them and showed them to his son and the stranger finished his meal and said to the old man that he might have those coins.

But ingratitude is more common than you might think and the harnessmaker wasnt satisfied and he began to question whether he ought not perhaps to have another such coin for his wife. The traveler pushed back his plate and turned in his chair and gave the old man a lecture and in this lecture the old man heard things he had once known but forgotten and he heard some new things to go with them. The traveler concluded by telling the old man that he was a loss to God and man alike and would remain so until he took his brother into his heart as he would take himself in and he come upon his own person in want in some desert place in the world.

Now as he was concluding this speech there passed in the road a nigger drawing a funeral hearse for one of his own kind and it was painted pink and the nigger was dressed in clothes of every color like a carnival clown and the young man pointed out this nigger passing in the road and he said that even a black nigger . . .

Here the judge paused. He had been looking into the fire and he raised his head and looked around him. His narration was much in the manner of a recital. He had not lost the thread of his tale. He smiled at the listeners about.

Said that even a crazy black nigger was not less than a man among men. And then the old man's son stood up and began an oration himself, pointing out at the road and calling for a place to be made for the nigger. He used those words. That a place be made. Of course by this time the nigger and hearse had passed on from sight.

With this the old man repented all over again and swore that the boy was right and the old woman who was seated by the fire was amazed at all she had heard and when the guest announced that the time had come for his departure she had tears in her eyes and the little girl came out from behind the bed and clung to his clothes.

The old man offered to walk him out the road so as to see him off on his journey and to apprise him of which fork in the road to take and which not for there were scarcely any waysigns in that part of the world.

As they walked out they spoke of life in such a wild place where such people as you saw you saw but one and never again and by and by they came to the fork in the road and here the traveler told the old man that he had come with him far enough and he thanked him and they took their departure each of the other and the stranger went on his way. But the harnessmaker seemed unable to suffer the loss of his company and he called to him and went with him again a little way upon the road. And by and by they came to a place where the road was darkened in a deep wood and in this place the old man killed the traveler.

He killed him with a rock and he took his clothes and he took his watch and his money and he buried him in a shallow grave by the side of the road. Then he went home.

On the way he tore his own clothes and bloodied himself with a flint and he told his wife they had been set upon by robbers and the young traveler murdered and him only escaped. She began to cry and after a while she made him take her to the place and she took wild primrose which grew in plenty thereabout and she put it on the stones and she came there many times until she was old.

The harnessmaker lived until his son was grown and never did anyone harm again. As he lay dying he called the son to him and told him what he had done. And the son said that he forgave him if it was his to do so and the old man said that it was his to do so and then he died.

But the boy was not sorry for he was jealous of the dead man and before he went away he visited that place and cast away the rocks and dug up the bones and scattered them in the forest and then he went away. He went away to the west and he himself became a killer of men.

The old woman was still living at the time and she knew none of what had passed and she thought that wild animals had dug the bones and scattered them. Perhaps she did not find all the bones but such as she did she restored to the grave and she covered them up and piled the stones over them and carried flowers to that place as before. When she was an old woman she told people that it was her son buried there and perhaps by that time it was so.

Here the judge looked up and smiled. There was a silence, then all began to shout at once with every kind of disclaimer.

He was no harnessmaker he was a shoemaker and he was cleared of them charges, called one.

And another: He never lived in no wilderness place, he had a shop dead in the center of Cumberland Maryland.

They never knew where them bones come from. The old woman was crazy, known to be so.

That was my brother in that casket and he was a minstrel dancer out of Cincinnati Ohio was shot to death over a woman.

And other protests until the judge raised both hands for silence. Wait now, he said. For there's a rider to the tale. There was a young bride waiting for that traveler with whose bones we are acquainted and she bore a child in her womb that was the traveler's son. Now this son whose father's existence in this world is historical and speculative even before the son has entered it is in a bad way. All his life he carries before him the idol of a perfection to which he can never attain. The father dead has euchered the son out of his patrimony. For it is the death of the father to which the son is entitled and to which he is heir, more so than his goods. He will not hear of the small mean ways that tempered the man in life. He will not see him struggling in follies of his own devising. No. The world which he inherits bears him false witness. He is broken before a frozen god and he will never find his way.

What is true of one man, said the judge, is true of many. The people who once lived here are called the Anasazi. The old ones. They quit these parts, routed by drought or disease or by wandering bands of marauders, quit these parts ages since and of them there is no memory. They are rumors and ghosts in this land and they are much revered. The tools, the art, the building—these things stand in judgement on the latter races. Yet there is nothing for them to grapple with. The old ones are gone like phantoms and the savages wander these canyons to the sound of an ancient laughter. In their crude huts they crouch in darkness and listen to the fear seeping out of the rock. All progressions from a higher to a lower order are marked by ruins and mystery and a residue of nameless rage. So. Here are the dead fathers. Their spirit is entombed in the stone. It lies upon the land with the same weight and the same ubiquity. For whoever makes a shelter of reeds and hides has joined his spirit to the common destiny of creatures and he will subside back into the primal mud with scarcely a cry. But who builds in stone seeks to alter the structure of the universe and so it was with these masons however primitive their works may seem to us.

None spoke. The judge sat half naked and sweating for all the night was cool. At length the expriest Tobin looked up.

It strikes me, he said, that either son is equal in the way of disadvantage. So what is the way of raising a child?

At a young age, said the judge, they should be put in a pit with wild dogs. They should be set to puzzle out from their proper clues the one of three doors that does not harbor wild lions. They should be made to run naked in the desert until . . .

Hold now, said Tobin. The question was put in all earnestness.

And the answer, said the judge. If God meant to interfere in the degeneracy of mankind would he not have done so by now? Wolves cull themselves, man. What other creature could? And is the race of man not more predacious yet? The way of the world is to bloom and to flower and die but in the affairs of men there is no waning and the noon of his expression signals the onset of night. His spirit is exhausted at the peak of its achievement. His meridian is at once his darkening and the evening of his day. He loves games? Let him play for stakes. This you see here, these ruins wondered at by tribes of savages, do you not think that this will be again? Aye. And again. With other people, with other sons.

The judge looked about him. He was sat before the fire naked save for his breeches and his hands rested palm down upon his knees. His eyes were empty slots. None among the company harbored any notion as to what this attitude implied, yet so like an icon was he in his sitting that they grew cautious

154

and spoke with circumspection among themselves as if they would not waken something that had better been left sleeping.

THE FOLLOWING evening as they rode up onto the western rim they lost one of the mules. It went skittering off down the canyon wall with the contents of the panniers exploding soundlessly in the hot dry air and it fell through sunlight and through shade, turning in that lonely void until it fell from sight into a sink of cold blue space that absolved it forever of memory in the mind of any living thing that was. Glanton sat his horse and studied the adamantine deep beneath him. A raven had set forth from the cliffs far below to wheel and croak. In the acute light the sheer stone wall wore strange contours and the horsemen on that promontory seemed very small even to themselves. Glanton looked upward, briefly, as if there were anything to ascertain in that perfect china sky, and then he chucked up his horse and they rode on.

Crossing the high mesas in the days to follow they began to come upon burnedout pits in the ground where the indians had cooked mescal and they rode through strange forests of maguey—the aloe or century plant—with immense flowering stalks that rose forty feet into the desert air. Each dawn as they saddled their horses they watched the pale mountains to the north and to the west for any trace of smoke. There was none. The scouts would be already gone, riding out in the dark before the sun rose, and they would not return until night, reckoning out the camp in that incoordinate waste by palest starlight or in blackness absolute where the company sat among the rocks without fire or bread or camaraderie any more than banded apes. They crouched in silence eating raw meat the Delawares had killed on the plain with arrows and they slept among the bones. A lobeshaped moon rose over the black shapes of the mountains dimming out the eastern stars and along the nearby ridge the white blooms of flowering yuccas moved in the wind and in the night bats came from some nether part of the world to stand on leather wings like dark satanic humming-birds and feed at the mouths of those flowers. Farther along the ridge and slightly elevated on a ledge of sandstone squatted the judge, pale and naked. He raised his hand and the bats flared in confusion and then he lowered it and sat as before and soon they were feeding again.

GLANTON WOULD NOT turn back. His calculations concerning the enemy included every duplicity. He spoke of ambushes. Even he in all his pride could not have believed that a company of nineteen men had evacuated an area of ten thousand square miles of every living human. Two days later when the scouts returned in the middle of the afternoon and reported finding the Apache villages abandoned he would not ride in. They camped on the mesa and made false fires and lay all night with their rifles on that stony heath. In the morning they caught up the horses and descended into a wild valley strewn with grass huts and the remains of old cookfires. They dismounted and moved among the shelters, frail structures of saplings and weeds stuck into the ground and bent to at the top to form a rounded hovel over which a few rags of hide or old blankets remained. The grounds were strewn with bones and knappings of flint or quartzite and they found pieces of jars and old baskets and broken stone mortars and rifts of dried beanpods from the mesquite and a child's straw doll and a primitive onestringed fiddle that had been crushed and a part of a necklace of dried melonseeds.

The hovel doors were waist high and faced the east and few of the shelters were tall enough to be stood in. The last one that Glanton and David Brown entered was defended by a large and vicious dog. Brown drew his belt pistol but Glanton stopped him. He dropped to one knee and spoke to the animal. It crouched against the rear wall of the hogan and bared its teeth and swung its head from side to side, the ears flattened alongside its skull.

He'll bite you, said Brown.

Get me a piece of jerky.

He crouched, talking to the dog. The dog watched him.

You wont man that son of a bitch, said Brown.

I can man anything that eats. Get me a piece of jerky.

When Brown came back with the dried meat the dog was looking about uneasily. When they rode west out of the canyon it was trotting with a slight limp at the heels of Glanton's horse.

They followed an old stone trail up out of the valley and through a high pass, the mules clambering along the ledges like goats. Glanton led his horse and called after the others, and yet darkness overtook them and they were benighted in that place, strung out along a fault in the wall of the gorge. He led them cursing upward through the profoundest dark but the way grew so narrow and the footing so treacherous they were obliged to halt. The Delawares came back afoot, having left their horses at the top of the pass, and Glanton threatened to shoot them all were they attacked in that place.

They passed the night each man at the feet of his horse where it stood in the trail between a sheer rise and a sheer fall. Glanton sat at the head of the column with his guns laid out before him. He watched the dog. In the morning they rose and went on, picking up the other scouts and their horses at the top of the pass and sending them on again. They rode through the mountains all that day and if Glanton slept none saw him do so.

The Delawares had reckoned the village empty ten days and the Gileños had decamped in small bands by every egress. There was no trail to follow. The company rode on through the mountains singlefile. The scouts were gone for two days. On the third day they rode into camp with their horses all but ruined. That morning they'd seen fires atop a thin blue mesa fifty miles to the south.

XII

Crossing the border – Storms – Ice and lightning –
The slain argonauts – The azimuth – Rendezvous –
Councils of war – Slaughter of the Gileños –
Death of Juan Miguel – The dead in the lake – The chief –
An Apache child – On the desert – Night fires – El virote –
A surgery – The judge takes a scalp – Un hacendado –
Gallego – Ciudad de Chihuahua.

FOR THE NEXT two weeks they would ride by night, they would
make no fire. They had struck the shoes from their horses and
filled the nailholes in with clay and those who still had tobacco
used their pouches to spit in and they slept in caves and on bare
stone. They rode their horses through the tracks of their dismounting and they buried their stool like cats and they barely
spoke at all. Crossing those barren gravel reefs in the night they
seemed remote and without substance. Like a patrol condemned
to ride out some ancient curse. A thing surmised from the
blackness by the creak of leather and the chink of metal.

They cut the throats of the packanimals and jerked and
divided the meat and they traveled under the cape of the wild
mountains upon a broad soda plain with dry thunder to the
south and rumors of light. Under a gibbous moon horse and

rider spanceled to their shadows on the snowblue ground and in each flare of lightning as the storm advanced those selfsame forms rearing with a terrible redundancy behind them like some third aspect of their presence hammered out black and wild upon the naked grounds. They rode on. They rode like men invested with a purpose whose origins were antecedent to them, like blood legatees of an order both imperative and remote. For although each man among them was discrete unto himself, conjoined they made a thing that had not been before and in that communal soul were wastes hardly reckonable more than those whited regions on old maps where monsters do live and where there is nothing other of the known world save conjectural winds.

They crossed the del Norte and rode south into a land more hostile yet. All day they crouched like owls under the niggard acacia shade and peered out upon that cooking world. Dust-devils stood on the horizon like the smoke of distant fires but of living thing there was none. They eyed the sun in its circus and at dusk they rode out upon the cooling plain where the western sky was the color of blood. At a desert well they dismounted and drank jaw to jaw with their horses and remounted and rode on. The little desert wolves yapped in the dark and Glanton's dog trotted beneath the horse's belly, its footfalls stitched precisely among the hooves.

That night they were visited with a plague of hail out of a faultless sky and the horses shied and moaned and the men dismounted and sat upon the ground with their saddles over their heads while the hail leaped in the sand like small lucent eggs concocted alchemically out of the desert darkness. When they resaddled and rode on they went for miles through cobbled ice while a polar moon rose like a blind cat's eye up over the rim of the world. In the night they passed the lights of a village on the plain but they did not alter from their course.

Toward the morning they saw fires on the horizon. Glanton

sent the Delawares. Already the dawnstar burned pale in the east. When they returned they squatted with Glanton and the judge and the Brown brothers and spoke and gestured and then all remounted and all rode on.

Five wagons smoldered on the desert floor and the riders dismounted and moved among the bodies of the dead argonauts in silence, those right pilgrims nameless among the stones with their terrible wounds, the viscera spilled from their sides and the naked torsos bristling with arrowshafts. Some by their beards were men but yet wore strange menstrual wounds between their legs and no man's parts for these had been cut away and hung dark and strange from out their grinning mouths. In their wigs of dried blood they lay gazing up with ape's eyes at brother sun now rising in the east.

The wagons were no more than embers armatured with the blackened shapes of hoop-iron and tires, the redhot axles quaking deep within the coals. The riders squatted at the fires and boiled water and drank coffee and roasted meat and lay down to sleep among the dead.

When the company set forth in the evening they continued south as before. The tracks of the murderers bore on to the west but they were white men who preyed on travelers in that wilderness and disguised their work to be that of the savages. Notions of chance and fate are the preoccupation of men engaged in rash undertakings. The trail of the argonauts terminated in ashes as told and in the convergence of such vectors in such a waste wherein the hearts and enterprise of one small nation have been swallowed up and carried off by another the expriest asked if some might not see the hand of a cynical god conducting with what austerity and what mock surprise so lethal a congruence. The posting of witnesses by a third and other path altogether might also be called in evidence as appearing to beggar chance, yet the judge, who had put his horse forward until he was abreast of the speculants, said that in this was expressed the very nature of the witness and that his proximity was no third thing but rather the prime, for what could be said to occur unobserved?

The Delawares went on ahead in the dusk and the Mexican John McGill led the column, dropping from time to time from his horse to lie flat on his belly and skylight the outriders on the desert before them and then remount again without halting his pony or the company which followed. They moved like migrants under a drifting star and their track across the land reflected in its faint arcature the movements of the earth itself. To the west the cloudbanks stood above the mountains like the dark warp of the very firmament and the starsprent reaches of the galaxies hung in a vast aura above the riders' heads.

Two mornings later the Delawares returned from their dawn reconnaissance and reported the Gileños camped along the shore of a shallow lake less than four hours to the south. They had with them their women and children and they were many. Glanton when he rose from this council walked out on the desert alone and stood for a long time looking out upon the darkness downcountry.

They saw to their arms, drawing the charges from their pieces and reloading them. They spoke in low voices among themselves although the desert round lay like a great barren plate gently quaking in the heat. In the afternoon a detachment led the horses out to water and led them back again and with dark Glanton and his lieutenants followed the Delawares out to scout the enemy's position.

They'd driven a stick into the ground on a rise north of the camp and when the angle of the Dipper had swung about to this inclination Toadvine and the Vandiemanlander set the company in motion and they rode forth south after the others trammeled to chords of rawest destiny.

They reached the north end of the lake in the cool hours before dawn and turned along the shore. The water was very black and along the beach there lay a wrack of foam and they could hear ducks talking far out on the lake. The embers of the encampment's fires lay below them in a gentle curve like the lights of a distant port. Before them on that lonely strand a solitary rider sat his horse. It was one of the Delawares and he turned his horse without speaking and they followed him up through the brush onto the desert.

The party was crouched in a stand of willow a half mile from the fires of the enemy. They had muffled the heads of the horses with blankets and the hooded beasts stood rigid and ceremonial behind them. The new riders dismounted and bound their own horses and they sat upon the ground while Glanton addressed them.

We got a hour, maybe more. When we ride in it's ever man to his own. Dont leave a dog alive if you can help it.

How many is there, John?

Did you learn to whisper in a sawmill?

There's enough to go around, said the judge.

Dont waste powder and ball on anything that caint shoot back. If we dont kill ever nigger here we need to be whipped and sent home.

This was the extent of their council. The hour that followed was a long hour. They led the blindfolded horses down and stood looking out over the encampment but they were watching the horizon to the east. A bird called. Glanton turned to his horse and unhooded it like a falconer at morning. A wind had risen and the horse lifted its head and sniffed the air. The other men followed. The blankets lay where they had fallen. They mounted, pistols in hand, saps of rawhide and riverrock looped about their wrists like the implements of some primitive equestrian game. Glanton looked back at them and then nudged forth his horse.

As they trotted out onto the white salt shore an old man rose from the bushes where he'd been squatting and turned to face them. The dogs that had been waiting on to contest his stool bolted yapping. Ducks began to rise by ones and pairs out on the lake. Someone clubbed the old man down and the riders put rowels to their mounts and lined out for the camp behind the dogs with their clubs whirling and the dogs howling in a tableau of some hellish hunt, the partisans nineteen in number bearing down upon the encampment where there lay sleeping upward of a thousand souls.

Glanton rode his horse completely through the first wickiup trampling the occupants underfoot. Figures were scrambling out of the low doorways. The raiders went through the village at full gallop and turned and came back. A warrior stepped into their path and leveled a lance and Glanton shot him dead. Three others ran and he shot the first two with shots so closely executed that they fell together and the third one seemed to be coming apart as he ran, hit by half a dozen pistolballs.

Within that first minute the slaughter had become general. Women were screaming and naked children and one old man tottered forth waving a pair of white pantaloons. The horsemen moved among them and slew them with clubs or knives. A hundred tethered dogs were howling and others were racing crazed among the huts ripping at one another and at the tied dogs nor would this bedlam and clamor cease or diminish from the first moment the riders entered the village. Already a number of the huts were afire and a whole enfilade of refugees had begun streaming north along the shore wailing crazily with the riders among them like herdsmen clubbing down the laggards first.

When Glanton and his chiefs swung back through the village people were running out under the horses' hooves and the horses were plunging and some of the men were moving on foot among the huts with torches and dragging the victims out, slathered and dripping with blood, hacking at the dying and decapitating those who knelt for mercy. There were in the camp a number of Mexican slaves and these ran forth calling out in Spanish and were brained or shot and one of the Delawares emerged from the smoke with a naked infant dangling in each hand and squatted at a ring of midden stones and swung them by the heels each in turn and bashed their heads against the stones so that the brains burst forth through the fontanel in a bloody spew and humans on fire came shrieking forth like berserkers and the riders hacked them down with their enormous knives and a young woman ran up and embraced the bloodied forefeet of Glanton's warhorse.

By now a small band of warriors had mounted themselves out of the scattered remuda and they advanced upon the village and rattled a drove of arrows among the burning huts. Glanton drew his rifle from its scabbard and shot the two lead horses and resheathed the rifle and drew his pistol and began to fire between the actual ears of his horse. The mounted indians floundered among the down and kicking horses and they milled and circled and were shot down one by one until the dozen survivors among them turned and fled up the lake past the groaning column of refugees and disappeared in a drifting wake of soda ash.

Glanton turned his horse. The dead lay awash in the shallows like the victims of some disaster at sea and they were strewn along the salt foreshore in a havoc of blood and entrails. Riders were towing bodies out of the bloody waters of the lake and the froth that rode lightly on the beach was a pale pink in the rising light. They moved among the dead harvesting the long black locks with their knives and leaving their victims rawskulled and strange in their bloody cauls. The loosed horses from the remuda came pounding down the reeking strand and disappeared in the smoke and after a while they came pounding back. Men were wading about in the red waters hacking aimlessly at the dead and some lay coupled to the bludgeoned bodies of young women dead or dying on the beach. One of the Delawares passed with a collection of heads like some strange vendor bound for market, the hair twisted about his wrist and the heads dangling and turning together. Glanton knew that every moment on this ground must be contested later in the desert and he rode among the men and urged them on.

McGill came out of the crackling fires and stood staring bleakly at the scene about. He had been skewered through with a lance and he held the stock of it before him. It was fashioned from a sotol stalk and the point of an old cavalry sword bound to the haft curved from out the small of his back. The kid waded out of the water and approached him and the Mexican sat down carefully in the sand.

Get away from him, said Glanton.

McGill turned to look at Glanton and as he did so Glanton leveled his pistol and shot him through the head. He reholstered the gun and stood his empty rifle upright against the saddle and held it with his knee while he measured powder down the barrels. Someone shouted to him. The horse trembled and stepped back and Glanton spoke to it softly and patched two balls and drove them home. He was watching a rise to the north where a band of mounted Apaches were grouped against the sky.

They were perhaps a quarter mile distant, five, six of them, their cries thin and lost. Glanton brought the rifle to the crook of his arm and capped one drum and rotated the barrels and capped the other. He did not take his eyes from the Apaches. Webster stepped from his horse and drew his rifle and slid the ramrod from the thimbles and went to one knee, the ramrod upright in the sand, resting the rifle's forestock upon the fist with which he held it. The rifle had set triggers and he cocked the rear one and laid his face against the cheekpiece. He reckoned the drift of the wind and he reckoned against the sun on the side of the silver foresight and he held high and touched off the piece. Glanton sat immobile. The shot was flat and dead in the emptiness and the gray smoke drifted away. The leader of the group on the rise sat his horse. Then he slowly pitched sideways and fell to the ground.

Glanton gave a whoop and surged forward. Four men followed. The warriors on the rise had dismounted and were lifting up the fallen man. Glanton turned in the saddle without taking his eyes from the indians and held out his rifle to the nearest man. This man was Sam Tate and he took the rifle and reined his horse so short he nearly threw it. Glanton and three rode on and Tate drew the ramrod for a rest and crouched and fired. The horse that carried the wounded chief faltered, ran on. He swiveled the barrels and fired the second charge and it plowed to the ground. The Apaches reined with shrill cries. Glanton leaned forward and spoke into his horse's ear. The indians raised up their leader to a new mount and riding double they flailed at their horses and set out again. Glanton had drawn his pistol and he gestured with it to the men behind and one pulled up his horse and leaped to the ground and went flat on his belly and drew and cocked his own pistol and pulled down the loading lever and stuck it in the sand and holding the gun in both hands with his chin buried in the ground he sighted along the barrel. The horses were two hundred yards out and moving fast. With the second shot the pony that bore the leader bucked and a rider alongside reached and took the reins. They were attempting to take the leader off the wounded animal in mid-stride when the animal collapsed.

Glanton was first to reach the dying man and he knelt with that alien and barbarous head cradled between his thighs like some reeking outland nurse and dared off the savages with his revolver. They circled on the plain and shook their bows and lofted a few arrows at him and then turned and rode on. Blood bubbled from the man's chest and he turned his lost eyes upward, already glazed, the capillaries breaking up. In those dark pools there sat each a small and perfect sun.

He rode back to the camp at the fore of his small column with the chief's head hanging by its hair from his belt. The men were stringing up scalps on strips of leather whang and some of the dead lay with broad slices of hide cut from their backs to be used for the making of belts and harness. The dead Mexican McGill had been scalped and the bloody skulls were already blackening in the sun. Most of the wickiups were burned to the ground and because some gold coins had been found a few of the men were kicking through the smoldering ashes. Glanton cursed them on, taking up a lance and mounting the head upon it where it bobbed and leered like a carnival head and riding up and back, calling to them to round up the caballado and move out. When he turned his horse he saw the judge sitting on the ground. The judge had taken off his hat and was drinking water from a leather bottle. He looked up at Glanton.

It's not him.

What's not?

The judge nodded. That.

Glanton turned the shaft. The head with its long dark locks swung about to face him.

Who do you think it is if it aint him?

The judge shook his head. It's not Gómez. He nodded toward the thing. That gentleman is sangre puro. Gómez is Mexican.

He aint all Mexican.

You cant be all Mexican. It's like being all mongrel. But that's not Gómez because I've seen Gómez and it's not him.

Will it pass for him?

No.

Glanton looked toward the north. He looked down at the judge. You aint seen my dog have ye? he said.

The judge shook his head. Do you intend to drive that stock?

Until I'm made to quit.

That might be soon.

That might be.

How long do you think it will take these yahoos to regroup?

Glanton spat. It wasnt a question and he didnt answer it. Where's your horse? he said.

Gone.

Well if you aim to ride with us you better be for gettin you another one. He looked at the head on the pole. You was some kind of goddamned chief, he said. He nudged the horse forward with his heels and rode out along the water's edge. The Delawares were wading about in the lake feeling for sunken bodies with their feet. He sat there a moment and then he turned the horse and rode up through the sacked encampment. He rode warily, his pistol across his thigh. He followed the tracks coming down from the desert where they'd ridden in. When he returned he had with him the scalp of the old man who had first stood up out of the bushes at dawn.

Within the hour they were mounted and riding south leaving behind them on the scourged shore of the lake a shambles of blood and salt and ashes and driving before them a half a thousand horses and mules. The judge rode at the head of the column bearing on the saddle before him a strange dark child covered with ash. Part of its hair was burned away and it rode mute and stoic watching the land advance before it with huge black eyes like some changeling. The men as they rode turned black in the sun from the blood on their clothes and their faces and then paled slowly in the rising dust until they assumed once more the color of the land through which they passed.

They rode all day with Glanton bringing up the rear of the column. Toward noon the dog caught them up. His chest was dark with blood and Glanton carried him on the pommel of the saddle until he could recruit himself. In the long afternoon he trotted in the shadow of the horse and in the twilight he trotted far out on the plain where the tall shapes of the horses skated over the chaparral on spider legs.

By now there was a thin line of dust to the north and they rode on into dark and the Delawares dismounted and lay with their ears to the ground and then they mounted up and all rode on again.

When they halted Glanton ordered fires built and the wounded seen to. One of the mares had foaled in the desert and this frail form soon hung skewered on a paloverde pole over the raked coals while the Delawares passed among themselves a gourd containing the curdled milk taken from its stomach. From a slight rise to the west of the camp the fires of the enemy were visible ten miles to the north. The company squatted in their bloodstiffened hides and counted the scalps and strung them on poles, the blueblack hair dull and clotted with blood. David Brown went among these haggard butchers as they crouched before the flames but he could find him no surgeon. He carried an arrow in his thigh, fletching and all, and none would touch it. Least of all would Doc Irving, for Brown called him a mortician and a barber and they kept their distance one from the other.

Boys, said Brown, I'd doctorfy it myself but I caint get no straight grip.

The judge looked up at him and smiled.

Will you do her, Holden?

No, Davy, I wont. But I tell you what I will do.

What's that.

I'll write a policy on your life against every mishap save the noose.

Damn you then.

The judge chuckled. Brown glared about him. Will none of ye help a man?

None spoke.

Damn all of ye then, he said.

He sat and stretched his leg out on the ground and looked at it, he bloodier than most. He gripped the shaft and bore down on it. The sweat stood on his forehead. He held his leg and swore softly. Some watched, some did not. The lad rose. I'll try her, he said.

Good lad, said Brown.

He fetched his saddle to lean against. He turned his leg to the fire for the light and folded his belt and held it and hissed down at the boy kneeling there. Grip her stout, lad. And drive her straight. Then he gripped the belt in his teeth and lay back.

The kid took hold of the shaft close to the man's thigh and pressed forward with his weight. Brown seized the ground on either side of him and his head flew back and his wet teeth shone in the firelight. The kid took a new grip and bore down again. The veins in the man's neck stood like ropes and he cursed the boy's soul. On the fourth essay the point of the arrow came through the flesh of the man's thigh and blood ran over the ground. The kid sat back on his heels and passed the sleeve of his shirt across his brow.

Brown let the belt fall from his teeth. Is it through? he said.

It is.

The point? Is it the point? Speak up, man.

The kid drew his knife and cut away the bloody point deftly and handed it up. Brown held it to the firelight and smiled. The point was of hammered copper and it was cocked in its blood-soaked bindings on the shaft but it had held.

Stout lad, ye'll make a shadetree sawbones yet. Now draw her.

The kid withdrew the shaft from the man's leg smoothly and the man bowed on the ground in a lurid female motion and wheezed raggedly through his teeth. He lay there a moment and then he sat up and took the shaft from the lad and threw it in the fire and rose and went off to make his bed.

When the kid returned to his own blanket the expriest leaned to him and hissed at his ear.

Fool, he said. God will not love ye forever.

The kid turned to look at him.

Dont you know he'd of took you with him? He'd of took you, boy. Like a bride to the altar.

THEY ROSE UP and moved on sometime after midnight. Glanton had ordered the fires built up and they rode out with the flames lighting all the grounds about and the shadowshapes of the desert brush reeling on the sands and the riders treading their thin and flaring shadows until they had crossed altogether into the darkness which so well became them.

The horses and mules were ranged far out over the desert and they picked them up for miles to the south and drove them on. The sourceless summer lightning marked out of the night dark mountain ranges at the rim of the world and the halfwild horses on the plain before them trotted in those bluish strobes like horses called forth quivering out of the abyss.

In the smoking dawn the party riding ragged and bloody with their baled peltries looked less like victors than the harried afterguard of some ruined army retreating across the meridians of chaos and old night, the horses stumbling, the men tottering asleep in the saddles. The broached day discovered the same barren countryside about and the smoke from their fires of the night before stood thin and windless to the north. The pale dust of the enemy who were to hound them to the gates of the city seemed no nearer and they shambled on through the rising heat driving the crazed horses before them.

Midmorning they watered at a stagnant pothole that had already been walked through by three hundred animals, the riders hazing them out of the water and dismounting to drink from their hats and then riding on again down the dry bed of the stream and clattering over the stony ground, dry rocks and boulders and then the desert soil again red and sandy and the constant mountains about them thinly grassed and grown with ocotillo and sotol and the secular aloes blooming like phantas-magoria in a fever land. At dusk they sent riders west to build fires on the prairie and the company lay down in the dark and slept while bats crossed silently overhead among the stars. When they rode on in the morning it was still dark and the horses all but fainting. Day found the heathen much advanced upon them. They fought their first stand the dawn following and they fought them running for eight days and nights on the plain and among the rocks in the mountains and from the walls and azoteas of abandoned haciendas and they lost not a man.

On the third night they crouched in the keep of old walls of slumped mud with the fires of the enemy not a mile distant on the desert. The judge sat with the Apache boy before the fire and it watched everything with dark berry eyes and some of the men played with it and made it laugh and they gave it jerky and it sat chewing and watching gravely the figures that passed above it. They covered it with a blanket and in the morning the judge was dandling it on one knee while the men saddled their horses. Toadvine saw him with the child as he passed with his saddle but when he came back ten minutes later leading his horse the child was dead and the judge had scalped it. Toadvine put the muzzle of his pistol against the great dome of the judge's head.

Goddamn you, Holden.

You either shoot or take that away. Do it now.

Toadvine put the pistol in his belt. The judge smiled and wiped the scalp on the leg of his trousers and rose and turned away. Another ten minutes and they were on the plain again in full flight from the Apaches.

On the afternoon of the fifth day they were crossing a dry pan at a walk, driving the horses before them, the indians behind just out of rifle range calling out to them in Spanish. From time to time one of the company would dismount with rifle and wiping stick and the indians would flare like quail, pulling their ponies around and standing behind them. To the east trembling in the heat stood the thin white walls of a hacienda and the trees thin and green and rigid rising from it like a scene viewed in a diorama. An hour later they were driving the horses—perhaps now a hundred head—along these walls and down a worn trail toward a spring. A young man rode out and welcomed them formally in Spanish. No one answered. The young rider looked down along the creek where the fields were laid out with acequias and where the workers in their dusty white costumes stood poised with hoes among the new cotton or waist-high corn. He looked back to the northwest. The Apaches, seventy, eighty of them, were just coming past the first of a row of jacales and defiling along the path and into the shade of the trees.

The peons in the fields saw them at about the same time. They flung their implements from them and began to run, some shrieking, some with their hands atop their heads. The young Don looked at the Americans and he looked at the approaching savages again. He called out something in Spanish. The Americans drove the horses up out of the spring and on through the grove of cottonwoods. The last they saw of him he had drawn a small pistol from his boot and had turned to face the indians.

That evening they led the Apaches through the town of Gallego, the street a mud gutter patrolled by swine and wretched hairless dogs. It appeared deserted. The young corn in the roadside fields had been washed by recent rains and stood white and luminous, bleached almost transparent by the sun. They rode most of the night and the next day the indians were still there.

They fought them again at Encinillas and they fought them in the dry passes going toward El Sauz and beyond in the low foothills from which they could already see the churchspires of the city to the south. On the twenty-first of July in the year eighteen forty-nine they rode into the city of Chihuahua to a hero's welcome, driving the harlequin horses before them through the dust of the streets in a pandemonium of teeth and whited eyes. Small boys ran among the hooves and the victors in their gory rags smiled through the filth and the dust and the caked blood as they bore on poles the desiccated heads of the enemy through that fantasy of music and flowers.

XIII

At the baths – Merchants – Trophies of war – The banquet –
Trias – The ball – North – Coyame – The border –
The Hueco tanks – Massacre of the Tiguas – Carrizal –
A desert spring – The Medanos – An inquest concerning teeth –
Nacori – The cantina – A desperate encounter –
Into the mountains – A village decimated – Mounted lancers –
A skirmish – Pursuing the survivors – The plains of Chihuahua –
Slaughter of the soldiers – A burial – Chihuahua – Westward.

THEIR PROGRESS was swelled by new riders, by boys on mule-
back and old men in plaited hats and a deputation that took
charge of the captured horses and mules and hazed them on
through the narrow streets toward the bullring where they
could be kept. The tattered campaigners surged on, some now
holding aloft cups that had been pressed upon them, waving to
the ladies clustered on the balconies their putrescent hats and
elevating the bobbing heads with those strange halflidded looks
of ennui into which the features had dried, all so hemmed about
now by the citizenry that they seemed the vanguard of some
ragged uprising and heralded before by a pair of drummers one
witless and both barefoot and by a trumpeter who marched with
one arm raised above his head in a martial gesture and playing

the while. In this manner they passed through the standing portals of the governor's palace, over the worn stone sills and into the courtyard where the broomed hooves of the mercenaries' shoeless horses subsided upon the cobbles with a curious turtlelike clatter.

Hundreds of onlookers pressed about as the dried scalps were counted out upon the stones. Soldiers with muskets kept back the crowds and young girls watched the Americans with huge black eyes and boys crept forth to touch the grisly trophies. There were one hundred and twenty-eight scalps and eight heads and the governor's lieutenant and his retinue came down into the courtyard to welcome them and admire their work. They were promised full payment in gold at the dinner to be held in their honor that evening at the Riddle and Stephens Hotel and with this the Americans sent up a cheer and mounted their horses again. Old women in black rebozos ran forth to kiss the hems of their reeking shirts and hold up their dark little hands in blessing and the riders wheeled their gaunted mounts and pushed through the clamoring multitude and into the street.

They moved on to the public baths where they descended one by one into the waters, each more pale than the one before and all tattooed, branded, sutured, the great puckered scars inaugurated God knows where by what barbarous surgeons across chests and abdomens like the tracks of gigantic millipedes, some deformed, fingers missing, eyes, their foreheads and arms stamped with letters and numbers as if they were articles requiring inventory. Citizens of both sexes withdrew along the walls and watched the water turn into a thin gruel of blood and filth and none could take their eyes from the judge who had disrobed last of all and now walked the perimeter of the baths with a cigar in his mouth and a regal air, testing the waters with one toe, surprisingly petite. He shone like the moon so pale he was and not a hair to be seen anywhere upon that vast corpus, not in any crevice nor in the great bores of his nose and not upon his chest nor in his ears nor any tuft at all above his eyes nor to the lids thereof. The immense and gleaming dome of his naked skull looked like a cap for bathing pulled down to the otherwise darkened skin of his face and neck. As that great bulk lowered itself into the bath the waters rose perceptibly and when he had submerged himself to the eyes he looked about with considerable pleasure, the eyes slightly crinkled, as if he were smiling under the water like some pale and bloated manatee surfaced in a bog while behind his small and close-set ear the wedged cigar smoked gently just above the waterline.

By now merchants had spread their wares all along the clay tiles behind them, suits of European cloth and cut and shirts of colored silks and closenapped beaver hats and fine Spanish leather boots, silverheaded canes and riding crops and silvermounted saddles and carven pipes and hideout guns and a group of Toledo swords with ivory hilts and nicely chased blades and barbers were setting up chairs to receive them, crying out the names of celebrated patrons upon whom they had attended, and all of these entrepreneurs assuring the company of credit on the most generous terms.

When they crossed the square attired in their new haberdashery, some with coatsleeves barely past their elbows, the scalps were being strung about the iron fretwork of the gazebo like decorations for some barbaric celebration. The severed heads had been raised on poles above the lampstandards where they now contemplated with their caved and pagan eyes the dry hides of their kinsmen and forebears strung across the stone facade of the cathedral and clacking lightly in the wind. Later when the lamps were lit the heads in the soft glare of the uplight assumed the look of tragic masks and within a few days they would become mottled white and altogether leprous with the droppings of the birds that roosted upon them.

*

THIS ANGEL TRIAS who was governor had been sent abroad as a young man for his education and was widely read in the classics and was a student of languages. He was also a man among men and the rough warriors he'd hired for the protection of the state seemed to warm something in him. When the lieutenant invited Glanton and his officers to dine Glanton replied that he and his men did not keep separate mess. The lieutenant yielded the point with a smile and Trias had done the same. They arrived in good order, shaved and shorn and turned out in their new boots and finery, the Delawares strangely austere and menacing in their morningcoats, all to gather about the table set for them. Cigars were presented and glasses of sherry poured and the governor standing at the head of the table made them welcome and issued orders to his chamberlain that every need be seen to. Soldiers attended them, fetching extra glasses, pouring the wine, lighting cigars from a wick in a silver holder designed for just that purpose. The judge arrived last of all, dressed in a well-cut suit of unbleached linen that had been made for him that very afternoon. Whole bolts of cloth exhausted and squads of tailors as well in that fabrication. His feet were encased in nicely polished gray kid boots and in his hand he held a panama hat that had been spliced together from two such lesser hats by such painstaking work that the joinery did scarcely show at all.

Trias had already taken his seat when the judge made his appearance but no sooner had the governor seen him than he rose again and they shook hands cordially and the governor had him seated at his right and they at once fell into conversation in a tongue none other in that room spoke at all saving for random vile epithets drifted down from the north. The expriest was sat opposite the kid and he raised his brows and motioned toward the head of the table with a swing of his eyes. The kid, in the first starched collar he'd ever owned and the first cravat, sat mute as a tailor's dummy at that board.

By now the table was fully commenced and there was a

178

tandem run of dishes, fish and fowl and beef and wild meats of the countryside and a roast shoat on a platter and casseroles of savories and trifles and glaces and bottles of wine and brandy from the vineyards at El Paso. Patriotic toasts were drunk, the governor's aides raising their glasses to Washington and Franklin and the Americans responding with yet more of their own country's heroes, ignorant alike of diplomacy and any name at all from the pantheon of their sister republic. They fell to and they continued to eat until they had exhausted first the banquet and then the larder of the hotel altogether. Couriers were sent abroad through the city to fetch more only to have this also vanish and more sent for until Riddle's cook barricaded the door with his body and the soldiers in attendance took to simply dumping great trays of pastries, fried meatskins, rounds of cheese—whatever they could find—out upon the table.

The governor had tapped his glass and risen to speak in his well-phrased english, but the bloated and belching mercenaries were leering about and were calling for more drink and some had not ceased to scream out toasts, now degenerated into obscene pledges to the whores of various southern cities. The bursar was introduced to cheers, catcalls, hoisted bumpers. Glanton took charge of the long canvas bag stamped with the state cartouche and cutting the governor short he rose and dumped the gold out onto the table among the bones and rinds and pools of spilled drink and in a brisk drumhead disbursement divided out the pile of gold with the blade of his knife so that each man was paid his spoken share and no further ceremony to it. A sort of skiffle band had struck up a lugubrious air in one corner of the hall and first up was the judge who ushered the players and their instruments into the adjoining ballroom where a number of ladies who had been sent for sat already about the walls on benches and fanned themselves without apparent alarm.

The Americans debouched into the dancing hall by ones and twos and by groups, chairs pushed back, chairs pushed over to lie where they fell. Wall lamps in their tin reflectors had been lit all about the room and the celebrants foregathered there cast conflicting shadows. The scalphunters stood grinning at the dames, churlishlooking in their shrunken clothes, sucking their teeth, armed with knives and pistols and mad about the eyes. The judge was in close conference with the band and soon a quadrille was struck up. A great lurching and stomping ensued while the judge, affable, gallant, squired first one and then another of the ladies through the steps with an easy niceness. By midnight the governor had excused himself and members of the band had begun to slip away. A blind street harpist stood terrified upon the banquet table among the bones and platters and a horde of luridlooking whores had infiltrated the dance. Pistolfire soon became general and Mr Riddle, who was acting American consul in the city, descended to remonstrate with the revelers and was warned away. Fights broke out. Furniture was disassembled, men waving chairlegs, candlestands. Two whores grappled and pitched into a sideboard and went to the floor in a crash of brandyglasses. Jackson, pistols drawn, lurched into the street vowing to Shoot the ass off Jesus Christ, the longlegged white son of a bitch. At dawn the shapes of insensate topers lay snoring about the floor among dark patches of drying blood. Bathcat and the harpist lay asleep upon the banquet table in one another's arms. A family of thieves were tiptoeing through the wreckage turning out the pockets of the sleepers and the remains of a bonfire that had consumed a good part of the hotel's furnishings smoldered in the street before the door.

These scenes and scenes like them were repeated night after night. The citizenry made address to the governor but he was much like the sorcerer's apprentice who could indeed provoke the imp to do his will but could in no way make him cease again. The baths had become bordellos, the attendants driven off. The white stone fountain in the plaza was filled at night with naked and drunken men. Cantinas were evacuated as if by fire with the appearance of any two of the company and the Americans found themselves in ghost taverns with drinks on the tables and cigars still burning in the clay ashtrays. Horses were ridden indoors and out and as the gold began to dwindle away shopkeepers found themselves presented with debits scrawled on butcherpaper in a foreign language for whole shelves of goods. Stores began to close. Charcoal scrawls appeared on the limewashed walls. Mejor los indios. The evening streets stood empty and there were no paseos and the young girls of the city were boarded up and seen no more.

On the fifteenth of August they rode out. A week later a company of drovers reported them investing the town of Coyame eighty miles to the northeast.

THE VILLAGE OF Coyame had for some years been laid under annual contribution by Gómez and his band. When Glanton and his men rode in they were fallen upon as saints. Women ran alongside the horses to touch their boots and presents of every kind were pressed upon them until each man rode with an embarrassment of melons and pastries and trussed chickens gathered in the bow of his saddle. When they rode out three days later the streets stood empty, not even a dog followed them to the gates.

They traveled northeast as far as the town of Presidio on the Texas border and they crossed the horses and rode dripping through the streets. A soil where Glanton was subject to arrest. He rode out alone on the desert and sat the horse and he and the horse and the dog looked out across the rolling scrubland and the barren peppercorn hills and the mountains and the flat brush country and running plain beyond where four hundred miles to the east were the wife and child that he would not see again. His shadow grew long before him on the banded wash of sand. He would not follow. He had taken off his hat for the evening wind to cool him and at length he put it on again and turned the horse and rode back.

They wandered the borderland for weeks seeking some sign

of the Apache. Deployed upon that plain they moved in a constant elision, ordained agents of the actual dividing out the world which they encountered and leaving what had been and what would never be alike extinguished on the ground behind them. Spectre horsemen, pale with dust, anonymous in the crenellated heat. Above all else they appeared wholly at venture, primal, provisional, devoid of order. Like beings provoked out of the absolute rock and set nameless and at no remove from their own loomings to wander ravenous and doomed and mute as gorgons shambling the brutal wastes of Gondwanaland in a time before nomenclature was and each was all.

They killed wild meat and they took what they required by way of commissary from the pueblos and estancias through which they passed. One evening almost within sight of the town of El Paso they looked off toward the north where the Gileños wintered and they knew they would not be going there. They camped that night at the Hueco tanks, a group of natural stone cisterns in the desert. The rocks about in every sheltered place were covered with ancient paintings and the judge was soon among them copying out those certain ones into his book to take away with him. They were of men and animals and of the chase and there were curious birds and arcane maps and there were constructions of such singular vision as to justify every fear of man and the things that are in him. Of these etchings—some bright yet with color—there were hundreds, and yet the judge went among them with assurance, tracing out the very ones which he required. When he had done and while there yet was light he returned to a certain stone ledge and sat a while and studied again the work there. Then he rose and with a piece of broken chert he scappled away one of the designs, leaving no trace of it only a raw place on the stone where it had been. Then he put up his book and returned to the camp.

In the morning they rode out to the south. Little was said, nor were they quarrelsome among themselves. In three days they would fall upon a band of peaceful Tiguas camped on the river and slaughter them every soul.

On the eve of that day they crouched about the fire where it hissed in a softly falling rain and they ran balls and cut patches as if the fate of the aborigines had been cast into shape by some other agency altogether. As if such destinies were prefigured in the very rock for those with eyes to read. No man stood to tender them a defense. Toadvine and the kid conferred together and when they rode out at noon the day following they trotted their horses alongside Bathcat. They rode in silence. Them sons of bitches aint botherin nobody, Toadvine said. The Vandiemanlander looked at him. He looked at the livid letters tattooed on his forehead and at the lank greasy hair that hung from his earless skull. He looked at the necklace of gold teeth at his chest. They rode on.

They approached those wretched pavilions in the long light of the day's failing, coming up from downwind along the south bank of the river where they could smell the woodsmoke of the cookfires. When the first dogs barked Glanton roweled his horse forward and they came out of the trees and across the dry scrub with the long necks of the horses leaning out of the dust avid as hounds and the riders quirting them on into the sun where the shapes of the women rising up from their tasks stood flat and rigid in silhouette for a moment before they could quite believe in the reality of that dusty pandemoniac pounding down upon them. They stood dumb, barefoot, clad in the unbleached cotton of the country. They clutched cooking ladles, naked children. At the first fire a dozen of them crumpled and fell.

The others had begun to run, old people flinging up their hands, children tottering and blinking in the pistolfire. A few young men ran out with drawn bows and were shot down and then the riders were all through the village trampling down the grass wickiups and bludgeoning the shrieking householders.

Long past dark that night when the moon was already up a

party of women that had been upriver drying fish returned to the village and wandered howling through the ruins. A few fires still smoldered on the ground and dogs slank off from among the corpses. An old woman knelt at the blackened stones before her door and poked brush into the coals and blew back a flame from the ashes and began to right the overturned pots. All about her the dead lay with their peeled skulls like polyps bluely wet or luminescent melons cooling on some mesa of the moon. In the days to come the frail black rebuses of blood in those sands would crack and break and drift away so that in the circuit of few suns all trace of the destruction of these people would be erased. The desert wind would salt their ruins and there would be nothing, nor ghost nor scribe, to tell to any pilgrim in his passing how it was that people had lived in this place and in this place died.

The Americans entered the town of Carrizal late in the afternoon of the second day following, their horses festooned with the reeking scalps of the Tiguas. This town had fallen almost to ruin. Many of the houses stood empty and the presidio was collapsing back into the earth out of which it had been raised and the inhabitants seemed themselves made vacant by old terrors. They watched the passing of that bloodstained argosy through their streets with dark and solemn eyes. Those riders seemed journeyed from a legendary world and they left behind a strange tainture like an afterimage on the eye and the air they disturbed was altered and electric. They passed along the ruinous walls of the cemetery where the dead were trestled up in niches and the grounds strewn with bones and skulls and broken pots like some more ancient ossuary. Other ragged folk appeared in the dusty streets behind them and stood looking after.

That night they camped at a warm spring atop a hill amid old traces of Spanish masonry and they stripped and descended like acolytes into the water while huge white leeches willowed away over the sands. When they rode out in the morning it was still dark. Lightning stood in ragged chains far to the south, silent, the staccato mountains bespoken blue and barren out of the void. Day broke upon a smoking reach of desert darkly clouded where the riders could count five separate storms spaced upon the shores of the round earth. They were riding in pure sand and the horses labored so hugely that the men were obliged to dismount and lead them, toiling up steep eskers where the wind blew the white pumice from the crests like the spume from sea swells and the sand was scalloped and fraily shaped and nothing else was there save random polished bones. They were all day among the dunes and in the evening coming down from the last low sandhills to the plain below among catclaw and crucifixion thorn they were a parched and haggard lot man and beast. Harpie eagles flew up screaming from a dead mule and wheeled off westward into the sun as they led the horses out onto the plain.

Two nights later bivouacked in a pass in the mountains they could see the distant lights of the city below them. They crouched along a shale ridge in the leeward wall of the gap while the fire sawed in the wind and they watched the lamps winking in the blue floor of the night thirty miles away. The judge crossed before them in the dark. Sparks from the fire ran down the wind. He took his seat among the scrabbled plates of shale out there and so they sat like beings from an older age watching the distant lamps dim out one by one until the city on the plain had shrunk to a small core of light that might have been a burning tree or some solitary encampment of travelers or perhaps no ponderable fire at all.

As they rode out through the tall wooden gates of the governor's palace two soldiers who had been standing there counting them past stepped forward and took Toadvine's horse by the headstall. Glanton passed him on the right and rode on. Toadvine stood in the saddle.

Glanton!

The riders clattered into the street. Glanton just beyond the gates looked back. The soldiers were speaking to Toadvine in Spanish and one held an escopeta on him.

I aint got nobody's teeth, Glanton said.

I'll shoot these two fools where they stand.

Glanton spat. He looked down the street and he looked at Toadvine. Then he dismounted and led his horse back into the courtyard. Vamonos, he said. He looked up at Toadvine. Get off your horse.

They rode out of town under escort two days later. Upward of a hundred soldiers herding them along the road, uneasy in their varied dress and arms, wrenching their horses about and booting them through the ford where the American horses had stopped to drink. In the foothills above the aqueduct they reined to one side and the Americans filed past and wound up through the rocks and nopal and diminished among the shadows and were gone.

They rode west into the mountains. They passed through small villages doffing their hats to folk whom they would murder before the month was out. Mud pueblos that lay like plague towns with the crops rotting in the fields and what stock not driven off by the indians wandering at will and none to herd or tend it and many villages almost wholly depopulated of male inhabitants where the women and children crouched in terror in their hovels listening until the last hoofclop died in the distance.

At the town of Nacori there was a cantina and here the company dismounted and crowded through the doorway and took tables. Tobin volunteered to guard the horses. He stood watching up and down the street. No one paid him any mind. These people had seen Americans in plenty, dusty laggard trains of them months out of their own country and half crazed with the enormity of their own presence in that immense and bloodslaked waste, commandeering meal and meat or indulging a latent taste for rape among the sloe-eyed girls of that country.

Now it was something near to an hour past noon and a number of workers and tradesmen were crossing the street toward the cantina. As they passed Glanton's horse Glanton's dog rose up bristling. They veered slightly and went on. At the same moment a deputation of dogs of the village had started across the plaza, five, six of them, their eyes on Glanton's dog. As they did so a juggler leading a funeral rounded the corner into the street and taking a rocket from among several under his arm he held it to the cigarillo in his mouth and tossed it into the plaza where it exploded. The pack of dogs shied and scrambled back save for two who continued into the street. Among the Mexican horses tethered at the bar before the cantina several shot out a hind leg and the rest stepped about nervously. Glanton's dog did not take his eyes from the men moving toward the door. None of the American horses even raised an ear. The pair of dogs that had crossed in front of the funeral procession veered off from the kicking horses and came on toward the cantina. Two more rockets exploded in the street and now the rest of the procession had swung into view, a fiddler and a cornetplayer leading with a quick and lively tune. The dogs were trapped between the funeral and the animals of the mercenaries and they halted and flattened their ears and began to sidle and trot. Finally they bolted across the street behind the pallbearers. These details should have stood the workers entering the cantina in better stead. They had turned and they stood now with their backs to the door holding their hats to their chests. The pallbearers passed carrying on their shoulders a bier and the watchers could see in her burial dress among the flowers the graylooking face of a young woman jostling along woodenly. Behind came her coffin, made from rawhide blacked with lampblack, carried by dark-clad porters and looking much like a rude hide boat. At the rear advanced a company of mourners, some of the men drinking, the old women in their dusty black shawls helped weeping over the potholes and children bearing flowers who looked shyly at the spectators in the street as they passed.

Within the cantina the Americans had no more than seated themselves before a muttered insult from a nearby table brought three or four of them to their feet. The kid addressed the table in his wretched Spanish and demanded which among those sullen inebriates had spoken. Before any could own it the first of the funeral rockets exploded in the street as told and the entire company of Americans made for the door. A drunk at the table rose to his feet with a knife and lurched after them. His friends called after him but he waved them away.

John Dorsey and Henderson Smith, two boys from Missouri, were the first into the street. They were followed by Charlie Brown and the judge. The judge could see over their heads and he raised one hand to those behind him. The bier was just passing. The fiddler and the cornetist were making little bows to each other and their steps suggested the martial style of the air they played. It's a funeral, said the judge. As he spoke the drunk with the knife now reeling in the doorway sank the blade deep into the back of a man named Grimley. None saw it but the judge. Grimley put a hand on the rough wood frame of the door. I'm killed, he said. The judge drew his belt pistol and leveled it above the heads of the men and shot the drunk through the middle of the forehead.

The Americans outside the door were all but looking down the barrel of the judge's pistol when he fired and most of them dove to the ground. Dorsey rolled clear and got to his feet and collided with the workers who'd been paying their respects to the passing cortege. They were putting their hats on when the judge fired. The dead man fell backward into the cantina, blood spouting from his head. When Grimley turned they could see the wooden handle of the knife protruding from his bloody shirt. Other knives were already in play. Dorsey was grappling with the Mexicans and Henderson Smith had drawn his bowie and half severed a man's arm with it and the man was standing with the dark arterial blood spraying between his fingers where he tried to hold the wound shut. The judge got Dorsey to his feet and they backed toward the cantina with the Mexicans feinting and jabbing at them with their knives. From inside came the uninterrupted sound of gunfire and the doorframe was filling up with smoke. The judge turned at the door and stepped over the several corpses sprawled there. Inside the huge pistols roared without intermission and the twenty or so Mexicans who'd been in the room were strewn about in every position, shot to pieces among the overturned chairs and the tables with the fresh splinters blown out of the wood and the mud walls pocked everywhere by the big conical bullets. The survivors were making for the daylight in the doorway and the first of these encountered the judge there and cut at him with his knife. But the judge was like a cat and he sidestepped the man and seized his arm and broke it and picked the man up by his head. He put him against the wall and smiled at him but the man had begun to bleed from the ears and the blood was running down between the judge's fingers and over his hands and when the judge turned him loose there was something wrong with his head and he slid to the floor and did not get up. Those behind him had meanwhile met with a great battery of gunfire and the doorway was jammed with the dead and dying when there was suddenly a great ringing silence in the room. The judge stood with his back to the wall. The smoke drifted through like fog and the shrouded figures stood frozen. In the center of the room Toadvine and the kid were standing back to back with their pistols at port like duellists. The judge stepped to the door and shouted across the stacked bodies to the expriest where he stood among the horses with his pistol drawn.

The laggards, Priest, the laggards.

They'd not have shot men in public in a town so large but there was no help for it. Three men were running down the street and two others were legging it across the square. Of other souls abroad there were none. Tobin stepped from between the horses and leveled the big pistol in both hands and began to fire, the pistol bucking and dropping back and the runners wobbling and pitching headlong. He shot the two in the plaza and swung and shot down the runners in the street. The last one fell in a doorway and Tobin turned and drew the other pistol from his belt and stepped to the other side of the horse and looked up the street and across the square for any sign of movement there or among the buildings. The judge stepped back from the doorway into the cantina where the Americans stood looking at each other and at the bodies in a sort of wonder. They looked at Glanton. His eyes cut across the smoking room. His hat lying on a table. He stepped over and got it and set it on his head and squared it. He looked about. The men were reloading the empty chambers in their pistols. Hair, boys, he said. The string aint run on this trade yet.

When they left the cantina ten minutes later the streets were deserted. They had scalped the entire body of the dead, sliding about in a floor that had been packed clay and was now a wine-colored mud. There were twenty-eight Mexicans inside the tavern and eight more in the street including the five the expriest had shot. They mounted up. Grimley sat slumped sideways against the mud wall of the building. He did not look up. He was holding his pistol in his lap and looking off down the street and they turned and rode out along the north side of the plaza and disappeared.

It was thirty minutes before anyone appeared in the street. They spoke in whispers. As they approached the cantina one of the men from inside appeared in the doorway like a bloody apparition. He had been scalped and the blood was all run down into his eyes and he was holding shut a huge hole in his chest where a pink froth breathed in and out. One of the citizens laid a hand on his shoulder.

A dónde vas? he said.

A casa, said the man.

✢

THE NEXT TOWN they entered was two days deeper into the sierras. They never knew what it was called. A collection of mud huts pitched on the naked plateau. As they rode in the people ran before them like harried game. Their cries to one another or perhaps the visible frailty of them seemed to incite something in Glanton. Brown watched him. He nudged forth his horse and drew his pistol and this somnolent pueblo was forthwith dragooned into a weltering shambles. Many of the people had been running toward the church where they knelt clutching the altar and from this refuge they were dragged howling one by one and one by one they were slain and scalped in the chancel floor. When the riders passed through this same village four days later the dead were still in the streets and buzzards and pigs were feeding on them. The scavengers watched in silence while the company picked their way past like supernumeraries in a dream. When the last of them was gone they commenced to feed again.

They went on through the mountains without resting. They trod a narrow trail through a black pine wood by day and by dark and in silence save for the creaking of tack and the breathing of the horses. A thin shell of a moon lay capsized over the jagged peaks. They rode down into a mountain town just before day where there was no lamp nor watchman nor dog. In the gray dawn they sat along a wall waiting for daylight. A rooster called. A door slammed. An old woman came down the lane past the daubed sty walls through the mist carrying a yoke of jars. They rose up. It was cold and their breath plumed about them. They took down the poles in the corral and led the horses out. They rode up the street. They halted. The animals sidled and stamped in the cold. Glanton had reined up and drawn his pistol.

A company of mounted troops passed out from behind a wall at the north end of the village and turned in to the street. They wore tall shakos faced with metal plates and horsehair plumes and they wore green coats trimmed with scarlet and scarlet sashes and they were armed with lances and muskets and their mounts were nicely caparisoned and they entered the street sidling and prancing, horsemen riding upon horses, all of them desirable young men. The company looked to Glanton. He holstered the pistol and drew his rifle. The captain of the lancers had raised his sabre to halt the column. The next instant the narrow street was filled with riflesmoke and a dozen of the soldiers lay dead or dying on the ground. The horses reared and screamed and fell back upon each other and men were unhorsed and rose up struggling to hold their mounts. A second fire tore through their ranks. They fell away in confusion. The Americans drew their pistols and booted their horses forward up the street.

The Mexican captain was bleeding from a gunshot wound in the chest and he stood in the stirrups to receive the charge with his sabre. Glanton shot him through the head and shoved him from his horse with his foot and shot down in succession three men behind him. A soldier on the ground had picked up a lance and ran at him with it and one of the riders leaned down out of that wild melee and cut his throat and passed on. In the morning dampness the sulphurous smoke hung over the street in a gray shroud and the colorful lancers fell under the horses in that perilous mist like soldiers slaughtered in a dream wide-eyed and wooden and mute.

Some among the rear guard had managed to turn their mounts and start back up the street and the Americans were clouting back with pistolbarrels the riderless horses and the horses surged and milled with the stirrups kicking out and they trumpeted with their long mouths and trampled underfoot the dead. They beat them back and urged their horses through and up the street to where it narrowed and turned up the mountain and they fired after the fleeing lancers as they skeltered up the trail in a rattle of small stones.

Glanton sent a detachment of five men to follow and he and the judge and Bathcat turned back. They met the rest of the company riding up and they turned back and they went down and looted the bodies where they lay in the street like dead bandsmen and they smashed their muskets against the walls of the houses and broke their swords and lances. As they rode out they met the five scouts returning. The lancers had quit the trail and scattered through the woods. Two nights later camped on a butte looking out over the broad central plain they could see a point of light out on that desert like the reflection of a single star in a lake of utter blackness.

They took council. On that raw tablestone the flames of their balefire swirled and circled and they studied the arrant blackness under them where it fell away like the sheer cloven face of the world.

How far do you make them, said Glanton.

Holden shook his head. They've made half a day on us. They number no more than twelve, fourteen. They wont send men ahead.

How far are we from Chihuahua City?

Four days. Three. Where's Davy?

Glanton turned. How far to Chihuahua, David?

Brown stood with his back to the fire. He nodded. If that's them they could be there in three days.

You reckon we can overhaul them?

I dont know. Might depend on whether they figure us to be after them.

Glanton turned and spat into the fire. The judge raised one pale and naked arm and pursued something in the pit of it with his fingers. If we can be off of this mountain by daylight, he said, I believe we can overtake them. Otherwise we had better make for Sonora.

They may be from Sonora.

Then we'd better go get them.

We could take these scalps to Ures.

The fire swept along the ground, it rose again. We'd better go get them, said the judge.

They rode onto the plain at dawn as the judge had said and

that night they could see the fire of the Mexicans reflected in the sky to the east beyond the curve of the earth. All the day following they rode and all that night, jerking and lurching like a deputation of spastics as they slept in their saddles. On the morning of the third day they could see the riders before them on the plain in silhouette against the sun and in the evening they could count their number struggling upon that desolate mineral waste. When the sun rose the walls of the city stood pale and thin in the rising light twenty miles to the east. They sat their horses. The lancers were strung out along the road several miles to the south of them. There was no reason for them to stop and no hope in it any more than there was in the riding but as they were riding they rode and the Americans put their horses forward once again.

For a while they rode almost parallel toward the gates of the city, the two parties bloody and ragged, the horses stumbling. Glanton called out to them to surrender but they rode on. He drew his rifle. They were shambling along the road like dumb things. He pulled up his horse and it stood with its legs spread and its flanks heaving and he leveled the rifle and fired.

They were for the most part no longer even armed. There were nine of them and they halted and turned and then they charged across that intermittent ground of rock and scrub and were shot down in the space of a minute.

The horses were caught and herded back to the road and the saddles and trappings cut away. The bodies of the dead were stripped and their uniforms and weapons burned along with the saddles and other gear and the Americans dug a pit in the road and buried them in a common grave, the naked bodies with their wounds like the victims of surgical experimentation lying in the pit gaping sightlessly at the desert sky as the dirt was pushed over them. They trampled the spot with their horses until it looked much like the road again and the smoking gunlocks and sabreblades and girthrings were dragged from the ashes of the fire and carried away and buried in a separate place and the riderless horses hazed off into the desert and in the evening the wind carried away the ashes and the wind blew in the night and fanned the last smoldering billets and drove forth the last fragile race of sparks fugitive as flintstrikings in the unanimous dark of the world.

They entered the city haggard and filthy and reeking with the blood of the citizenry for whose protection they had contracted. The scalps of the slain villagers were strung from the windows of the governor's house and the partisans were paid out of the all but exhausted coffers and the Sociedad was disbanded and the bounty rescinded. Within a week of their quitting the city there would be a price of eight thousand pesos posted for Glanton's head. They rode out on the north road as would parties bound for El Paso but before they were even quite out of sight of the city they had turned their tragic mounts to the west and they rode infatuate and half fond toward the red demise of that day, toward the evening lands and the distant pandemonium of the sun.

XIV

Mountain storms – Tierras quemadas, tierras despobladas –
Jesús María – The inn – Shopkeepers – A bodega – The fiddler –
The priest – Las Animas – The procession – Cazando las almas –
Glanton takes a fit – Dogs for sale – The judge prestidigitant –
The flag – A shootout – An exodus – The conducta –
Blood and mercury – At the ford – Jackson restored –
The jungle – An herbalist – The judge collects specimens –
The point of view for his work as a scientist – Ures – The populace –
Los pordioseros – A fandango – Pariah dogs – Glanton and judge.

ALL TO THE NORTH the rain had dragged black tendrils down
from the thunderclouds like tracings of lampblack fallen in a
beaker and in the night they could hear the drum of rain miles
away on the prairie. They ascended through a rocky pass and
lightning shaped out the distant shivering mountains and lightning rang the stones about and tufts of blue fire clung to the
hordes like incandescent elementals that would not be driven
off. Soft smelterlights advanced upon the metal of the harness,
lights ran blue and liquid on the barrels of the guns. Mad
jackhares started and checked in the blue glare and high among
those clanging crags jokin roehawks crouched in their feathers
or cracked a yellow eye at the thunder underfoot.

They rode for days through the rain and they rode through rain and hail and rain again. In that gray storm light they crossed a flooded plain with the footed shapes of the horses reflected in the water among clouds and mountains and the riders slumped forward and rightly skeptic of the shimmering cities on the distant shore of that sea whereon they trod miraculous. They climbed up through rolling grasslands where small birds shied away chittering down the wind and a buzzard labored up from among bones with wings that went whoop whoop whoop like a child's toy swung on a string and in the long red sunset the sheets of water on the plain below them lay like tidepools of primal blood.

They passed through a highland meadow carpeted with wildflowers, acres of golden groundsel and zinnia and deep purple gentian and wild vines of blue morninglory and a vast plain of varied small blooms reaching onward like a gingham print to the farthest serried rimlands blue with haze and the adamantine ranges rising out of nothing like the backs of seabeasts in a devonian dawn. It was raining again and they rode slouched under slickers hacked from greasy halfcured hides and so cowled in these primitive skins before the gray and driving rain they looked like wardens of some dim sect sent forth to proselytize among the very beasts of the land. The country before them lay clouded and dark. They rode through the long twilight and the sun set and no moon rose and to the west the mountains shuddered again and again in clattering frames and burned to final darkness and the rain hissed in the blind night land. They went up through the foothills among pine trees and barren rock and they went up through juniper and spruce and the rare great aloes and the rising stalks of the yuccas with their pale blooms silent and unearthly among the evergreens.

In the night they followed a mountain torrent in a wild gorge choked with mossy rocks and they rode under dark grottoes where the water dripped and spattered and tasted of iron and they saw the silver filaments of cascades divided upon the faces of distant buttes that appeared as signs and wonders in the heavens themselves so dark was the ground of their origins. They crossed the blackened wood of a burn and they rode through a region of cloven rock where great boulders lay halved with smooth uncentered faces and on the slopes of those ferric grounds old paths of fire and the blackened bones of trees assassinated in the mountain storms. On the day following they began to encounter holly and oak, hardwood forests much like those they had quit in their youth. In pockets on the north slopes hail lay nested like tectites among the leaves and the nights were cool. They traveled through the high country deeper into the mountains where the storms had their lairs, a fiery clangorous region where white flames ran on the peaks and the ground bore the burnt smell of broken flint. At night the wolves in the dark forests of the world below called to them as if they were friends to man and Glanton's dog trotted moaning among the endlessly articulating legs of the horses.

Nine days out of Chihuahua they passed through a gap in the mountains and began to descend by a trail that ran carved along the solid stone face of a bluff a thousand feet above the clouds. A great stone mammoth watched from the gray escarpment above them. They picked their way down singlefile. They passed through a tunnel hewn in the rock and on the other side miles below them in a gorge lay the roofs of a town.

They descended by rocky switchbacks and across the beds of streams where small trout stood on their pale fins and studied the noses of the drinking horses. Sheets of mist that smelled and tasted of metal rose out of the gorge and crossed over them and moved on through the woods. They nudged the horses through the ford and down the trace and at three oclock in the afternoon in a thin and drizzling rain they rode into the old stone town of Jesús María.

They clattered over the rainwashed cobbles stuck with leaves and crossed a stone bridge and rode up the street under the dripping eaves of the galleried buildings and along a mountain torrent that ran through the town. Small oremills had been ground into the polished rocks in the river and the hills above the town were everywhere tunneled and scaffolded and scarred with drifts and tailings. The raggletag advent of the riders was howled about by a few wet dogs crouched in doorways and they turned into a narrow street and halted dripping before the door of an inn.

Glanton pounded on the door and it opened and a young boy looked out. A woman appeared and looked at them and went back in. Finally a man came and opened the gate. He was slightly drunk and he held the gate while the horsemen rode through one by one into the little flooded courtyard and then he closed the gate behind them.

In the morning the rain had stopped and they appeared in the streets, tattered, stinking, ornamented with human parts like cannibals. They carried the huge pistols stuck in their belts and the vile skins they wore were deeply stained with blood and smoke and gunblack. The sun was out and the old women on their knees with bucket and rag washing the stones before the shopdoors turned and looked after them and shopkeepers setting out their wares nodded them a wary good morning. They were a strange clientele among such commerce. They stood blinking before the doorways where finches hung in small withy cages and green and brassy parrots that stood on one foot and croaked uneasily. There were ristras of dried fruit and peppers and clusters of tinware that hung like chimes and there were hog-skins filled with pulque that swung from the beams like bloated swine in a knacker's yard. They sent for cups. A fiddler appeared and crouched on a stone doorsill and began to saw out some Moorish folktune and none who passed on their morning errands could take their eyes from those pale and rancid giants.

By noon they'd found a bodega run by a man named Frank Carroll, a low doggery once a stable whose shed doors stood open to the street to admit the only light. The fiddler had followed in what seemed a great sadness and he took up his station just without the door where he could watch the out-landers drink and clack their gold doubloons on the board. In the doorway there was an old man taking the sun and he leaned with a goathorn eartrumpet to the rising din within and nodded in continual agreement although no word was spoken in any language he had understanding of.

The judge had spied the musician and he called to him and tossed a coin that clinked upon the stones. The fiddler held it briefly to the light as if it might not serve and then slipped it away among his clothes and fitted his instrument beneath his chin and struck up an air that was old among the mountebanks of Spain two hundred years before. The judge stepped into the sunlit doorway and executed upon the stones a series of steps with a strange precision and he and the fiddler seemed alien minstrels met by chance in this medieval town. The judge removed his hat and bowed to a pair of ladies detoured into the street to bypass the doggery and he pirouetted hugely on his mincing feet and poured pulque from his cup into the old man's eartrumpet. The old man quickly stoppered the horn with the ball of his thumb and he held the horn with care before him while he augered his ear with one finger and then he drank.

By dark the streets were filled with besotted bedlamites lurching and cursing and ringing the churchbells with pistolballs in a godless charivari until the priest emerged bearing before him the crucified Christ and exhorting them with fragments of latin in a singsong chant. This man was drubbed in the street and prodded obscenely and they flung gold coins at him as he lay clutching his image. When he rose he disdained to take up the coins until some small boys ran out to gather them and then he ordered them brought to him while the barbarians whooped and drank him a toast.

Spectators drifted away, the narrow street emptied. Some of the Americans had wandered into the cold waters of the stream and were splashing about and they clambered dripping into the street and stood dark and smoking and apocalyptic in the dim lampfall. The night was cold and they shambled steaming through the cobbled town like fairybook beasts and it had begun to rain again.

The day that followed was the feast of Las Animas and there was a parade through the streets and a horsedrawn cart that bore a rude Christ in a stained and ancient catafalque. Lay acolytes followed all in company and the priest went before ringing a small bell. A barefoot brotherhood clad in black marched in the rear bearing sceptres of weeds. The Christ jostled past, a poor figure of straw with carven head and feet. He wore a crown of mountain briars and on his brow were painted drops of blood and on his old dry wooden cheeks blue tears. The villagers knelt and blessed themselves and some stepped forward and touched the garment the figure wore and kissed their fingertips. The parade trundled past mournfully and small children sat in the doorways eating pastry skulls and watching the parade and the rain in the streets.

The judge sat alone in the cantina. He also watched the rain, his eyes small in his great naked face. He'd filled his pockets with little candy deathsheads and he sat by the door and offered these to children passing on the walk under the eaves but they shied away like little horses.

In the evening groups of townfolk descended from the cemetery on the side of the hill and later in the dark by candle or lamp light they emerged again and made their way up to the church to pray. None but passed clutches of Americans crazed with drink and these grimy visitants would doff their hats oafishly and totter and grin and make obscene suggestions to the young girls. Carroll had closed his squalid bistro at dusk but opened it again to save the doors being stove. Sometime in the night a party of horsemen bound for California arrived, every man of them slumped in exhaustion. Yet within the hour they'd ridden out again. By midnight when the souls of the dead were rumored to be about the scalphunters were again howling in the streets and discharging their pistols in spite of rain or death and this continued sporadically until dawn.

By noon the day following Glanton in his drunkenness was taken with a kind of fit and he lurched crazed and disheveled into the little courtyard and began to open fire with his pistols. In the afternoon he lay bound to his bed like a madman while the judge sat with him and cooled his brow with rags of water and spoke to him in a low voice. Outside voices called across the steep hillsides. A little girl was missing and parties of citizens had turned out to search the mineshafts. After a while Glanton slept and the judge rose and went out.

It was gray and raining, leaves were blowing down. A ragged stripling stepped from a doorway by a wooden rainspout and tugged at the judge's elbow. He had two pups in his shirtfront and these he offered for sale, dragging one forth by the neck.

The judge was looking off up the street. When he looked down at the boy the boy hauled forth the other dog. They hung limply. Perros a vende, he said.

Cuánto quieres? said the judge.

The boy looked at one and then the other of the animals. As if he'd pick one to suit the judge's character, such dogs existing somewhere perhaps. He thrust forth the lefthand animal. Cincuenta centavos, he said.

The pup squirmed and drew back in his fist like an animal backing down a hole, its pale blue eyes impartial, befrighted alike of the cold and the rain and the judge.

Ambos, said the judge. He sought in his pockets for coins.

The dogvendor took this for a bargaining device and studied the dogs anew to better determine their worth, but the judge had dredged from his polluted clothes a small gold coin worth a bushel of suchpriced dogs. He laid the coin in the palm of his hand and held it out and with the other hand took the pups from their keeper, holding them in one fist like a pair of socks. He gestured with the gold.

Andale, he said.

The boy stared at the coin.

The judge made a fist and opened it. The coin was gone. He wove his fingers in the empty air and reached behind the boy's ear and took the coin and handed it to him. The boy held the coin in both hands before him like a small ciborium and he looked up at the judge. But the judge had set forth, dogs dangling. He crossed upon the stone bridge and he looked down into the swollen waters and raised the dogs and pitched them in.

At the farther end the bridge gave onto a small street that ran along the river. Here the Vandiemenlander stood urinating from a stone wall into the water. When he saw the judge commit the dogs from the bridge he drew his pistol and called out.

The dogs disappeared in the foam. They swept one and the next down a broad green race over sheets of polished rock into the pool below. The Vandiemenlander raised and cocked the pistol. In the clear waters of the pool willow leaves turned like jade dace. The pistol bucked in his hand and one of the dogs leaped in the water and he cocked it again and fired again and a pink stain diffused. He cocked and fired the pistol a third time and the other dog also blossomed and sank.

The judge continued on across the bridge. When the boy ran up and looked down into the water he was still holding the coin. The Vandiemenlander stood in the street opposite with his pizzle in one hand and the revolver in the other. The smoke had drifted off downstream and there was nothing in the pool at all.

Sometime in the late afternoon Glanton woke and managed to struggle free of his bindings. The first news they had of him was in front of the cuartel where he cut down the Mexican flag with his knife and tied it to the tail of a mule. Then he mounted the mule and goaded it through the square dragging the sacred bandera in the mud behind him.

He made a circuit of the streets and emerged in the plaza again, kicking the animal viciously in the flanks. As he turned a shot rang out and the mule fell stone dead under him with a musketball lodged in its brain. Glanton rolled clear and scrambled to his feet firing wildly. An old woman sank soundlessly to the stones. The judge and Tobin and Doc Irving came from Frank Carroll's on a dead run and knelt in the shadow of a wall and began to fire at the upper windows. Another half dozen Americans came around the corner at the far side of the square and in a flurry of gunfire two of them fell. Slags of lead were whining off the stones and gunsmoke hung over the streets in the damp air. Glanton and John Gunn had made their way along the walls to the shed behind the posada where the horses were stabled and they began bringing the animals out. Three more of the company entered the yard at a run and commenced to tote gear out of the building and to saddle horses. Gunfire was now continual in the street and two Americans lay dead and others lay calling out. When the company rode out thirty minutes later they ran a gantlet of ragged fusil fire and rocks and bottles and they left six of their number behind.

An hour later Carroll and another American named Sanford who'd been residing in the town caught them up. The citizens had torched the saloon. The priest had baptized the wounded Americans and then stood back while they were shot through the head.

Before dark they encountered laboring up the western slope of the mountain a conducta of one hundred and twenty-two mules bearing flasks of quicksilver for the mines. They could hear the whipcrack and cry of the arrieros on the switchbacks far below them and they could see the burdened animals plodding like goats along a faultline in the sheer rock wall. Bad luck. Twenty-six days from the sea and less than two hours out from the mines. The mules wheezed and scrabbled in the talus and the drivers in their ragged and colorful costumes harried them on. When the first of them saw the riders above them he stood in the stirrups and looked back. The column of mules wound down the trail for a half mile or more and as they bunched and halted there were sections of the train visible on the separate switchbacks far below, eight and ten mules, facing now this way, now that, the tails of the animals picked clean as bones by those behind and the mercury within the guttapercha flasks pulsing heavily as if they carried secret beasts, things in pairs that stirred and breathed uneasily within those bloated satchels. The muleteer turned and looked up the trail. Already Glanton was upon him. He greeted the American cordially. Glanton rode past without speaking, taking the upper side in that rocky strait and shouldering the drover's mule dangerously among the loose shales. The man's face clouded and he turned and called back down the trail. The other riders were now pushing past him, their eyes narrow and their faces black as stokers with gunsoot. He stood down off his mule and drew his escopeta from under the fender of the saddle. David Brown was opposite him at this point, his pistol already in his hand at the off side of his horse. He swung it over the pommel and shot the man squarely in the chest. The man sat down heavily and Brown shot him again and he pitched off down the rocks into the abyss below.

The others of the company hardly turned to advise themselves of what had occurred. Every man of them was firing point blank at the muleteers. They fell from their mounts and lay in the trail or slid from the escarpment and vanished. The drivers below got their animals turned and were attempting to flee back down the trail and the laden packmules were beginning to clamber white-eyed at the sheer wall of the bluff like enormous rats. The riders pushed between them and the rock and methodically rode them from the escarpment, the animals dropping silently as martyrs, turning sedately in the empty air and exploding on the rocks below in startling bursts of blood and silver as the flasks broke open and the mercury loomed wobbling in the air in great sheets and lobes and small trembling satellites and all its forms grouping below and racing in the stone arroyos like the imbreachment of some ultimate alchemic work decocted from out the secret dark of the earth's heart, the fleeing stag of the ancients fugitive on the mountainside and bright and quick in the dry path of the storm channels and shaping out the sockets in the rock and hurrying from ledge to ledge down the slope shimmering and deft as eels.

The muleteers benched out in a swag on the trail where the precipice was almost negotiable and they rode and fell crashing down through the scrub juniper and pine in a confusion of cries while the horsemen herded the lag mules off after them and rode wildly down the rock trail like men themselves at the mercy of something terrible. Carroll and Sanford had become detached from the company and when they reached the bench where the last of the arrieros had disappeared they reined their horses and looked back up the trail. It was empty save for a few dead men from the conducta. Half a hundred mules had been ridden off the escarpment and in the curve of the bluff they could see the broken shapes of the animals strewn down the rocks and they could see the bright shapes of the quicksilver pooled in the evening light. The horses stamped and arched their necks. The riders looked off down into that calamitous gulf and they looked at each other but they required no conference and they pulled the mouths of the horses about and roweled them on down the mountain.

They caught up with the company at dusk. They were dismounted at the far side of a river and the kid and one of the Delawares were hazing the lathered horses back from the edge of the water. They put their animals to the ford and crossed, the water up under the horses bellies and the horses picking their way over the rocks and glancing wildly upstream where a cataract thundered out of the darkening forest into the flecked and seething pool below. When they rode up out of the ford the judge stepped forward and took Carroll's horse by the jaw.

Where's the nigger? he said.

He looked at the judge. They were all but at eyelevel and he on horseback. I dont know, he said.

The judge looked at Glanton. Glanton spat.

How many men did you see in the square?

I didnt have time to take no headcount. There was three or four shot that I know of.

But not the nigger?

I never saw him.

Sanford pushed his horse forward. There was no nigger in the square, he said. I seen them shoot them boys and they were ever one white as you and me.

The judge turned loose Carroll's horse and went to get his own animal. Two of the Delawares detached themselves from the company. When they rode out up the trail it was almost dark and the company had pulled back into the woods and posted videttes at the ford and they made no fire.

No riders came down the trail. The early part of the night was dark but the first relief at the ford saw it begin to clear and the moon came out over the canyon and they saw a bear come down and pause at the far side of the river and test the air with his nose and turn back. About daybreak the judge and the Delawares returned. They had the black with them. He was naked save for a blanket he'd wrapped himself in. He didnt even have boots. He was riding one of the bonetailed packmules from the conducta and he was shivering with cold. The only thing he'd saved was his pistol. He was holding it against his chest under the blanket for he had no other place to carry it.

THE WAY DOWN out of the mountains toward the western sea led them through green gorges thick with vines where paroquets and gaudy macaws leered and croaked. The trail followed a river and the river was up and muddy and there were many fords and they crossed and recrossed the river continually. Pale cascades hung down the sheer mountain wall above them, blowing off of the high slick rock in wild vapors. In eight days they passed no other riders. On the ninth they saw an old man trying to get off the trail below them, caning a pair of burros through the woods. As they came abreast of this spot they halted and Glanton turned into the woods where the wet leaves were shuffled up and he tracked down the old man sitting in the shrubbery solitary as a gnome. The burros looked up and twitched their ears and then lowered their heads to browse again. The old man watched him.

Por qué se esconde? said Glanton.

The old man didnt answer.

De dónde viene?

The old man seemed unwilling to reckon even with the idea of a dialogue. He squatted in the leaves with his arms folded. Glanton leaned and spat. He gestured with his chin at the burros.

Qué tiene allá?

The old man shrugged. Hierbas, he said.

Glanton looked at the animals and he looked at the old man. He turned his horse back toward the trail to rejoin the party.

Por qué me busca? called the old man after him.

They moved on. There were eagles and other birds in the valley and many deer and there were wild orchids and brakes of bamboo. The river here was sizeable and it swept past enormous boulders and waterfalls fell everywhere out of the high tangled jungle. The judge had taken to riding ahead with one of the Delawares and he carried his rifle loaded with the small hard seeds of the nopal fruit and in the evening he would dress expertly the colorful birds he'd shot, rubbing the skins with gunpowder and stuffing them with balls of dried grass and packing them away in his wallets. He pressed the leaves of trees and plants into his book and he stalked tiptoe the mountain butterflies with his shirt outheld in both hands, speaking to them in a low whisper, no curious study himself. Toadvine sat watching him as he made his notations in the ledger, holding the book toward the fire for the light, and he asked him what was his purpose in all this.

The judge's quill ceased its scratching. He looked at Toad-vine. Then he continued to write again.

Toadvine spat into the fire.

The judge wrote on and then he folded the ledger shut and laid it to one side and pressed his hands together and passed them down over his nose and mouth and placed them palm down on his knees.

Whatever exists, he said. Whatever in creation exists without my knowledge exists without my consent.

He looked about at the dark forest in which they were bivouacked. He nodded toward the specimens he'd collected. These anonymous creatures, he said, may seem little or nothing in the world. Yet the smallest crumb can devour us. Any smallest thing beneath yon rock out of men's knowing. Only nature can enslave man and only when the existence of each last entity is routed out and made to stand naked before him will he be properly suzerain of the earth.

What's a suzerain?

A keeper. A keeper or overlord.

Why not say keeper then?

Because he is a special kind of keeper. A suzerain rules even where there are other rulers. His authority countermands local judgements.

Toadvine spat.

The judge placed his hands on the ground. He looked at his inquisitor. This is my claim, he said. And yet everywhere upon it are pockets of autonomous life. Autonomous. In order for it to be mine nothing must be permitted to occur upon it save by my dispensation.

Toadvine sat with his boots crossed before the fire. No man can acquaint himself with everthing on this earth, he said.

The judge tilted his great head. The man who believes that the secrets of the world are forever hidden lives in mystery and fear. Superstition will drag him down. The rain will erode the deeds of his life. But that man who sets himself the task of singling out the thread of order from the tapestry will by the decision alone have taken charge of the world and it is only by such taking charge that he will effect a way to dictate the terms of his own fate.

I dont see what that has to do with catchin birds.

The freedom of birds is an insult to me. I'd have them all in zoos.

That would be a hell of a zoo.

The judge smiled. Yes, he said. Even so.

In the night a caravan passed, the heads of the horses and mules muffled in serapes, led along silently in the dark, the riders cautioning one to the other with their fingers to their lips. The judge atop a great boulder overlooking the trail watched them go.

In the morning they rode on. They forded the muddy Yaqui River and they rode through stands of sunflowers tall as a man on horseback, the dead faces dished toward the west. The country began to open up and they began to come upon plantings of corn on the hillsides and a few clearings in the wilderness where there were grass huts and orange and tamarind trees. Of humans they saw none. On the second of December of eighteen forty-nine they rode into the town of Ures, capital of the state of Sonora.

They'd not trotted half the length of the town before they had drawn about them a following of rabble unmatched for variety and sordidness by any they had yet encountered, beggars and proctors of beggars and whores and pimps and vendors and filthy children and whole deputations of the blind and the maimed and the importunate all crying out por dios and some who rode astride the backs of porters and hied them after and great numbers of folk of every age and condition who were merely curious. Females of domestic reputation lounged upon the balconies they passed with faces gotten up in indigo and almagre gaudy as the rumps of apes and they peered from behind their fans with a kind of lurid coyness like transvestites in a madhouse. The judge and Glanton rode at the head of the little column and conferred between themselves. The horses cantered nervously and if the riders roweled an occasional hand clutching at the trappings of their mounts those hands withdrew in silence.

They put up that night at a hostel at the edge of the town run by a German who turned over the premises to them entirely and was seen no more for either service or payment. Glanton wandered through the tall and dusty rooms with their withy ceilings and at length he found an old criada cowering in what must have passed for a kitchen although it contained nothing culinary save a brazier and a few clay pots. He set her to work heating water for baths and pressed a handful of silver coins on her and charged her with setting them some kind of board. She stared at the coins without moving until he shooed her away and she went off down the hallway holding the coins cupped in her hands like a bird. She disappeared up the stairwell calling out and soon there were a number of women busy about the place.

When Glanton turned to go back down the hall there were four or five horses standing in it. He slapped them away with his hat and went to the door and looked out at the silent mob of spectators.

Mozos de cuadra, he called. Venga. Pronto.

Two boys pushed through and approached the door and a number of others followed. Glanton motioned the tallest of them forward and placed one hand on top of his head and turned him around and looked at the others.

Este hombre es el jefe, he said. The jefe stood solemnly, his eyes cutting about. Glanton turned his head around and looked at him.

Te encargo todo, entiendes? Caballos, sillas, todo.

Sí. Entiendo.

Bueno. Andale. Hay caballos en la casa.

The jefe turned and shouted out the names of his friends and half a dozen came forward and they entered the house.

When Glanton went down the hall they were leading those animals—known mankillers some—toward the door, scolding them, the least of the boys hardly taller than the legs of the animal he'd taken in charge. Glanton went out to the back of the building and looked about for the expriest whom it pleased him to send for whores and drink but he could not be found. In trying to arrive at a detail which might reasonably be expected to return at all he settled on Doc Irving and Shelby and gave them a fistful of coins and returned to the kitchen again.

By dark there were a half dozen young goats roasting on spits in the yard behind the hostel, their blackened figures shining in the smoky light. The judge strolled the grounds in his linen suit and directed the chefs with a wave of his cigar and he in turn was followed by a string band of six musicians, all of them old, all serious, who stayed with him at every turn some three paces to the rear and playing the while. A skin of pulque hung from a tripod in the center of the yard and Irving had returned with between twenty and thirty whores of every age and size and there were deployed before the door of the building whole trains of wagons and carts overseen by impromptu sutlers crying out each his bill of particulars and surrounded by a shifting gallery of townspeople and dozens of halfbroken horses for trade that reared and whinnied and desolatelooking cattle and sheep and pigs together with their owners until the town that Glanton and the judge had hoped to lay clear of was almost entirely at their door in a carnival underwritten with that mood of festivity and growing ugliness common to gatherings in that quarter of the world. The bonfire in the courtyard had been stoked to such heights that from the street the entire rear of the premises appeared to be in flames and new merchants with their goods and new spectators were arriving regularly together with sullen groups of Yaqui indians in loincloths who would be hired for their labor.

By midnight there were fires in the street and dancing and drunkenness and the house rang with the shrill cries of the

whores and rival packs of dogs had infiltrated the now partly
darkened and smoking yard in the back where a vicious dogfight
broke out over the charred racks of goatbones and where the
first gunfire of the night erupted and wounded dogs howled and
dragged themselves about until Glanton himself went out and
killed them with his knife, a lurid scene in the flickering light,
the wounded dogs silent save for the pop of their teeth, dragging
themselves across the lot like seals or other things and crouching
under the walls while Glanton walked them down and clove
their skulls with the huge copperbacked beltknife. He was no
more than back inside the house before new dogs were muttering at the spits.

By the small hours of the morning most of the lamps within
the hostel had smoked out and the rooms were filled with
drunken snoring. The sutlers and their carts were gone and
the blackened rings of the burnedout fires lay in the road like
bomb-craters, the smoldering billets dragged forth to sustain the
one last fire about which sat old men and boys smoking and
exchanging tales. As the mountains to the east began to shape
themselves out of the dawn these figures too drifted away.
In the yard at the rear of the premises the surviving dogs had
dragged the bones about everywhere and the dead dogs lay in
dark shingles of their own blood dried in the dust and cocks
had begun to crow. When the judge and Glanton appeared at
the front door in their suits, the judge in white and Glanton in
black, the only person about was one of the small hostlers asleep
on the steps.

Joven, said the judge.

The boy leaped up.

Eres mozo del caballado?

Sí señor. A su servicio.

Nuestros caballos, he said. He would describe the animals
but the boy was already on the run.

It was cold and a wind was blowing. The sun not up. The
judge stood at the steps and Glanton walked up and down

213

studying the ground. In ten minutes the boy and another appeared leading the two horses saddled and groomed at a nice trot up the street, the boys at a dead run, barefoot, the breath of the horses pluming and their heads turning smartly from side to side.

XV

ON THE FIFTH OF December they rode out north in the cold darkness before daybreak carrying with them a contract signed by the governor of the state of Sonora for the furnishing of Apache scalps. The streets were silent and empty. Carroll and Sanford had defected from the company and with them now rode a boy named Sloat who had been left sick to die in this place by one of the gold trains bound for the coast weeks earlier. When Glanton asked him if he were kin to the commodore of that name the boy spat quietly and said No, nor him to me. He rode near the head of the column and he must have counted himself well out of that place yet if he gave thanks to any god at all it was ill timed for the country was not done with him.

They rode north onto the broad Sonoran desert and in that

cauterized waste they wandered aimlessly for weeks pursuing rumor and shadow. A few small scattered bands of Chiricahua raiders supposedly seen by herdsmen on some squalid and desolate ranch. A few peons waylaid and slain. Two weeks out they massacred a pueblo on the Nacozari River and two days later as they rode toward Ures with the scalps they encountered a party of armed Sonoran cavalry on the plains west of Baviácora under General Elias. A running fight ensued in which three of Glanton's party were killed and another seven wounded, four of whom could not ride.

That night they could see the fires of the army less than ten miles to the south. They sat out the night in darkness and the wounded called for water and in the cold stillness before dawn the fires out there were still burning. At sunrise the Delawares rode into the camp and sat on the ground with Glanton and Brown and the judge. In the eastern light the fires on the plain faded like an evil dream and the country lay bare and sparkling in the pure air. Elias was moving upon them out there with over five hundred troops.

They rose and began to saddle the horses. Glanton fetched down a quiver made from ocelot skin and counted out the arrows in it so that there was one for each man and he tore a piece of red flannel into strips and tied these about the footings of four of the shafts and then replaced the counted arrows into the quiver.

He sat on the ground with the quiver upright between his knees while the company filed past. When the kid selected among the shafts to draw one he saw the judge watching him and he paused. He looked at Glanton. He let go the arrow he'd chosen and sorted out another and drew that one. It carried the red tassel. He looked at the judge again and the judge was not watching and he moved on and took his place with Tate and Webster. They were joined finally by a man named Harlan from Texas who had drawn the last arrow and the four of them stood together while the rest saddled their horses and led them out.

Of the wounded men two were Delawares and one a Mexican. The fourth was Dick Shelby and he alone sat watching the preparations for departure. The Delawares remaining in the company conferred among themselves and one of them approached the four Americans and studied them each in turn. He walked past them and turned and came back and took the arrow from Webster. Webster looked at Glanton where he stood with his horse. Then the Delaware took Harlan's arrow. Glanton turned and with his forehead against the ribs of his horse he tightened the girthstraps and then mounted up. He adjusted his hat. No one spoke. Harlan and Webster went to get their animals. Glanton sat his horse while the company filed past and then he turned and followed them out onto the plain.

The Delaware had gone for his horse and he brought it up still hobbled through the wallowed places in the sand where the men had slept. Of the wounded indians one was silent, breathing heavily with his eyes closed. The other was chanting rhythmically. The Delaware let drop the reins and took down his warclub from his bag and stepped astraddle of the man and swung the club and crushed his skull with a single blow. The man humped up in a little shuddering spasm and then lay still. The other was dispatched in the same way and then the Delaware raised the horse's leg and undid the hobble and slid it clear and rose and put the hobble and the club in the bag and mounted up and turned the horse. He looked at the two men standing there. His face and chest were freckled with blood. He touched up the horse with his heels and rode out.

Tate squatted in the sand, his hands dangling in front of him. He turned and looked at the kid.

Who gets the Mexican? he said.

The kid didnt answer. They looked at Shelby. He was watching them.

Tate had a clutch of small pebbles in his hand and he let them drop one by one into the sand. He looked at the kid.

Go on if you want to, the kid said.

He looked at the Delawares dead in their blankets. You might not do it, he said.

That aint your worry.

Glanton might come back.

He might.

Tate looked over to where the Mexican was lying and he looked at the kid again. I'm still held to it, he said.

The kid didnt answer.

You know what they'll do to them?

The kid spat. I can guess, he said.

No you caint.

I said you could go. You do what you want.

Tate rose and looked to the south but the desert there lay in all its clarity uninhabited by any approaching armies. He shrugged up his shoulders in the cold. Injins, he said. It dont mean nothin to them. He crossed the campground and brought his horse around and led it up and mounted it. He looked at the Mexican, wheezing softly, a pink froth on his lips. He looked at the kid and then he nudged the pony up through the scraggly acacia and was gone.

The kid sat in the sand and stared off to the south. The Mexican was shot through the lungs and would die anyway but Shelby had had his hip shattered by a ball and he was clear in his head. He lay watching the kid. He was from a prominent Kentucky family and had attended Transylvania College and like many another young man of his class he'd gone west because of a woman. He watched the kid and he watched the enormous sun where it sat boiling on the edge of the desert. Any roadagent or gambler would have known that the first to speak would lose but Shelby had already lost it all.

Why dont you just get on with it? he said.

The kid looked at him.

If I had a gun I'd shoot you, Shelby said.

The kid didnt answer.

You know that, dont you?

You aint got a gun, the kid said.

He looked to the south again. Something moving, perhaps the first lines of heat. No dust in the morning so early. When he looked at Shelby again Shelby was crying.

You wont thank me if I let you off, he said.

Do it then you son of a bitch.

The kid sat. A light wind was blowing out of the north and some doves had begun to call in the thicket of greasewood behind them.

If you want me just to leave you I will.

Shelby didnt answer.

He pushed a furrow in the sand with the heel of his boot. You'll have to say.

Will you leave me a gun?

You know I caint leave you no gun.

You're no better than him. Are you?

The kid didnt answer.

What if he comes back.

Glanton.

Yes.

What if he does.

He'll kill me.

You wont be out nothin.

You son of a bitch.

The kid rose.

Will you hide me?

Hide you?

Yes.

The kid spat. You caint hide. Where you goin to hide at?

Will he come back?

I dont know.

This is a terrible place to die in.

Where's a good one?

Shelby wiped his eyes with the back of his wrist. Can you see them? he said.

Not yet.

Will you pull me up under that bush?

The kid turned and looked at him. He looked off down-country again and then he crossed the basin and squatted behind Shelby and took him up under the arms and raised him. Shelby's head rolled back and he looked up and then he snatched at the butt of the pistol stuck in the kid's belt. The kid seized his arm. He let him down and stepped away and turned him loose. When he returned through the basin leading the horse the man was crying again. He took the pistol from his belt and jammed it among his belongings lashed to the cantle and took his canteen down and went to him.

He had his face turned away. The kid filled his flask from his own and reseated the stopper where it hung by its thong and drove it home with the heel of his hand. Then he rose and looked off to the south.

Yonder they come, he said.

Shelby raised up on one elbow.

The kid looked at him and he looked at the faint and formless articulation along the horizon to the south. Shelby lay back. He was staring up at the sky. A dark overcast was moving down from the north and the wind was up. A clutch of leaves scuttled out of the willow bracken at the edge of the sand and then scuttled back again. The kid crossed to where the horse stood waiting and took the pistol and stuck it in his belt and hung the canteen over the saddlehorn and mounted up and looked back at the wounded man. Then he rode out.

HE WAS TROTTING north on the plain when he saw another horseman on the grounds before him perhaps a mile distant. He could not make him out and he rode more slowly. After a while he saw that the rider was leading the horse and after a while he could see that the horse was not walking right.

It was Tate. He sat by the wayside watching the kid as he

rode up. The horse stood on three legs. Tate said nothing. He took off his hat and looked inside it and put it on again. The kid was turned in the saddle and he was looking to the south. Then he looked at Tate.

Can he walk?

Not much.

He got down and drew up the horse's leg. The frog of the hoof was split and bloody and the animal's shoulder quivered. He let the hoof down. The sun was about two hours high and now there was dust on the horizon. He looked at Tate.

What do you want to do?

I dont know. Lead him awhile. See how he does.

He aint goin to do.

I know it.

We could ride and tie.

You might just keep ridin.

I might anyway.

Tate looked at him. Go on if you want, he said.

The kid spat. Come on, he said.

I hate to leave the saddle. Hate to leave the horse far as that goes.

The kid picked up the trailing reins of his own animal. You might change your mind about what you hate to leave, he said.

They set out leading both horses. The damaged animal kept wanting to stop. Tate coaxed it along. Come on fool, he said. You aint goin to like them niggers a bit more than me.

By noon the sun was a pale blur overhead and a cold wind was blowing out of the north. They leaned into it man and animal. The wind bore stinging bits of grit and they set their hats low over their faces and pushed on. Dried desert chaff passed along with the seething migrant sands. Another hour and there was no track visible from the main party of riders before them. The sky lay gray and of a piece in every direction as far as they could see and the wind did not abate. After a while it began to snow.

The kid had taken down his blanket and wrapped himself in it. He turned and stood with his back to the wind and the horse leaned and laid its cheek against his. Its eyelashes were thatched with snow. When Tate came up he stopped and they stood looking out downwind where the snow was blowing. They could see no more than a few feet.

Aint this hell, he said.

Will your horse lead?

Hell no. I caint hardly make him foller.

We get turned around we might just run plumb into the Spaniards.

I never saw it turn so cold so quick.

What do you want to do.

We better go on.

We could pull for the high country. As long as we keep goin uphill we'll know we aint got in a circle.

We'll get cut off. We never will find Glanton.

We're cut off now.

Tate turned and stared bleakly to where the whirling flakes blew down from the north. Let's go, he said. We caint stand here.

They led the horses on. Already the ground was white. They took turns riding the good horse and leading the lame. They climbed for hours up a long rocky wash and the snow did not diminish. They began to come upon piñon and dwarf oak and open parkland and the snow on those high meadows was soon a foot deep and the horses were blowing and smoking like steamengines and it was colder and growing dark.

They were rolled in their blankets asleep in the snow when the scouts from Elias's forward company came upon them. They'd ridden all night the only track there was, pushing on not to lose the march of those shallow pans as they filled with snow. They were five men and they came up through the evergreens in the dark and all but stumbled upon the sleepers, two mounds in the snow one of which broke open and up out of which a figure sat suddenly like some terrible hatching.

The snow had stopped falling. The kid could see them and their animals clearly on that pale ground, the men in midstride and the horses blowing cold. He had his boots in one hand and his pistol in the other and he came up out of the blanket and leveled the pistol and discharged it into the chest of the man nearest him and turned to run. His feet slid and he went to one knee. A musket fired behind him. He rose again, running down a darkened slash of piñon and turning out along the face of the slope. There were other shots behind him and when he turned he could see a man coming down through the trees. The man stopped and raised his elbows and the kid dove headlong. The musketball went racketing off among the branches. He rolled over and cocked the pistol. The barrel must have been full of snow because when he fired a hoop of orange light sprang out about it and the shot made a strange sound. He felt to see if the gun had burst but it had not. He could not see the man any more and he picked himself up and ran on. At the foot of the slope he sat gasping in the cold air and pulled on the boots and watched back among the trees. Nothing moved. He rose and stuck the pistol in his belt and went on.

THE RISING SUN found him crouched under a rocky promontory watching the country to the south. He sat so for an hour or more. A group of deer moved up the far side of the arroyo feeding and feeding moved on. After a while he rose and went on along the ridge.

He walked all day through those wild uplands, eating handfuls of snow from the evergreen boughs as he went. He followed gametrails through the firs and in the evening he hiked along the rimrock where he could see the tilted desert to the southwest patched with shapes of snow that roughly reproduced the patterns of cloud cover already moved on to the south. Ice had frozen on the rock and the myriad icicles among the conifers glistened blood red in the reflected light of the sunset spread across the prairie to the west. He sat with his back to a rock and felt the warmth of the sun on his face and watched it pool and flare and drain away dragging with it all that pink and rose and crimson sky. An icy wind sprang up and the junipers darkened suddenly against the snow and then there was just stillness and cold.

He rose and moved on, hurrying along the shaly rocks. He walked all night. The stars swung counterclockwise in their course and the Great Bear turned and the Pleiades winked in the very roof of the vault. He walked until his toes grew numb and fairly rattled in his boots. His path upon the rimrock was leading him deeper into the mountains along the edge of a great gorge and he could see no place to descend out of that country. He sat and wrestled off the boots and held his frozen feet each by turn in his arms. They did not warm and his jaw was in a seizure of cold and when he went to put the boots back on again his feet were like clubs to poke into them. When he got them on and stood up and stamped numbly he knew that he could not stop again until the sun rose.

It grew colder and the night lay long before him. He kept moving, following in the darkness the naked chines of rock blown bare of snow. The stars burned with a lidless fixity and they drew nearer in the night until toward dawn he was stumbling among the whinstones of the uttermost ridge to heaven, a barren range of rock so enfolded in that gaudy house that stars lay awash at his feet and migratory spalls of burning matter crossed constantly about him on their chartless reckonings. In the predawn light he made his way out upon a promontory and there received first of any creature in that country the warmth of the sun's ascending.

He slept curled among the stones, the pistol clutched to his chest. His feet thawed and burned and he woke and lay staring up at a sky of china blue where very high there circled two black hawks about the sun slowly and perfectly opposed like paper birds upon a pole.

He moved north all day and in the long light of the evening he saw from that high rimland the collision of armies remote and silent upon the plain below. The dark little horses circled and the landscape shifted in the paling light and the mountains beyond brooded in darkening silhouette. The distant horsemen rode and parried and a faint drift of smoke passed over them and they moved on up the deepening shade of the valley floor leaving behind them the shapes of mortal men who had lost their lives in that place. He watched all this pass below him mute and ordered and senseless until the warring horsemen were gone in the sudden rush of dark that fell over the desert. All that land lay cold and blue and without definition and the sun shone solely on the high rocks where he stood. He moved on and soon he was in darkness himself and the wind came up off the desert and frayed wires of lightning stood again and again along the western terminals of the world. He made his way along the escarpment until he came to a break in the wall cut through by a canyon running back into the mountains. He stood looking down into this gulf where the tops of the twisted evergreens hissed in the wind and then he started down.

The snow lay in deep pockets on the slope and he floundered down through them, steadying himself along the naked rocks until his hands were numb with cold. He crossed with care a gravel slide and made his way down the far side among the rubble stone and small gnarled trees. He fell and fell again, scrabbling for a handpurchase in the dark, rising and feeling in his belt for the pistol. He was at this work the night long. When he reached the benchland above the canyon floor he could hear a stream running in the gorge below him and he went stumbling along with his hands in his armpits like a fugitive in a madman's waistcoat. He reached a sandy wash and followed it down and it took him at last out upon the desert again where he stood tottering in the cold and casting about dumbly for some star in the overcast.

Most of the snow had blown or melted from off the plain on which he found himself. Tandem storms were blowing down-country from the north and the thunder trundled away in the distance and the air was cold and smelled of wet stone. He struck out across the barren pan, nothing but sparse tufts of grass and the widely scattered palmilla standing solitary and silent against the lowering sky like other beings posted there. To the east the mountains stood footed blackly into the desert and before him were bluffs or promontories that ran out like headlands massive and sombre upon the desert floor. He clopped on woodenly, half frozen, his feet senseless. He'd been without food for almost two days and he'd had little rest. He cited the terrain before him in the periodic flare of the lightning and trudged on and in this manner he rounded a dark cape of rock off to his right and came to a halt, shivering and blowing into his clawed and palsied hands. In the distance before him a fire burned on the prairie, a solitary flame frayed by the wind that freshened and faded and shed scattered sparks down the storm like hot scurf blown from some unreckonable forge howling in the waste. He sat and watched it. He could not judge how far it was. He lay on his stomach to skylight the terrain to see what men were there but there was no sky and no light. He lay for a long time watching but he saw nothing move.

When he went on again the fire seemed to recede before him. A troop of figures passed between him and the light. Then again. Wolves perhaps. He went on.

It was a lone tree burning on the desert. A heraldic tree that the passing storm had left afire. The solitary pilgrim drawn up before it had traveled far to be here and he knelt in the hot sand and held his numbed hands out while all about in that circle attended companies of lesser auxiliaries routed forth into the inordinate day, small owls that crouched silently and stood from foot to foot and tarantulas and solpugas and vinegarroons and the vicious mygale spiders and beaded lizards with mouths black as a chowdog's, deadly to man, and the little desert basilisks that jet blood from their eyes and the small sandvipers like seemly gods, silent and the same, in Jeda, in Babylon. A constellation of ignited eyes that edged the ring of light all bound in a precarious truce before this torch whose brightness had set back the stars in their sockets.

When the sun rose he was asleep under the smoldering skeleton of a blackened scrog. The storm had long passed off to the south and the new sky was raw and blue and the spire of smoke from the burnt tree stood vertically in the still dawn like a slender stylus marking the hour with its particular and faintly breathing shadow upon the face of a terrain that was without other designation. All the creatures that had been at vigil with him in the night were gone and about him lay only the strange coral shapes of fulgurite in their scorched furrows fused out of the sand where ball lightning had run upon the ground in the night hissing and stinking of sulphur.

Seated tailorwise in the eye of that cratered waste he watched the world tend away at the edges to a shimmering surmise that ringed the desert round. After a while he rose and made his way to the edge of the pan and up the dry course of an arroyo, following the small demonic tracks of javelinas until he came upon them drinking at a standing pool of water. They flushed snorting into the chaparral and he lay in the wet trampled sand and drank and rested and drank again.

In the afternoon he started across the valley floor with the weight of the water swinging in his gut. Three hours later he stood in the long arc of horsetracks coming up from the south where the party had passed. He followed the edge of the tracks and sorted out single riders and he reckoned their number and he reckoned them to be riding at a canter. He followed the trace for several miles and he could tell by the alternation of tracks ridden over that all these riders had passed together and he could tell by the small rocks overturned and holes stepped into that they had passed in the night. He stood looking out from under his hand long downcountry for any dust or rumor of Elias. There was nothing. He went on. A mile further and he came upon a strange blackened mass in the trail like a burnt carcass of some ungodly beast. He circled it. The tracks of wolves and coyotes had walked through the horse and boot prints, little sallies and sorties that fetched up to the edge of that incinerated shape and flared away again.

It was the remains of the scalps taken on the Nacozari and they had been burned unredeemed in a green and stinking bonfire so that nothing remained of the poblanos save this charred coagulate of their preterite lives. The cremation had been sited upon a rise of ground and he studied every quarter of the terrain about but there was nothing to be seen. He went on, following the tracks with their suggestion of pursuit and darkness, trailing them through the deepening twilight. With sunset it grew cold, yet nothing like so cold as in the mountains. His fast had weakened him and he sat in the sand to rest and woke sprawled and twisted on the ground. The moon was up, a half moon that sat like a child's boat in the gap of the black paper mountains to the east. He rose and went on. Coyotes were yapping out there and his feet reeled beneath him. An hour more of such progress and he came upon a horse.

It had been standing in the trace and it moved off in the dark and stood again. He halted with his pistol drawn. The horse went past, a dark shape, rider or none he could not tell. It circled and came back.

He spoke to it. He could hear its deep pulmonary breathing out there and he could hear it move and when it came back he could smell it. He followed it about for the better part of an hour, talking to it, whistling, holding out his hands. When he got near enough to touch it at last he took hold of it by the mane and it went trotting as before and he ran alongside and clung to it and finally wrapped his legs about one foreleg and brought it to the ground in a heap.

He was the first up. The animal was struggling to rise and he thought it was injured in the fall but it was not. He cinched his belt about its muzzle and mounted it and it rose and stood trembling under him with its legs spread. He patted it along the withers and spoke to it and it moved forward uncertainly.

He reckoned it one of the packhorses purchased in Ures. It stopped and he urged it forward but it did not go. He brought his bootheels sharply up under its ribs and it squatted on its hindquarters and went crabbing sideways. He reached and undid the belt from its muzzle and kicked it forward and gave it a whack with the belt and it stepped out right smartly. He twisted a good handful of the mane in his fist and jammed the pistol securely in his waist and rode on, perched upon the raw spine of the animal with the vertebra articulating palpable and discrete under the hide.

In their riding they were joined by another horse that came off the desert and walked alongside them and it was still there when dawn broke. In the night too the tracks of the riders had been joined by a larger party and it was a broad and trampled causeway that now led up the valley floor to the north. With daylight he leaned down with his face against the horse's shoulder and studied the tracks. They were unshod indian ponies and there were perhaps a hundred of them. Nor had they joined the riders but rather been joined by them. He pushed on. The little horse that had come to them in the night had moved off some leagues and now paced them with a watchful eye and the horse he rode was nervous and ill for want of water.

By noon the animal was failing. He tried to coax it out of the track to catch the other horse but it would not quit the course it was set upon. He sucked on a pebble and surveyed the countryside. Then he saw riders ahead of him. They'd not been there, then they were there. He realized it was their vicinity that was the source of the unrest in the two horses and he rode on watching now the animals and now the skyline to the north. The hack that he straddled trembled and pushed ahead and after a while he could see that the riders wore hats. He urged the horse on and when he rode up the party were halted and seated on the ground all watching his approach.

They looked bad. They were used up and bloody, and black about the eyes and they had bound up their wounds with linens that were filthy and bloodstained and their clothes were crusted with dried blood and powderblack. Glanton's eyes in their dark sockets were burning centroids of murder and he and his haggard riders stared balefully at the kid as if he were no part of them for all they were so like in wretchedness of circumstance. The kid slid down from the horse and stood among them gaunt and parched and crazedlooking. Someone threw him a canteen.

They had lost four men. The others were ahead on scout. Elias had forced on through the mountains all night and all the day following and had ridden upon them through the snow in the dark on the plain forty miles to the south. They'd been harried north over the desert like cattle and had deliberately taken the track of the warparty in order to lose their pursuers. They did not know how far the Mexicans were behind them and they did not know how far the Apaches were ahead.

He drank from the canteen and looked them over. Of the missing he'd no way of knowing which were ahead with the scouts and which were dead in the desert. The horse that Toadvine brought him was the one the recruit Sloat had ridden out of Ures. When they moved out a half hour later two of the horses would not rise and were left behind. He sat a hideless and rickety saddle astride the dead man's horse and he rode slumped and tottering and soon his legs and arms were dangling and he jostled along in his sleep like a mounted marionette. He woke to find the expriest alongside him. He slept again. When he woke next it was the judge was there. He too had lost his hat and he rode with a woven wreath of desert scrub about his head like some egregious saltland bard and he looked down upon the refugee with the same smile, as if the world were pleasing even to him alone.

They rode all the rest of that day, up through low rolling hills covered with cholla and whitethorn. From time to time one of the spare horses would stop and stand swaying in the track and grow small behind them. They rode down a long north slope in the cold blue evening and through a barren bajada grown only with sporadic ocotillo and stands of grama and they made camp in the flat and all night the wind blew and they could see other fires burning on the desert to the north. The judge walked out and looked over the horses and selected from that sorry remuda the animal least likely in appearance and caught it up. He led it past the fire and called for someone to come hold it. No one rose. The expriest leaned to the kid.

Pay him no mind lad.

The judge called again from the dark beyond the fire and the expriest placed a cautionary hand upon the kid's arm. But the kid rose and spat into the fire. He turned and eyed the expriest.

You think I'm afraid of him?

The expriest didnt answer and the kid turned and went out into the darkness where the judge waited.

He stood holding the horse. Just his teeth glistened in the firelight. Together they led the animal off a little ways and the kid held the woven reata while the judge took up a round rock weighing perhaps a hundred pounds and crushed the horse's skull with a single blow. Blood shot out of its ears and it slammed to the ground so hard that one of its forelegs broke under it with a dull snap.

They skinned out the hindquarters without gutting the animal and the men cut steaks from it and roasted them over the fire and cut the rest of the meat in strips and hung it to smoke. The scouts did not come in and they posted videttes and turned in to sleep each man with his weapons at his breast.

Midmorning of the day following they crossed an alkali pan whereon were convoked an assembly of men's heads. The company halted and Glanton and the judge rode forward. The heads were eight in number and each wore a hat and they formed a ring all facing outward. Glanton and the judge circled them and the judge halted and stepped down and pushed over one of the heads with his boot. As if to satisfy himself that no man stood buried in the sand beneath it. The other heads glared blindly out of their wrinkled eyes like fellows of some righteous initiate given up to vows of silence and of death.

The riders looked off to the north. They rode on. Beyond a shallow rise in cold ash lay the blackened wreckage of a pair of wagons and the nude torsos of the party. The wind had shifted the ashes and the iron axletrees marked the shapes of the wagons as keelsons do the bones of ships on the sea's floors. The bodies had been partly eaten and rooks flew up as the riders approached and a pair of buzzards began to trot off across the sand with their wings outheld like soiled chorines, their boiled-looking heads jerking obscenely.

They went on. They crossed a dry estuary of the desert flat and in the afternoon they rode up through a series of narrow defiles into a rolling hill country. They could smell the smoke of piñonwood fires and before dark they rode into the town of Santa Cruz.

This town like all the presidios along the border was much reduced from its former estate and many of the buildings were uninhabited and ruinous. The coming of the riders had been cried before them and the way stood lined with inhabitants watching dumbly as they passed, the old women in black rebozos and the men armed with old muskets and miquelets or guns fabricated out of parts rudely let into stocks of Cottonwood that had been shaped with axes like clubhouse guns for boys. There were even guns among them with no locks at all that were fired by jamming a cigarillo against the vent in the barrel, sending the gunstones from the riverbed with which they were loaded whissing through the air on flights of their own eccentric selection like the paths of meteorites. The Americans pushed their horses forward. It had begun to snow again and a cold wind blew down the narrow street before them. Even in their wretched state they glared from their saddles at this falstaffian militia with undisguised contempt.

They stood among their horses in the squalid little alameda while the wind ransacked the trees and the birds nesting in the gray twilight cried out and clutched the limbs and the snow swirled and blew across the little square and shrouded the shapes of the mud buildings beyond and made mute the cries of the vendors who'd followed them. Glanton and the Mexican he'd set out with returned and the company mounted up and filed out down the street until they came to an old wooden gate that led into a courtyard. The courtyard was dusted with snow and within were contained barnyard fowl and animals—goats, a burro—that clawed and scrabbled blindly at the walls as the riders entered. In one corner stood a tripod of blackened sticks and there was a large bloodstain that had been partly snowed over and showed a faint pale rose in the last light. A man came out of the house and he and Glanton spoke and the man talked with the Mexican and then he motioned them in out of the weather.

They sat in the floor of a long room with a high ceiling and smokestained vigas while a woman and a girl brought bowls of guisado made from goat and a clay plate heaped with blue tortillas and they were served bowls of beans and of coffee and a cornmeal porridge in which sat little chunks of raw brown peloncillo sugar. Outside it was dark and the snow swirled down. There was no fire in the room and the food steamed ponderously. When they had eaten they sat smoking and the women gathered up the bowls and after a while a boy came with a lantern and led them out.

They crossed the yard among the snuffling horses and the boy opened a rough wooden door in an adobe shed and stood by holding the lamp aloft. They brought their saddles and their blankets. In the yard the horses stamped in the cold.

The shed held a mare with a suckling colt and the boy would have put her out but they called to him to leave her. They carried straw from a stall and pitched it down and he held the lamp for them while they spread their bedding. The barn smelled of clay and straw and manure and in the soiled yellow light of the lamp their breath rolled smoking through the cold. When they had arranged their blankets the boy lowered the lamp and stepped into the yard and pulled the door shut behind, leaving them in profound and absolute darkness.

No one moved. In that cold stable the shutting of the door may have evoked in some hearts other hostels and not of their choosing. The mare sniffed uneasily and the young colt stepped about. Then one by one they began to divest themselves of their outer clothes, the hide slickers and raw wool serapes and vests, and one by one they propagated about themselves a great crackling of sparks and each man was seen to wear a shroud of palest fire. Their arms aloft pulling at their clothes were luminous and each obscure soul was enveloped in audible shapes of light as if it had always been so. The mare at the far end of the stable snorted and shied at this luminosity in beings so endarkened and the little horse turned and hid his face in the web of his dam's flank.

XVI

IT WAS COLDER YET in the morning when they rode out. There was no one in the streets and there were no tracks in the new snow. At the edge of the town they saw where wolves had crossed the road.

They rode out by a small river, skim ice, a frozen marsh where ducks walked up and back muttering. That afternoon they traversed a lush valley where the dead winter grass reached to the horses' bellies. Empty fields where the crops had rotted and orchards of apple and quince and pomegranate where the fruit had dried and fallen to the ground. They found deer yarded up in the meadows and the tracks of cattle and that night as they sat about their fire roasting the ribs and haunches of a young doe they could hear the lowing of bulls in the dark.

The following day they rode past the ruins of the old hacienda at San Bernardino. On that range they saw wild bulls so old that they bore Spanish brands on their hips and several of these animals charged the little company and were shot down and left on the ground until one came out of a stand of acacia in a wash and buried its horns to the boss in the ribs of a horse ridden by James Miller. He'd lifted his foot out of the near stirrup when he saw it coming and the impact all but jarred him from the saddle. The horse screamed and kicked but the bull had planted its feet and it lifted the animal rider and all clear of the ground before Miller could get his pistol free and when he put the muzzle to the bull's forehead and fired and the whole grotesque assembly collapsed he stepped clear of the wreckage and walked off in disgust with the smoking gun dangling in his hand. The horse was struggling to rise and he went back and shot it and put the gun in his belt and commenced to unbuckle the girthstraps. The horse was lying square atop the dead bull and it took him some tugging to get the saddle free. The other riders had stopped to watch and someone hazed forward the last spare horse out of the remuda but other than that they offered him no help.

They rode on, following the course of the Santa Cruz, up through stands of immense riverbottom cottonwoods. They did not cut the sign of the Apache again and they found no trace of the missing scouts. The following day they passed the old mission at San José de Tumacacori and the judge rode off to look at the church which stood about a mile off the track. He'd given a short disquisition on the history and architecture of the mission and those who heard it would not believe that he had never been there. Three of the party rode with him and Glanton watched them go with dark misgiving. He and the others rode on a short distance and then he halted and turned back.

The old church was in ruins and the door stood open to the high walled enclosure. When Glanton and his men rode through the crumbling portal four horses stood riderless in the empty compound among the dead fruit trees and grapevines. Glanton rode with his rifle upright before him, the buttplate on his thigh. His dog heeled to the horse and they approached cautiously the sagging walls of the church. They would have ridden their horses through the door but as they reached it there was a rifleshot from inside and pigeons flapped up and they slipped down from their mounts and crouched behind them with their rifles. Glanton looked back at the others and then walked his horse forward to where he could see into the interior. Part of the upper wall was fallen in and most of the roof and there was a man lying in the floor. Glanton led the horse into the sacristy and stood looking down with the others.

The man in the floor was dying and he was dressed altogether in homemade clothes of sheephide even to boots and a strange cap. They turned him over on the cracked clay tiles and his jaw moved and a bloody spittle formed along his lower lip. His eyes were dull and there was fear in them and there was something else. John Prewett stood the butt of his rifle in the floor and swung his horn about to recharge the piece. I seen anothern run, he said. They's two of em.

The man in the floor began to move. He had one arm lying in his groin and he moved it slightly and pointed. At them or at the height from which he had fallen or to his destination in eternity they did not know. Then he died.

Glanton looked about the ruins. Where did this son of a bitch come from? he said.

Prewett nodded toward the crumbling mud parapet. He was up yonder. I didnt know what he was. Still dont. I shot the son of a bitch out of there.

Glanton looked at the judge.

I think he was an imbecile, the judge said.

Glanton led his horse through the church and out by a small door in the nave into the yard. He was sitting there when they brought the other hermit out. Jackson prodded him forward with the barrel of his rifle, a small thin man, not young. The one they'd killed was his brother. They had jumped ship on the coast long ago and made their way to this place. He was terrified and he spoke no english and little Spanish. The judge spoke to him in german. They had been here for years. The brother had his wits stole in this place and the man now before them in his hides and his peculiar bootees was not altogether sane. They left him there. As they rode out he was trotting up and back in the yard calling out. He seemed not to be aware that his brother was dead in the church.

The judge caught Glanton up and they rode side by side out to the road.

Glanton spat. Ort to of shot that one too, he said.

The judge smiled.

I dont like to see white men that way, Glanton said. Dutch or whatever. I dont like to see it.

They rode north along the river trace. The woods were bare and the leaves on the ground clutched little scales of ice and the mottled and bony limbs of the cottonwoods were stark and heavy against the quilted desert sky. In the evening they passed through Tubac, abandoned, wheat dead in the winter fields and grass growing in the street. There was a blind man on a stoop watching the plaza and as they passed he raised his head to listen.

They rode out onto the desert to camp. There was no wind and the silence out there was greatly favored by every kind of fugitive as was the open country itself and no mountains close at hand for enemies to black themselves against. They were caught up and saddled in the morning before light, all riding together, their arms at the ready. Each man scanned the terrain and the movements of the least of creatures were logged into their collective cognizance until they were federated with invisible wires of vigilance and advanced upon that landscape with a single resonance. They passed abandoned haciendas and road-side graves and by midmorning they had picked up the track of the Apaches again coming in off the desert to the west and advancing before them through the loose sand of the river-bottom. The riders got down and pinched up samples of the forced sand at the rim of the tracks and tested it between their fingers and calibrated its moisture against the sun and let it fall and looked off up the river through the naked trees. They remounted and rode on.

They found the lost scouts hanging head downward from the limbs of a fireblacked paloverde tree. They were skewered through the cords of their heels with sharpened shuttles of green wood and they hung gray and naked above the dead ashes of the coals where they'd been roasted until their heads had charred and the brains bubbled in the skulls and steam sang from their noseholes. Their tongues were drawn out and held with sharpened sticks thrust through them and they had been docked of their ears and their torsos were sliced open with flints until the entrails hung down on their chests. Some of the men pushed forward with their knives and cut the bodies down and they left them there in the ashes. The two darker forms were the last of the Delawares and the other two were the Vandiemenlander and a man from the east named Gilchrist. Among their barbarous hosts they had met with neither favor nor discrimination but had suffered and died impartially.

They rode that night through the mission of San Xavier del Bac, the church solemn and stark in the starlight. Not a dog barked. The clusters of Papago huts seemed without tenant. The air was cold and clear and the country there and beyond lay in a darkness unclaimed by so much as an owl. A pale green meteor came up the valley floor behind them and passed overhead and vanished silently in the void.

At dawn on the outskirts of the presidio of Tucson they passed the ruins of several haciendas and they passed more roadside markers where people had been murdered. Out on the plain stood a small estancia where the buildings were still smoking and along the segments of a fence constructed from the bones of cactus sat vultures shoulder to shoulder facing east to the promised sun, lifting one foot and then the other and holding out their wings like cloaks. They saw the bones of pigs that had died in a claywalled lot and they saw a wolf in a melonpatch that crouched between its thin elbows and watched them as they passed. The town lay on the plain to the north in a thin line of pale walls and they grouped their horses along a low esker of gravel and surveyed it and the country and the naked ranges of mountains beyond. The stones of the desert lay in dark tethers of shadow and a wind was blowing out of the sun where it sat squat and pulsing at the eastern reaches of the earth. They chucked up their horses and sallied out onto the flat as did the Apache track before them two days old and a hundred riders strong.

They rode with their rifles on their knees, fanned out, riding abreast. The desert sunrise flared over the ground before them and ringdoves rose out of the chaparral by ones and by pairs and whistled away with thin calls. A thousand yards out and they could see the Apaches camped along the south wall. Their animals were grazing among the willows in the periodic river basin to the west of the town and what seemed to be rocks or debris under the wall was the sordid collection of leantos and wickiups thrown up with poles and hides and wagonsheets.

They rode on. A few dogs had begun to bark. Glanton's dog was quartering back and forth nervously and a deputation of riders had set out from the camp.

They were Chiricahuas, twenty, twenty-five of them. Even with the sun up it was not above freezing and yet they sat their horses half naked, naught but boots and breechclouts and the plumed hide helmets they wore, stoneage savages daubed with clay paints in obscure charges, greasy, stinking, the paint on the horses pale under the dust and the horses prancing and blowing cold. They carried lances and bows and a few had muskets and they had long black hair and dead black eyes that cut among the riders studying their arms, the sclera bloodshot and opaque.

None spoke even to another and they shouldered their horses through the party in a sort of ritual movement as if certain points of ground must be trod in a certain sequence as in a child's game yet with some terrible forfeit at hand.

The leader of these jackal warriors was a small dark man in cast-off Mexican military attire and he carried a sword and he carried in a torn and gaudy baldric one of the Whitneyville Colts that had belonged to the scouts. He sat his horse before Glanton and assessed the position of the other riders and then asked in good Spanish where were they bound. He'd no sooner spoken than Glanton's horse leaned its jaw forward and seized the man's horse by the ear. Blood flew. The horse screamed and reared and the Apache struggled to keep his seat and drew his sword and found himself staring into the black lemniscate that was the paired bores of Glanton's doublerifle. Glanton slapped the muzzle of his horse twice hard and it tossed its head with one eye blinking and blood dripping from its mouth. The Apache wrenched his pony's head around and when Glanton spun to look at his men he found them frozen in deadlock with the savages, they and their arms wired into a construction taut and fragile as those puzzles wherein the placement of each piece is predicated upon every other and they in turn so that none can move for bringing down the structure entire.

The leader was the first to speak. He gestured at the bloodied ear of his mount and spoke angrily in apache, his dark eyes avoiding Glanton. The judge pushed his horse forward.

Vaya tranquilo, he said. Un accidente, nada más.

Mire, said the Apache. Mire la oreja de mi caballo.

He steadied the animal's head to show it but it jerked loose and slung the broken ear about so that blood sprayed the riders. Horseblood or any blood a tremor ran that perilous architecture and the ponies stood rigid and quivering in the reddened sunrise and the desert under them hummed like a snaredrum. The tensile properties of this unratified truce were abused to the utmost of their enduring when the judge stood slightly in the saddle and raised his arm and spoke out a greeting beyond them.

Another eight or ten mounted warriors had ridden out from the wall. Their leader was a huge man with a huge head and he was dressed in overalls cut off at the knees to accommodate the leggingtops of his moccasins and he wore a checked shirt and a red scarf. He carried no arms but the men at either side of him were armed with shortbarreled rifles and they also carried the saddle pistols and other accoutrements of the murdered scouts. As they approached the other savages deferred and gave way before them. The indian whose horse had been bitten pointed out this injury to them but the leader only nodded affably. He turned his mount quarterwise to the judge and it arched its neck and he sat it well. Buenos días, he said. De dónde viene?

The judge smiled and touched the withered garland at his brow, forgetting possibly that he had no hat. He presented his chief Glanton very formally. Introductions were exchanged. The man's name was Mangas and he was cordial and spoke Spanish well. When the rider of the injured horse again put forth his claim for consideration this man dismounted and took hold of the animal's head and examined it. He was bandylegged for all his height and he was strangely proportioned. He looked up at the Americans and he looked at the other riders and waved his hand at them.

Andale, he said. He turned to Glanton. Ellos son amigables. Un poco borracho, nada más.

The Apache riders had begun to extricate themselves from among the Americans like men backing out of a thornthicket. The Americans stood their rifles upright and Mangas led the injured horse forward and turned its head up, containing the animal solely with his hands and the white eye rolling crazily. After some discussion it became plain that whatever the assessment of damage levied there was no specie acceptable by way of payment other than whiskey.

Glanton spat and eyed the man. No hay whiskey, he said.

Silence fell. The Apaches looked from one to the other. They looked at the saddle wallets and canteens and gourds. Cómo? said Mangas.

No hay whiskey, said Glanton.

Mangas let go the rough hide headstall of the horse. His men watched him. He looked toward the walled town and he looked at the judge. No whiskey? he said.

No whiskey.

His among the clouded faces seemed unperturbed. He looked over the Americans, their gear. In truth they did not look like men who might have whiskey they hadnt drunk. The judge and Glanton sat their mounts and offered nothing further in the way of parley.

Hay whiskey en Tucson, said Mangas.

Sin duda, said the judge. Y soldados también. He put forward his horse, his rifle in one hand and the reins in the other. Glanton moved. The horse behind him shifted into motion. Then Glanton stopped.

Tiene oro? he said.

Sí.

Cuánto.

Bastante.

Glanton looked at the judge then at Mangas again. Bueno, he said. Tres días. Aquí. Un barril de whiskey.

Un barril?

Un barril. He nudged the pony and the Apaches gave way and Glanton and the judge and those who followed rode single-file toward the gates of the squalid mud town that sat burning in the winter sunrise on the plain.

THE LIEUTENANT in charge of the little garrison was named Couts. He had been to the coast with Major Graham's command and returned here four days ago to find the town under an informal investment by the Apaches. They were drunk on tiswin they'd brewed and there had been shooting in the night two nights running and an incessant clamor for whiskey. The garrison had a twelvepound demiculverin loaded with musketballs mounted on the revetment and Couts expected the savages would withdraw when they could get nothing more to drink. He was very formal and he addressed Glanton as Captain. None of the tattered partisans had even dismounted. They looked about at the bleak and ruinous town. A blindfolded burro tethered to a pole was turning a pugmill, circling endlessly, the wooden millshaft creaking in its blocks. Chickens and smaller birds were scratching at the base of the mill. The pole was a good four feet off the ground yet the birds ducked or squatted each time it passed overhead. In the dust of the plaza lay a number of men apparently asleep. White, indian, Mexican. Some covered with blankets and some not. At the far end of the square there was a public whippingpost that was dark about its base where dogs had pissed on it. The lieutenant followed their gaze. Glanton pushed back his hat and looked down from his horse.

Where in this pukehole can a man get a drink? he said.

It was the first word any of them had spoken. Couts looked them over. Haggard and haunted and blacked by the sun. The lines and pores of their skin deeply grimed with gunblack where they'd washed the bores of their weapons. Even the horses looked alien to any he'd ever seen, decked as they were in human hair and teeth and skin. Save for their guns and buckles and a few pieces of metal in the harness of the animals there was nothing about these arrivals to suggest even the discovery of the wheel.

There are several places, said the lieutenant. None open yet though, I'm afraid.

They're fixin to get that way, said Glanton. He nudged the horse forward. He did not speak again and none of the others

244

had spoken at all. As they crossed the plaza a few vagrants raised their heads up out of their blankets and looked after them.

The bar they entered was a square mud room and the proprietor set about serving them in his underwear. They sat on a bench at a wooden table in the gloom drinking sullenly.

Where you all from? said the proprietor.

Glanton and the judge went out to see if they could recruit any men from the rabble reposing in the dust of the square. Some of them were sitting, squinting in the sun. A man with a bowieknife was offering to cut blades with anyone at a wager to see who had the better steel. The judge went among them with his smile.

Captain what all you got in them saddlegrips?

Glanton turned. He and the judge carried their valises across their shoulders. The man who'd spoken was propped against a post with one knee drawn up to support his elbow.

These bags? said Glanton.

Them bags.

These here bags are full of gold and silver, said Glanton, for they were.

The idler grinned and spat.

That's why he's a wantin to go to Californy, said another. Account of he's done got a satchel full of gold now.

The judge smiled benignly at the wastrels. You're liable to take a chill out here, he said. Who's for the gold fields now.

One man rose and took a few steps away and began to piss in the street.

Maybe the wild man'll go with ye, called another. Him and Cloyce'll make ye good hands.

They been tryin to go for long enough.

Glanton and the judge sought them out. A rude tent thrown up out of an old tarp. A sign that said: See The Wild Man Two Bits. They passed behind a wagonsheet where within a crude cage of paloverde poles crouched a naked imbecile. The floor of the cage was littered with filth and trodden food and flies clambered about everywhere. The idiot was small and misshapen and his face was smeared with feces and he sat peering at them with dull hostility silently chewing a turd.

The owner came from the rear shaking his head at them. Aint nobody allowed in here. We aint open.

Glanton looked about the wretched enclosure. The tent smelled of oil and smoke and excrement. The judge squatted to study the imbecile.

Is that thing yours? Glanton said.

Yes. Yes he is.

Glanton spat. Man told us you was wantin to go to Californy.

Well, said the owner. Yes, that's right. That is right.

What do you figure to do with that thing?

Take him with me.

How you aim to haul him?

Got a pony and cart. To haul him in.

You got any money?

The judge raised up. This is Captain Glanton, he said. He's leading an expedition to California. He's willing to take a few passengers under the protection of his company provided they can find themselves adequately.

Well now yes. Got some money. How much money are we talking about?

How much have you got? said Glanton.

Well. Adequate, I would say. I'd say adequate in money.

Glanton studied the man. I'll tell you what I'll do with you, he said. Are you wantin to go to Californy or are you just mouth?

California, said the owner. By all means.

I'll carry ye for a hundred dollars, paid in advance.

The man's eyes shifted from Glanton to the judge and back. I like some of having that much, he said.

We'll be here a couple of days, said Glanton. You find us some more fares and we'll adjust your tariff accordingly.

The captain will treat you right, said the judge. You can be assured of that.

Yessir, said the owner.

As they passed out by the cage Glanton turned to look at the idiot again. You let women see that thing? he said.

I dont know, said the owner. There's none ever asked.

By noon the company had moved on to an eatinghouse. There were three or four men inside when they entered and they got up and left. There was a mud oven in the lot behind the building and the bed of a wrecked wagon with a few pots and a kettle on it. An old woman in a gray shawl was cutting up beefribs with an axe while two dogs sat watching. A tall thin man in a bloodstained apron entered the room from the rear and looked them over. He leaned and placed both hands on the table before them.

Gentlemen, he said, we dont mind servin people of color. Glad to do it. But we ast for em to set over here at this other table here. Right over here.

He stepped back and held out one hand in a strange gesture of hospice. His guests looked at one another.

What in the hell is he talkin about?

Just right over here, said the man.

Toadvine looked down the table to where Jackson sat. Several looked toward Glanton. His hands were at rest on the board in front of him and his head was slightly bent like a man at grace. The judge sat smiling, his arms crossed. They were all slightly drunk.

He thinks we're niggers.

They sat in silence. The old woman in the court had commenced wailing some dolorous air and the man was standing with his hand outheld. Piled just within the door were the satchels and holsters and arms of the company.

Glanton raised his head. He looked at the man.

What's your name? he said.

Name's Owens. I own this place.

Mr Owens, if you was anything at all other than a goddamn fool you could take one look at these here men and know for a stone fact they aint a one of em goin to get up from where they're at to go set somewheres else.

Well I caint serve you.

You suit yourself about that. Ask her what she's got, Tommy.

Harlan was sitting at the end of the table and he leaned out and called to the old woman at her pots and asked her in Spanish what she had to eat.

She looked toward the house. Huesos, she said.

Huesos, said Harlan.

Tell her to bring em, Tommy.

She wont bring you nothin without I tell her to. I own this place.

Harlan was calling out the open door.

I know for a fact that man yonder's a nigger, said Owens.

Jackson looked up at him.

Brown turned toward the owner.

Have you got a gun? he said.

A gun?

A gun. Have you got a gun.

Not on me I aint.

Brown pulled a small fiveshot Colt from his belt and pitched it to him. He caught it and stood holding it uncertainly.

You got one now. Now shoot the nigger.

Wait a goddamn minute, said Owens.

Shoot him, said Brown.

Jackson had risen and he pulled one of the big pistols from his belt. Owens pointed the pistol at him. You put that down, he said.

You better forget about givin orders and shoot the son of a bitch.

Put it down. Goddamn, man. Tell him to put it down.

Shoot him.

He cocked the pistol.

Jackson fired. He simply passed his left hand over the top of the revolver he was holding in a gesture brief as flintspark and tripped the hammer. The big pistol jumped and a double handful of Owens's brains went out the back of his skull and plopped in the floor behind him. He sank without a sound and lay crumpled up with his face in the floor and one eye open and the blood welling up out of the destruction at the back of his head. Jackson sat down. Brown rose and retrieved his pistol and let the hammer back down and put it in his belt. Most terrible nigger I ever seen, he said. Find some plates, Charlie. I doubt the old lady is out there any more.

They were drinking in a cantina not a hundred feet from this scene when the lieutenant and a half dozen armed troopers entered the premises. The cantina was a single room and there was a hole in the ceiling where a trunk of sunlight fell through onto the mud floor and figures crossing the room steered with care past the edge of this column of light as if it might be hot to the touch. They were a hardbit denizenry and they shambled to the bar and back in their rags and skins like cavefolk exchanging at some nameless trade. The lieutenant circled this reeking solarium and stood before Glanton.

Captain, we're going to have to take whoever's responsible for the death of Mr Owens into custody.

Glanton looked up. Who's Mr Owens? he said.

Mr Owens is the gentleman who ran the eatinghouse down here. He's been shot to death.

Sorry to hear it, said Glanton. Set down.

Couts ignored the invitation. Captain, you dont aim to deny that one of your men shot him do you?

I aim exactly that, said Glanton.

Captain, it wont hold water.

The judge emerged from the darkness. Evening, Lieutenant, he said. Are these men the witnesses?

Couts looked at his corporal. No, he said. They aint witnesses.

Hell, Captain. You all were seen to enter the premises and seen to leave after the shot was fired. Are you going to deny that you and your men took your dinner there?

Deny ever goddamned word of it, said Glanton.

Well by god I believe I can prove that you ate there.

Kindly address your remarks to me, Lieutenant, said the judge. I represent Captain Glanton in all legal matters. I think you should know first of all that the captain does not propose to be called a liar and I would think twice before I involved myself with him in an affair of honor. Secondly I have been with him all day and I can assure you that neither he nor any of his men have ever set foot in the premises to which you allude.

The lieutenant seemed stunned at the baldness of these disclaimers. He looked from the judge to Glanton and back again. I will be damned, he said. Then he turned and pushed past the men and quit the place.

Glanton tilted his chair and leaned his back to the wall. They'd recruited two men from among the town's indigents, an unpromising pair that sat gawking at the end of the bench with their hats in their hands. Glanton's dark eye passed over them and alighted on the owner of the imbecile who sat alone across the room watching him.

You a drinkin man? said Glanton.

How's that?

Glanton exhaled slowly through his nose.

Yes, said the owner. Yes I am.

There was a common wooden pail on the table before Glanton with a tin dipper in it and it was about a third full of wagonyard whiskey drawn off from a cask at the bar. Glanton nodded toward it.

I aint a carryin it to ye.

The owner rose and picked up his cup and came across to the table. He took up the dipper and poured his cup and set the dipper back in the bucket. He gestured slightly with the cup and raised and drained it.

Much obliged.

Where's your ape at?

The man looked at the judge. He looked at Glanton again.

I dont take him out much.

Where'd you get that thing at?

He was left to me. Mama died. There was nobody to take him to raise. They shipped him to me. Joplin Missouri. Just put him in a box and shipped him. Took five weeks. Didnt bother him a bit. I opened up the box and there he set.

Get ye another drink there.

He took up the dipper and filled his cup again.

Big as life. Never hurt him a bit. I had him a hair suit made but he ate it.

Aint everbody in this town seen the son of a bitch?

Yes. Yes they have. I need to get to California. I may charge four bits out there.

You may get tarred and feathered out there.

I've been that. State of Arkansas. Claimed I'd given him something. Drugged him. They took him off and waited for him to get better but of course he didnt do it. They had a special preacher come and pray over him. Finally I got him back. I could have been somebody in this world wasnt for him.

Do I understand you correctly, said the judge, that the imbecile is your brother?

Yessir, said the man. That's the truth of the matter.

The judge reached and took hold of the man's head in his hands and began to explore its contours. The man's eyes darted about and he held onto the judge's wrists. The judge had his entire head in his grip like an immense and dangerous faith healer. The man was standing tiptoe as if to better accommodate him in his investigations and when the judge let go of him he took a step back and looked at Glanton with eyes that were white in the gloom. The recruits at the end of the bench sat watching with their jaws down and the judge narrowed an eye at the man and studied him and then reached and gripped him again, holding him by the forehead while he prodded along the back of his skull with the ball of his thumb. When the judge put him down the man stepped back and fell over the bench and the recruits commenced to bob up and down and to wheeze and croak. The owner of the idiot looked about the tawdry grogshop, passing up each face as if it did not quite suffice. He picked himself up and moved past the end of the bench. When he was halfway across the room the judge called out to him.

Has he always been like that? said the judge.

Yessir. He was born that way.

He turned to go. Glanton emptied his cup and set it before him and looked up. Were you? he said. But the owner pushed open the door and vanished in the blinding light without.

The lieutenant came again in the evening. He and the judge sat together and the judge went over points of law with him. The lieutenant nodded, his lips pursed. The judge translated for him latin terms of jurisprudence. He cited cases civil and martial. He quoted Coke and Blackstone, Anaximander, Thales.

In the morning there was new trouble. A young Mexican girl had been abducted. Parts of her clothes were found torn and bloodied under the north wall, over which she could only have been thrown. In the desert were drag marks. A shoe. The father of the child knelt clutching a bloodstained rag to his chest and none could persuade him to rise and none to leave. That night fires were lit in the streets and a beef killed and Glanton and his men were host to a motley collection of citizens and soldiers and reduced indians or tontos as their brothers outside the gates would name them. A keg of whiskey was broached and soon men were reeling aimlessly through the smoke. A merchant of that town brought forth a litter of dogs one of whom had six legs and another two and a third with four eyes in its head. He offered these for sale to Glanton and Glanton warned the man away and threatened to shoot them.

The beef was stripped to the bones and the bones themselves carried off and vigas were dragged from the ruined buildings and piled onto the blaze. By now many of Glanton's men were naked and lurching about and the judge soon had them dancing while he fiddled on a crude instrument he'd commandeered and the filthy hides of which they'd divested themselves smoked and stank and blackened in the flames and the red sparks rose like the souls of the small life they'd harbored.

By midnight the citizens had cleared out and there were armed and naked men pounding on doors demanding drink and women. In the early morning hours when the fires had burned to heaps of coals and a few sparks scampered in the wind down the cold clay streets feral dogs trotted around the cookfire snatching out the blackened scraps of meat and men lay huddled naked in the doorways clutching their elbows and snoring in the cold.

By noon they were abroad again, wandering red-eyed in the streets, fitted out for the most part in new shirts and breeches. They collected the remaining horses from the farrier and he stood them to a drink. He was a small sturdy man named Pacheco and he had for anvil an enormous iron meteorite shaped like a great molar and the judge on a wager lifted the thing and on a further wager lifted it over his head. Several men pushed forward to feel the iron and to rock it where it stood, nor did the judge lose this opportunity to ventilate himself upon the ferric nature of heavenly bodies and their powers and claims. Two lines were drawn in the dirt ten feet apart and a third round of wagers was laid, coins from half a dozen countries in both gold and silver and even a few boletas or notes of discounted script from the mines near Tubac. The judge seized that great slag wandered for what millennia from what unreckonable corner of the universe and he raised it overhead and stood tottering and then lunged forward. It cleared the mark by a foot and he shared with no one the specie piled on the saddleblanket at the farrier's feet for not even Glanton had been willing to underwrite this third trial.

XVII

Leaving Tucson – A new cooperage – An exchange –
Sguaro forests – Glanton at the fire – Garcia's command –
The paraselene – The godfire – The expriest on astronomy –
The judge on the extraterrestrial, on order, on teleology in
the universe – A coin trick – Glanton's dog – Dead animals –
The sands – A crucifixion – The judge on war – The priest
does not say – Tierras quebradas, tierras desamparadas – The
Tinajas Atlas – Un hueso de piedra – The Colorado –
Argonauts – Yumas – The ferrymen – To the Yuma camp.

THEY RODE OUT at dusk. The corporal in the gatehouse above
the portal came out and called to them to halt but they did not.
They rode twenty-one men and a dog and a little flatbed cart
aboard which the idiot and his cage had been lashed as if for a
sea journey. Lashed on behind the cage rode the whiskey keg
they'd drained the night before. The keg had been dismantled
and rebound by a man Glanton had appointed cooper pro-tem
to the expedition and it now contained within it a flask made
from a common sheep's stomach and holding perhaps three
quarts of whiskey. This flask was fitted to the bung at the inside
and the rest of the keg was filled with water. So provisioned
they passed out through the gates and beyond the walls onto the

prairie where it lay pulsing in the banded twilight. The little cart jostled and creaked and the idiot clutched at the bars of his cage and croaked hoarsely after the sun.

Glanton rode at the fore of the column in a new Ringgold saddle ironbound that he'd traded for and he wore a new hat which was black and became him. The recruits now five in number grinned at one another and looked back at the sentry. David Brown rode at the rear and he was leaving his brother here for what would prove forever and his mood was foul enough for him to have shot the sentry with no provocation at all. When the sentry called again he swung about with his rifle and the man had the sense to duck under the parapet and they heard no more from him. In the long dusk the savages rode out to meet them and the whiskey was exchanged for upon a Saltillo blanket spread on the ground. Glanton paid little attention to the proceedings. When the savages had counted out gold and silver to the judge's satisfaction Glanton stepped onto the blanket and kicked the coins together with his bootheel and then stepped away and directed Brown to take up the blanket. Mangas and his lieutenants exchanged dark looks but the Americans mounted up and rode out and none looked back save the recruits. They'd become privy to the details of the business and one of them fell in alongside Brown and asked if the Apaches would not follow them.

They wont ride at night, said Brown.

The recruit looked back at the figures gathered about the keg in that scoured and darkening waste.

Why wont they? he said.

Brown spat. Because it's dark, he said.

They rode west from the town across the base of a small mountain through a dogtown strewn with old broken earthenware from a crockery furnace that once had been there. The keeper of the idiot rode downside of the trestled cage and the idiot clutched the poles and watched the land pass in silence.

They rode that night through forests of saguaro up into the

hills to the west. The sky was all overcast and those fluted columns passing in the dark were like the ruins of vast temples ordered and grave and silent save for the soft cries of elf owls among them. The terrain was thick with cholla and clumps of it clung to the horses with spikes that would drive through a bootsole to the bones within and a wind came up through the hills and all night it sang with a wild viper sound through that countless reach of spines. They rode on and the land grew more spare and they reached the first of a series of jornadas where there would be no water at all and there they camped. That night Glanton stared long into the embers of the fire. All about him his men were sleeping but much was changed. So many gone, defected or dead. The Delawares all slain. He watched the fire and if he saw portents there it was much the same to him. He would live to look upon the western sea and he was equal to whatever might follow for he was complete at every hour. Whether his history should run concomitant with men and nations, whether it should cease. He'd long forsworn all weighing of consequence and allowing as he did that men's destinies are given yet he usurped to contain within him all that he would ever be in the world and all that the world would be to him and be his charter written in the urstone itself he claimed agency and said so and he'd drive the remorseless sun on to its final endarkenment as if he'd ordered it all ages since, before there were paths anywhere, before there were men or suns to go upon them.

Across from him sat the vast abhorrence of the judge. Half naked, scribbling in his ledger. In the thornforest through which they'd passed the little desert wolves yapped and on the dry plain before them others answered and the wind fanned the coals that he watched. The bones of cholla that glowed there in their incandescent basketry pulsed like burning holothurians in the phosphorous dark of the sea's deeps. The idiot in his cage had been drawn close to the fire and he watched it tirelessly.

When Glanton raised his head he saw the kid across the fire from him, squatting in his blanket, watching the judge.

Two days later they encountered a ragged legion under the command of Colonel Garcia. They were troops from Sonora seeking a band of Apaches under Pablo and they numbered close to a hundred riders. Of these some were without hats and some without pantaloons and some were naked under their coats and they were armed with derelict weapons, old fusils and Tower muskets, some with bows and arrows or nothing more than ropes with which to garrote the enemy.

Glanton and his men reviewed this company with stony amazement. The Mexicans pressed about with their hands out-held for tobacco and Glanton and the colonel exchanged rudimentary civilities and then Glanton pushed on through that importunate horde. They were of another nation, those riders, and all that land to the south out of which they'd originated and whatever lands to the east toward which they were bound were dead to him and both the ground and any sojourners upon it remote and arguable of substance. This feeling communicated itself through the company before Glanton had moved entirely clear of them and each man turned his horse and each man followed and not even the judge spoke to excuse himself from out of that encounter.

They rode on into the darkness and the moonblanched waste lay before them cold and pale and the moon sat in a ring overhead and in that ring lay a mock moon with its own cold gray and nacre seas. They made camp on a low bench of land where walls of dry aggregate marked an old river course and they struck up a fire about which they sat in silence, the eyes of the dog and of the idiot and certain other men glowing red as coals in their heads where they turned. The flames sawed in the wind and the embers paled and deepened and paled and deepened like the bloodbeat of some living thing eviscerate upon the ground before them and they watched the fire which does contain within it something of men themselves inasmuch as they are less without it and are divided from their origins and are exiles. For each fire is all fires, the first fire and the last ever to be. By and by the judge rose and moved away on some obscure mission and after a while someone asked the expriest if it were true that at one time there had been two moons in the sky and the expriest eyed the false moon above them and said that it may well have been so. But certainly the wise high God in his dismay at the proliferation of lunacy on this earth must have wetted a thumb and leaned down out of the abyss and pinched it hissing into extinction. And could he find some alter means by which the birds could mend their paths in the darkness he might have done with this one too.

The question was then put as to whether there were on Mars or other planets in the void men or creatures like them and at this the judge who had returned to the fire and stood half naked and sweating spoke and said that there were not and that there were no men anywhere in the universe save those upon the earth. All listened as he spoke, those who had turned to watch him and those who would not.

The truth about the world, he said, is that anything is possible. Had you not seen it all from birth and thereby bled it of its strangeness it would appear to you for what it is, a hat trick in a medicine show, a fevered dream, a trance bepopulate with chimeras having neither analogue nor precedent, an itinerant carnival, a migratory tentshow whose ultimate destination after many a pitch in many a mudded field is unspeakable and calamitous beyond reckoning.

The universe is no narrow thing and the order within it is not constrained by any latitude in its conception to repeat what exists in one part in any other part. Even in this world more things exist without our knowledge than with it and the order in creation which you see is that which you have put there, like a string in a maze, so that you shall not lose your way. For existence has its own order and that no man's mind can compass, that mind itself being but a fact among others.

Brown spat into the fire. That's some more of your craziness, he said.

The judge smiled. He placed the palms of his hands upon his chest and breathed the night air and he stepped closer and squatted and held up one hand. He turned that hand and there was a gold coin between his fingers.

Where is the coin, Davy?

I'll notify you where to put the coin.

The judge swung his hand and the coin winked overhead in the firelight. It must have been fastened to some subtle lead, horsehair perhaps, for it circled the fire and returned to the judge and he caught it in his hand and smiled.

The arc of circling bodies is determined by the length of their tether, said the judge. Moons, coins, men. His hands moved as if he were pulling something from one fist in a series of elongations. Watch the coin, Davy, he said.

He flung it and it cut an arc through the firelight and was gone in the darkness beyond. They watched the night where it had vanished and they watched the judge and in their watching some the one and some the other they were a common witness.

The coin, Davy, the coin, whispered the judge. He sat erect and raised his hand and smiled around.

The coin returned back out of the night and crossed the fire with a faint high droning and the judge's raised hand was empty and then it held the coin. There was a light slap and it held the coin. Even so some claimed that he had thrown the coin away and palmed another like it and made the sound with his tongue for he was himself a cunning old malabarista and he said himself as he put the coin away what all men knew that there are coins and false coins. In the morning some did walk over the ground where the coin had gone but if any man found it he kept it to himself and with sunrise they were mounted and riding again.

The cart with the idiot in his cage trundled along at the rear and now Glanton's dog fell back to trot alongside, perhaps out of some custodial instinct such as children will evoke in animals. But Glanton called the dog to him and when it did not come he dropped back along the little column and leaned down and quirted it viciously with his hobble rope and drove it out before him.

They began to come upon chains and packsaddles, single-trees, dead mules, wagons. Saddletrees eaten bare of their rawhide coverings and weathered white as bone, a light chamfering of miceteeth along the edges of the wood. They rode through a region where iron will not rust nor tin tarnish. The ribbed frames of dead cattle under their patches of dried hide lay like the ruins of primitive boats upturned upon that shoreless void and they passed lurid and austere the black and desiccated shapes of horses and mules that travelers had stood afoot. These parched beasts had died with their necks stretched in agony in the sand and now upright and blind and lurching askew with scraps of blackened leather hanging from the fretwork of their ribs they leaned with their long mouths howling after the endless tandem suns that passed above them. The riders rode on. They crossed a vast dry lake with rows of dead volcanoes ranged beyond it like the works of enormous insects. To the south lay broken shapes of scoria in a lava bed as far as the eye could see. Under the hooves of the horses the alabaster sand shaped itself in whorls strangely symmetric like iron filings in a field and these shapes flared and drew back again, resonating upon that harmonic ground and then turning to swirl away over the playa. As if the very sediment of things contained yet some residue of sentience. As if in the transit of those riders were a thing so profoundly terrible as to register even to the uttermost granulation of reality.

On a rise at the western edge of the playa they passed a crude wooden cross where Maricopas had crucified an Apache. The mummied corpse hung from the crosstree with its mouth gaped in a raw hole, a thing of leather and bone scoured by the pumice winds off the lake and the pale tree of the ribs showing through the scraps of hide that hung from the breast. They rode on. The horses trudged sullenly the alien ground and the round earth rolled beneath them silently milling the greater void wherein they were contained. In the neuter austerity of that terrain all phenomena were bequeathed a strange equality and no one thing nor spider nor stone nor blade of grass could put forth claim to precedence. The very clarity of these articles belied their familiarity, for the eye predicates the whole on some feature or part and here was nothing more luminous than another and nothing more enshadowed and in the optical democracy of such landscapes all preference is made whimsical and a man and a rock become endowed with unguessed kinships.

They grew gaunted and lank under the white suns of those days and their hollow burnedout eyes were like those of noctambulants surprised by day. Crouched under their hats they seemed fugitives on some grander scale, like beings for whom the sun hungered. Even the judge grew silent and speculative. He'd spoke of purging oneself of those things that lay claim to a man but that body receiving his remarks counted themselves well done with any claims at all. They rode on and the wind drove the fine gray dust before them and they rode an army of gray-beards, gray men, gray horses. The mountains to the north lay sunwise in corrugated folds and the days were cool and the nights were cold and they sat about the fire each in his round of darkness in that round of dark while the idiot watched from his cage at the edge of the light. The judge cracked with the back of an axe the shinbone on an antelope and the hot marrow dripped smoking on the stones. They watched him. The subject was war.

The good book says that he that lives by the sword shall perish by the sword, said the black.

The judge smiled, his face shining with grease. What right man would have it any other way? he said.

The good book does indeed count war an evil, said Irving. Yet there's many a bloody tale of war inside it.

It makes no difference what men think of war, said the judge. War endures. As well ask men what they think of stone. War was always here. Before man was, war waited for him. The ultimate trade awaiting its ultimate practitioner. That is the way it was and will be. That way and not some other way.

He turned to Brown, from whom he'd heard some whispered slur or demurrer. Ah Davy, he said. It's your own trade we honor here. Why not rather take a small bow. Let each acknowledge each.

My trade?

Certainly.

What is my trade?

War. War is your trade. Is it not?

And it aint yours?

Mine too. Very much so.

What about all them notebooks and bones and stuff?

All other trades are contained in that of war.

Is that why war endures?

No. It endures because young men love it and old men love it in them. Those that fought, those that did not.

That's your notion.

The judge smiled. Men are born for games. Nothing else. Every child knows that play is nobler than work. He knows too that the worth or merit of a game is not inherent in the game itself but rather in the value of that which is put at hazard. Games of chance require a wager to have meaning at all. Games of sport involve the skill and strength of the opponents and the humiliation of defeat and the pride of victory are in themselves sufficient stake because they inhere in the worth of the principals and define them. But trial of chance or trial of worth all games aspire to the condition of war for here that which is wagered swallows up game, player, all.

Suppose two men at cards with nothing to wager save their

lives. Who has not heard such a tale? A turn of the card. The whole universe for such a player has labored clanking to this moment which will tell if he is to die at that man's hand or that man at his. What more certain validation of a man's worth could there be? This enhancement of the game to its ultimate state admits no argument concerning the notion of fate. The selection of one man over another is a preference absolute and irrevocable and it is a dull man indeed who could reckon so profound a decision without agency or significance either one. In such games as have for their stake the annihilation of the defeated the decisions are quite clear. This man holding this particular arrangement of cards in his hand is thereby removed from existence. This is the nature of war, whose stake is at once the game and the authority and the justification. Seen so, war is the truest form of divination. It is the testing of one's will and the will of another within that larger will which because it binds them is therefore forced to select. War is the ultimate game because war is at last a forcing of the unity of existence. War is god.

Brown studied the judge. You're crazy Holden. Crazy at last.

The judge smiled.

Might does not make right, said Irving. The man that wins in some combat is not vindicated morally.

Moral law is an invention of mankind for the disenfranchisement of the powerful in favor of the weak. Historical law subverts it at every turn. A moral view can never be proven right or wrong by any ultimate test. A man falling dead in a duel is not thought thereby to be proven in error as to his views. His very involvement in such a trial gives evidence of a new and broader view. The willingness of the principals to forgo further argument as the triviality which it in fact is and to petition directly the chambers of the historical absolute clearly indicates of how little moment are the opinions and of what great moment the divergences thereof. For the argument is indeed trivial, but not so the separate wills thereby made manifest. Man's vanity may well approach the infinite in capacity but his knowledge remains imperfect and howevermuch he comes to value his judgements ultimately he must submit them before a higher court. Here there can be no special pleading. Here are considerations of equity and rectitude and moral right rendered void and without warrant and here are the views of the litigants despised. Decisions of life and death, of what shall be and what shall not, beggar all question of right. In elections of these magnitudes are all lesser ones subsumed, moral, spiritual, natural.

The judge searched out the circle for disputants. But what says the priest? he said.

Tobin looked up. The priest does not say.

The priest does not say, said the judge. Nihil dicit. But the priest has said. For the priest has put by the robes of his craft and taken up the tools of that higher calling which all men honor. The priest also would be no godserver but a god himself.

Tobin shook his head. You've a blasphemous tongue, Holden. And in truth I was never a priest but only a novitiate to the order.

Journeyman priest or apprentice priest, said the judge. Men of god and men of war have strange affinities.

I'll not secondsay you in your notions, said Tobin. Dont ask it.

Ah Priest, said the judge. What could I ask of you that you've not already given?

ON THE DAY FOLLOWING they crossed the malpais afoot, leading the horses upon a lakebed of lava all cracked and reddish black like a pan of dried blood, threading those badlands of dark amber glass like the remnants of some dim legion scrabbling up out of a land accursed, shouldering the little cart over the rifts and ledges, the idiot clinging to the bars and calling hoarsely after the sun like some queer unruly god abducted from a race of degenerates. They crossed a cinderland of caked slurry and volcanic ash imponderable as the burnedout floor of hell and they climbed up through a low range of barren granite hills to a stark promontory where the judge, triangulating from known points of landscape, reckoned anew their course. A gravel flat stretched away to the horizon. Far to the south beyond the black volcanic hills lay a lone albino ridge, sand or gypsum, like the back of some pale seabeast surfaced among the dark archipelagos. They went on. In a day's ride they reached the stone tanks and the water they sought and they drank and bailed water down from the higher tanks to the dry ones below for the horses.

At all desert watering places there are bones but the judge that evening carried to the fire one such as none there had ever seen before, a great femur from some beast long extinct that he'd found weathered out of a bluff and that he now sat measuring with the tailor's tape he carried and sketching into his log. All in that company had heard the judge on paleontology save for the new recruits and they sat watching and putting to him such queries as they could conceive of. He answered them with care, amplifying their own questions for them, as if they might be apprentice scholars. They nodded dully and reached to touch that pillar of stained and petrified bone, perhaps to sense with their fingers the temporal immensities of which the judge spoke. The keeper led the imbecile down from its cage and tethered it by the fire with a braided horsehair rope that it could not chew through and it stood leaning in its collar with its hands outheld as if it yearned for the flames. Glanton's dog rose and sat watching it and the idiot swayed and drooled with its dull eyes falsely brightened by the fire. The judge had been holding the femur upright in order to better illustrate its analogies to the prevalent bones of the country about and he let it fall in the sand and closed his book.

There is no mystery to it, he said.

The recruits blinked dully.

Your heart's desire is to be told some mystery. The mystery is that there is no mystery.

He rose and moved away into the darkness beyond the fire. Aye, said the expriest watching, his pipe cold in his teeth. And no mystery. As if he were no mystery himself, the bloody old hoodwinker.

THREE DAYS LATER they reached the Colorado. They stood at the edge of the river watching the roiled and claycolored waters coming down in a flat and steady seething out of the desert. Two cranes rose from the shore and flapped away and the horses and mules led down the bank ventured uncertainly into the eddying shoals and stood drinking and looking up with their muzzles dripping at the passing current and the shore beyond.

Upriver they encountered in camp the remnants of a wagon train laid waste by cholera. The survivors moved among their noonday cookfires or stared hollowly at the ragged dragoons riding up out of the willows. Their chattels were scattered about over the sand and the wretched estates of the deceased stood separate to be parceled out among them. There were in the camp a number of Yuma indians. The men wore their hair hacked to length with knives or plastered up in wigs of mud and they shambled about with heavy clubs dangling in their hands. Both they and the women were tattooed of face and the women were naked save for skirts of willowbark woven into string and many of them were lovely and many more bore the marks of syphilis.

Glanton moved through this balesome depot with his dog at heel and his rifle in his hand. The Yumas were swimming the few sorry mules left to the party across the river and he stood on the bank and watched them. Downriver they'd drowned one of the animals and towed it ashore to be butchered. An old man in a shacto coat and a long beard sat with his boots at his side and his feet in the river.

Where's your all's horses? said Glanton.

We ate them.

Glanton studied the river.

How do you aim to cross?

On the ferry.

He looked crossriver to where the old man gestured. What does he get to cross ye? he said.

Dollar a head.

Glanton turned and studied the pilgrims on the beach. The dog was drinking from the river and he said something to it and it came up and sat by his knee.

The ferryboat put out from the far bank and crossed to a landing upstream where there was a deadman built of driftlogs. The boat was contrived from a pair of old wagonboxes fitted together and caulked with pitch. A group of people had shouldered up their dunnage and stood waiting. Glanton turned and went up the bank to get his horse.

The ferryman was a doctor from New York state named Lincoln. He was supervising the loading, the travelers stepping aboard and squatting along the rails of the scow with their parcels and looking out uncertainly at the broad water. A half-mastiff dog sat on the bank watching. At Glanton's approach it stood bristling. The doctor turned and shaded his eyes with his hand and Glanton introduced himself. They shook hands. A pleasure, Captain Glanton. I am at your service.

Glanton nodded. The doctor gave instructions to the two men working for him and he and Glanton walked out along the downriver path, Glanton leading the horse and the doctor's dog following some ten paces behind.

Glanton's party was camped on a bench of sand partially shaded by river willows. As he and the doctor approached the idiot rose in his cage and seized the bars and commenced hooting as if he'd warn the doctor back. The doctor went wide of the thing, glancing at his host, but Glanton's lieutenants had come forward and soon the doctor and the judge were deep in discourse to the exclusion of anyone else.

In the evening Glanton and the judge and a detail of five men rode downriver into the Yuma encampment. They rode through a pale wood of willow and sycamore flaked with clay from the high water and they rode past old acequias and small winter fields where the dry husks of corn rattled lightly in the wind and they crossed the river at the Algodones ford. When the dogs announced them the sun was already down and the western land red and smoking and they rode singlefile in cameo detailed by the winey light with their dark sides to the river. Cookfires from the camp smoldered among the trees and a delegation of mounted savages rode out to meet them.

They halted and sat their horses. The party approaching were clad in such fool's regalia and withal bore themselves with such aplomb that the paler riders were hard put to keep their composure. The leader was a man named Caballo en Pelo and this old mogul wore a belted wool overcoat that would have served a far colder climate and beneath it a woman's blouse of embroidered silk and a pair of pantaloons of gray cassinette. He was small and wiry and he had lost an eye to the Maricopas and he presented the Americans with a strange priapic leer that may have at one time been a smile. At his right rode a lesser chieftain named Pascual in a frogged coat out at the elbows and who wore in his nose a bone hung with small pendants. The third man was Pablo and he was clad in a scarlet coat with tarnished braiding and tarnished epaulettes of silver wire. He was barefooted and bare of leg and he wore on his face a pair of round green goggles. In this attire they arranged themselves before the Americans and nodded austerely.

Brown spat on the ground in disgust and Glanton shook his head.

Aint you a crazylookin bunch of niggers, he said.

Only the judge seemed to weigh them up at all and he was sober in the doing, judging as perhaps he did that things are seldom what they seem.

Buenas tardes, he said.

The mogul tossed his chin, a small gesture darkened with a certain ambiguity. Buenas tardes, he said. De dónde viene?

XVIII

*The return to camp – The idiot delivered – Sarah Borginnis –
A confrontation – Bathed in the river – The tumbril burned –
James Robert in camp – Another baptism – Judge and fool.*

WHEN THEY RODE OUT of the Yuma camp it was in the dark
of early morning. Cancer, Virgo, Leo raced the ecliptic down
the southern night and to the north the constellation of Cassi-
opeia burned like a witch's signature on the black face of the
firmament. In the nightlong parley they'd come to terms with
the Yumas in conspiring to seize the ferry. They rode upriver
among the floodstained trees talking quietly among themselves
like men returning late from a social, from a wedding or a
death.

By daylight the women at the crossing had discovered the
idiot in his cage. They gathered about him, apparently unap-
palled by the nakedness and filth. They crooned to him and
they consulted among themselves and a woman named Sarah
Borginnis led them to seek out the brother. She was a huge
woman with a great red face and she read him riot.

What's your name anyways? she said.

Cloyce Bell mam.

What's his.

His name's James Robert but there dont anybody call him it.

If your mother was to see him what do you reckon she'd say.

I dont know. She's dead.

Aint you ashamed?

No mam.

Dont you sass me.

I'm not trying to. You want him just take him. I'll give him to you. I cant do any more than what I've done.

Damn if you aint a sorry specimen. She turned to the other women.

You all help me. We need to bathe him and get some clothes on him. Somebody run get some soap.

Mam, said the keeper.

You all just take him on to the river.

TOADVINE and the kid passed them as they were dragging the cart along. They stepped off the path and watched them go by. The idiot was clutching the bars and hooting at the water and some of the women had started up a hymn.

Where are they takin it? said Toadvine.

The kid didnt know. They were backing the cart through the loose sand toward the edge of the river and they let it down and opened the cage. The Borginnis woman stood before the imbecile.

James Robert come out of there.

She reached in and took him by the hand. He peered past her at the water, then he reached for her.

A sigh went up from the women, several of whom had hiked their skirts and tucked them at the waist and now stood in the river to receive him.

She handed him down, him clinging to her neck. When his feet touched the ground he turned to the water. She was smeared with feces but she seemed not to notice. She looked back at those on the riverbank.

Burn that thing, she said.

Someone ran to the fire for a brand and while they led James Robert into the waters the cage was torched and began to burn.

He clutched at their skirts, he reached with a clawed hand, gibbering, drooling.

He sees hisself in it, they said.

Shoo. Imagine having this child penned up like a wild animal.

The flames from the burning cart crackled in the dry air and the noise must have caught the idiot's attention for he turned his dead black eyes upon it. He knows, they said. All agreed. The Borginnis woman waded out with her dress ballooning about her and took him deeper and swirled him about grown man that he was in her great stout arms. She held him up, she crooned to him. Her pale hair floated on the water.

His old companions saw him that night before the migrants' fires in a coarse woven wool suit. His thin neck turned warily in the collar of his outsized shirt. They'd greased his hair and combed it flat upon his skull so that it looked painted on. They brought him sweets and he sat drooling and watched the fire, greatly to their admiration. In the dark the river ran on and a fishcolored moon rose over the desert east and set their shadows by their sides in the barren light The fires drew down and the smoke stood gray and chambered in the night. The little jackal wolves cried from across the river and the camp dogs stirred and muttered. The Borginnis took the idiot to his pallet under a wagon-sheet and stripped him to his new underwear and she tucked him into his blanket and kissed him goodnight and the camp grew quiet. When the idiot crossed that blue and smoky amphitheatre he was naked once again, shambling past the fires like a balden groundsloth. He paused and tested the air and he shuffled on. He went wide of the landing and stumbled through the shore willows, whimpering and pushing with his thin arms at things in the night Then he was standing alone on the shore. He hooted softly and his voice passed from him like a gift that was also needed so that no sound of it echoed back. He entered the water. Before the river reached much past his waist he'd lost his footing and sunk from sight.

Now the judge on his midnight rounds was passing along at just this place stark naked himself—such encounters being commoner than men suppose or who would survive any crossing by night—and he stepped into the river and seized up the drowning idiot, snatching it aloft by the heels like a great midwife and slapping it on the back to let the water out. A birth scene or a baptism or some ritual not yet inaugurated into any canon. He twisted the water from its hair and he gathered the naked and sobbing fool into his arms and carried it up into the camp and restored it among its fellows.

XIX

THE DOCTOR had been bound for California when the ferry fell into his hands for the most by chance. In the ensuing months he'd amassed a considerable wealth in gold and silver and jewelry. He and the two men who worked for him had taken up residence on the west bank of the river overlooking the ferrylanding among the abutments of an unfinished hillside fortification made from mud and rock. In addition to the pair of freightwagons he'd inherited from Major Graham's command he had also a mountain howitzer—a bronze twelvepounder with a bore the size of a saucer—and this piece stood idle and unloaded in its wooden truck. In the doctor's crude quarters he and Glanton and the judge together with Brown and Irving sat drinking tea and Glanton sketched for the doctor a few of their Indian adventures and advised him strongly to secure his position. The doctor demurred. He claimed to get along well with the Yumas. Glanton told him to his face that any man who trusted an indian was a fool. The doctor colored but he held his tongue. The judge intervened. He asked the doctor did he consider the pilgrims huddled on the far shore to be under his protection. The doctor said that he did so consider them. The judge spoke reasonably and with concern and when Glanton and his detail returned down the hill to cross to their camp they had the doctor's permission to fortify the hill and charge the howitzer and to this end they set about running the last of their lead until they had close on to a hatful of rifleballs.

They loaded the howitzer that evening with something like a pound of powder and the entire cast of shot and they trundled the piece to a place of advantage overlooking the river and the landing below.

Two days later the Yumas attacked the crossing. The scows were on the west bank of the river discharging cargo as arranged and the travelers stood by to claim their goods. The savages came both mounted and afoot out of the willows with no warning and swarmed across the open ground toward the ferry. On the hill above them Brown and Long Webster swung the howitzer and steadied it and Brown crammed his lighted cigar into the touch-hole.

Even over that open terrain the concussion was immense. The howitzer in its truck leaped from the ground and clattered smoking backward across the packed clay. On the floodplain below the fort a terrible destruction had passed and upward of a dozen of the Yumas lay dead or writhing in the sand. A great howl went up among them and Glanton and his riders defiled out of the wooded littoral upriver and rode upon them and they cried out in rage at their betrayal. Their horses began to mill and they pulled them about and loosed arrows at the approaching dragoons and were shot down in volleys of pistolfire and the debarkees at the crossing scrabbled up their arms from among the dunnage and knelt and set up a fire from that quarter while the women and children lay prone among the trunks and freightboxes. The horses of the Yumas reared and screamed and churned about in the loose sand with their hoopshaped nostrils and whited eyes and the survivors made for the willows from which they'd emerged leaving on the field the wounded and the dying and the dead. Glanton and his men did not pursue them. They dismounted and walked methodically among the fallen dispatching them man and horse alike each with a pistolball through the brain while the ferry travelers watched and then they took the scalps.

The doctor stood on the low parapet of the works in silence and watched the bodies dragged down the landing and booted and shoved into the river. He turned and looked at Brown and Webster. They'd hauled the howitzer back to its position and Brown sat easily on the warm barrel smoking his cigar and watching the activity below. The doctor turned and walked back to his quarters.

Nor did he appear the following day. Glanton took charge of the operation of the ferry. People who had been waiting three days to cross at a dollar a head were now told that the fare was four dollars. And even this tariff was in effect for no more than a few days. Soon they were operating a sort of procrustean ferry where the fares were tailored to accommodate the purses of the travelers. Ultimately all pretense was dropped and the immigrants were robbed outright. Travelers were beaten and their arms and goods appropriated and they were sent destitute and beggared into the desert. The doctor came down to remonstrate with them and was paid his share of the revenues and sent back. Horses were taken and women violated and bodies began to drift past the Yuma camp downriver. As these outrages multiplied the doctor barricaded himself in his quarters and was seen no more.

In the following month a company from Kentucky under General Patterson arrived and disdaining to bargain with Glanton constructed a ferry downriver and crossed and moved on. This ferry was taken over by the Yumas and operated for them by a man named Callaghan, but within days it was burned and Callaghan's headless body floated anonymously downriver, a vulture standing between the shoulderblades in clerical black, silent rider to the sea.

Easter in that year fell on the last day of March and at dawn on that day the kid together with Toadvine and a boy named Billy Carr crossed the river to cut willow poles at a place where they grew upstream from the encampment of immigrants. Passing through this place before it was yet good light they encountered a party of Sonorans up and about and they saw hanging from a scaffold a poor Judas fashioned from straw and old rags who wore on his canvas face a painted scowl that reflected in the hand that had executed it no more than a child's conception of the man and his crime. The Sonorans had been up since midnight drinking and they had lit a bonfire on the bench of loam where the gibbet stood and as the Americans passed along the edge of their camp they called out to them in Spanish. Someone had brought a long cane from the fire tipped with lighted tow and the Judas was being set afire. Its raggedy clothes were packed with squibs and rockets and as the fire took hold it began to blow apart piece by piece in a shower of burning rags and straw. Until at last a bomb in its breeches went off and blew the thing to pieces in a stink of soot and sulphur and the men cheered and small boys threw a few last stones at the blackened remnants dangling from the noose. The kid was the last to pass through the clearing and the Sonorans called out to him and offered him wine from a goatskin but he shrugged up his rag of a coat about his shoulders and hurried on.

By now Glanton had enslaved a number of Sonorans and he kept crews of them working at the fortification of the hill. There were also detained in their camp a dozen or more indian and

Mexican girls, some little more than children. Glanton supervised with some interest the raising of the walls about him but otherwise left his men to pursue the business at the crossing with a terrible latitude. He seemed to take little account of the wealth they were amassing although daily he'd open the brass lock with which the wood and leather trunk in his quarters was secured and raise the lid and empty whole sacks of valuables into it, the trunk already holding thousands of dollars in gold and silver coins as well as jewelry, watches, pistols, raw gold in little leather stives, silver in bars, knives, silverware, plate, teeth.

On the second of April David Brown with Long Webster and Toadvine set out for the town of San Diego on the old Mexican coast for the purpose of obtaining supplies. They took with them a string of packanimals and they left at sunset, riding up out of the trees and looking back at the river and then walking the horses sideways down the dunes into the cool blue dusk.

They crossed the desert in five days without incident and rode up through the coastal range and led the mules through the snow in the gap and descended the western slope and entered the town in a slow drizzle of rain. Their hide clothing was heavy with water and the animals were stained with the silt that had leached out of them and their trappings. Mounted U S cavalry passed them in the mud of the street and in the distance beyond they could hear the sea boom shuddering on the gray and stony coast.

Brown took from the horn of his saddle a fibre morral filled with coins and the three of them dismounted and entered a whiskey grocer's and unannounced they upended the sack on the grocer's board.

There were doubloons minted in Spain and in Guadalajara and half doubloons and gold dollars and tiny gold half dollars and French coins of ten franc value and gold eagles and half eagles and ring dollars and dollars minted in North Carolina and Georgia that were twenty-two carats pure. The grocer weighed them out by stacks in a common scale, sorted by their mintings, and he drew corks and poured measures round in small tin cups whereon the gills were stamped. They drank and set down the cups again and he pushed the bottle across the raw sashmilled boards of the counter.

They had drafted a list of supplies to be contracted for and when they'd agreed on the price of flour and coffee and a few other staples they turned into the street each with a bottle in his fist. They went down the plankboard walkway and crossed through the mud and they went past rows of rawlooking shacks and crossed a small plaza beyond which they could see the low sea rolling and a small encampment of tents and a street where the squatting houses were made of hides ranged like curious dorys along the selvage of sea oats above the beach and quite black and shining in the rain.

It was in one of these that Brown woke the next morning. He had little recollection of the prior night and there was no one in the hut with him. The remainder of their money was in a bag around his neck. He pushed open the framed hide door and stepped out into the darkness and the mist. They'd neither put up nor fed their animals and he made his way back to the grocer's where they were tied and sat on the walkway and watched the dawn come down from the hills behind the town.

Noon he was red-eyed and reeking before the alcalde's door demanding the release of his companions. The alcalde vacated out the back of the premises and shortly there arrived an American corporal and two soldiers who warned him away. An hour later he was at the farriery. Standing warily in the doorway peering into the gloom until he could make out the shape of things within.

The farrier was at his bench and Brown entered and laid before him a polished mahogany case with a brass nameplate bradded to the lid. He unsnapped the catches and opened the case and raised from their recess within a pair of shotgun barrels and he took up the stock with the other hand. He hooked the barrels into the patent breech and stood the shotgun on the bench and pushed the fitted pin home to secure the forearm. He cocked the hammers with his thumbs and let them fall again. The shotgun was English made and had damascus barrels and engraved locks and the stock was burl mahogany. He looked up. The farrier was watching him.

You work on guns? said Brown.

I do some.

I need these barrels cut down.

The man took the gun and held it in his hands. There was a raised center rib between the barrels and inlaid in gold the maker's name, London. There were two platinum bands in the patent breech and the locks and the hammers were chased with scrollwork cut deeply in the steel and there were partridges engraved at either end of the maker's name there. The purple barrels were welded up from triple skelps and the hammered iron and steel bore a watered figure like the markings of some alien and antique serpent, rare and beautiful and lethal, and the wood was figured with a deep red feather grain at the butt and held a small springloaded silver capbox in the toe.

The farrier turned the gun in his hands and looked at Brown. He looked down at the case. It was lined with green baize and there were little fitted compartments that held a wadcutter, a pewter powderflask, cleaning jags, a patent pewter capper.

You need what? he said.

Cut the barrels down. Long about in here. He held a finger across the piece.

I cant do that.

Brown looked at him. You cant do it?

No sir.

He looked around the shop. Well, he said. I'd of thought any damn fool could saw the barrels off a shotgun.

There's something wrong with you. Why would anybody want to cut the barrels off a gun like this?

What did you say? said Brown.

The man tendered the gun nervously. I just meant that I dont see why anybody would want to ruin a good gun like this here. What would you take for it?

It aint for sale. You think there's something wrong with me?

No I dont. I didnt mean it that way.

Are you goin to cut them barrels down or aint ye?

I cant do that.

Cant or wont?

You pick the one that best suits you.

Brown took the shotgun and laid it on the bench.

What would you have to have to do it? he said.

I aint doin it.

If a man wanted it done what would be a fair price?

I dont know. A dollar.

Brown reached into his pocket and came up with a handful of coins. He laid a two and a half dollar gold piece on the bench. Now, he said. I'm payin you two and a half dollars.

The farrier looked at the coin nervously. I dont need your money, he said. You cant pay me to butcher that there gun.

You done been paid.

No I aint.

Yonder it lays. Now you can either get to sawin or you can default. In the case of which I aim to take it out of your ass.

The farrier didnt take his eyes off Brown. He began to back away from the bench and then he turned and ran.

When the sergeant of the guard arrived Brown had the shotgun chucked up in the benchvise and was working at the barrels with a hacksaw. The sergeant walked around to where he could see his face. What do you want, said Brown.

This man says you threatened his life.

What man?

This man. The sergeant nodded toward the door of the shed.

Brown continued to saw. You call that a man? he said.

I never give him no leave to come in here and use my tools neither, said the farrier.

How about it? said the sergeant.

How about what?

How do you answer to this man's charges?

He's a liar.

You never threatened him?

That's right.

The hell he never.

I dont threaten people. I told him I'd whip his ass and that's as good as notarized.

You dont call that a threat?

Brown looked up. It was not no threat. It was a promise.

He bent to the work again and another few passes with the saw and the barrels dropped to the dirt. He laid down the saw and backed off the jaws of the vise and lifted out the shotgun and unpinned the barrels from the stock and fitted the pieces into the case and shut the lid and latched it.

What was the argument about? said the sergeant.

Wasnt no argument that I know of.

You better ask him where he got that gun he's just ruined. He's stole that somewheres, you can wager on it.

Where'd you get the shotgun? said the sergeant.

Brown bent down and picked up the severed barrels. They were about eighteen inches long and he had them by the small end. He came around the bench and walked past the sergeant. He put the guncase under his arm. At the door he turned. The farrier was nowhere in sight. He looked at the sergeant.

I believe that man has done withdrawed his charges, he said. Like as not he was drunk.

As he was crossing the plaza toward the little mud cabildo he encountered Toadvine and Webster newly released. They were wildlooking and they stank. The three of them went down to the beach and sat looking out at the long gray swells and passing Brown's bottle among them. They'd none of them seen an ocean before. Brown walked down and held his hand to the sheet of spume that ran up the dark sand. He lifted his hand and tasted the salt on his fingers and he looked downcoast and up and then they went back up the beach toward the town.

They spent the afternoon drinking in a lazarous bodega run by a Mexican. Some soldiers came in. An altercation took place. Toadvine was on his feet, swaying. A peacemaker rose from among the soldiers and soon the principals were seated again. But minutes later Brown on his way back from the bar poured a pitcher of aguardiente over a young soldier and set him afire with his cigar. The man ran outside mute save for the whoosh of the flames and the flames were pale blue and then invisible in the sunlight and he fought them in the street like a man beset with bees or madness and then he fell over in the road and burned up. By the time they got to him with a bucket of water he had blackened and shriveled in the mud like an enormous spider.

Brown woke in a dark little cell manacled and crazed with thirst. The first thing he consulted for was the bag of coins. It was still inside his shirt. He rose up from the straw and put one eye to the judas hole. It was day. He called out for someone to come. He sat and with his chained hands counted out the coins and put them back in the bag.

In the evening he was brought his supper by a soldier. The soldier's name was Petit and Brown showed him his necklace of ears and he showed him the coins. Petit said he wanted no part of his schemes. Brown told him how he had thirty thousand dollars buried in the desert. He told him of the ferry, installing himself in Glanton's place. He showed him the coins again and he spoke familiarly of their places of origin, supplementing the judge's reports with impromptu data. Even shares, he hissed. You and me.

He studied the recruit through the bars. Petit wiped his forehead with his sleeve. Brown scooped the coins back into the poke and handed them out to him.

You think we caint trust one another? he said.

The boy stood holding the sack of coins uncertainly. He tried to push it back through the bars. Brown stepped away and held his hands up.

Dont be a fool, he hissed. What do you think I'd of give to have had such a chance at your age?

When Petit was gone he sat in the straw and looked at the thin metal plate of beans and the tortillas. After a while he ate. Outside it was raining again and he could hear riders passing in the mud of the street and soon it was dark.

They left two nights later. They had each a passable saddle-horse and a rifle and blanket and they had a mule that carried provisions of dried corn and beef and dates. They rode up into the dripping hills and in the first light Brown raised the rifle and shot the boy through the back of the head. The horse lurched forward and the boy toppled backward, the entire foreplate of his skull gone and the brains exposed. Brown halted his mount and got down and retrieved the sack of coins and took the boy's knife and took his rifle and his powderflask and his coat and he cut the ears from the boy's head and strung them onto his scapular and then he mounted up and rode on. The packmule followed and after a while so did the horse the boy had been riding.

WHEN WEBSTER and Toadvine rode into the camp at Yuma they had neither provisions nor the mules they'd left with. Glanton took five men and rode out at dusk leaving the judge in charge of the ferry. They reached San Diego in the dead of night and were directed to the alcalde's house. This man came to the door in nightshirt and stockingcap holding a candle before him. Glanton pushed him back into the parlor and sent his men on to the rear of the house from whence they heard directly a woman's screams and a few dull slaps and then silence.

The alcalde was a man in his sixties and he turned to go to

his wife's aid and was struck down with a pistolbarrel. He stood up again holding his head. Glanton pushed him on to the rear room. He had in his hand a rope already fashioned into a noose and he turned the alcalde around and put the noose over his head and pulled it taut. The wife was sitting up in bed and at this she commenced to scream again. One of her eyes was swollen and closing rapidly and now one of the recruits hit her flush in the mouth and she fell over in the tousled bedding and put her hands over her head. Glanton held the candle aloft and directed one of the recruits to boost the other on his shoulders and the boy reached along the top of one of the vigas until he found a space and he fitted the end of the rope through and let it down and they hauled on it and raised the mute and struggling alcalde into the air. They'd not tied his hands and he groped wildly overhead for the rope and pulled himself up to save strangling and he kicked his feet and revolved slowly in the candlelight.

Válgame Dios, he gasped. Qué quiere?

I want my money, said Glanton. I want my money and I want my packmules and I want David Brown.

Cómo? wheezed the old man.

Someone had lit a lamp. The old woman raised up and saw first the shadow and then the form of her husband dangling from the rope and she began to crawl across the bed toward him.

Dígame, gasped the alcalde.

Someone reached to seize the wife but Glanton motioned him away and she staggered out of the bed and took hold of her husband about the knees, to hold him up. She was sobbing and praying for mercy to Glanton and to God impartially.

Glanton walked around to where he could see the man's face. I want my money, he said. My money and my mules and the man I sent out here. El hombre que tiene usted. Mi compañero.

No no, gasped the hanged man. Búscale. No man is here.

Where is he?

He is no here.

Yes he's here. In the juzgado.

No no. Madre de Jesús. No here. He is gone. Siete, ocho días.

Where is the juzgado?

Cómo?

El juzgado. Dónde está?

The old woman turned loose with one arm long enough to point, her face pressed to the man's leg. Allá, she said. Allá.

Two men went out, one holding the stub of the candle and shielding the flame with his cupped hand before him. When they came back they reported the little dungeon in the building out back empty.

Glanton studied the alcalde. The old woman was visibly tottering. They'd halfhitched the rope about the tailpost of the bed and he loosed the rope and the alcalde and the wife collapsed into the floor.

They left them bound and gagged and rode out to visit the grocer. Three days later the alcalde and the grocer and the alcalde's wife were found tied and lying in their own excrement in an abandoned hut at the edge of the ocean eight miles south of the settlement They'd been left a pan of water from which they drank like dogs and they had howled at the booming surf in that wayplace until they were mute as stones.

Glanton and his men were two days and nights in the streets crazed with liquor. The sergeant in charge of the small garrison of American troops confronted them in a drinking exchange on the evening of the second day and he and the three men with him were beaten senseless and stripped of their arms. At dawn when the soldiers kicked in the hostel door there was no one in the room.

Glanton returned to Yuma alone, his men gone to the gold fields. On that bonestrewn waste he encountered wretched parcels of foot-travelers who called out to him and men dead where they'd fallen and men who would die and groups of folks clustered about a last wagon or cart shouting hoarsely at the mules or oxen and goading them on as if they bore in those frail caissons the covenant itself and these animals would die and the people with them and they called out to that lone horseman to warn him of the danger at the crossing and the horseman rode on all contrary to the tide of refugees like some storied hero toward what beast of war or plague or famine with what set to his relentless jaw.

When he reached Yuma he was drunk. Behind him on a string were two small jacks laden with whiskey and biscuit. He sat his horse and looked down at the river who was keeper of the crossroads of all that world and his dog came to him and nuzzled his foot in the stirrup.

A young Mexican girl was crouched naked under the shade of the wall. She watched him ride past, covering her breasts with her hands. She wore a rawhide collar about her neck and she was chained to a post and there was a clay bowl of blackened meatscraps beside her. Glanton tied the jacks to the post and rode inside on the horse.

There was no one about. He rode down to the landing. While he was watching the river the doctor came scrambling down the bank and seized Glanton by the foot and began to plead with him in a senseless jabber. He'd not seen to his person in weeks and he was filthy and disheveled and he tugged at Glanton's trouserleg and pointed toward the fortifications on the hill. That man, he said. That man.

Glanton slid his boot from the stirrup and pushed the doctor away with his foot and turned the horse and rode back up the hill. The judge was standing on the rise in silhouette against the evening sun like some great balden archimandrite. He was wrapped in a mantle of freeflowing cloth beneath which he was naked. The black man Jackson came out of one of the stone bunkers dressed in a similar garb and stood beside him. Glanton rode back up along the crest of the hill to his quarters.

All night gunfire drifted intermittently across the water and laughter and drunken oaths. When day broke no one appeared. The ferry lay at its moorings and across the river a man came down to the landing and blew a horn and waited and then went back.

The ferry stood idle all that day. By evening the drunkenness and revelry had begun afresh and the shrieks of young girls carried across the water to the pilgrims huddled in their camp. Someone had given the idiot whiskey mixed with sarsaparilla and this thing which could little more than walk had commenced to dance before the fire with loping simian steps, moving with great gravity and smacking its loose wet lips.

At dawn the black walked out to the landing and stood urinating in the river. The scows lay downstream against the bank with a few inches of sandy water standing in the floorboards. He pulled his robes about him and stepped aboard the thwart and balanced there. The water ran over the boards toward him. He stood looking out. The sun was not up and there was a low skein of mist on the water. Downstream some ducks moved out from the willows. They circled in the eddy water and then flapped out across the open river and rose and circled and bent their way upstream. In the floor of the scow was a small coin. Perhaps once lodged under the tongue of some passenger. He bent to fetch it. He stood up and wiped the grit from the piece and held it up and as he did so a long cane arrow passed through his upper abdomen and flew on and fell far out in the river and sank and backed to the surface again and began to turn and to drift downstream.

He faced around, his robes sustained about him. He was holding his wound and with his other hand he ravaged among his clothes for the weapons that were not there and were not there. A second arrow passed him on the left and two more struck and lodged fast in his chest and in his groin. They were a full four feet in length and they lofted slightly with his movements like ceremonial wands and he seized his thigh where the dark arterial blood was spurting along the shaft and took a step toward the shore and fell sideways into the river.

The water was shallow and he was moving weakly to regain his feet when the first of the Yumas leaped aboard the scow. Completely naked, his hair dyed orange, his face painted black with a crimson line dividing it from widow's peak to chin. He stamped his feet twice on the boards and flared his arms like some wild thaumaturge out of an atavistic drama and reached and seized the black by his robes where he lay in the reddening waters and raised him up and stove in his head with his warclub.

They swarmed up the hill toward the fortifications where the Americans lay sleeping and some were mounted and some afoot and all of them armed with bows and clubs and their faces blacked or pale with fard and their hair bound up in clay. The first quarters they entered were Lincoln's. When they emerged a few minutes later one of them carried the doctor's dripping head by the hair and others were dragging behind them the doctor's dog, bound at the muzzle, jerking and bucking across the dry clay of the concourse. They entered a wickiup of willow-poles and canvas and slew Gunn and Wilson and Henderson Smith each in turn as they reared up drunkenly and they moved on among the rude half walls in total silence glistening with paint and grease and blood among the bands of light where the risen sun now touched the higher ground.

When they entered Glanton's chamber he lurched upright and glared wildly about him. The small clay room he occupied was entirely filled with a brass bed he'd appropriated from some migrating family and he sat in it like a debauched feudal baron while his weapons hung in a rich array from the finials. Caballo en Pelo mounted into the actual bed with him and stood there while one of the attending tribunal handed him at his right side a common axe the hickory helve of which was carved with pagan motifs and tasseled with the feathers of predatory birds. Glanton spat.

Hack away you mean red nigger, he said, and the old man

raised the axe and split the head of John Joel Glanton to the thrapple.

When they entered the judge's quarters they found the idiot and a girl of perhaps twelve years cowering naked in the floor. Behind them also naked stood the judge. He was holding leveled at them the bronze barrel of the howitzer. The wooden truck stood in the floor, the straps pried up and twisted off the pillow-blocks. The judge had the cannon under one arm and he was holding a lighted cigar over the touch-hole. The Yumas fell over one another backward and the judge put the cigar in his mouth and took up his portmanteau and stepped out the door and backed past them and down the embankment. The idiot, who reached just to his waist, stuck close to his side, and together they entered the wood at the base of the hill and disappeared from sight.

THE SAVAGES built a bonfire on the hill and fueled it with the furnishings from the white men's quarters and they raised up Glanton's body and bore it aloft in the manner of a slain champion and hurled it onto the flames. They'd tied his dog to his corpse and it was snatched after in howling suttee to disappear crackling in the rolling greenwood smoke. The doctor's torso was dragged up by the heels and raised and flung onto the pyre and the doctor's mastiff also was committed to the flames. It slid struggling down the far side and the thongs with which it was tied must have burnt in two for it began to crawl charred and blind and smoking from the fire and was flung back with a shovel. The other bodies eight in number were heaped onto the fire where they sizzled and stank and the thick smoke rolled out over the river. The doctor's head had been mounted upon a paling and carried about but at the last it too was thrown onto the blaze. The guns and clothing were divided upon the clay and divided too were the gold and silver out of the hacked and splintered chest that they'd dragged forth. All else was heaped on the flames and while the sun rose and glistened on their gaudy faces they sat upon the ground each with his new goods before him and they watched the fire and smoked their pipes as might some painted troupe of mimefolk recruiting themselves in such a wayplace far from the towns and the rabble hooting at them across the smoking footlamps, contemplating towns to come and the poor fanfare of trumpet and drum and the rude boards upon which their destinies were inscribed for these people were no less bound and indentured and they watched like the prefiguration of their own ends the carbonized skulls of their enemies incandescing before them bright as blood among the coals.

XX

TOADVINE AND the kid fought a running engagement upriver
through the shore bracken with arrows clattering through the
cane all about them. They came out of the willow brakes and
climbed the dunes and descended the far side and reappeared
again, two dark figures anguishing upon the sands, now trotting,
now stooping, the report of the pistol flat and dead in the open
country. The Yumas who crested out on the dunes were four
in number and they did not follow but rather fixed them upon
the terrain to which they had committed themselves and then
turned back.

The kid carried an arrow in his leg and it was butted against
the bone. He stopped and sat and broke off the shaft a few
inches from the wound and then he got up again and they went

on. At the crest of the rise they stopped and looked back. The Yumas had already left the dunes and they could see the smoke rising darkly along the river bluff. To the west the country was all rolling sandhills where a man might lie in hiding but there was no place the sun would not find him and only the wind could hide his tracks.

Can you walk? said Toadvine.

I aint got no choice.

How much water you got?

Not much.

What do you want to do?

I dont know.

We could ease back to the river and lay up, said Toadvine.

Till what?

He looked toward the fort again and he looked at the broken shaft in the kid's leg and the welling blood. You want to try and pull that?

No.

What do you want to do?

Go on.

They mended their course and picked up the trail the wagon parties followed and they went on through the long forenoon and the day and the evening of the day. By dark their water was gone and they labored on beneath the slow wheel of stars and slept shivering among the dunes and rose in the dawn and went on again. The kid's leg had stiffened and he hobbled after with a section of wagontongue for a crutch and twice he told Toadvine to go on but he would not. Before noon the aborigines appeared.

They watched them assemble upon the trembling drop of the eastern horizon like baleful marionettes. They were without horses and they seemed to be moving at a trot and within the hour they were lofting arrows upon the refugees.

They went on, the kid with his pistol drawn, stepping and ducking the shafts where they fell out of the sun, the lengths of them glistening against the pale sky and foreshortening in a reedy flutter and then suddenly quivering dead in the ground. They snapped off the shafts against their being used again and they labored on sideways over the sand like crabs until the arrows coming so thick and close they made a stand. The kid dropped onto his elbows and cocked and leveled the revolver. The Yumas were over a hundred yards out and they set up a cry and Toadvine dropped to one knee alongside the kid. The pistol bucked and the gray smoke hung motionless in the air and one of the savages went down like a player through a trap. The kid had cocked the pistol again but Toadvine put his hand over the barrel and the kid looked up at him and lowered the hammer and then sat and reloaded the empty chamber and pushed himself up and recovered his crutch and they went on. Behind them on the plain they could hear the thin clamor of the aborigines as they clustered about the one he'd shot.

That painted horde dogged their steps the day long. They were twenty-four hours without water and the barren mural of sand and sky was beginning to shimmer and swim and the periodic arrows sprang aslant from the sands about them like the tufted stalks of mutant desert growths propagating angrily into the dry desert air. They did not stop. When they reached the wells at Alamo Mucho the sun was low before them and there was a figure seated at the rim of the basin. This figure rose and stood warped in the quaking lens of that world and held out one hand, in welcome or warning they had no way to know. They shielded their eyes and limped on and the figure at the well called out to them. It was the expriest Tobin.

He was alone and unarmed. How many are ye? he said.

What you see, said Toadvine.

All the rest gone under? Glanton? The judge?

They didnt answer. They slid down to the floor of the well where there stood a few inches of water and they knelt and drank.

The pit in which the well was sunk was perhaps a dozen feet

in diameter and they posted themselves about the inner slope of this salient and watched while the indians fanned out over the plain, moving past in the distance at a slow lope. Assembled in small groups at cardinal points out there they began to launch their arrows upon the defenders and the Americans called out the arrival of the incoming shafts like artillery officers, lying there on the exposed bank and watching out across the pit toward the assailants in that quarter, their hands clawed at either side of them and their legs cocked, rigid as cats. The kid held his fire altogether and soon those savages on the western shore who were more favored by the light began to move in.

About the well were hillocks of sand from old diggings and the Yumas may have meant to try to reach them. The kid left his post and moved to the west rim of the excavation and began to fire on them where they stood or squatted on their haunches like wolves out there on the shimmering pan. The expriest knelt by the kid's side and watched behind them and held his hat between the sun and the foresight of the kid's pistol and the kid steadied the pistol in both hands on the edge of the works and let off the rounds. At the second fire one of the savages fell over and lay without moving. The next shot spun another one around and he sat down and then rose and took a few steps and sat down again. The expriest whispered encouragement at his elbow and the kid thumbed back the hammer and the expriest adjusted the hat to shade gunsight and sight eye with the one shadow and the kid fired again. He'd drawn his sight upon the wounded man sitting on the pan and his shot stretched him out dead. The expriest gave a low whistle.

Aye, you're a cool one, he whispered. But it's cunning work all the same and wouldnt it take the heart out of ye.

The Yumas seemed immobilized by these misfortunes and the kid cocked the pistol and shot down another of their number before they began to collect themselves and to move back, taking their dead with them, lofting a flurry of arrows and howling out bloodoaths in their stoneage tongue or invocations to whatever gods of war or fortune they'd the ear of and retreating upon the pan until they were very small indeed.

The kid shouldered up his flask and shotpouch and slid down the pitch to the floor of the well where he dug a second small basin with the old shovel there and in the water that seeped in he washed the bores of the cylinder and washed the barrel and ran pieces of his shirt through the bore with a stick until they came clean. Then he reassembled the pistol, tapping the barrel pin until the cylinder was snug and laying the piece in the warm sand to dry.

Toadvine had made his way around the excavation until he reached the expriest and they lay watching the retreat of the savages through the heat shimmering off the pan in the late sunlight.

He's a deadeye aint he?

Tobin nodded. He looked down the pit to where the kid sat loading the pistol, turning the powderfilled chambers and measuring them with his eye, seating the balls with the sprues down.

How do you stand by way of ammunition?

Poorly. We got a few rounds, not many.

The expriest nodded. Evening was coming on and in the red land to the west the Yumas were gathering in silhouette before the sun.

All night their watchfires burned on the dark circlet of the world and the kid unpinned the barrel from the pistol and using it for a spyglass he went around the warm sand selvage of the well and studied the separate fires for movement. There is hardly in the world a waste so barren but some creature will not cry out at night, yet here one was and they listened to their breathing in the dark and the cold and they listened to the systole of the rubymeated hearts that hung within them. When day broke the fires had burned out and slender terminals of smoke stood from the plain at three separate points of the compass and the enemy had gone. Crossing the dry pan toward them from the east was a large figure attended by a smaller. Toadvine and the expriest watched.

What do you make it to be?

The expriest shook his head.

Toadvine cupped his hand and whistled sharply down at the kid. He sat up with the pistol. He clambered up the slope with his stiff leg. The three of them lay watching.

It was the judge and the imbecile. They were both of them naked and they neared through the desert dawn like beings of a mode little more than tangential to the world at large, their figures now quick with clarity and now fugitive in the strangeness of that same light. Like things whose very portent renders them ambiguous. Like things so charged with meaning that their forms are dimmed. The three at the well watched mutely this transit out of the breaking day and even though there was no longer any question as to what it was that approached yet none would name it. They lumbered on, the judge a pale pink beneath his talc of dust like something newly born, the imbecile much the darker, lurching together across the pan at the very extremes of exile like some scurrilous king stripped of his vestiture and driven together with his fool into the wilderness to die.

Those who travel in desert places do indeed meet with creatures surpassing all description. The watchers at the well rose the better to witness these arrivals. The imbecile was fairly loping along to keep the pace. The judge on his head wore a wig of dried river mud from which protruded bits of straw and grass and tied upon the imbecile's head was a rag of fur with the blackened blood side out. The judge carried in one hand a small canvas satchel and he was bedraped with meat like some medieval penitent. He hove up at the diggings and nodded them a good morning and he and the idiot slid down the bank and knelt and began to drink.

Even the idiot, who must be fed by hand. He knelt beside the judge and sucked noisily at the mineral water and raised his dark larval eyes to the three men crouched above him at the rim of the pit and then bent and drank again.

The judge threw off his bandoliers of sunblacked meat and his skin beneath was strangely mottled pink and white in the shapes of them. He set by the little mud cap and laved water over his burnt and peeling skull and over his face and he drank again and sat in the sand. He looked up at his old companions. His mouth was cracked and his tongue swollen.

Louis, he said. What will you take for that hat?

Toadvine spat. It aint for sale, he said.

Everything's for sale, said the judge. What will you take?

Toadvine looked uneasily at the expriest. He looked down into the well. Got to have my hat, he said.

How much?

Toadvine gestured with his chin at the strings of meat. I reckon you want to trade some of that rug for it.

Not at all, said the judge. Such as is here is for everybody. How much for the hat?

What'll you give? said Toadvine.

The judge studied him. I'll give one hundred dollars, he said.

No one spoke. The idiot crouched on its haunches seemed also to be awaiting the outcome of this exchange. Toadvine took off the hat and looked at it. His lank black hair clove to the sides of his head. It wont fit ye, he said.

The judge quoted him some term in latin. He smiled. Not your concern, he said.

Toadvine put the hat on and adjusted it. I reckon that's what you got in that there satchel, he said.

You reckon correctly, said the judge.

Toadvine looked off toward the sun.

I'll make it a hundred and a quarter and wont ask you where you got it, said the judge.

Let's see your color.

The judge unclasped the satchel and tipped and emptied it out on the sand. It contained a knife and perhaps a half a bucketful of gold coins of every value. The judge pushed the knife to one side and spread the coins with the palm of his hand and looked up.

Toadvine took off the hat. He made his way down the slope. He and the judge squatted on either side of the judge's trove and the judge put forward the coins agreed upon, advancing them with the back of his hand forward like a croupier. Toadvine handed up the hat and gathered the coins and the judge took the knife and slit the band of the hat at the rear and cut through the brim and opened up the crown and then set the hat on his head and looked up at Tobin and the kid.

Come down, he said. Come down and share this meat.

They didnt move. Toadvine already had a piece of it in both hands and was tugging at it with his teeth. It was cool in the well and the morning sun fell only upon the upper rim. The judge scooped the remaining coins back into the satchel and stood it aside and bent to drink again. The imbecile had been watching its reflection in the pool and it watched the judge drink and it watched the water calm itself once more. The judge wiped his mouth and looked at the figures above him.

How are you fixed for weapons? he said.

The kid had set one foot over the edge of the pit and now he drew it back. Tobin did not move. He was watching the judge.

We've just the one pistol, Holden.

We? said the judge.

The lad here.

The kid had risen to his feet again. The expriest stood by him.

The judge in the floor of the well likewise rose and he adjusted his hat and gripped the valise under his arm like some immense and naked barrister whom the country had crazed.

Weigh your counsel, Priest, he said. We are all here together. Yonder sun is like the eye of God and we will cook impartially upon this great siliceous griddle I do assure you.

I'm no priest and I've no counsel, said Tobin. The lad is a free agent.

The judge smiled. Quite so, he said. He looked at Toadvine and he smiled up at the expriest again. What then? he said. Are we to drink at these holes turn about like rival bands of apes?

The expriest looked at the kid. They stood facing the sun. He squatted, the better to address the judge below.

Do you think that there is a registry where you can file on the wells of the desert?

Ah Priest, you'd know those offices more readily than I. I've no claim here. I've told you before, I'm a simple man. You know you're welcome to come down here and to drink and to fill your flask.

Tobin didnt move.

Let me have the canteen, said the kid. He'd taken the pistol from his belt and he handed it to the expriest and took the leather bottle and descended the bank.

The judge followed him with his eyes. The kid circled the floor of the well, no part of which was altogether beyond the judge's reach, and he knelt opposite the imbecile and pulled the stopper from the flask and submerged the flask in the basin. He and the imbecile watched the water run in at the neck of the flask and they watched it bubble and they watched it cease. The kid stoppered the flask and leaned and drank from the pool and then he sat back and looked at Toadvine.

Are you goin with us?

Toadvine looked at the judge. I dont know, he said. I'm subject to arrest. They'll arrest me in California.

Arrest ye?

Toadvine didnt answer. He was sitting in the sand and he made a tripod of three fingers and stuck them in the sand before him and then he lifted and turned them and poked them in again so that there were six holes in the form of a star or a hexagon and then he rubbed them out again. He looked up.

You wouldnt think that a man would run plumb out of country out here, would ye?

The kid rose and slung the flask by its strap over his shoulder. His trouserleg was black with blood and the bloody stump of the shaft jutted from his thigh like a peg for hanging implements upon. He spat and wiped his mouth with the back of his hand and he looked at Toadvine. It aint country you've run out of, he said. Then he made his way across the sink and up the bank. The judge followed him with his eyes and when the kid reached the sunlight at the top he turned and looked back and the judge was holding open the satchel between his naked thighs.

Five hundred dollars, he said. Powder and ball included.

The expriest was at the kid's side. Do him, he hissed.

The kid took the pistol but the expriest clung to his arm whispering and when the kid pulled away he spoke aloud, such was his fear.

You'll get no second chance lad. Do it He is naked. He is unarmed. God's blood, do you think you'll best him any other way? Do it, lad. Do it for the love of God. Do it or I swear your life is forfeit.

The judge smiled, he tapped his temple. The priest, he said. The priest has been too long in the sun. Seven-fifty and that's my best offer. It's a seller's market.

The kid put the pistol in his belt. Then with the expriest at his elbow importunate he circled the crater and they set out west across the pan. Toadvine climbed up and watched them. After a while there was nothing to see.

That day their way took them upon a vast mosaic pavement cobbled up from tiny blocks of jasper, carnelian, agate. A thousand acres wide where the wind sang in the groutless interstices. Traversing this ground toward the east riding one horse and leading another came David Brown. The horse he led was saddled and bridled and the kid stood with his thumbs in his belt and watched while he rode up and looked down at his old companions.

We heard you were in the juzgado, said Tobin.

I was, said Brown. I aint now. His eyes catalogued them in every part. He looked at the piece of arrowshaft protruding from the kid's leg and he looked into the expriest's eyes. Where's your outfits? he said.

You're lookin at them.

You fall out with Glanton?

Glanton's dead.

Brown spat a dry white spot in that vast and broken plateland. He had a small stone in his mouth against the thirst and he shifted it with his jaw and looked at them. The Yumas, he said.

Aye, said the expriest.

All rubbed out?

Toadvine and the judge are at the well back yonder.

The judge, said Brown.

The horses stared bleakly at the crazed stone floor whereon they stood.

The rest gone under? Smith? Dorsey? The nigger?

All, said Tobin.

Brown looked east across the desert. How far to the well?

We left about an hour past daybreak.

Is he armed?

He is not.

He studied their faces. The priest dont lie, he said.

No one spoke. He sat fingering the scapular of dried ears. Then he turned the horse and rode on, leading the riderless animal behind. He rode watching back at them. Then he stopped again.

Did you see him dead? he called. Glanton?

I did, called the expriest. For he had so.

He rode on, turned slightly in the saddle, the rifle on his knee. He kept watch behind him on those pilgrims and they on him. When he was well diminished on the pan they turned and went on.

BY NOON the day following they had begun to come again upon abandoned gear from the caravans, cast shoes and pieces of harness and bones and the dried carcasses of mules with the alparejas still buckled about. They trod the faint arc of an ancient lake shore where broken shells lay like bits of pottery frail and ribbed among the sands and in the early evening they descended among a series of dunes and spoilbanks to Carrizo Creek, a seep that welled out of the stones and ran off down the desert and vanished again. Thousands of sheep had perished here and the travelers made their way among the yellowed bones and carcasses with their rags of tattered wool and they knelt among bones to drink. When the kid raised his dripping head from the water a rifleball dished his reflection from the pool and the echoes of the shot clattered about the bonestrewn slope and clanged away in the desert and died.

He spun on his belly and clambered sideways, scanning the skyline. He saw the horses first, standing nose to nose in a notch among the dunes to the south. He saw the judge clad in the gusseted clothing of his recent associates. He was holding the mouth of the upright rifle in his fist and pouring powder from a flask down the bore. The imbecile, naked save for a hat, squatted in the sands at his feet.

The kid scuttled to a low place in the ground and lay flat with the pistol in his fist and the creek trickling past his elbow. He turned to look for the expriest but he could not find him. He could see through the lattice of bones the judge and his charge on the hill in the sun and he raised the pistol and rested it in the saddle of a rancid pelvis and fired. He saw the sand jump on the slope behind the judge and the judge leveled the rifle and fired and the rifleball whacked through the bones and the shots rolled away over the dunelands.

The kid lay with his heart hammering in the sand. He thumbed back the hammer again and raised his head. The idiot sat as before and the judge was trudging sedately along the skyline looking over the windrowed bones below him for an advantage. The kid began to move again. He moved into the creek on his belly and lay drinking, holding up the pistol and the powderflask and sucking at the water. Then he moved out the far side and down a trampled corridor through the sands where wolves had gone to and fro. Off to his left he thought he heard the expriest hiss at him and he could hear the creek and he lay listening. He set the hammer at halfcock and rotated the cylinder and recharged the empty chamber and capped the piece and raised up to look. The shallow ridge along which the judge had advanced was empty and the two horses were coming toward him across the sand to the south. He cocked the pistol and lay watching. They approached freely over the barren pitch, nudging the air with their heads, their tails whisking. Then he saw the idiot shambling along behind them like some dim neolithic herdsman. To his right he saw the judge appear from the dunes and reconnoitre and drop from sight again. The horses continued on and there was a scrabbling behind him and when the kid turned the expriest was in the corridor hissing at him.

Shoot him, he called.

The kid spun about to look for the judge but the expriest called again in his hoarse whisper.

The fool. Shoot the fool.

He raised his pistol. The horses stepped one and the next through a break in the yellowed palings and the imbecile shambled after and disappeared. He looked back at Tobin but the expriest was gone. He moved along the corridor until he came to the creek again, already slightly roiled from the drinking horses above him. His leg had begun to bleed and he lay soaking it in the cold water and he drank and palmed water over the back of his neck. The marblings of blood that swung from his thigh were like thin red leeches in the current. He looked at the sun.

Hello called the judge, his voice off to the west. As if there were new riders to the creek and he addressed them.

The kid lay listening. There were no new riders. After a while the judge called out again. Come out, he called. There's plenty of water for everybody.

The kid had swung the powderflask around to his back to keep it out of the creek and he held the pistol up and waited. Upstream the horses had stopped drinking. Then they started drinking again.

When he moved out on the far side of the creek he came upon the hand and foot tracks left by the expriest among the prints of cats and foxes and the little desert pigs. He entered a clearing in that senseless midden and sat listening. His leather clothes were heavy and stiff with water and his leg was throbbing. A horse's head came up streaming water at the muzzle a hundred feet away over the bones and dropped from sight again. When the judge called out his voice was in a new place. He called out for them to be friends. The kid watched a small caravan of ants bearing off among the arches of sheepribs. In the watching his eyes met the eyes of a small viper coiled under a flap of hide. He wiped his mouth and began to move again. In a culdesac the tracks of the expriest terminated and came back. He lay listening. It was hours till dark. After a while he heard the idiot slobbering somewhere among the bones.

He heard the wind coming in off the desert and he heard his own breathing. When he raised his head to look out he saw the expriest stumbling among the bones and holding aloft a cross he'd fashioned out of the shins of a ram and he'd lashed them together with strips of hide and he was holding the thing before him like some mad dowser in the bleak of desert and calling out in a tongue both alien and extinct.

The kid stood up, the revolver in both hands. He wheeled. He saw the judge and the judge was in another quarter altogether and he had the rifle already at his shoulder. When he fired Tobin turned around facing the way he'd come and sat down still holding the cross. The judge put down the rifle and took up another. The kid tried to steady the barrel of the pistol and he let off the shot and then dropped to the sand. The heavy ball of the rifle passed overhead like an asteroid and chattered and chopped among the bones fanned over the rise of ground beyond. He raised to his knees and looked for the judge but the judge was not there. He reloaded the empty chamber and began to move again on his elbows toward the spot where he'd seen the expriest fall, taking his bearings by the sun and pausing from time to time to listen. The ground was trampled with the tracks of predators come in from the plains for the carrion and the wind carrying through the breaks bore with it a sour reek like the stink of a rancid dishclout and there was no sound except the wind anywhere at all.

He found Tobin kneeling in the creek bathing his wound with a piece of linen torn from his shirt. The ball had passed completely through his neck. It had narrowly missed the carotid artery yet he could not make the blood to stop. He looked at the kid crouched among the skulls and upturned ribtines.

You've got to kill the horses, he said. You've no other chance out of here. He'll ride you down.

We could take the horses.

Dont be a fool lad. What other bait has he?

We can get out as soon as it comes dark.

Do you think there'll be no day again?

The kid watched him. Will it not stop? he said.

It will not.

What do you think?

I've got to stop it.

The blood was running between his fingers.

Where is the judge? said the kid.

Where indeed.

If I kill him we can take the horses.

You'll not kill him. Dont be a fool. Shoot the horses.

The kid looked off up the shallow sandy creek.

Go on lad.

He looked at the expriest and at the slow gouts of blood dropping in the water like roseblooms how they swelled and were made pale. He moved away up the creek.

When he came to where the horses had entered the water they were gone. The sand on the side where they'd gone out was still wet. He pushed the revolver along before him, moving on the heels of his hands. For all his caution he found the idiot watching him before ever he saw it.

It was sitting motionless in a bower of bones with the broken sunlight stenciled over its vacant face and it was watching like a wild thing in a wood. The kid looked at it and then he shoved on past in the tracks of the horses. The loose neck swiveled slowly and the dull jaw drooled. When he looked back it was still watching. Its wrists were lying in the sand before it and although there was no expression to its face yet it seemed a creature beset with a great woe.

When he saw the horses they were standing on a rise of ground above the creek and looking toward the west. He lay quietly and studied the terrain. Then he moved out along the edge of the wash and sat with his back to the bone salients and cocked the pistol and took a rest with his elbows on his knees.

The horses had seen him come out of the wash and they were watching him. When they heard the pistol cock they pricked their ears and began to walk toward him across the sand. He shot the forward horse in the chest and it fell over and lay breathing heavily with the blood running out of its nose. The other one stopped and stood uncertainly and he cocked the pistol and shot it as it turned. It began to trot among the dunes and he shot it again and its front legs buckled and it pitched forward and rolled onto its side. It raised its head once and then it lay still.

He sat listening. Nothing moved. The first horse lay as it had fallen, the sand about its head darkening with blood. The smoke drifted away down the draw and thinned and vanished. He moved back down the wash and crouched under the ribs of a dead mule and recharged the pistol and then moved on toward the creek again. He did not go back the way he'd come and he did not see the imbecile again. When he came to the creek he drank and bathed his leg and lay listening as before.

Throw that gun out now, said the judge.

He froze.

The voice was not fifty feet away.

I know what you've done. The priest put you up to it and I'll take that as a mitigation in the act and the intent. Which I would any man in his wrongdoing. But there's the question of property. You bring me the pistol now.

The kid lay without moving. He heard the judge wade the creek upstream. He lay counting slowly under his breath. When the roiled water reached him he stopped counting and let go on the current a dry twist of grass and tolled it away downstream. At that same count it was scarcely out of sight among the bones. He moved out of the water and looked at the sun and began to make his way back to where he'd left Tobin.

He found the expriest's tracks still wet where he'd left the creek and the way of his progress marked with blood. He followed through the sand until he came to that place where the expriest had circled upon himself and lay hissing at him from his place of cover.

Did you do for them lad?

He raised his hand.

Aye. I heard the shots all three. The fool as well, aye lad?

He didnt answer.

Good lad, hissed the expriest. He'd bound up his neck in his shirt and he was naked to the waist and he squatted among those rancid pickets and eyed the sun. The shadows were long on the dunes and in the shadow the bones of the beasts that had died there lay skewed in a curious congress of garbled armatures upon the sands. They'd close to two hours till dark and the expriest said so. They lay under the boardlike hide of a dead ox and listened to the judge calling to them. He called out points of jurisprudence, he cited cases. He expounded upon those laws pertaining to property rights in beasts mansuete and he quoted from cases of attainder insofar as he reckoned them germane to the corruption of blood in the prior and felonious owners of the horses now dead among the bones. Then he spoke of other things. The expriest leaned to the kid. Dont listen, he said.

I aint listenin.

Stop your ears.

Stop yours.

The priest cupped his hands over his ears and looked at the kid. His eyes were bright from the bloodloss and he was possessed of a great earnestness. Do it, he whispered. Do you think he speaks to me?

The kid turned away. He marked the sun squatting at the western rim of the waste and they spoke no more until it was dark and then they rose and made their way out.

They stole up from the basin and set off across the shallow dunes and they looked a last time back at the valley where flickering in the wind at the edge of the revetment stood the judge's nightfire for all to see. They did not speculate as to what it fed upon for fuel and they were well advanced on the desert before the moon rose.

There were wolves and jackals in that region and they cried all the forepart of the night until the moon came up and then they ceased as if surprised by its rising. Then they began again. The pilgrims were weak from their wounds. They lay down to rest but never for long and never without scanning the skyline to the east for any figure intruded upon it and they shivered in the barren desert wind coming out of whatever godless quadrant cold and sterile and bearing news of nothing at all. When day came they made their way to a slight rise on that endless flat and squatted in the loose shale and watched the sun's rising. It was cold and the expriest in his rags and his collar of blood hugged himself. On this small promontory they slept and when they woke it was midmorning and the sun well advanced. They sat up and looked out. Coming toward them over the plain in the middle distance they could see the figure of the judge, the figure of the fool.

XXI

Desert castaways – The backtrack – A hideout –
The wind takes a side – The judge returns – An address –
Los Diegueños – San Felipe – Hospitality of the savages –
Into the mountains – Grizzlies – San Diego – The sea.

THE KID LOOKED AT Tobin but the expriest sat without expression. He was drawn and wretchedlooking and the approaching travelers seemed to evoke in him no recognition. He raised his head slightly and he spoke without looking at the kid. Go on, he said. Save yourself.

The kid took the water bottle from the shales and unstoppered it and drank and handed it across. The expriest drank and they sat watching and then they rose and turned and set out again.

They were much reduced by their wounds and their hunger and they made a poor show as they staggered onward. By noon their water was gone and they sat studying the barrenness about. A wind blew down from the north. Their mouths were dry. The desert upon which they were entrained was desert absolute and it was devoid of feature altogether and there was nothing to mark their progress upon it. The earth fell away on every side equally in its arcature and by these limits were they circumscribed and of them were they locus. They rose and went on. The sky was luminous. There was no trace to follow other than the bits of cast-off left by travelers even to the bones of men drifted out of their graves in the scalloped sands. In the afternoon the terrain began to rise before them and at the crest of a shallow esker they stood and looked back to see the judge much as before some two miles distant on the plain. They went on.

The approach to any watering place in that desert was marked by the carcasses of perished animals in increasing number and so it was now, as if the wells were ringed about by some hazard lethal to creatures. The travelers looked back. The judge was out of sight beyond the rise. Before them lay the whitened boards of a wagon and further on the shapes of mule and ox with the hide scoured bald as canvas by the constant abrasion of the sand.

The kid stood studying this place and then he backtracked some hundred yards and stood looking down at his shallow footprints in the sand. He looked upon the drifted slope of the esker which they had descended and he knelt and held his hand against the ground and he listened to the faint silica hiss of the wind.

When he lifted his hand there was a thin ridge of sand that had drifted against it and he watched this ridge slowly vanish before him.

The expriest when he returned to him presented a grave appearance. The kid knelt and studied him where he sat.

We got to hide, he said.

Hide?

Yes.

Where do you aim to hide?

Here. We'll hide here.

You cant hide, lad.

We can hide.

You think he cant follow your track?

The wind's taking it. It's gone from the slope yonder.

Gone?

Ever trace.

The expriest shook his head.

Come on. We got to get goin.

You cant hide.

Get up.

The expriest shook his head. Ah lad, he said.

Get up, said the kid.

Go on, go on. He waved his hand.

The kid spoke to him. He aint nothin. You told me so your-self. Men are made of the dust of the earth. You said it was no pair . . . pair . . .

Parable.

No parable. That it was a naked fact and the judge was a man like all men.

Face him down then, said the expriest. Face him down if he is so.

And him with a rifle and me with a pistol. Him with two rifles. Get up from there.

Tobin rose. He stood unsteadily, he leaned against the kid. They set out, veering off from the drifted track and down past the wagon.

They passed the first of the racks of bones and went on to where a pair of mules lay dead in the traces and here the kid knelt with a piece of board and began to scoop them a shelter, watching the skyline to the east as he worked. Then they lay prone in the lee of those sour bones like sated scavengers and awaited the arrival of the judge and the passing of the judge if he would so pass.

They'd not long to wait. He appeared upon the rise and paused momentarily before starting down, he and his drooling manciple. The ground before him was drifted and rolling and although it could be fairly reconnoitred from the rise the judge did not scan the country nor did he seem to miss the fugitives from his purview. He descended the ridge and started across the flats, the idiot before him on a leather lead. He carried the two rifles that had belonged to Brown and he wore a pair of canteens crossed upon his chest and he carried a powderhorn and flask and his portmanteau and a canvas rucksack that must have belonged to Brown also. More strangely he carried a parasol made from rotted scraps of hide stretched over a framework of rib bones bound with strips of tug. The handle had been the foreleg of some creature and the judge approaching was clothed in little more than confetti so rent was his costume to accommodate his figure. Bearing before him that morbid umbrella with the idiot in its rawhide collar pulling at the lead he seemed some degenerate entrepreneur fleeing from a medicine show and the outrage of the citizens who'd sacked it.

They advanced across the flats and the kid on his belly in the sand wallow watched them through the ribs of the dead mules. He could see his own tracks and Tobin's coming across the sand, dim and rounded but tracks for that, and he watched the judge and he watched the tracks and he listened to the sand moving on the desert floor. The judge was perhaps a hundred yards out when he stopped and surveyed the ground. The idiot squatted on all fours and leaned into the lead like some naked species of lemur. It swung its head and sniffed at the air, as if it were being used for tracking. It had lost its hat, or perhaps the judge had replevined it, for he now wore a rough and curious pair of pampooties cut from a piece of hide and strapped to the soles of his feet with wrappings of hemp salvaged from some desert wreck. The imbecile lunged in its collar and croaked, its forearms dangling at its chest. When they passed the wagon and continued on the kid knew they were beyond the point where he and Tobin had turned off from the trace. He looked at the tracks. Faint shapes that backed across the sands and vanished. The expriest at his side seized his arm and hissed and gestured toward the passing judge and the wind rattled the scraps of hide at the carcass and the judge and the idiot passed on across the sands and disappeared from sight.

They lay without speaking. The expriest raised himself slightly and looked out and he looked at the kid. The kid lowered the hammer of the pistol.

Ye'll get no such a chance as that again.

The kid put the pistol in his belt and rose onto his knees and looked out.

And what now?

The kid didnt answer.

He'll be waiting at the next well.

Let him wait.

We could go back to the creek.

And do what.

Wait for a party to come through.

Through from where? There aint no ferry.

There's game comes to the creek.

Tobin was looking out through the bones and hide. When the kid didnt answer he looked up. We could go there, he said.

I got four rounds, the kid said.

He rose and looked out across the scavenged ground and the expriest rose and looked with him. What they saw was the judge returning.

The kid swore and dropped to his belly. The expriest crouched. They pushed down into the wallow and with their chins in the sand like lizards they watched the judge traverse again the grounds before them.

With his leashed fool and his equipage and the parasol dipping in the wind like a great black flower he passed among the wreckage until he was again upon the slope of the sand esker. At the crest he turned and the imbecile squatted at his knees and the judge lowered the parasol before him and addressed the countryside about.

The priest has led you to this, boy. I know you would not hide. I know too that you've not the heart of a common assassin.

I've passed before your gunsights twice this hour and will pass a third time. Why not show yourself?

No assassin, called the judge. And no partisan either. There's a flawed place in the fabric of your heart. Do you think I could not know? You alone were mutinous. You alone reserved in your soul some corner of clemency for the heathen.

The imbecile stood and raised its hands to its face and yammered weirdly and sat again.

You think I've killed Brown and Toadvine? They are alive as you and me. They are alive and in possession of the fruits of their election. Do you understand? Ask the priest. The priest knows. The priest does not lie.

The judge raised the parasol and adjusted his parcels. Perhaps, he called, perhaps you have seen this place in a dream. That you would die here. Then he descended the esker and passed once more across the boneyard led by the tethered fool until the two were shimmering and insubstantial in the waves of heat and then they were gone altogether.

THEY WOULD HAVE died if the indians had not found them. All the early part of the night they'd kept Sirius at their left on the southwest horizon and Cetus out there fording the void and Orion and Betelgeuse turning overhead and they had slept curled and shivering in the auburn of the plains and woke to find the heavens all changed and the stars by which they'd traveled not to be found, as if their sleep had encompassed whole seasons. In the auburn dawn they saw the halfnaked savages crouched or standing all in a row along a rise to the north. They got up and went on, their shadows so long and so narrow raising with mock stealth each thin articulated leg. The mountains to the west were whited out against the daybreak. The aborigines moved along the sand ridge. After a while the expriest sat down and the kid stood over him with the pistol and the savages came down from the dunes and approached by starts and checks across the plain like painted sprites.

They were Diegueños. They were armed with short bows and they drew about the travelers and knelt and gave them water out of a gourd. They'd seen such pilgrims before and with sufferings more terrible. They eked a desperate living from that land and they knew that nothing excepting some savage pursuit could drive men to such plight and they watched each day for that thing to gather itself out of its terrible incubation in the house of the sun and muster along the edge of the eastern world and whether it be armies or plague or pestilence or something altogether unspeakable they waited with a strange equanimity.

They led the refugees into their camp at San Felipe, a collection of crude huts made from reeds and housing a population of filthy and beggarly creatures dressed largely in the cotton shirts of the argonauts who'd passed there, shirts and nothing more. They fetched them a stew of lizards and pocket-mice hot in clay bowls and a sort of piñole made from dried and pounded grasshoppers and they crouched about and watched them with great solemnity as they ate.

One reached and touched the grips of the pistol in the kid's belt and drew back again. Pistola, he said.

The kid ate.

The savages nodded.

Quiero mirar su pistola, the man said.

The kid didnt answer. When the man reached for the pistol he intercepted his hand and put it from him. When he turned loose the man reached again and the kid pushed his hand away again.

The man grinned. He reached a third time. The kid set the bowl between his legs and drew the pistol and cocked it and put the muzzle against the man's forehead.

They sat quite still. The others watched. After a while the kid lowered the pistol and let down the hammer and put it in his belt and picked up the bowl and commenced eating again. The man gestured toward the pistol and spoke to his friends and they nodded and then they sat as before.

Qué pasó con ustedes.

The kid watched the man over the rim of the bowl with his dark and hollow eyes.

The indian looked at the expriest.

Qué pasó con ustedes.

The expriest in his black and crusted cravat turned his whole torso to look at the man who'd spoken. He looked at the kid. He'd been eating with his fingers and he licked them and wiped them on the filthy leg of his trousers.

Las Yumas, he said.

They sucked in air and clucked their tongues.

Son muy malos, said the speaker.

Claro.

No tiene compañeros?

The kid and the expriest eyed each other.

Sí, said the kid. Muchos. He waved his hand to the east. Llegaran. Muchos compañeros.

The indians received this news without expression. A woman brought more of the piñole but they had been without food too long to have appetites and they waved her away.

In the afternoon they bathed in the creek and slept on the ground. When they woke they were being watched by a group of naked children and a few dogs. When they went up through the camp they saw the indians sitting along a ledge of rock watching tirelessly the land to the east for whatever might come out of it. No one spoke to them of the judge and they did not ask. The dogs and children followed them out of the camp and they took the trail up into the low hills to the west where the sun was already going.

They reached Warner's Ranch late the following day and they restored themselves at the hot sulphur springs there. There was no one about. They moved on. The country to the west was rolling and grassy and beyond were mountains running to the coast. They slept that night among dwarf cedars and in the morning the grass was frozen and they could hear the wind in the frozen grass and they could hear the cries of birds that seemed a charm against the sullen shores of the void out of which they had ascended.

All that day they climbed through a highland park forested with joshua trees and rimmed about by bald granite peaks. In the evening flocks of eagles went up through the pass before them and they could see on those grassy benches the great shambling figures of bears like cattle grazing on some upland heath. There were skifts of snow in the lee of the stone ledges and in the night a light snow fell upon them. Reefs of mist were blowing across the slopes when they set out shivering in the dawn and in the new snow they saw the tracks of the bears that had come down to take their wind just before daylight.

That day there was no sun only a paleness in the haze and the country was white with frost and the shrubs were like polar isomers of their own shapes. Wild rams ghosted away up those rocky draws and the wind swirled down cold and gray from the snowy reeks above them, a smoking region of wild vapors blowing down through the gap as if the world up there were all afire. They spoke less and less between them until at last they were silent altogether as is often the way with travelers approaching the end of a journey. They drank from the cold mountain streams and bathed their wounds and they shot a young doe at a spring and ate what they could and smoked thin sheets of the meat to carry with them. Although they saw no more bears they saw sign of their vicinity and they moved off over the slopes a good mile from their meatcamp before they put down for the night. In the morning they crossed a bed of thunderstones clustered on that heath like the ossified eggs of some primal groundbird. They trod the shadowline under the mountains keeping just in the sun for the warmth of it and that afternoon they first saw the sea, far below them, blue and serene under clouds.

The trail went down through the low hills and picked up the wagontrack and they followed where the locked wheels had skidded and the iron tires scarred the rock and the sea down there darkened to black and the sun fell and all the land about went blue and cold. They slept shivering under a wooded boss among owlcries and a scent of juniper while the stars swarmed in the bottomless night.

It was evening of the following day when they entered San Diego. The expriest turned off to find them a doctor but the kid wandered on through the raw mud streets and out past the houses of hide in their rows and across the gravel strand to the beach.

Loose strands of ambercolored kelp lay in a rubbery wrack at the tideline. A dead seal. Beyond the inner bay part of a reef in a thin line like something foundered there on which the sea was teething. He squatted in the sand and watched the sun on the hammered face of the water. Out there island clouds emplaned upon a salmoncolored othersea. Seafowl in silhouette. Downshore the dull surf boomed. There was a horse standing there staring out upon the darkening waters and a young colt that cavorted and trotted off and came back.

He sat watching while the sun dipped hissing in the swells. The horse stood darkly against the sky. The surf boomed in the dark and the sea's black hide heaved in the cobbled starlight and the long pale combers loped out of the night and broke along the beach.

He rose and turned toward the lights of the town. The tidepools bright as smelterpots among the dark rocks where the phosphorescent seacrabs clambered back. Passing through the salt grass he looked back. The horse had not moved. A ship's light winked in the swells. The colt stood against the horse with its head down and the horse was watching, out there past men's knowing, where the stars are drowning and whales ferry their vast souls through the black and seamless sea.

XXII

*Under arrest – The judge pays a call – An arraignment –
Soldier, priest, magistrate – On his own recognizance –
He sees a surgeon – The arrowshaft removed from his leg –
Delirium – He journeys to Los Angeles – A public hanging –
Los ahorcados – Looking for the expriest – Another fool –
The scapular – To Sacramento – A traveler in the west –
He abandons his party – The penitent brothers – The deathcart –
Another massacre – The eldress in the rocks.*

GOING BACK THROUGH the streets past the yellow windowlights and barking dogs he encountered a detachment of soldiers
but they took him for an older man in the dark and passed on.
He entered a tavern and sat in a darkened corner watching the
groups of men at the tables. No one asked him what he wanted
in that place. He seemed to be waiting for someone to come for
him and after a while four soldiers entered and arrested him.
They didnt even ask him his name.

In his cell he began to speak with a strange urgency of things
few men have seen in a lifetime and his jailers said that his mind
had come uncottered by the acts of blood in which he had
participated. One morning he woke to find the judge standing at
his cage, hat in hand, smiling down at him. He was dressed in a

321

suit of gray linen and he wore new polished boots. His coat was unbuttoned and in his waistcoat he carried a watchchain and a stickpin and in his belt a leathercovered clip that held a small silvermounted derringer stocked in rosewood. He looked down the hallway of the crude mud building and donned the hat and smiled again at the prisoner.

Well, he said. How are you?

The kid didnt answer.

They wanted to know from me if you were always crazy, said the judge. They said it was the country. The country turned them out.

Where's Tobin?

I told them that the cretin had been a respected Doctor of Divinity from Harvard College as recently as March of this year. That his wits had stood him as far west as the Aquarius Mountains. It was the ensuing country that carried them off. Together with his clothes.

And Toadvine and Brown. Where are they?

In the desert where you left them. A cruel thing. Your companions in arms. The judge shook his head.

What do they aim to do with me?

I believe it is their intention to hang you.

What did you tell them?

Told them the truth. That you were the person responsible. Not that we have all the details. But they understand that it was you and none other who shaped events along such a calamitous course. Eventuating in the massacre at the ford by the savages with whom you conspired. Means and ends are of little moment here. Idle speculations. But even though you carry the draft of your murderous plan with you to the grave it will nonetheless be known in all its infamy to your Maker and as that is so so shall it be made known to the least of men. All in the fullness of time.

You're the one that's crazy, said the kid.

The judge smiled. No, he said. It was never me. But why

322

lurk there in the shadows? Come here where we can talk, you and me.

The kid stood against the far wall. Hardly more than a shadow himself.

Come up, said the judge. Come up, for I've yet more to tell you.

He looked down the hallway. Dont be afraid, he said. I'll speak softly. It's not for the world's ears but for yours only. Let me see you. Dont you know that I'd have loved you like a son?

He reached through the bars. Come here, he said. Let me touch you.

The kid stood with his back to the wall.

Come here if you're not afraid, whispered the judge.

I aint afraid of you.

The judge smiled. He spoke softly into the dim mud cubicle. You came forward, he said, to take part in a work. But you were a witness against yourself. You sat in judgement on your own deeds. You put your own allowances before the judgements of history and you broke with the body of which you were pledged a part and poisoned it in all its enterprise. Hear me, man. I spoke in the desert for you and you only and you turned a deaf ear to me. If war is not holy man is nothing but antic clay. Even the cretin acted in good faith according to his parts. For it was required of no man to give more than he possessed nor was any man's share compared to another's. Only each was called upon to empty out his heart into the common and one did not. Can you tell me who that one was?

It was you, whispered the kid. You were the one.

The judge watched him through the bars, he shook his head. What joins men together, he said, is not the sharing of bread but the sharing of enemies. But if I was your enemy with whom would you have shared me? With whom? The priest? Where is he now? Look at me. Our animosities were formed and waiting before ever we two met. Yet even so you could have changed it all.

You, said the kid. It was you.

It was never me, said the judge. Listen to me. Do you think Glanton was a fool? Dont you know he'd have killed you?

Lies, said the kid. Lies, by god lies.

Think again, said the judge.

He never took part in your craziness.

The judge smiled. He took his watch from his waistcoat and opened it and held it to the failing light.

For even if you should have stood your ground, he said, yet what ground was it?

He looked up. He pressed the case shut and restored the instrument to his person. Time to be going, he said. I have errands.

The kid closed his eyes. When he opened them the judge was gone. That night he called the corporal to him and they sat on either side of the bars while the lad told the soldier of the horde of gold and silver coins hid in the mountains not far from this place. He talked for a long time. The corporal had set the candle on the floor between them and he watched him as one might watch a glib and lying child. When he was finished the corporal rose and took the candle with him, leaving him in darkness.

He was released two days later. A Spanish priest had come to baptize him and had flung water at him through the bars like a priest casting out spirits. An hour later when they came for him he grew giddy with fear. He was taken before the alcalde and this man spoke to him in a fatherly manner in the Spanish language and then he was turned out into the streets.

The doctor that he found was a young man of good family from the east. He cut open his trouserleg with scissors and looked at the blackened shaft of the arrow and moved it about. A soft fistula had formed about it.

Do you have any pain? he said.

The kid didnt answer.

He pressed about the wound with his thumb. He said that

he could perform the surgery and that it would cost one hundred dollars.

The kid rose from the table and limped out.

The day following as he sat in the plaza a boy came and led him again to the shack behind the hotel and the doctor told him that they would operate in the morning.

He sold the pistol to an Englishman for forty dollars and woke at dawn in a lot underneath some boards where he'd crawled in the night. It was raining and he went down through the empty mud streets and hammered at the grocer's door until the man let him in. When he appeared at the surgeon's office he was very drunk, holding onto the doorjamb, a quart bottle half full of whiskey clutched in his hand.

The surgeon's assistant was a student from Sinaloa who had apprenticed himself here. An altercation ensued at the door until the surgeon himself came from the rear of the premises.

You'll have to come back tomorrow, he said.

I dont aim to be no soberer then.

The surgeon studied him. All right, he said. Let me have the whiskey.

He entered and the apprentice shut the door behind him.

You wont need the whiskey, said the doctor. Let me have it.

Why wont I need it?

We have spirits of ether. You wont need the whiskey.

Is it stronger?

Much stronger. In any case I cant operate on a man and him dead drunk.

He looked at the assistant and then he looked at the surgeon. He set the bottle on the table.

Good, said the surgeon. I want you to go with Marcelo. He will draw you a bath and give you clean linen and show you to a bed.

He pulled his watch from his vest and held it in his palm and read it.

It is a quarter past eight. We'll operate at one. Get some rest. If you require anything please let us know.

The assistant led him across the courtyard to a whitewashed adobe building in the rear. A bay that held four iron beds all empty. He bathed in a large riveted copper boiler that looked to have been salvaged from a ship and he lay on the rough mattress and listened to children playing somewhere beyond the wall. He did not sleep. When they came for him he was still drunk. He was led out and laid on a trestle in an empty room adjoining the bay and the assistant pressed an icy cloth to his nose and told him to breathe deeply.

In that sleep and in sleeps to follow the judge did visit. Who would come other? A great shambling mutant, silent and serene. Whatever his antecedents he was something wholly other than their sum, nor was there system by which to divide him back into his origins for he would not go. Whoever would seek out his history through what unraveling of loins and ledgerbooks must stand at last darkened and dumb at the shore of a void without terminus or origin and whatever science he might bring to bear upon the dusty primal matter blowing down out of the millennia will discover no trace of any ultimate atavistic egg by which to reckon his commencing. In the white and empty room he stood in his bespoken suit with his hat in his hand and he peered down with his small and lashless pig's eyes wherein this child just sixteen years on earth could read whole bodies of decisions not accountable to the courts of men and he saw his own name which nowhere else could he have ciphered out at all logged into the records as a thing already accomplished, a traveler known in jurisdictions existing only in the claims of certain pensioners or on old dated maps.

In his delirium he ransacked the linens of his pallet for arms but there were none. The judge smiled. The fool was no longer there but another man and this other man he could never see in his entirety but he seemed an artisan and a worker in metal. The judge enshadowed him where he crouched at his trade but he was a coldforger who worked with hammer and die, perhaps under some indictment and an exile from men's fires, hammering out like his own conjectural destiny all through the night of his becoming some coinage for a dawn that would not be. It is this false moneyer with his gravers and burins who seeks favor with the judge and he is at contriving from cold slag brute in the crucible a face that will pass, an image that will render this residual specie current in the markets where men barter. Of this is the judge judge and the night does not end.

THE LIGHT IN the room altered, a door closed. He opened his eyes. His leg was swathed in sheeting and it was propped up with small rolls of reed matting. He was desperate with thirst and his head was booming and his leg was like an evil visitant in the bed with him such was the pain. By and by the assistant came with water for him. He did not sleep again. The water that he drank ran out through his skin and drenched the bedding and he lay without moving as if to outwit the pain and his face was gray and drawn and his long hair damp and matted.

A week more and he was hobbling through the town on crutches provided him by the surgeon. He inquired at every door for news of the expriest but no one knew him.

In June of that year he was in Los Angeles quartered in a hostel that was no more than a common dosshouse, he and forty other men of every nationality. On the morning of the eleventh all rose up still in darkness and turned out to witness a public hanging at the carcel. When he arrived it was paling light and already such a horde of spectators at the gate that he could not well see the proceedings. He stood at the edge of the crowd while day broke and speeches were said. Then abruptly two bound figures rose vertically from among their fellows to the top of the gatehouse and there they hung and there they died. Bottles were handed about and the witnesses who had stood in silence began to talk again.

In the evening when he returned to that place there was no one there at all. A guard leaned in the gatehouse portal chewing tobacco and the hanged men at their rope-ends looked like effigies for to frighten birds. As he drew near he saw that it was Toadvine and Brown.

He'd little money and then he'd none but he was in every dramhouse and gamingroom, every cockpit and doggery. A quiet youth in a suit too large and the same broken boots he'd come off the desert in. Standing just within the door of a foul saloon with his eyes shifting under the brim of the hat he wore and the light from a wallsconce on the side of his face he was taken for a male whore and set up to drinks and then shown to the rear of the premises. He left his patron senseless in a mudroom there where there was no light. Other men found him on their own sordid missions and other men took his purse and watch. Later still someone took his shoes.

He heard no news of the priest and he'd quit asking. Returning to his lodging one morning at daybreak in a gray rain he saw a face slobbering in an upper window and he climbed the stairwell and rapped at the door. A woman in a silk kimono opened the door and looked out at him. Behind her in the room a candle burned at a table and in the pale light at the window a halfwit sat in a pen with a cat. It turned to look at him, not the judge's fool but just some other fool. When the woman asked him what he wanted he turned without speaking and descended the stairwell into the rain and the mud in the street.

With his last two dollars he bought from a soldier the scapular of heathen ears that Brown had worn to the scaffold. He was wearing them the next morning when he hired out to an independent conductor from the state of Missouri and he was wearing them when they set out for Fremont on the Sacramento River with a train of wagons and packanimals. If the conductor had any curiosity about the necklace he kept it to himself.

He was at this employment for some months and he left it

without notice. He traveled about from place to place. He did not avoid the company of other men. He was treated with a certain deference as one who had got onto terms with life beyond what his years could account for. By now he'd come by a horse and a revolver, the rudiments of an outfit. He worked at different trades. He had a bible that he'd found at the mining camps and he carried this book with him no word of which could he read. In his dark and frugal clothes some took him for a sort of preacher but he was no witness to them, neither of things at hand nor things to come, he least of any man. They were remote places for news that he traveled in and in those uncertain times men toasted the ascension of rulers already deposed and hailed the coronation of kings murdered and in their graves. Of such corporal histories even as these he bore no tidings and although it was the custom in that wilderness to stop with any traveler and exchange the news he seemed to travel with no news at all, as if the doings of the world were too slanderous for him to truck with, or perhaps too trivial.

He saw men killed with guns and with knives and with ropes and he saw women fought over to the death whose value they themselves set at two dollars. He saw ships from the land of China chained in the small harbors and bales of tea and silks and spices broken open with swords by small yellow men with speech like cats. On that lonely coast where the steep rocks cradled a dark and muttersome sea he saw vultures at their soaring whose wingspan so dwarfed all lesser birds that the eagles shrieking underneath were more like terns or plovers. He saw piles of gold a hat would scarcely have covered wagered on the turn of a card and lost and he saw bears and lions turned loose in pits to fight wild bulk to the death and he was twice in the city of San Francisco and twice saw it burn and never went back, riding out on horseback along the road to the south where all night the shape of the city burned against the sky and burned again in the black waters of the sea where dolphins rolled through the flames, fire in the lake, through the fall of burning timbers and the cries of the lost. He never saw the expriest again. Of the judge he heard rumor everywhere.

In the spring of his twenty-eighth year he set out with others upon the desert to the east, he one of five at hire to see a party through the wilderness to their homes halfway across the continent. Seven days from the coast at a desert well he left them. They were just a band of pilgrims returning to their homes, men and women, already dusty and travelworn.

He set the horse's face north toward the stone mountains running thinly under the edge of the sky and he rode the stars down and the sur up. It was no country he had ever seen and there was no track to follow into those mountains and there was no track out. Yet in the deepest fastness of those rocks he met with men who seemed unable to abide the silence of the world.

He first saw them laboring over the plain in the dusk among flowering ocotillo that burned in the final light like homed candelabra. They were led by a pitero piping a reed and then in procession a clanging of tambourines and matracas and men naked to the waist in black capes and hoods who flailed themselves with whips of braided yucca and men who bore on their naked backs great loads of cholla and a man tied to a rope who was pulled this way and that by his companions and a hooded man in a white robe who bore a heavy wooden cross on his shoulders. They were all of them barefoot and they left a trail of blood across the rocks and they were followed by a rude carreta in which sat a carved wooden skeleton who rattled along stiffly holding before him a bow and arrow. He shared his cart with a load of stones and they went trundling over the rocks drawn by ropes tied to the heads and ankles of the bearers and accompanied by a deputation of women who carried small desert flowers in their folded hands or torches of sotol or primitive lanterns of pierced tin.

This troubled sect traversed slowly the ground under the

bluff where the watcher stood and made their way over the broken scree of a fan washed out of the draw above them and wailing and piping and clanging they passed between the granite walls into the upper valley and disappeared in the coming darkness like heralds of some unspeakable calamity leaving only bloody footprints on the stone.

He bivouacked in a barren swale and he and the horse lay down together and all night the dry wind blew down the desert and the wind was all but silent for there was nothing of resonance among those rocks. In the dawn he and the horse stood watching the east where the light commenced and then he saddled the horse and led it down a scrabbled trail through a canyon where he found a tank deep under a pitch of boulders. The water lay in darkness and the stones were cool and he drank and fetched water for the horse in his hat. Then he led the animal up onto the ridge and they went on, the man watching the tableland to the south and the mountains to the north and the horse clattering along behind.

By and by the horse began to toss its head and soon it would not go. He stood holding the hackamore and studying the country. Then he saw the pilgrims. They were scattered about below him in a stone coulee dead in their blood. He took down his rifle and squatted and listened. He led the horse under the shade of the rock wall and hobbled it and moved along the rock and down the slope.

The company of penitents lay hacked and butchered among the stones in every attitude. Many lay about the fallen cross and some were mutilated and some were without heads. Perhaps they'd gathered under the cross for shelter but the hole into which it had been set and the cairn of rocks about its base showed how it had been pushed over and how the hooded alter-christ had been cut down and disemboweled who now lay with the scraps of rope by which he had been bound still tied about his wrists and ankles.

The kid rose and looked about at this desolate scene and then he saw alone and upright in a small niche in the rocks an old woman kneeling in a faded rebozo with her eyes cast down.

He made his way among the corpses and stood before her. She was very old and her face was gray and leathery and sand had collected in the folds of her clothing. She did not look up. The shawl that covered her head was much faded of its color yet it bore like a patent woven into the fabric the figures of stars and quartermoons and other insignia of a provenance unknown to him. He spoke to her in a low voice. He told her that he was an American and that he was a long way from the country of his birth and that he had no family and that he had traveled much and seen many things and had been at war and endured hardships. He told her that he would convey her to a safe place, some party of her countrypeople who would welcome her and that she should join them for he could not leave her in this place or she would surely die.

He knelt on one knee, resting the rifle before him like a staff. Abuelita, he said. No puedes escúcharme?

He reached into the little cove and touched her arm. She moved slightly, her whole body, light and rigid. She weighed nothing. She was just a dried shell and she had been dead in that place for years.

XXIII

IN THE LATE WINTER of eighteen seventy-eight he was on the plains of north Texas. He crossed the Double Mountain Fork of the Brazos River on a morning when skim ice lay along the sandy shore and he rode through a dark dwarf forest of black and twisted mesquite trees. He made his camp that night on a piece of high ground where there was a windbreak formed of a tree felled by lightning. He'd no sooner got his fire to burn than he saw across the prairie in the darkness another fire. Like his it twisted in the wind, like his it warmed one man alone.

It was an old hunter in camp and the hunter shared tobacco with him and told him of the buffalo and the stands he'd made against them, laid up in a sag on some rise with the dead animals scattered over the grounds and the herd beginning to mill and the riflebarrel so hot the wiping patches sizzled in the bore and the animals by the thousands and tens of thousands and the hides pegged out over actual square miles of ground and the teams of skinners spelling one another around the clock and the shooting and shooting weeks and months till the bore shot slick and the stock shot loose at the tang and their shoulders were yellow and blue to the elbow and the tandem wagons groaned away over the prairie twenty and twenty-two ox teams and the flint hides by the ton and hundred ton and the meat rotting on the ground and the air whining with flies and the buzzards and ravens and the night a horror of snarling and feeding with the wolves half crazed and wallowing in the carrion.

I seen Studebaker wagons with six and eight ox teams headed out for the grounds not haulin a thing but lead. Just pure galena. Tons of it. On this ground alone between the Arkansas River and the Concho there was eight million carcasses for that's how many hides reached the railhead. Two year ago we pulled out from Griffin for a last hunt. We ransacked the country. Six weeks. Finally found a herd of eight animals and we killed them and come in. They're gone. Ever one of them that God ever made is gone as if they'd never been at all.

The ragged sparks blew down the wind. The prairie about them lay silent. Beyond the fire it was cold and the night was clear and the stars were falling. The old hunter pulled his blanket about him. I wonder if there's other worlds like this, he said. Or if this is the only one.

WHEN HE CAME UPON the bonepickers he'd been riding three days in a country he'd never seen. The plains were sere and burntlooking and the small trees black and misshapen and haunted by ravens and everywhere the ragged packs of jackal wolves and the crazed and sunchalked bones of the vanished herds. He dismounted and led the horse. Here and there within

the arc of ribs a few flat discs of darkened lead like old medal-
lions of some order of the hunt. In the distance teams of oxen
bore along slowly and the heavy wagons creaked dryly. Into
these barrows the pickers tossed the bones, kicking down the
calcined architecture, breaking apart the great frames with axes.
The bones clattered in the wagons, they plowed on in a pale
dust. He watched them pass, ragged, filthy, the oxen galled and
madlooking. None spoke to him. In the distance he could see a
train of wagons moving off to the northeast with great tottering
loads of bones and further to the north other teams of pickers at
their work.

He mounted and rode on. The bones had been gathered into
windrows ten feet high and hundreds long or into great conical
hills topped with the signs or brands of their owners. He
overtook one of the lumbering carts, a boy riding the near wheel
ox and driving with a jerkline and a jockeystick. Two youths
squatting atop a mound of skulls and pelvic bones leered down
at him.

Their fires dotted the plain that night and he sat with his
back to the wind and drank from an army canteen and ate a
handful of parched corn for his supper. All across those reaches
the yammer and yap of the starving wolves relayed and to the
north the silent lightning rigged a broken lyre upon the world's
dark rim. The air smelled of rain but no rain fell and the
creaking bonecarts passed in the night like darkened ships and
he could smell the oxen and hear their breath. The sour smell
of the bones was everywhere. Toward midnight a party hailed
him as he squatted at his coals.

Come up, he said.

They came up out of the dark, sullen wretches dressed in
skins. They carried old military guns save for one who had a
buffalo rifle and they had no coats and one of them wore green
hide boots peeled whole from the hocks of some animal and the
toes gathered shut with leader.

Evenin stranger, called out the eldest child among them.

He looked at them. They were four and a halfgrown boy and they halted at the edge of the light and arranged themselves there.

Come up, he said.

They shuffled forward. Three of them squatted and two stood.

Where's ye outfit? said one.

He aint out for bones.

You aint got nary chew of tobacca about your clothes have ye?

He shook his head.

Nary drink of whiskey neither I dont reckon.

He aint got no whiskey.

Where ye headed mister?

Are you headed twards Griffin?

He looked them over. I am, he said.

Goin for the whores I'll bet ye.

He aint goin for the whores.

It's full of whores, Griffin is.

Hell, he's probably been there more'n you.

You been to Griffin mister?

Not yet.

Full of whores. Full plumb up.

They say you can get clapped a day's ride out when the wind is right.

They set in a tree in front of this here place and you can look up and see their bloomers. I've counted high as eight in that tree early of a evenin. Set up there like coons and smoke cigarettes and holler down at ye.

It's set up to be the biggest town for sin in all Texas.

It's as lively a place for murders as you'd care to visit.

Scrapes with knives. About any kind of meanness you can name.

He looked at them from one to the other. He reached and

took up a stick and roused the fire with it and put the stick in the flames. You all like meanness? he said.

We dont hold with it.

Like to drink whiskey?

He's just talkin. He aint no whiskey drinker.

Hell, you just now seen him drink it not a hour ago.

I seen him puke it back up too. What's them things around your neck there mister?

He pulled the aged scapular from his shirtfront and looked at it. It's ears, he said.

It's what?

Ears.

What kind of ears?

He tugged at the thong and looked down at them. They were perfectly black and hard and dry and of no shape at all.

Humans, he said. Human ears.

Aint done it, said the one with the rifle.

Dont call him a liar Elrod, he's liable to shoot ye. Let's see them things mister if you dont care.

He slipped the scapular over his head and handed it across to the boy who'd spoken. They pressed about and felt the strange dried pendants.

Niggers, aint it? they said.

Docked them niggers' ears so they'd know em when they run off.

How many is there mister?

I dont know. Used to be near a hundred.

They held the thing up and turned it in the firelight.

Nigger ears, by god.

They aint niggers.

They aint?

No.

What are they?

Injins.

The hell they are.

Elrod you done been told.

How come them to be so black as that if they aint niggers.

They turned that way. They got blacker till they couldnt black no more.

Where'd you get em at?

Killed them sons of bitches. Didnt ye mister?

You been a scout on the prairies, aint ye?

I bought them ears in California off a soldier in a saloon didnt have no money to drink on.

He reached and took the scapular from them.

Shoot. I bet he's been a scout on the prairie killed ever one of them sons of bitches.

The one called Elrod followed the trophies with his chin and sniffed the air. I dont see what you want with them things, he said. I wouldnt have em.

The others looked at him uneasily.

You dont know where them ears come from. That old boy you bought em off of might of said they was injins but that dont make it so.

The man didnt answer.

Them ears could of come off of cannibals or any other land of foreign nigger. They tell me you can buy the whole heads in New Orleans. Sailors brings em in and you can buy em for five dollars all day long them heads.

Hush Elrod.

The man sat holding the necklace in his hands. They wasnt cannibals, he said. They was Apaches. I knowed the man that docked em. Knowed him and rode with him and seen him hung.

Elrod looked at the others and grinned. Apaches, he said. I bet them old Apaches would give a watermelon a pure fit, what about you all?

The man looked up wearily. You aint callin me a liar are ye son?

I aint ye son.

338

How old are you?

That's some more of your business.

How old are you?

He's fifteen.

You hush your damn mouth.

He turned to the man. He dont speak for me, he said.

He's done spoke. I was fifteen year old when I was first shot.

I ain't never been shot.

You aint sixteen yet neither.

You aim to shoot me?

I aim to try to keep from it.

Come on Elrod.

You aint goin to shoot nobody. Maybe in the back or them asleep.

Elrod we're gone.

I knowed you for what you was when I seen ye.

You better go on.

Set there and talk about shootin somebody. They aint nobody done it yet.

The other four stood at the limits of the firelight. The youngest of them was casting glances out at the dark sanctuary of the prairie night.

Go on, the man said. They're waitin on ye.

He spat into the man's fire and wiped his mouth. Out on the prairie to the north a train of yoked wagons was passing and the oxen were pale and silent in the starlight and the wagons creaked faintly in the distance and a lantern with a red glass followed them out like an alien eye. This country was filled with violent children orphaned by war. His companions had started back to fetch him and perhaps this emboldened him the more and perhaps he said other things to the man for when they got to the fire the man had risen to his feet. You keep him away from me, he said. I see him back here I'll kill him.

When they had gone he built up the fire and caught the horse and took the hobbles off and tied it and saddled it and

339

then he moved off apart and spread his blanket and lay down in the dark.

When he woke there was still no light in the east. The boy was standing by the ashes of the fire with the rifle in his hand. The horse had snuffed and now it snuffed again.

I knowed you'd be hid out, the boy called.

He pushed back the blanket and rolled onto his stomach and cocked the pistol and leveled it at the sky where the clustered stars were burning for eternity. He centered the foresight in the milled groove of the framestrap and holding the piece so he swung it through the dark of the trees with both hands to the darker shape of the visitor.

I'm right here, he said.

The boy swung with the rifle and fired.

You wouldnt of lived anyway, the man said.

It was gray dawn when the others came up. They had no horses. They led the halfgrown boy to where the dead youth was lying on his back with his hands composed upon his chest.

We dont want no trouble mister. We just want to take him with us.

Take him.

I knowed we'd bury him on this prairie.

They come out here from Kentucky mister. This tyke and his brother. His momma and daddy both dead. His grandaddy was killed by a lunatic and buried in the woods like a dog. He's never knowed good fortune in his life and now he aint got a soul in this world.

Randall you take a good look at the man that has made you a orphan.

The orphan in his large clothes holding the old musket with the mended stock stared at him woodenly. He was maybe twelve years old and he looked not so much dullwitted as insane. Two of the others were going through the dead boy's pockets.

Where's his rifle at mister?

The man stood with his hand on his belt. He nodded to where the rifle stood against a tree.

They brought it over and presented it to the brother. It was a Sharp's fifty calibre and holding it and the musket he stood inanely armed, his eyes skittering.

One of the older boys handed him the dead boy's hat and then he turned to the man. He give forty dollars for that rifle in Little Rock. You can buy em in Griffin for ten. They aint worth nothin. Randall, are you ready to go?

He did not assist as a bearer for he was too small. When they set out across the prairie with his brother's body carried up on their shoulders he followed behind carrying the musket and the dead boy's rifle and the dead boy's hat. The man watched them go. Out there was nothing. They were simply bearing the body off over the bonestrewn waste toward a naked horizon. The orphan turned once to look back at him and then he hurried to catch up.

IN THE AFTERNOON he rode through the McKenzie crossing of the Clear Fork of the Brazos River and he and the horse walked side by side down the twilight toward the town where in the long red dusk and in the darkness the random aggregate of the lamps formed slowly a false shore of hospice cradled on the low plain before them. They passed enormous ricks of bones, colossal dikes composed of horned skulls and the crescent ribs like old ivory bows heaped in the aftermath of some legendary battle, great levees of them curving away over the plain into the night.

They entered the town in a light rain falling. The horse nickered and snuffed shyly at the hocks of the other animals standing at stall before the lamplit bagnios they passed. Fiddle-music issued into the solitary mud street and lean dogs crossed before them from shadow to shadow. At the end of the town he led the horse to a rail and tied it among others and stepped up the low wooden stairs into the dim light that fell from the doorway there. He looked back a last time at the street and at the random windowlights let into the darkness and at the last pale light in the west and the low dark hills around. Then he pushed open the door and entered.

A dimly seething rabble had coagulated within. As if the raw board structure erected for their containment occupied some ultimate sink into which they had gravitated from off the surrounding flatlands. An old man in a tyrolean costume was shuffling among the rough tables with his hat outheld while a little girl in a smock cranked a barrel organ and a bear in a crinoline twirled strangely upon a board stage defined by a row of tallow candles that dripped and sputtered in their pools of grease.

He made his way through the crowd to the bar where several men in gaitered shirts were drawing beer or pouring whiskey. Young boys worked behind them fetching crates of bottles and racks of glasses steaming from the scullery to the rear. The bar was covered with zinc and he placed his elbows upon it and spun a silver coin before him and slapped it flat.

Speak or forever, said the barman.

A whiskey.

Whiskey it is. He set up a glass and uncorked a bottle and poured perhaps half a gill and took the coin.

He stood looking at the whiskey. Then he took his hat off and placed it on the bar and took up the glass and drank it very deliberately and set the empty glass down again. He wiped his mouth and turned around and placed his elbows on the bar behind him.

Watching him across the layered smoke in the yellow light was the judge.

He was sitting at one of the tables. He wore a round hat with a narrow brim and he was among every kind of man, herder and bullwhacker and drover and freighter and miner and hunter and soldier and pedlar and gambler and drifter and drunkard and thief and he was among the dregs of the earth in beggary a thousand years and he was among the scapegrace scions of eastern dynasties and in all that motley assemblage he sat by them and yet alone as if he were some other sort of man entire and he seemed little changed or none in all these years.

He turned away from those eyes and stood looking down at the empty tumbler between his fists. When he looked up the barman was watching him. He raised his forefinger and the barman brought the whiskey.

He paid, he lifted the glass and drank. There was a mirror along the backbar but it held only smoke and phantoms. The barrel organ was groaning and creaking and the bear with tongue aloll was revolving heavily on the boards.

When he turned the judge had risen and was speaking with other men. The showman made his way through the throng shaking the coins in his hat. Garishly clad whores were going out through a door at the rear of the premises and he watched them and he watched the bear and when he looked back across the room the judge was not there. The showman seemed to be in altercation with the men standing at the table. Another man rose. The showman gestured with his hat. One of them pointed toward the bar. He shook his head. Their voices were incoherent in the din. On the boards the bear was dancing for all that his heart was worth and the girl cranked the organ handle and the shadow of the act which the candlelight constructed upon the wall might have gone begging for referents in any daylight world. When he looked back the showman had donned the hat and he stood with his hands on his hips. One of the men had drawn a longbarreled cavalry pistol from his belt. He turned and leveled the pistol toward the stage.

Some dove for the floor, some reached for their own arms. The owner of the bear stood like a pitchman at a shooting gallery. The shot was thunderous and in the afterclap all sound in that room ceased. The bear had been shot through the midsection. He let out a low moan and he began to dance faster, dancing in silence save for the slap of his great footpads on the planks. Blood was running down his groin. The little girl strapped into the barrel organ stood frozen, the crank at rest on the upswing. The man with the pistol fired again and the pistol bucked and roared and the black smoke rolled and the bear groaned and began to reel drunkenly. He was holding his chest and a thin foam of blood swung from his jaw and he began to totter and to cry like a child and he took a few last steps, dancing, and crashed to the boards.

Someone had seized the pistol arm of the man who'd done the shooting and the gun was waving aloft. The owner of the bear stood stunned, clutching the brim of his oldworld hat.

Shot the goddamned bear, said the barman.

The little girl had unbuckled herself out of the barrel organ and it clattered wheezing to the floor. She ran forward and knelt and gathered the great shaggy head up in her arms and began to rock back and forth sobbing. Most of the men in the room had risen and they stood in the smoky yellow space with their hands on their sidearms. Whole flocks of whores were scuttling toward the rear and a woman mounted to the boards and stepped past the bear and held out her hands.

It's all over, she said. It's all over.

Do you believe it's all over, son?

He turned. The judge was standing at the bar looking down at him. He smiled, he removed his hat. The great pale dome of his skull shone like an enormous phosphorescent egg in the lamplight.

The last of the true. The last of the true. I'd say they're all gone under now saving me and thee. Would you not?

He tried to see past him. That great corpus enshadowed him from all beyond. He could hear the woman announcing the commencement of dancing in the hall to the rear.

And some are not yet born who shall have cause to curse

the Dauphin's soul, said the judge. He turned slightly. Plenty of time for the dance.

I aint studyin no dance.

The judge smiled.

The tyrolean and another man were bent over the bear. The girl was sobbing, the front of her dress dark with blood. The judge leaned across the bar and seized a bottle and snapped the cork out of it with his thumb. The cork whined off into the blackness above the lamps like a bullet. He rifled a great drink down his throat and leaned back against the bar. You're here for the dance, he said.

I got to go.

The judge looked aggrieved. Go? he said.

He nodded. He reached and took hold of his hat where it lay on the bar but he did not take it up and he did not move.

What man would not be a dancer if he could, said the judge. It's a great thing, the dance.

The woman was kneeling and had her arm around the little girl. The candles sputtered and the great hairy mound of the bear dead in its crinoline lay like some monster slain in the commission of unnatural acts. The judge poured the tumbler full where it stood empty alongside the hat and nudged it forward.

Drink up, he said. Drink up. This night thy soul may be required of thee.

He looked at the glass. The judge smiled and gestured with the bottle. He took up the glass and drank.

The judge watched him. Was it always your idea, he said, that if you did not speak you would not be recognized?

You seen me.

The judge ignored this. I recognized you when I first saw you and yet you were a disappointment to me. Then and now. Even so at the last I find you here with me.

I aint with you.

The judge raised his bald brow. Not? he said. He looked about him in a puzzled and artful way and he was a passable thespian.

I never come here huntin you.

What then? said the judge.

What would I want with you? I come here same reason as any man.

And what reason is that?

What reason is what?

That these men are here.

They come here to have a good time.

The judge watched him. He began to point out various men in the room and to ask if these men were here for a good time or if indeed they knew why they were here at all.

Everbody dont have to have a reason to be someplace.

That's so, said the judge. They do not have to have a reason. But order is not set aside because of their indifference.

He regarded the judge warily.

Let me put it this way, said the judge. If it is so that they themselves have no reason and yet are indeed here must they not be here by reason of some other? And if this is so can you guess who that other might be?

No. Can you?

I know him well.

He poured the tumbler full once more and he took a drink himself from the bottle and he wiped his mouth and turned to regard the room. This is an orchestration for an event. For a dance in fact. The participants will be apprised of their roles at the proper time. For now it is enough that they have arrived. As the dance is the thing with which we are concerned and contains complete within itself its own arrangement and history and finale there is no necessity that the dancers contain these things within themselves as well. In any event the history of all is not the history of each nor indeed the sum of those histories and none here can finally comprehend the reason for his presence for he has no way of knowing even in what the event consists. In fact, were he to know he might well absent himself and you can see that that cannot be any part of the plan if plan there be.

He smiled, his great teeth shone. He drank.

An event, a ceremony. The orchestration thereof. The overture carries certain marks of decisiveness. It includes the slaying of a large bear. The evening's progress will not appear strange or unusual even to those who question the rightness of the events so ordered.

A ceremony then. One could well argue that there are not categories of no ceremony but only ceremonies of greater or lesser degree and deferring to this argument we will say that this is a ceremony of a certain magnitude perhaps more commonly called a ritual. A ritual includes the letting of blood. Rituals which fail in this requirement are but mock rituals. Here every man knows the false at once. Never doubt it. That feeling in the breast that evokes a child's memory of loneliness such as when the others have gone and only the game is left with its solitary participant. A solitary game, without opponent. Where only the rules are at hazard. Dont look away. We are not speaking in mysteries. You of all men are no stranger to that feeling, the emptiness and the despair. It is that which we take arms against, is it not? Is not blood the tempering agent in the mortar which bonds? The judge leaned closer. What do you think death is, man? Of whom do we speak when we speak of a man who was and is not? Are these blind riddles, or are they not some part of every man's jurisdiction? What is death if not an agency? And whom does he intend toward? Look at me.

I dont like craziness.

Nor I. Nor I. Bear with me. Look at them now. Pick a man, any man. That man there. See him. That man hatless. You know his opinion of the world. You can read it in his face, in his stance. Yet his complaint that a man's life is no bargain masks the actual case with him. Which is that men will not do as he wishes them to. Have never done, never will do. That's the way of things with him and his life is so balked about by difficulty and become so altered of its intended architecture that he is little more than a walking hovel hardly fit to house the human spirit at all. Can he say, such a man, that there is no malign thing set against him? That there is no power and no force and no cause? What manner of heretic could doubt agency and claimant alike? Can he believe that the wreckage of his existence is unentailed? No liens, no creditors? That gods of vengeance and of compassion alike lie sleeping in their crypt and whether our cries are for an accounting or for the destruction of the ledgers altogether they must evoke only the same silence and that it is this silence which will prevail? To whom is he talking, man? Cant you see him?

The man was indeed muttering to himself and peering balefully about the room wherein it seemed there was no friend to him.

A man seeks his own destiny and no other, said the judge. Will or nill. Any man who could discover his own fate and elect therefore some opposite course could only come at last to that selfsame reckoning at the same appointed time, for each man's destiny is as large as the world he inhabits and contains within it all opposites as well. This desert upon which so many have been broken is vast and calls for largeness of heart but it is also ultimately empty. It is hard, it is barren. Its very nature is stone.

He poured the tumbler full. Drink up, he said. The world goes on. We have dancing nightly and this night is no exception. The straight and the winding way are one and now that you are here what do the years count since last we two met together? Men's memories are uncertain and the past that was differs little from the past that was not.

He took up the tumbler the judge had poured and he drank and set it down again. He looked at the judge. I been everwhere, he said. This is just one more place.

The judge arched his brow. Did you post witnesses? he said.

To report to you on the continuing existence of those places once you'd quit them?

That's crazy.

Is it? Where is yesterday? Where is Glanton and Brown and where is the priest? He leaned closer. Where is Shelby, whom you left to the mercies of Elias in the desert, and where is Tate whom you abandoned in the mountains? Where are the ladies, ah the fair and tender ladies with whom you danced at the governor's ball when you were a hero anointed with the blood of the enemies of the republic you'd elected to defend? And where is the fiddler and where the dance?

I guess you can tell me.

I tell you this. As war becomes dishonored and its nobility called into question those honorable men who recognize the sanctity of blood will become excluded from the dance, which is the warrior's right, and thereby will the dance become a false dance and the dancers false dancers. And yet there will be one there always who is a true dancer and can you guess who that might be?

You aint nothin.

You speak truer than you know. But I will tell you. Only that man who has offered up himself entire to the blood of war, who has been to the floor of the pit and seen horror in the round and learned at last that it speaks to his inmost heart, only that man can dance.

Even a dumb animal can dance.

The judge set the bottle on the bar. Hear me, man, he said. There is room on the stage for one beast and one alone. All others are destined for a night that is eternal and without name. One by one they will step down into the darkness before the footlamps. Bears that dance, bears that dont.

HE DRIFTED WITH the crowd toward the door at the rear. In the anteroom sat men at cards, dim in the smoke. He moved on. A woman was taking chits from the men as they passed through to the shed at the rear of the building. She looked up at him. He had no chit. She directed him to a table where a woman was selling the chits and stuffing the money with a piece of shingle through a narrow slit into an iron strongbox. He paid his dollar and took the stamped brass token and rendered it up at the door and passed through.

He found himself in a large hall with a platform for the musicians at one end and a large homemade sheetiron stove at the other. Whole squadrons of whores were working the floor. In their stained peignoirs, in their green stockings and melon-colored drawers they drifted through the smoky oil light like makebelieve wantons, at once childlike and lewd. A dark little dwarf of a whore took his arm and smiled up at him.

I seen you right away, she said. I always pick the one I want.

She led him through a door where an old Mexican woman was handing out towels and candles and they ascended like refugees of some sordid disaster the darkened plankboard stairwell to the upper rooms.

Lying in the little cubicle with his trousers about his knees he watched her. He watched her take up her clothes and don them and he watched her hold the candle to the mirror and study her face there. She turned and looked at him.

Let's go, she said. I got to go.

Go on.

You cant lay there. Come on. I got to go.

He sat up and swung his legs over the edge of the little iron cot and stood and pulled his trousers up and buttoned them and buckled his belt. His hat was on the floor and he picked it up and slapped it against the side of his leg and put it on.

You need to get down there and get you a drink, she said. You'll be all right.

I'm all right now.

He went out. He turned at the end of the hallway and looked back. Then he went down the stairs. She had come to the door.

She stood in the hallway holding the candle and brushing her hair back with one hand and she watched him descend into the dark of the stairwell and then she pulled the door shut behind her.

He stood at the edge of the dancefloor. A ring of people had taken the floor and were holding hands and grinning and calling out to one another. A fiddler sat on a stool on the stage and a man walked up and down calling out the order of the dance and gesturing and stepping in the way he wished them to go. Outside in the darkened lot groups of wretched Tonkawas stood in the mud with their faces composed in strange lost portraits within the sashwork of the windowlights. The fiddler rose and set the fiddle to his jaw. There was a shout and the music began and the ring of dancers began to rotate ponderously with a great shuffling. He went out the back.

The rain had stopped and the air was cold. He stood in the yard. Stars were falling across the sky myriad and random, speeding along brief vectors from their origins in night to their destinies in dust and nothingness. Within the hall the fiddle squealed and the dancers shuffled and stomped. In the street men were calling for the little girl whose bear was dead for she was lost. They went among the darkened lots with lanterns and torches calling out to her.

He went down the walkboard toward the jakes. He stood outside listening to the voices fading away and he looked again at the silent tracks of the stars where they died over the darkened hills. Then he opened the rough board door of the jakes and stepped in.

The judge was seated upon the closet. He was naked and he rose up smiling and gathered him in his arms against his immense and terrible flesh and shot the wooden barlatch home behind him.

In the saloon two men who wanted to buy the hide were looking for the owner of the bear. The bear lay on the stage in an immense pool of blood. All the candles had gone out save one and it guttered uneasily in its grease like a votive lamp. In the dancehall a young man had joined the fiddler and he kept the measure of the music with a pair of spoons which he clapped between his knees. The whores sashayed half naked, some with their breasts exposed. In the mudded dogyard behind the premises two men went down the boards toward the jakes. A third man was standing there urinating into the mud.

Is someone in there? the first man said.

The man who was relieving himself did not look up. I wouldnt go in there if I was you, he said.

Is there somebody in there?

I wouldnt go in.

He hitched himself up and buttoned his trousers and stepped past them and went up the walk toward the lights. The first man watched him go and then opened the door of the jakes.

Good God almighty, he said.

What is it?

He didnt answer. He stepped past the other and went back up the walk. The other man stood looking after him. Then he opened the door and looked in.

In the saloon they had rolled the dead bear onto a wagon-sheet and there was a general call for hands. In the anteroom the tobacco smoke circled the lamps like an evil fog and the men bid and dealt in a low mutter.

There was a lull in the dancing and a second fiddler took the stage and the two plucked their strings and turned the little hardwood pegs until they were satisfied. Many among the dancers were staggering drunk through the room and some had rid themselves of shirts and jackets and stood barechested and sweating even though the room was cold enough to cloud their breath. An enormous whore stood clapping her hands at the bandstand and calling drunkenly for the music. She wore nothing but a pair of men's drawers and some of her sisters were likewise clad in what appeared to be trophies—hats or pantaloons or blue twill cavalry jackets. As the music sawed up there was a lively cry from all and a caller stood to the front and called out the dance and the dancers stomped and hooted and lurched against one another.

And they are dancing, the board floor slamming under the jackboots and the fiddlers grinning hideously over their canted pieces. Towering over them all is the judge and he is naked dancing, his small feet lively and quick and now in doubletime and bowing to the ladies, huge and pale and hairless, like an enormous infant. He never sleeps, he says. He says he'll never die. He bows to the fiddlers and sashays backwards and throws back his head and laughs deep in his throat and he is a great favorite, the judge. He wafts his hat and the lunar dome of his skull passes palely under the lamps and he swings about and takes possession of one of the fiddles and he pirouettes and makes a pass, two passes, dancing and fiddling at once. His feet are light and nimble. He never sleeps. He says that he will never die. He dances in light and in shadow and he is a great favorite. He never sleeps, the judge. He is dancing, dancing. He says that he will never die.

THE END

Epilogue

IN THE DAWN there is a man progressing over the plain by means of holes which he is making in the ground. He uses an implement with two handles and he chucks it into the hole and he enkindles the stone in the hole with his steel hole by hole striking the fire out of the rock which God has put there. On the plain behind him are the wanderers in search of bones and those who do not search and they move haltingly in the light like mechanisms whose movements are monitored with escapement and pallet so that they appear restrained by a prudence or reflectiveness which has no inner reality and they cross in their progress one by one that track of holes that runs to the rim of the visible ground and which seems less the pursuit of some continuance than the verification of a principle, a validation of sequence and causality as if each round and perfect hole owed its existence to the one before it there on that prairie upon which are the bones and the gatherers of bones and those who do not gather. He strikes fire in the hole and draws out his steel. Then they all move on again.

PICADOR CLASSIC

CHANGE YOUR MIND

PICADOR CLASSIC

On 6 October 1972, Picador published its first list of eight paperbacks. It was a list that demonstrated ambition as well as cultural breadth, and included great writing from Latin America (Jorge Luis Borges's *A Personal Anthology*), Europe (Hermann Hesse's *Rosshalde*), America (Richard Brautigan's *Trout Fishing in America*) and Britain (Angela Carter's *Heroes and Villains*). Within a few years, Picador had established itself as one of the pre-eminent publishers of contemporary fiction, non-fiction and poetry.

What defines Picador is the unique nature of each of its authors' voices. The Picador Classic series highlights some of those great voices and brings neglected classics back into print. New introductions - personal recommendations if you will - from writers and public figures illuminate these works, as well as putting them into a wider context. Many of the Picador Classic editions also include afterwords from their authors which provide insight into the background to their original publication, and how that author identifies with their work years on.

Printed on high quality paper stock and with thick cover boards, the Picador Classic series is also a celebration of the physical book.

Whether fiction, journalism, memoir or poetry, Picador Classic represents timeless quality and extraordinary writing from some of the world's greatest voices.

Discover the history of the Picador Classic series and
the stories behind the books themselves at
www.picador.com/classic